ACCLAIM FO

The Winter Wedding Plan

"A charming holiday tale of fresh starts, friendship, and love with a heroine even Scrooge couldn't resist."

— Sheila Roberts, *New York Times* bestselling author

One Week To The Wedding

"An emotional ride for all of the characters in this amazing story... This book took me through an array of emotions, laughter, tears, and in the end, my heart was light with the love between these friends and families."

— HarlequinJunkie.com

"A poignant tale of forgiveness and moving forward."

— WritingPearls.com

"I was hooked from page one and did not want to stop reading. I love Ms. Olivia Miles's writing."

— AlwaysReadingReview.blogspot.com

"The town of Misty Point comes to life with charm, heart, and a sweet romance."

— *RT Book Reviews*

The Winter Wedding Plan

OLIVIA MILES

FOREVER

New York   Boston

Copyright © 2017 by Megan Leavell
Excerpt from *One Week to the Wedding* copyright © 2017 by Megan Leavell

Cover photograph © Shutterstock.
Cover design by Brian Lemus.
Cover copyright © 2017 by Hachette Book Group, Inc.

Forever
Hachette Book Group
1290 Avenue of the Americas, New York, NY 10104
forever-romance.com
twitter.com/foreverromance

First Edition: September 2017

Forever is an imprint of Grand Central Publishing. The Forever name and logo are trademarks of Hachette Book Group, Inc.

The publisher is not responsible for websites (or their content) that are not owned by the publisher.

The Hachette Speakers Bureau provides a wide range of authors for speaking events. To find out more, go to www.hachettespeakersbureau.com or call (866) 376-6591.

Library of Congress Control Number: 2017942516

ISBNs: 978-1-4555-6726-3 (trade pbk.), 978-1-4555-6724-9 (ebook)

Printed in the United States of America

LSC-C

10 9 8 7 6 5 4 3 2 1

To my darling little girl, Avery

Acknowledgments

When I finished writing this book, I knew that it had become one of my favorites. I'm so grateful to my editor, Michele Bidelspach, for connecting with this project and understanding my characters and giving me an opportunity to share this story with my readers, just as I had envisioned it.

Thank you, Paige Wheeler, agent extraordinaire, who has been an invaluable resource and friend to me from day one, and who gave me the confidence to send this manuscript to my editor in the first place.

I'd like to thank to my copy editor, Lori Paximadis; my production editor, Carolyn Kurek; and everyone at Grand Central who has a hand in polishing my books and making them shine.

And thank you, as ever, to my readers.

Chapter One

Perhaps it was the laundry pile, which had grown so high that only two choices could be made—do it or wear yesterday's clothes. Or perhaps it was the stack of unpaid bills, tucked under a pile of picture books and nearly forgotten until the baby discovered them and used the credit card statement as a teething ring. Or perhaps it was the call from her landlord, reminding her about the rent check. Charlotte couldn't be sure. But one thing she could be sure of was that today things were going to change in the Daniels residence. Sure, it was only Thanksgiving, and typically big resolutions didn't come about for another five weeks, but she didn't exactly have five weeks at the rate things were going, so today would just have to do.

First up: She'd organize her apartment. Get the closets in order and make the bed every morning before work—in other words, customary adult responsibilities that she just didn't seem to have time for these days, but would make time for, starting today! Next (and this was a big one), she'd get her finances together and pay back that loan her parents had so generously given her for a security deposit on an apartment when she'd moved back to Misty Point last summer. And third, she'd focus on the future, not the past with all its icky mistakes, and start building the life that her daughter deserved.

It started today. About a month before Christmas. *Baby's first Christmas,* she thought with a smile as she walked into her parents' dining room and tucked Audrey into the nicked wooden high chair that had been passed down from her sister, Kate, to her, and now to her seven-month-old daughter. Charlotte felt her eyes begin to mist when she thought of how her family had opened their arms to her surprise baby girl. It was more than Audrey's father had ever done . . . Not that any of them would be discussing him today. Or any other day for that matter. No, he was part of her past. Not her future. And she wasn't going to be dwelling on her past anymore, was she?

Nope. It was on the list. A resolution. One she was sticking to.

"Doesn't Audrey look sweet in her new Thanksgiving dress!" Charlotte's father grinned as he carried two bottles of wine into the room and set them on the table her mother had covered in an orange linen cloth just for the occasion. The moment his hands were free, he reached for the camera that was within arm's reach at all times, and began snapping some candids of Audrey, who was happily chewing on her fingers, a habit she'd picked up when she started teething. Charlotte stifled a sigh and leaned in close, smiling into the lens and hoping that the dark circles under her eyes from lack of sleep weren't accentuated by the overhead lighting.

"It fits perfectly," Charlotte commented once Frank had reluctantly turned off the camera and positioned it close to his place setting. There was no denying that Audrey was the best-dressed baby in their small Rhode Island town, not that Charlotte could take any of the credit. Any money she had went to the necessities, but soon that would all change. Soon she hoped to give her only child all that she deserved. She'd already started by giving her the gift of family. Next it would be a nice home. And after that . . . Well, some might say that a father figure would benefit Audrey, but Charlotte wasn't taking any risks in that department any time soon. If ever.

Charlotte's mother came into the room with a bowl of roasted squash. "Before you leave tonight, remind me that I have a few more things to give you."

"Mom." Charlotte felt her face flush. She darted her eyes to the doorway, happy that the friends and family who had gathered for the day were still in the kitchen, snacking on appetizers. Her mother was forever buying gifts lately, and while the clothes and toys were understandable, things like paper towels and laundry detergent made her always feel a strange mix of gratitude and humiliation.

Maura winked. "Just a few little things I couldn't pass up. On sale for a steal. I couldn't resist!"

Charlotte inwardly cringed. It wouldn't be exactly easy to ask for yet another favor tonight when her parents were already offering up so much.

She wrapped a bib around Audrey's neck—another gift, this one from her sister, Kate, and her fiancé, Alec—and snapped it closed. Her stomach felt funny as she mentally rehearsed the speech she would give. It had all seemed so much easier when she'd practiced in the shower this morning while Audrey took a brief nap.

"Turkey coming through!" Kate cried out now as their uncle Bill carried the large bird into the room and set it down on the center of the table.

Her cousin Bree, a strict vegetarian, hovered in the doorway, her top lip curling slightly. "Please tell me I will be eating more than mashed potatoes today."

"There's bread." Her mother, Charlotte's aunt Ellen, handed Bree a basket of rolls and disappeared back into the kitchen.

"Yum. Bread." Bree's older but considerably less mature brother, Matt, snatched one and took a large bite, causing Bree to swat him on the arm.

"It's a good thing I had the sense to bring a salad," Bree muttered.

"Out of curiosity," Alec said as he came into the room. "Would you ever date a carnivore, Bree?"

Bree's cheeks turned pink at the question. "Why? Did you have someone specific in mind?"

Now it was Alec's turn to look uncomfortable. "Just curious is all." He pulled out a chair and quickly settled himself into it.

Bree pinched her lips as she dropped the basket onto the table. "Good. The last thing I need right now is to be set up."

Charlotte quietly seconded that sentiment as everyone took their seats, which wasn't an easy feat this year with so many people tucked around the table. This year Alec's brother, William, and his wife, also Kate's best friend, Elizabeth, had joined with Elizabeth's parents and brother. The two families were merging in a way, expanding the holiday cheer, and Charlotte was happy for it. She liked William. And she'd always liked Elizabeth. Even if she did make her feel a little uncomfortable these days.

She slid into the chair next to Elizabeth, feeling out the

situation. Sure enough, Elizabeth's smile was a little strained. Well, who could blame her? She was a loyal friend. And Charlotte . . . well, Charlotte hadn't exactly been the most loyal sister in the recent past. And rectifying that was her top resolution.

"I think we're ready to eat!" Frank said, his eyes shining as he practically licked his lips. Charlotte glanced over at Bree to see if she'd caught the gesture, and the horror widening in her cousin's eyes told her that she had.

"The potatoes!" Maura suddenly cried as she started to push back her chair.

Charlotte, who had bent to pick up the spoon Audrey had dropped, stood and set her hand on her mother's shoulders. "Allow me."

It was the least she could do, considering that the pumpkin cheesecake she'd baked that morning had inexplicably curdled in the oven while the graham cracker crust had burnt to a crisp, causing the smoke alarms in her apartment to go off until she'd been forced to open the front door for thirty straight minutes and then sit with Audrey in the car to stay warm. The one thing she was asked to contribute, and she'd managed to ruin it. She'd brought a bottle of wine instead. Nice. Traditional. Perfectly acceptable once she'd wiped off the dust and checked the label, hoping that the age of it was a good thing, since it had been sitting in the back of her pantry for months and *might* have belonged to the former tenants.

She walked into the kitchen, her eyes coming to rest on Kate's magazine-cover-worthy apple tart, complete with a perfect lattice crust and no doubt homemade vanilla bean ice cream to accompany it—something Kate had whipped up when it was announced that Charlotte wouldn't be bringing the dessert after all.

Charlotte grumbled under her breath. Then, because she couldn't resist, she flung open the freezer door and narrowed her eyes on the simple white carton that rested primly on the second shelf. Suspicion confirmed.

"I forgot the cranberries, too!" Her mother sighed as she came up behind her, but she paused when she noticed Charlotte's frown. "Honey, what's wrong?"

Charlotte closed the freezer with a guilty shrug. "Nothing." Yet so much all at once. "I just feel bad about my cheesecake." It was the first thing that came to mind, but she was horrified to realize a single hot tear had slipped down her cheek.

"Honey!" Maura's laugh was good-natured as she brushed the tear away with the pad of her thumb. "It's the thought that counts. Besides, we have this apple tart to enjoy. It looks beautiful, doesn't it?"

"Hmm." Charlotte felt her lips thin. She had spent Audrey's entire morning nap carefully following the recipe she had printed at the office yesterday. She'd even made a special trip to the grocery store for the ingredients last night, which had cost a pretty penny. By the time she'd pulled the mess from the oven and stared at it in complete bewilderment, wondering where exactly she had gone wrong, Audrey had started crying again, needing to be changed and fed. And then the smoke alarm started to blare . . .

Now Charlotte set a hand to her forehead. She was just tired, that was all. Running on interrupted sleep for months on end could do that to anyone. She was crying over a cheesecake, of all things. A curdled, inedible, burnt-to-the-edges cheesecake.

But she knew from the ache in her chest that it really was about so much more.

"I guess I just wonder if I'll ever get anything right," she said as she spooned the mashed potatoes from the pot that was still warm on the stovetop into one of her mother's best serving bowls.

"We all make mistakes, Charlotte. Don't let them define you." Her mother's hand on her shoulder was kind, but her words were firm, and ones that Charlotte knew she should heed.

She finished filling the bowl slowly, wondering if now was the time to ask about moving back home for a while, just until she landed on steadier ground. No need to admit the extent of her mess. But even though she knew she had to ask—today— she couldn't bring her mouth to form the words. To admit that she'd tried. And failed. Again.

"I have the cranberries," Maura announced. "All set with the potatoes?"

The moment now lost, Charlotte nodded briskly and took a deep breath before following her mother back into the dining room, where everyone was clutching their forks, eager for the meal to begin.

As they did every Thanksgiving, each person went around the table and said what they were thankful for as her father carved the massive bird, which was a bit larger than usual this year.

"I'm thankful for the new additions to our Thanksgiving table," Maura said, giving Audrey a little kiss on the head. "We don't just have this precious little baby with us this year; we also have a fine young man and his parents. Alec, we're so happy to welcome you to the family."

Charlotte raised her glass to toast the happy couple on cue, but she couldn't help but feel a little uneasy at the turn of events. Her sister was engaged (for the second time, but no need to harp on those details just now), and Charlotte was sitting pretty all alone. No man was waiting for her at home tonight. No man had gotten down on one knee and popped the question.

Jake Lambert hadn't even met his daughter, much less acknowledged that she was his. Not that Charlotte would be admitting that to anyone. They all assumed he was contributing something, and she let them all think so. It was easier that way.

Alec's turn was next. "I'm grateful for a short engagement," he said with a mischievous grin.

"Oh, isn't that sweet," Maura said, tilting her head as she smiled wistfully.

"It's not for the reason you think, Mom," Kate corrected. She held out her plate as their father piled turkey onto it. "It's not that he can't wait to be married. It's that he knows he only has to tolerate all my wedding planning for another eight weeks."

Alec held up his palms. "Guilty as charged. Who knew there were so many varieties of roses?"

From beside her, Bree raised her hand, eliciting a laugh from the table. "Alec, I could tell you just how many varieties of roses there are, but I don't think we have enough wine to keep you from panicking. Besides, I am happy to let you know that Kate has already been into my shop and she has narrowed down her choices to two different looks. Two very different looks, I might add, but all the same, two."

Really? Charlotte frowned, wondering why she hadn't been let it on this earlier. So Kate had gone to Bree's flower shop, chatted about colors and arrangements and all that fun stuff, while Charlotte was either filing paperwork at the office they shared or sitting in her apartment with Audrey. Either way, she hadn't been invited.

She glanced at Elizabeth, who was nodding along casually. Sure enough.

"Well, if it were up to me, we'd have gone to city hall last month when I proposed," Alec said ruefully.

"That's what Frank and I did, and I've always regretted it," Maura said.

"That's what I try telling Alec." Kate shook her head. "But he's too practical."

"Aw, now . . . " Alec roped an arm over Kate's shoulders and gave her a peck on the cheek. "You know I want you to have the wedding of your dreams. I just don't want you losing sleep over it while you're planning it!"

Kate gave a resigned smile. "It's true that I have been losing some sleep. There are just so many hours in the day, and with client weddings to plan and Christmas parties, too, there's always something to take my attention away from our big day." She poked at her plate. "Maybe we should have planned for something for spring. But I had my heart set on a winter wedding."

"January is a wonderful month to get married," Maura said. "A new year. A new beginning. And Misty Point is so pretty when it's covered with snow."

"I can help," Charlotte offered, eager to make herself useful, and not just because she wanted to preserve the good standing she had with her sister. She'd been working part-time in Kate's new event planning company since August, and every extra assignment would go that much further to bettering her circumstances and, from the sound of it, Kate's, too.

"I don't want to put too much pressure on you, with a new

baby and all that..." Kate looked uncertain, and Charlotte had to clench her teeth from blurting out that the income from the event company was all she had in this world, now that she'd gone through the loan their parents had given her, at an alarming rate, mind you. That there were no monthly stipends from Jake. That if anyone wanted to talk about pressure, it came in the form of the landlord breathing down her neck for November's rent check.

She forced a reassuring smile. "It's no pressure at all! I'm eager to build up my resume, and I really enjoy the work, Kate." Sure, it was a struggle to balance her schedule with Audrey at times. Her sitter wasn't always available, and she didn't have the funds for day care just yet, but she needed to work. And she wanted to work. To prove to herself that she could stick with something. And to prove to Kate—and everyone else at this table—that she wasn't the girl she'd once been.

"Well, next week is gearing up to be a tough one for me with two holiday parties and a fitting with my newest bridezilla. And I *had* hoped to finalize those floral arrangements..."

"Finally!" Bree blurted, shaking her head. She grabbed another roll from the basket and added it to her plate, which consisted solely of mashed potatoes and squash. The salad she had brought sat untouched at the far end of the table.

Kate eyed Charlotte, as if weighing her options. "All right, I'll bring you in full-time through the month, starting Monday."

Monday morning. Charlotte hoped the panic she felt didn't show in her face. She hadn't expected to go into the office until Tuesday afternoon, as usual, and she knew that her sitter was currently away for the holiday weekend in Connecticut. She supposed she could call her anyway, but Lisa hated short notice—always charged more for it, too, savvy opportunist that she was.

She squeezed the napkin in her lap, working through the logistics, and decided she had no alternative. Her mother still worked at the town library during the week. There was no one else to call on for a last-minute favor. And really, what choice did she have?

"Monday morning it is, then," she said, feeling her spirits lift at the thought of a steadier paycheck.

"Wow, I feel like a load has been lifted from my shoulders already," Kate said through a smile, and Charlotte felt her heart warm as it did every time her sister paid her a compliment.

"Your turn, Kate," Frank said, steering the conversation back to the holiday tradition.

Kate reached over and slipped her hand onto Alec's. "I'm grateful for second chances," she said, and Charlotte found it hard to swallow the food she was chewing.

A second chance. That's what this was, all right. And she wasn't about to blow it. Last Thanksgiving Charlotte had been pregnant and alone, in a dark and musty basement apartment in Boston, twisted with anxiety, wondering if she would ever again be welcome in her childhood home. And now she was about to ask to move back into it. To admit that her second attempt to swing it on her own wasn't working out.

She reached for her wineglass and allowed herself a sip— only because she wouldn't be driving for a while. She'd stick around and help clean up after the rest of the family left. She'd explain to her parents that money was tight, and she wanted to build up her savings. She'd offer to pay a bit of rent, or help out around the house. Tidying up had never been her strong suit—that was more Kate's area—but she could learn. Or at least, try.

She set her wineglass down, wondering if it would be that easy. Or if they'd ask why Jake's child support payments weren't enough, given what he was worth, and where she was spending the money. Even if they didn't say it, she knew they'd wonder if she was being irresponsible. The way she used to be.

"What about you, Charlotte?" her mother asked.

Her heart felt heavy as she considered her response. There were so many things she could say, but only one thing mattered, really. "I'm just grateful to be here."

No one said anything, but she knew that everyone at the table understood. It had been a rough year, for all of them in many ways, but this holiday, like Kate's upcoming wedding, sparked a new beginning.

She eyed her sister, thinking of the rough times they'd been through, and how far they'd come. Everything had fallen into place...well, for Kate. As for herself, Charlotte was almost there. Soon she'd be finished paying for her mistakes. She'd move back in. Save some money. And then...And then things would be better.

"Since we're all gathered together, we have some news to share." Frank eyed Maura knowingly, and Charlotte shot her sister a look of alarm. No good news started with an announcement like that. Unless it was a marriage or a birth. And she very much doubted either of those were on the table for her parents.

"As you know, Grandma Daniels hasn't been doing well for a while," her father continued, and Charlotte murmured her sympathy, feeling all at once like a heel for panicking. Of course. Her grandmother had struggled with her health for a while now.

It had been a source of stress to her father, who, as the only child, was forever hopping on a plane to tend to her, or worrying about her from afar. Charlotte looked around the table, thinking it was a shame that Granny couldn't have joined them today.

She looked at her father, waiting for him to continue, wondering if he would announce that Granny was moving up to Rhode Island, to maybe live with them. She chewed her lip, selfishly wondering if that would impact her plans to move back in herself, but then decided that she and Audrey would just have to share her old bedroom while Granny took Kate's. Not ideal, but what was anymore?

"It's been a tough decision, but... Well, there's no easy way to say it. We've decided to move to Florida to be with her."

Silence fell over the room, and all that Charlotte could hear was the pounding of her own heart. She looked at her mother, then Kate, who seemed almost more bewildered than Charlotte herself felt.

"The warm air is better for her, and she needs family right now."

Charlotte glanced at her baby daughter, who had only started to bond with her grandparents, and felt her eyes sting. She reached for her water glass with a shaking hand and brought it to her lips. There was nothing she could say. Nothing that wouldn't sound completely selfish.

"When do you plan to go?" Kate finally asked, breaking the silence.

"Sunday," her mother replied, and Charlotte nearly choked on the water. She coughed, and her mother slid her a strange look. "We've been talking about it for a while, and there just never seemed to be a good time to bring it up. It won't be forever. We're keeping the house—"

Oh, sweet Heaven. Thank goodness for small blessings. Charlotte closed her eyes, slumping back in her chair, feeling her panic subside.

"But we're renting it out."

"Will you be able to find a renter at this time of year?" Kate asked. Everyone knew that Misty Point was a summer destination.

Her mother looked to Ellen, and Charlotte felt another prickle of panic. Aunt Ellen was a real estate agent. And she'd clearly been let in on these plans long before everyone else had. "Thanks to my sister's help, a couple came forward for a December first lease. We'd thought we'd go down south in January after the wedding, but, well, we decided to move up our plans!"

The conversation seemed to go on and on, but Charlotte stopped listening. Her head felt murky and her heart was racing, but despite all the questions she had and all the confusion, one thing was very clear: she was in trouble. Again.

Chapter Two

⚬⚬⚬⚬

Bree Callahan was a proud vegetarian. And a florist, by default. And, as of recently, a homeowner, by inheritance. She was also thirty-two years old and dangerously close to becoming a spinster.

She wouldn't feel that way if her prospects didn't seem so bleak. In theory, she had time before her eggs dried up and her crow's-feet took over. But Misty Point was small, and it wasn't like she was leaving it anytime soon. She loved her hometown. She loved the cobblestone streets that ran through the quaint downtown lined with shops, and the smell of the salt water that lingered in the air, even now, when the first snow had already fallen. She loved that her family and friends were close by, and she loved her routine. Her life was simple. Perfect, really.

So why was she standing in the front hall of her aunt and uncle's beautiful home, blinking back tears as she gripped a plastic container of leftover stuffing (that she was emphatically informed hadn't been stuffed in the bird) in both hands?

"Are you on your way out, too?" Kate asked as she slid her feet into suede boots. "I think you're parked behind us."

Us. A word so short and concise and yet so full of possibility.

Bree managed a smile as she took her coat from her father, who would stick around for a while after the "kids" had left. Matt had been the first to leave, of course. He didn't say where he was going, but then he rarely did. He was going to meet a woman, Bree was sure, but as with the others, he'd never bring her home to meet the family. The poor girl. Bree felt sorry for whoever it was.

See, Bree? Better to be alone than led on by a man like your brother, right?

She wished that thought was more comforting. Instead it just felt confusing and strange.

So Matt was off, having his fun. Charlotte had left in a hurry, too, promising to come back on Sunday, the day her parents were moving. She was upset, Bree could tell, but did her best not to show it. Her smile was just a notch too bright, her eyes a tad too shiny. It made Bree sad in a way. Sometimes she missed the old Charlotte, who spoke her mind and was a little bit selfish in an endearing sort of way, and who didn't always seem like she was holding back some secret.

"We're heading out, too," Alec's brother, William, called out. "You want to stop over for drinks?"

"Sure!" Kate nodded her enthusiasm and, catching Bree's eye, said, "Want to join us?"

Us. Bree gave an apologetic smile as her mind spun to find a plausible excuse. Hanging out with two sets of lovebirds was hardly her idea of fun, even if Kate was her cousin and Elizabeth was a close friend.

"I have to do some paperwork tonight," she said, wondering how many times she could pull out that excuse. "Brunch this Saturday?" In other words: girl time.

"I might have a fitting with one of my brides. I'll double-check and get back to you tomorrow," Kate said with a grin.

And then they were off. Out the door. Walking along the snowy, slippery path toward the driveway. William and Elizabeth in front, holding hands. Kate and Alec just behind, arms linked through thick wool coats. And Bree. Trailing behind. Clutching a pile of leftovers.

She managed to wave and smile and be downright cheerful as everyone went to their respective cars, and then, sweet relief, she was inside her own car. Alone.

She turned on the radio. Blasted the heat. Checked her rearview mirror to make sure William had pulled away before shifting gears and backing out. The road was paved, the street empty, and lights glowed in windows from the houses on either side.

It was a perfect late-fall night. Usually her favorite kind. But instead of feeling uplifted by a few hours spent with her favorite people, her heart was heavy at the prospect of going home to a dark, empty house that didn't even feel like it belonged to her. It was her gran's house, really. She had taken occupancy of it in September with the hope of starting over. But instead, she felt lost in all the rooms, like a visitor. Sometimes she missed her one-bedroom apartment that was walking distance to town.

And she was feeling sorry for herself again ...

She knew it was foolish to be so upset right now, but she couldn't help it. When Alec made that comment about her ever dating a carnivore, all her ethical resolve and strident stance on cage-free eggs and hunting for sport evaporated, and her mind was filled with the image of a square jaw, floppy brown hair, kind blue eyes, and, for some reason, wire-framed glasses. She had a thing for men in glasses.

Simon had worn glasses. Good God, she was picturing Simon.

She gave the rubber band on her wrist a quick snap. Sadly, she didn't even flinch anymore. Instead, her skin was turning calloused from the number of times she thought of her ex. Physical evidence of the pathetic fact that she just wasn't over him yet, despite the fact that he was well over her, and possibly hadn't ever been all that interested to begin with.

More like probably. Actually, more like certainly.

But she...she'd adored him.

Her grandmother had given her a harsh piece of advice when Bree was only twelve or thirteen. She could still remember where they were when she'd said it. They were in the flower shop, and Gran was pulling together a big bouquet for a twenty-fifth wedding anniversary. Suddenly, she'd stopped what she was doing, turned to Bree, and said, "Relationships work best if the man loves the woman just this much more than she loves him." She'd drawn her pointer finger close to her thumb to demonstrate the distance, careful to leave a one-inch gap. Bree had been indignant, claiming that was hardly fair. "Fair has nothing to do with it," Gran had remarked. "It's just the way love works."

Oh, Gran, Bree thought. She would have been *so* disappointed in her only granddaughter.

She shuddered when she thought of the flowers she'd sent Simon on what would have been their one-year anniversary last month, two months after they had split up. She sent a dozen perfect red roses to his office, so she wouldn't have to deliver them to his door.

That's right, Gran, you gave me your business, your home, and every bit of advice you'd ever saved up. And I went and sent a man flowers.

She could almost hear her grandmother's squawk of horror over her granddaughter doing such a thing. *Or buying ridiculously expensive tickets to a hockey game under the guise of having spontaneously come into possession of them, as desperation disguised as a casual excuse to get together when said man hadn't called in six days.*

Bree shuddered, imagining how the conversation would play out.

"Flowers! Sent to a man!"

"Not just any man, Gran. My ex-boyfriend. I sent him one dozen perfect red roses and then I sat clutching my phone and waited for three days to see if he would call to..." To what?

"In all my days running that shop, I never once fulfilled such an outrageous request."

"But you'll be proud of me, Gran."

A snort, followed by a hesitation.

"I resisted calling his office to check up on the order. I could have." In fact, she'd rehearsed the script. She'd call during the lunch break, when the usual gossipy receptionist whom Bree had always suspected had a thing for Simon took her lunch break, and old Hazel McClain, who had been the assistant to the founder of the law firm since it first opened its doors back in the forties, took over. Hazel was practically blind, didn't know how to operate a computer, and had no interest in office drama, especially when half the time she couldn't remember anyone's names. She'd never remember that Simon, who was tucked away in patent law, far down the hall from the senior partner's office that Hazel guarded, had just ceremoniously broken another girl's heart. Or that this girl worked in a flower shop, namely, the one that was calling to check up on the order.

Bree could hear Gran *tsk* her disapproval. "Flowers to a man."

She couldn't stop muttering it. No doubt, if there was a bridge club in the afterlife, the entire club would be aghast in no time.

"It was my birthday," Bree protested, out loud. Because yeah, she talked to herself now, frequently, and had imaginary conversations with Gran. And sadly, Simon. "Thirty-two." She cringed at the reminder. As if anything more needed to be said.

"Thirty-two! At that age, I had six children and was already a widow," Gran would have said, as she had been keen to point out every chance she had.

Now Bree was gripping the steering wheel. Sure, it wasn't conventional to send a seventy-dollar bouquet to your ex-boyfriend, but surely it couldn't be *that* shocking.

She imagined Simon finding them on his desk. The surprise in his eyes. The expression when he read the card.

The card! Dear God, she hadn't considered that piece of hard evidence. Had it been passed around? Discovered in the trash by the gossipy receptionist? Oh my God, oh my God...

She was thirty-two. She'd spent the better part of a year dating that man, dreaming of a future together.

This was never how it was supposed to go.

"My birthday wasn't the happiest one, Gran. So you can understand why I freaked out. I...I snapped. I thought..." She didn't frankly know what she'd been thinking. But she'd clearly had one too many glasses of pinot grigio.

Gran was giving her one of those knowing looks, down the length of her nose, her gray eyes a little hooded, her mouth a thin line of complete disapproval. "You were thinking he may have had a change of heart. That he just needed a nudge."

Gran knew her so well. "Yes, Gran, that's exactly what I had been hoping."

Pinched lips. Here it came. "Interested men don't need a nudge, Bree."

No. They didn't. And respectable women didn't try to woo them, either.

It been a lapse in judgment. A moment of crazy. Well, it wouldn't happen again.

Up ahead, William's car was turning onto Thackeray Lane. Behind her, Alec's would soon do the same. She could join them, of course. Forgo the imaginary paperwork and sit on Elizabeth's lovely overstuffed slipcovered couch, complete with the chunky chenille throws in soft neutral colors and everything else that felt so adult and accomplished in comparison with Bree's own meager belongings, most of which were handed down from good old Gran. There would be carols playing in the background from their surround-sound system. She'd have a glass of eggnog in one of the mugs Elizabeth had registered for. Christmas had officially launched now that Thanksgiving was behind them.

And wasn't that depressing? She'd dared to think perhaps this Christmas she and Simon might be engaged. And instead, she had nothing to look forward to but a poinsettia delivery tomorrow. And she didn't even like poinsettias. In fact, she rather hated the look of them.

Right. The slippery slope. No going there. After all, the night was hers! She could fill it however she wished! She could slip into her least flattering yet comfiest pajamas, heat up a mug of cider, add of splash of something extra, and watch a movie.

Or...she could do a drive-by of Simon's parents' house.

It wasn't that outrageous, after all. She was practically passing by it on her way back into town, give or take a mile or two.

She pulled up to the stop sign and flicked her blinker. Soon, she was cruising down Glen Oak Drive, at roughly four miles an hour, her eyes scanning the left side of the street. Her breath caught when she spotted his car, a black newer-model Volvo, and in panic, she pressed her foot on the accelerator, barely managing a look-see as she whizzed past at a rate that wasn't common on residential streets.

Her heart was still pounding when she turned onto the next street, which carried her back to the main road. He was there. At his parents' house. Of course he was. It was Thanksgiving!

But was he alone? Or had he brought a date? Last Thanksgiving they hadn't felt that they knew each other well enough to share the holidays. But that wouldn't stop him from having a change of heart this time around.

She turned back onto the main road, in the opposite direction of home, and this time, kept her slow pace as she turned back down Glen Oak, her tires crunching on the frozen pavement, the radio on low.

The lights were on in the house, and she could make out some people in the back room. The dining room, perhaps? Most likely. There was a man and...

Damn it! She'd passed the house. Too late to see now. Still, she felt reassured with her findings. Nothing wild going on in there. Simon was probably in the kitchen, helping his mother clean up. Or in the study, having a drink with his dad.

Or in his childhood bedroom, getting busy with her replacement.

She followed the street up to the main road and stopped at the stop sign. She flicked her signal in the direction of home, chewing on her bottom lip as she waited for the traffic to clear.

The radio switched over to a Christmas song, one of the sad ones designed to remind people that merry Christmases weren't for everyone.

She switched it off and gripped the steering wheel tighter.

Well, maybe just one more lap around the block.

Chapter Three

At ten o'clock Sunday morning, Charlotte swerved to a stop in front of Bree's house, only at that point realizing that their plans had been made for eleven. She cursed under her breath, then, alarmed, glanced up at the rearview mirror to see if Audrey had caught any of Mommy's potty talk. But Audrey was sound asleep. Of course. Daytime was her favorite time to sleep. She was nocturnal, Charlotte had come to realize. And Charlotte was running on empty, and clearly not thinking straight.

She eyed the clock on the dashboard, deciding if she should use the hour to grab a coffee in town or take a nap in the car, when she heard her name being called, and there was Bree, standing in the doorway, clutching a steaming mug in both hands, beckoning her to hurry up already.

Charlotte blinked in confusion. Maybe it had been ten o'clock after all. Right. Another thing to add to her resolutions. Starting today, she'd keep a calendar. And this time she wouldn't just say she was going to keep it; this time she would actually stick with it. Cross things off and everything. She could hardly wait.

Buoyed by the thought of getting things back under control, she killed the engine. Audrey didn't stir as she released the car seat from its base and hooked it over her forearm. The walk up the stone path to Bree's front door was short, and despite the flurries that were starting to dance in the wind, a few colorful potted mums still anchored the front stoop.

"Asleep?" Bree asked, glancing down at Audrey and giving her an adoring smile. She shook her head as she closed the door behind them. "Aren't you lucky, Charlotte. I have a friend who said her baby *never* sleeps."

Charlotte gave her cousin a long, hard stare, and fought with her mouth not to say something fresh. Bree didn't have a clue. But then, she supposed she hadn't either . . . until recently.

"Audrey is a good baby," she agreed as she set the carrier down on the floor so she could remove her shoes.

"A good baby? She's perfect!" Bree used the opportunity to crouch and get a better look at Audrey. Charlotte winced as her cousin fiddled with the blanket and cooed over the pink snowsuit she'd given as an impromptu gift, which did look rather adorable on the baby. Audrey's eyelids fluttered, and for a moment Charlotte felt a twinge of panic. She just needed ten minutes . . . five even!

"She is perfect." Charlotte grinned. "But I do wish she'd sleep more at night."

"Can't you nap when she naps?" Bree stood and shrugged, as if it were just that obvious.

Charlotte stopped unbuttoning her coat, counted to three, and pulled in a measured breath. She'd used the same trick last week when Bree had complained about only getting five hours of sleep due to a rush of holiday orders. "I suppose I could. If I wasn't at work."

"But weekends?"

There was no use arguing. "Weekends, sure." Because of course she could get by on a few hours of sleep. Two days a week.

Her eyelids began to droop as she hung her coat in the small closet Bree had crammed with coats for every season, and what seemed like every pair of shoes she owned, too, right down to her leopard-print stilettos, which Charlotte hoped to borrow someday, if she ever had occasion to wear them, that is. Right now, she'd happily trade a proper night of sleep for a fancy restaurant.

She eyed the creamy off-white living room sofa eagerly as they rounded the corner. What she wouldn't give to lie down right now, just rest her head for a moment on one of Bree's colorful throw pillows. Instead she motioned to Bree's mug. "Any more of that, by chance?"

"A whole pot in the kitchen." Bree grinned. "And I have your favorite flavor of creamer, too."

Ah, bless her. Charlotte had been sleeping even worse than usual since the big Thanksgiving announcement, but this morning brought a new source of hope. This morning, she was going to ask Bree if she could move in here. Temporarily.

After all, the place was far too big for just one person. It had once belonged to Bree's paternal grandmother, who'd taken a special liking to her only granddaughter over her many grandsons (once a prickly issue during holiday gatherings that had eventually faded to a family joke) and gave Bree not only her flower shop but also her home. It had taken more than a year since her passing for Bree to take occupancy of the old cedar-sided Colonial. At first, Charlotte had assumed that Bree didn't want to take liberties, or perhaps couldn't bear to part with some of the antique items, but as she followed her cousin down the hall that led to the kitchen, she began to wonder...

Boxes of all sizes lined the passageway, confining the space to single-file, none visibly marked, but all haphazardly arranged. Inside the kitchen, cans of paint were stacked on the island and several of the oak cabinets were missing their doors. Bree said nothing as she casually reached for a mug from an open shelf, as if the house weren't in some strange sense of disarray, and nothing was amiss.

"Are you...painting?" Charlotte latched on to the most obvious and motioned toward the paint cans.

Bree smiled. "Renovating." She reached for the coffeepot and filled a mug for Charlotte before topping herself off.

"The kitchen?" Charlotte inquired, wondering if the boxes in the hall meant she had finally gotten around to that attic.

"The entire house!" Bree beamed, as if this was the most natural statement she could make at ten in the morning, when Charlotte was running on about three hours of sleep in twenty-four hours. When she was hoping to move in. To a construction site. With a baby. A baby who could crawl.

Her hand shook a little as she reached for the vanilla creamer that Bree set on the counter. Her cousin kept one on hand in her flower shop, too, for Charlotte's frequent visits: some professional errands, but most of a more personal nature.

But in all their recent chats, she'd failed to mention this.

"You hired a local crew then?" Charlotte asked pleasantly. Maybe it would be finished quickly, she dared to hope. After all, the house was in decent enough shape. Or at least it had been, as of last month, when Charlotte had brought Audrey over for a much-needed stop on their trick-or-treat run. Bree had fussed over Audrey in her pumpkin costume and added five extra candies to the trick-or-treat bag, which of course Charlotte later consumed on the couch in her apartment, relishing that little parenting perk.

"Oh, no. That would be much too expensive!" Bree clucked her tongue. "I'm doing it myself."

"Yourself?" Charlotte closed her gaping mouth. Bree looked so proud. Who was she to burst her bubble?

"Yup. Come see what I'm doing to the master bath. I've been watching videos on my laptop, taking down notes. You'd be amazed what you can learn off the internet! How to clean a furnace. How to anchor a heavy mirror to plaster walls! You should see me with my drill. I've even learned how to spot asbestos. And it's a good thing I did." She chuckled knowingly.

Oh, dear God. Bracing herself, Charlotte grabbed her mug and retraced her path through the front hall and up the winding stairs to the top landing, her eyes widening with each step. A ladder was facedown on the floor, next to an open toolbox, and she caught the glint of sunlight reflecting off some spilled nails. Gingerly climbing over the equipment, she followed Bree into the master bedroom, trying to murmur some encouragement and support, but all words were lost when she spotted the open door to the bathroom.

What once had been wall tile of an ancient, peachy hue was now exposed pipes and irregularly shaped holes where drywall had been. A few tiles remained. "Couldn't get those off for the life of me. Yet," Bree explained, without having to be asked, and Charlotte's head started to spin when she saw that her cousin was still grinning.

"How long is all this going to take?" she finally asked.

Bree shrugged. "I don't know. However long it does, I suppose."

Oh, the luxury. To live without a care in the world. To live only for yourself and your own whims.

Charlotte backed away from the bathroom door after noticing the loose wires and enormous hole where a light fixture and medicine cabinet had once hung. "Well. This is quite a project." To put it mildly...

Bree nodded. "I'm learning as I go. Part of home ownership!"

Was it? Charlotte wasn't so sure.

"Besides," Bree said, a little more subdued. "It gives me something to do."

"But you have the flower shop," Charlotte said, puzzled.

"In the evenings, I meant." Bree gave a little sigh, and looked around the room. "It was overdue for a change, anyway."

Charlotte gave a little smile. Of course. Bree was lonely. And who wouldn't be living in this big old house all by herself? Moving in with Audrey would have been the perfect solution for everyone... if it wasn't a gigantic safety hazard.

She felt her shoulders drop. Gone were the fantasies she had of watching chick flicks with Bree, having someone to talk to at the end of the day, surrounding Audrey with family at Christmastime.

She'd just have to figure something else out.

"How's business going, by the way?" she ventured as she gripped the stair rail tightly, following Bree back downstairs to the living room, her eyes scanning for stray nails or loose floorboards.

"The holidays are always busy, but I have seasonal help lined up."

So much for picking up a few extra weekend shifts at the flower shop. Charlotte was happy to see that Audrey was still sleeping as she settled into an armchair near the fireplace and sipped her coffee. She supposed it was time to discuss the reason she was here. Technically. "I received all the RSVP notes. It looks like everyone can make Kate's shower next weekend."

"Oh, good!" Bree perked up. "And I talked to Elizabeth and she's excited she'll be hosting. No doubt she's been looking for another opportunity to use all her wedding registry goods."

Charlotte managed a wan smile. Elizabeth was her sister's best friend, and while they'd always had a close relationship, she felt a little uneasy in her company these days. Still, she thought as she rearranged the cushion behind her back, careful not to spill her coffee, she wouldn't let that interfere with Kate's wedding shower. Nothing could interfere with it. Not on her watch.

"She thinks I'm picking her up to go to a movie that night," Bree continued. "Alec has promised not to spill a word and to keep William entertained for the evening."

Charlotte knew she should be happy that Bree was so on top of things, but she couldn't help but frown a little. Kate was her sister, after all, and she had hoped to use this wedding shower as a way to bridge the gap between them and set the right tone for this upcoming wedding. The kind that said, *I'm your sister, your pinnacle of support, the one who will do anything and everything to make this perfect for you*. And now she was just a guest. At Elizabeth's house. She wouldn't even have a say in the decorations.

She took another sip of coffee, telling herself not to get sensitive. What mattered was that Kate had a good time.

"I'm happy to oversee the menu—"

"Already on it!" Bree said, leaning over to hand Charlotte a sheet of paper from a stack she had on the coffee table. "Everyone's offered to bring something."

Charlotte scanned the list to see what she could contribute that hadn't already been taken. The only spot open was for drinks. Well, how boring was that? She may as well be in charge of napkins.

"You're not upset that I went ahead and got things moving, are you? I know you're busy with the baby, and I hated to add more to your plate, and well...It gives me something to do." Bree looked a little rattled for a moment, and Charlotte eyed her carefully.

"It's not easy getting over someone." Wasn't that the truth? Even though Jake's behavior, from start to finish, had been deplorable, there was still a part of her that wished the phone would ring and he would apologize and say that he wanted to be a real family. That he was ready for midnight feedings, diaper changes, and all the other not-so-glamorous stuff you never really consider before you have a baby.

Yes, she thought it. When she was lying in bed at night, just about to drift off, and Audrey started to whimper...she thought it. And when she was walking down Harbor Street on Sunday mornings and saw all those sappy, happy couples at Jojo's Café, eating pancake breakfasts, she thought it. And she wanted it. There. It was out. She wanted Jake to pick up that phone and call her and apologize. Or turn up at her door with about five dozen red roses and a bashful grin and... *tears* in his eyes. Oh yes, there needed to be tears. In fact, she wanted him sobbing into those roses.

Pathetic. Really, pathetic. And definitely not something she would admit aloud.

"It's fine. Fine." Bree's smile was unnaturally bright. "Besides, now that I'm not busy primping for dates or shaving my legs, I have all this extra time to finally get this house in order."

Get the house in order? More like create a giant mess.

"Well, I for one think it's great that you have such a positive attitude. There's far too much expectation that a woman's life is not complete until she's landed a man. I like to think I'm setting a far better role model for my daughter by showing her that I can be a strong independent woman." But was she? Charlotte gulped her coffee. It was liberating to make such an announcement, but not true per se, was it? It wasn't like she was exactly standing on her own two feet, after all. And she wasn't independent either. But she was swinging it on her own.

What choice did she have?

"Good for you, Charlotte," Bree said earnestly. "If I had a drink, I'd toast to that, but I've cut myself off from wine until at least noon." She laughed.

Charlotte nodded her sympathy. "You just need to establish a new routine."

"I know it's crazy. But we were together for a year and... I thought I'd be over it by now."

"I understand." And she did. Far better than she'd ever led her cousin—or anyone else—to believe. It was bad enough that she'd fallen for Jake's charms, believing him when he'd sidled up next to her in a bar one early summer night, claiming Kate had broken his heart, when it was later determined that it was all part of his plan to call off the wedding. It was even worse when she'd let Jake buy her a few rounds, and blushed when he'd told her how pretty she was, how much better she was making him feel. It was downright stupid of her to accept his ride home, when she knew darn well what he meant by that. But it was downright foolish to ever think that he'd be excited to learn he was going to be a father.

And it was nothing short of pathetic that she'd followed him back to Boston a few weeks later, thinking he'd eventually have a change of heart.

Yes, a part of her still held on to that glimmer of hope. But did Bree—or anyone else for that matter—need to know that? After what Jake had done to her sister, then her, well, she'd probably be told she needed to have her head examined.

"At least you have your baby to keep you busy," Bree said cheerfully. "And Kate's wedding, I'm sure."

Kate! Charlotte had almost forgotten. She glanced at her watch, her heart slowing when she realized she still had fifteen minutes to spare. "I'm supposed to meet my sister at my parents' house soon. They're packing up today."

Bree shook her head. "Right before the holidays. But they'll be back. And you and Kate have each other."

Charlotte said nothing as she took a sip of her coffee, the weight of sadness settling in her chest. She had a sister, yes. A sister who employed her and who loved her daughter and who knew her. Too well at times. But it wasn't the same as having someone to confide in. And that was entirely her fault.

★ ★ ★

Kate was standing in her parents' empty kitchen, surrounded by packing boxes, when Charlotte scooted past the moving men, holding Audrey in the crook of her arm as she managed to feed her a bottle. Kate glanced up from the newspaper she was holding, blinking in distraction for a moment, but as soon as her gaze fell on her niece, her expression transformed.

She quickly folded the newspaper and shoved it into her black leather tote. "May I?" she asked, glancing at Charlotte for approval.

"Of course." Charlotte handed over the baby, who started to wail as the bottle was teased from her mouth, until Kate quickly popped it back in. "Any good leads in the society section today?"

Kate looked startled. "What? Oh, no. I have my hands full anyway." She looked back at Audrey quickly, and Charlotte felt that familiar sense of unease that she often had when she was alone with her sister anymore. Yes, they'd moved forward, but there was still something there, under the surface, reminding her that things were different now.

"Where are Mom and Dad?" She scanned the adjacent rooms, seeing no sign of them. Was this how it would be when they were gone? At the office, the sisters at least had matters to discuss. But when the workday was over, they were left with stilted chitchat and bad memories.

"They're down in the basement. You know I won't go down there."

Charlotte laughed in spite of herself. Kate had always been afraid of that basement, ever since Charlotte had locked her down there for a few hours, after Kate had tattled on her for eating all of the brownies her mother had made for the school bake sale the next morning.

"We must have been what, eight and ten then?"

Kate shook her head. "It could have been yesterday. I kept waiting for Mom to hear me pounding on the door."

Charlotte looked at her sister guiltily. "She was next door at Mrs. Paulsen's house. That lady could talk."

Kate laughed. "She still can! Careful, I saw her prowling around out front when the moving vans pulled up."

Charlotte looked at her sister thoughtfully. "You never told on me for locking you down there, did you?"

"No." Kate slipped her a smile. "I figured we were sort of even."

Even. If only it were so easy to settle the score now.

"Well." She shifted the weight on her feet, uncomfortable. She didn't like thinking of all the times she went wrong, and all the times Kate still took her back. "I suppose we should go up to our rooms and save what we can."

They walked up the stairs in silence. Audrey was gurgling behind her, happy to be in her aunt's arms. Usually the sound of her daughter's voice cheered her, but as Charlotte skimmed her hand up the banister, her heart felt heavy. She'd only just finally made it home after a year away. And now that home was being taken from her again.

No more Thanksgiving meals gathered at the dining room table. Or Christmas, for that matter.

"Who will host Christmas?" she asked aloud as she reached the landing.

"I suppose I will," Kate said. "Or maybe Aunt Ellen can have us over. Between you and me, I don't really feel up to guests this holiday. Not with my wedding in January."

Charlotte nodded mutely. Of course. Kate wouldn't want the trouble of being hostess, not when she took the role so seriously. She wouldn't be the kind to put out a plate of cheese and crackers and a bottle of wine the way Charlotte would. No, Kate liked details. Lots of them. So of course she couldn't take on the responsibility of entertaining right now.

Any more than she could probably take on the responsibility of a houseguest. Or two.

Good thing that Charlotte wasn't planning to ask.

Her stomach felt a little sick when she thought of her options. She walked into her room and sat down on her bed. Or the mattress, really. Her mother had taken the bedding to the Goodwill the day after Thanksgiving, supposedly. She knew she had no use for twin-sized bedding, and she of all people should know how much something pretty could mean to someone in need, but she couldn't fight the hot tears that welled in her eyes when she thought of all the times she dropped onto this very bed, on her pink-striped bedding. She'd line her dolls up in a precise order against the frilly throw pillows, kissing each one before she left for school. Later, when the dolls were dumped in the closet, she'd lay on this bed and stare at the posters of teen idols she'd ripped from glossy magazines. Might have even kissed a few of them on her way to school, too, come to think of it.

The pressure in her chest was heavy. She stood up, opened a few drawers and cracked the closet door, but everything had been cleared out. To think that just a few days ago she had imagined herself living in this room again.

Kate was standing in the doorway when Charlotte closed the closet. She jumped at the sight of her sister. "Nothing left to take," she said.

Kate sighed. "It's strange. Seeing the house empty this way. It feels like a lifetime of memories are just...gone. I mean, I know they say they are coming back, and most of everything went into storage, but it still feels permanent."

Charlotte pointed to the closet door frame. "Remember the way Dad used to measure us? Every birthday and the first day of school." She crouched to look at the faded lines on the white paint. At the passing of time etched in pencil. And she suddenly wondered if she'd ever have the security of living in a place long enough to mark her own child's growth over the years.

The thought of it saddened her, and she turned away.

"Remember how you tried to paint your bedroom black that one time, and Mom smelled the fumes from downstairs and caught you before you'd made three brushstrokes?"

Charlotte burst out laughing and crossed the room to slide the dresser over a few feet. Sure enough, a big smear of black paint was slashed across the wallpaper. "She had to rearrange my entire room. It was that or put up new wallpaper."

"I don't know which idea was worse. Painting it black, or trying to paint over wallpaper."

Charlotte shook her head. "I've certainly put everyone through a lot of grief over the years."

Kate didn't meet her eyes, and Charlotte knew it was on purpose. "Well, teenagers. You'll have your own someday." She grinned and, so help her, Audrey giggled.

"No. No, Audrey will be different." Charlotte was adamant.

"Sure she will!" Kate said, rolling her eyes.

Her mother's voice could be heard in the hall now, ordering the movers in the direction of her room.

Kate opened the door. "I think I'll go see if Dad needs help. He'll probably want to take a few more pictures of Audrey, too."

In the hall, Charlotte could hear Kate talking to her mother in low tones, and finally, heard her descending the stairs. Charlotte swept her eyes over the room once more and then, with one last glance at the height chart, closed the door behind her.

It wasn't forever, she told herself. And maybe it was for the best. If she'd moved back home now, would she ever have dared to try things on her own again?

This was a nudge. A big one. Another one. And she wasn't sure how much further she could be pushed.

Her mother's smile was strained when Charlotte met her in the hall. "I was going to save this for Audrey for Christmas, but, well, I thought you might want to take it with you." She held out a small cloth doll that had been Charlotte's favorite as a toddler.

"Nina!" Charlotte gasped, taking the small toy. "Where'd you find her?"

"In the basement, in that old, broken bassinet. I washed it by hand, but I'm afraid she's well loved."

That was putting it mildly. Her pink dress was faded and a few threads had come loose, but Charlotte didn't care. She stroked the cloth. It was still soft. "She's going to cherish this. Thank you." She gave a watery smile as her mother's forehead creased. "It's going to be okay, Mom."

Was it? She wasn't so sure. And from the look on her mother's face, she wasn't, either.

"I know your father's mother needs us, but this all just happened so much more quickly than I expected it would. And during the holidays..." From downstairs there was the peal of a baby's giggle, and Maura put her hand to her heart. "I'm going to miss my girls."

"And we'll miss you, Mom. But we'll be fine." Her smile felt brittle.

"And it's only temporary."

Charlotte nodded. "I know."

"And we'll be back for Christmas. We're spending Christmas Eve with Granny, and then we'll fly back to Misty Point that night. We'll stay with Kate," her mother added, as if there were any possibility of her parents staying at her cramped one-bedroom apartment.

"That's only a few weeks away." Charlotte brightened at the thought.

"Tomorrow's December first!" Maura announced, but the words hit Charlotte like a jolt of cold water.

She hadn't paid November rent yet. And now December's would be due. If she didn't get her act together soon, her parents wouldn't be the only ones staying with Kate for the holidays.

She frowned at the thought of resorting to asking her sister for anything more than she'd already given.

"Baby's first Christmas," her mother was saying now as she took the box from Charlotte's arms and began carrying it down the stairs. "It's going to be the best Christmas ever!"

Charlotte hesitated with her hand on the rail. Best Christmas ever.

Suddenly that felt very far from possible.

Chapter Four

⌇⌇⌇

Gregory Frost stood in the middle of the great room of his Misty Point home, not concerned with the tarps that covered the furnishings and the layer of dust that had accumulated on the mantel and windowsills, not even the slightest bit distracted by the sweeping views of the icy waves crashing against the rocky cliffs at the edge of his estate. Coffee in hand, he rocked back on his heels and scowled into the mug, then looked up and assessed the twelve-foot spruce wedged in the corner of the room with a curl of his lip.

"What's this?" he asked, when the family's long-time care-taker, Marlene, came into the room.

She pulled a tarp off an armchair and gave the seat cushion a hard punch. In the glow of the morning light filtering through the windows, Greg watched as the dust particles danced through the air. "What's what?" she asked. She folded the tarp and set it on the floor.

Greg casually pointed in the direction of the offensive object, and Marlene's soft gray eyes widened in surprise. "Well, it's a

Christmas tree, of course!" She smiled quizzically and resumed her task with a less-than-subtle shake of her head.

"Yes, I know it's a Christmas tree," Greg said wearily, "but what is it doing here?"

"It's tradition to set up the tree right after Thanksgiving in my family," Marlene said with a fond smile. She unveiled a large honey-colored suede sofa and tossed the tarp next to the others. "When you said you were returning to Misty Point for the holidays, I had it ordered."

"Well, I wish you wouldn't have," Greg said, frowning. "With everything that's happened recently, I'm not really feeling the holiday spirit this year."

Marlene paused midtask and regarded him hesitantly. She'd been with the family for years, taking care of the house even when it wasn't in use, which was often, and she was the only person outside of Greg's circle of friends in Boston who knew the circumstances of his return. "Of course. I don't know what I was thinking. I'll have it taken away, if that's what you prefer."

"Thank you."

With an apologetic smile, Marlene swept up the tarps and left the room, leaving Greg once again to himself. He wandered to the front of the room, where tall windows looked out onto the snow-covered lawn, and sighed deeply. The last time he'd been to Misty Point was Labor Day weekend. He had come with Rebecca, of course. They'd relaxed on the deck, drank sangria and eaten lobster rolls, and chatted casually about their wedding plans until the sun had faded over the bluffs and fallen into the sea.

He turned away from the window. There was no need to think about that anymore.

"Greg?" Marlene stood in the entranceway to the hall. "Your mother's on the phone. Would you prefer me to take a message?"

Recovering quickly, Greg shook his head. "No, I'll take it," he said, accepting the house phone. When he'd seen her at Thanksgiving, she'd seemed more distant than usual—something only he would have been able to decipher. Rita was not exactly a warm and fuzzy, milk and cookies kind of mom, after all. She was formal, petite, and always immaculately groomed. Careful with her words, too. Even around her only child. But last Thursday she'd been especially stiff, as if there was something weighing on her mind, and despite it just being the two of them for the meal, she'd revealed nothing more than a tight smile. Perhaps the red-eye back to Los Angeles had settled her spirit, or perhaps she was finally ready to tell him what was bothering her. He braced himself.

"Hello, Mother." He dropped into an armchair that he quickly realized lent an unfortunate view of that ridiculous oversized tree. The thing belonged in a forest, not in a house, he thought. The sooner it was out of here, the better.

"I was surprised to hear you left for Misty Point over the weekend." Rita Frost's voice sounded distant and muffled. Speaker phone, of course. He could picture his mother sitting in her corner office of the West Coast office of Frost Greeting Cards, replying to an email or skimming a contract while she pretended to give him her full attention. It was only five on the West Coast, but that never stopped his mother from being at her desk, ready to start the day. "I've been trying your cell phone, but it kept going to voice mail. I tried you at the office, and your assistant said you were working from home today. I assumed she meant your apartment. But no, she told me you were here."

Greg had intentionally silenced the ringer of his cell phone. He just needed a day of peace. A day to clear his head. One day to recover from the stress of the past few weeks. So much for that. "The city was getting too noisy for me. I figured I'd try the old homestead for a while."

He knew she had no room for argument. The East Coast office of Frost Greetings Cards, which Greg oversaw, was located halfway between Boston and Misty Point—not exactly a glamorous central city location, but it was adjacent to their warehouse and allowed for ample space for company growth; it had nearly doubled in the past ten years, thanks to Rita's perseverance.

He typically reverse-commuted each day from his Beacon Hill condo, but there was no reason why he couldn't live here in the family's country house permanently, if he wished to.

He sipped his coffee. It was a tempting thought.

"I see." His mother sounded distracted. Normally, she wasn't shy to voice her opinion, even over something as trivial as a few days in Misty Point. Her sharp mind would home in and start to spur questions, and she'd want to know why... why he was in Misty Point, not Boston. But today, she seemed completely satisfied with the bare facts.

Greg frowned. Something must really be wrong.

There was a shuffling on the other end of the line before his mother's suddenly crystal-clear voice whispered directly into the receiver, "We've got a *big* problem, Gregory."

Greg forced himself up to a straighter position. Other than illness, there was only one thing that could be important enough for his mother to admit there was a problem, and considering it was already the first day of December, it had to be the national campaign and the bid for next year's Christmas spotlight at Burke's department stores.

"I came into the office this morning to find a holiday greeting from Darling Cards," Rita continued.

Greg set down his mug on a coaster that was conveniently placed on an end table, well trained not to leave any rings on the wooden surfaces. "And?"

"And it's not your typical corporate greeting. I'm looking at a photo of the entire Darling family, from the grandparents down to the wailing infant in the CEO's arms! And you know what this means, Gregory, right? If I received one, you can bet the CEO of Burke's did, too. And a company like Burke's, which identifies itself with a family image, is going to lap this up." She chuckled mirthlessly, her laughter shrill with hysteria. "They're even wearing matching clothes! All twenty-nine of them in designer tartan! That clown Edgar Darling even has a jaunty little cap perched right on top of his inflated head!"

It was no secret that Rita Frost and Edgar Darling were lifelong rivals. For as long as Greg could remember, his mother was aware of all the comings and goings of poor old Edgar, from which account he'd landed to which marketing genius he'd snagged. They recruited staff off each other, had probing lunches with mutual acquaintances, each gleaning for a piece of information that would give their company an edge. At industry events, they hugged and laughed and toasted with drinks like old friends, and then watched each other with narrowed eyes over the rims of their Champagne flutes for the entire cocktail hour. Rita never slept after seeing Edgar. The agitation was palpable. Edgar Darling was the only man Greg had ever known who could shake up the unflappable Rita Frost.

Greg rubbed his forehead. "So? Frost Greeting Cards has been around for generations, too. I highly doubt Burke's would give Darling Cards the account based solely on the size of their family."

"It's not about size, Gregory; it's about *image*, and right now Darling Cards is consistent with the image Burke's department stores portrays for itself. *So.*" She took the opportunity for a dramatic pause. "The question now is, how do we trump this?"

Greg stifled a groan. It had been his maternal grandfather who started Frost Greeting Cards, and when his mother had taken over as CEO nearly thirty years ago, she had single-handedly turned the company around, expanding its product line to include ornaments, crafts, toys, and gift-wrapping paper. She had brought the company to an international level and pushed everyone to the brink to ensure its success.

"I think we should do the VIP Christmas party in Misty Point," she said, in response to her own question.

Greg felt his jaw slack. "*Here?* But there must be at least two hundred guests on that list!"

"And the Burke family is at the very top. You know how important this deal is. I can't think of a better atmosphere to highlight the essence of our company's values. From one family-run business to another, what would impress them more than welcoming them into our family home, rather than some stuffy hotel ballroom?"

Family home. Since when had this been their *home*? Rita loathed the place. She had barely returned since her parents had passed, claiming it gave her the chills, and not just because of the draft. She was a city girl, through and through. But it seemed that small-town life suddenly had its advantages...

"This was never our family home," he said gruffly. Not that he would have minded if it had been. He'd always had good times in this house, even if they had been infrequent and short-lived.

"Nonsense! It was your grandparents' summer home, and you always liked it. Too drafty for me..." She sighed. "Honestly, let's finally make the old thing useful for something."

Greg had returned to Misty Point to be alone, to reflect on his life and his future, and truth to be told, to run away—not to host a frivolous party. "Christmas is a means to an end, Mother. You know that as well as I do." Sometimes he thought the only reason his mother had even flown into Boston for Thanksgiving was so rumors wouldn't spread in the office that she had skipped turkey day, that she wasn't buying the lifestyle she was selling.

"Gregory," Rita continued. "I think we should use this party as an opportunity to announce your engagement to, um, oh...Sorry, dear, I have a lot on my mind, and it's not like I've had a chance to meet her yet."

Greg froze.

"It will be perfect. Rumors of you taking over are already circulating, and your engagement will put the Burke's people's mind at ease and cement the image of the family values Frost prides itself on. The holidays are a time for family, or so we say. We're in the business of selling Christmas, Gregory. Let's drive it *home* this year. Literally!"

Home. It was true that Misty Point felt more like his home than the city brownstone he'd grown up in. When he thought of home, he thought of laughter and conversation and banter. He didn't think of empty rooms and overwhelming quiet. Or silent meals for two with a giant turkey on the table and avoiding as much eye contact as humanly possible.

Greg felt his left eye begin to twitch. "I don't—"

"With my retirement plan in place for the end of the year, I was beginning to worry I'd be forced to pass the reins to Drew instead of you."

Well, now she'd gone too far! "*Drew?* But he's your second cousin!"

"Technically he's my first cousin once removed. And a relative with three children," his mother pointed out pertly.

Gregory clenched his jaw. She wouldn't...

Except she would. Well, what the hell was he going to do now? He could try to win back Rebecca, but the thought was so ludicrous and so unwanted, he realized, that it brought a bitter smile to his lips. He could make up an excuse, claim she was out of town for the holidays, but that would only lead to suspicion. And it certainly wouldn't meet his mother's goal. Or his, by extension.

"Well, good thing we don't have to worry about hypothetical scenarios since you're getting married," his mother was saying, and Greg sat straighter, forcing himself to focus. "Do you have a date set yet by the way? You'll want to have that figured out before the party." Without waiting for an answer, she continued. "So you'll host the event, and Burke's will see what a long legacy our company has. It's not just cards we're selling. It's an American tradition," she said, quoting the company's tagline.

He gripped the phone tighter in his fist, feeling the blood rush in his ears, wondering what he could say that would change his mother's mind and knowing there was nothing that could.

When Rita Frost latched on to an idea, she didn't let go of it—at least not until a better one came along.

Greg stared out the window, as if searching for an answer in the rolling waves. He needed to win the Burke's account. His mother couldn't argue about passing the company to him then. But first, he needed a fiancée. And fast.

Chapter Five

At eleven thirty-seven—only seven minutes past the time she was supposed to arrive, she noted in satisfaction—Charlotte pulled to a stop at the end of the long, brick-paved driveway edged with boxwood and looked up at the Frost house—mansion, really.

When Kate asked her to take this last-minute meeting, Charlotte had assumed her sister was throwing her a bone by passing off something small, but looking up at the stone monstrosity set far back from the main road that hugged the shoreline, she hesitated. This was the real deal. And she wasn't so sure she was fit for the role.

She reached for her handbag to see if she'd at least remembered to bring a notebook or scrap of paper, and frowned at the blinking light on her cell phone that was resting in the cup holder. She scrolled through the missed calls list, feeling her stomach tighten with dread. Three messages so far today. All from her landlord.

Charlotte quickly deleted the messages without listening to

them, and then tossed the phone back into her bag. She checked her watch—shoot, another minute had gone by—climbed out of the car, and hurried over the stone walkway to the double front door. She pressed the bell and waited, shivering in her coat and knowing deep down that Kate would never have been eight minutes late for a meeting with a client like this, or with any client, for that matter. But what Kate didn't understand was that being anywhere within fifteen minutes of when she was supposed to be was a victory in itself these days.

But she had managed it, she reminded herself, forcing her shoulders back. Thankfully she had remembered to get gas for her car yesterday, even if that did max out her second credit card. And she would have actually been early, if she hadn't gotten stuck in that long line at the post office and then remembered she had better pick up some more baby food as she was passing the grocery store, just in case she didn't have time to do so before relieving the sitter tonight. She was all but on time, really, considering different clocks ran on different settings. Gregory Frost wanted to plan a party? Well, she was the girl for the job!

Yes, she thought, grinning to herself. She could do this. She *had* to do this. Kate was finally giving her a chance, and it couldn't have come at a better time. In fact, it couldn't have waited even two more days...

She raised her hand to press the bell again, wondering if it could be heard through this ridiculously large house, but the door flung open before her finger could reach it. She stepped back, startled. "Hello."

Deep brown eyes bore through her, strong brows pinched to a point, and the frown on the man's otherwise handsome face told her she was already in trouble. "You're late."

"Oh." She inhaled sharply, quickly flitting through a mental Rolodex of truly plausible excuses she could give for her tardiness, like the fact that when her sister had called and told her to prepare for a meeting rather than come into the office, she had tried on five pairs of prebaby pants before she finally found a pair that fit without cutting off circulation or breaking the zipper, and that by then she had cried off her mascara and had just begun to reapply it, only to realize her seven-month-old had taken control of the lipstick that in her rush Charlotte had left on the edge of the nightstand, and drawn all over herself with it. Then Audrey had to be given a bath before going to the sitter's because, really, was leaving her like that an option? Yes, she had many reasons to be truly *celebrated* for arriving only eight minutes late—if you could even call that late—but she would swallow her own feelings and instead try to channel what her sister would do. Kate, the ever unflappable, cool, and professional Kate. "I apologize. I hope I didn't keep you waiting."

He studied her for a long moment, his features slowly relaxing into a broad grin.

Uh-oh. This was how it always began, every time. A look, then a smile, then a little flutter . . .

"Charlotte Daniels," she said crisply, forcing out her arm and giving the man's perfectly smooth, perfectly strong and warm hand a good hard shake.

"Gregory Frost. Greg, if you'd like." He stepped back to let her pass into the house.

"Gregory," she said, determined to keep things professional, "you mentioned that you wanted to have the party here, in the house?" She was standing in an entrance hall that could easily house her entire apartment, complete with a grandfather

clock and center table bearing an oversized floral arrangement.
A sweeping staircase was set far back, and every which way her
eyes darted, there seemed to be wide hallways opening to even
bigger rooms.

Well. Crap.

She turned to look him square in the eye, but instead of giving her a response, he just stared at her, a shadow passing over
his features. Finally, he shook his head, his grin turning bashful.
"Sorry, you'll have to repeat that. I'm afraid my mind's all over
the place right now."

Her smile came easier. Something in common, then. "The
party? You want it here in the house?"

He nodded and Charlotte reached into her bag for her notebook and pen and began jotting notes. "How many guests are
you expected to have?"

Greg—make that Gregory, or better yet, *Mr. Frost*—frowned.
"Oh, I think the final list was about two hundred."

"Two hundred!" Charlotte exclaimed, and then, catching the
panic in her voice, said a little quieter, "Two hundred. Excellent round number." Oh no. He was looking at her a little oddly
now. "And the party is—"

"On Saturday, the thirteenth," Greg finished for her.

Less than two weeks. She wrote down the date, noting the
shakiness of her letters. She angled the book a little closer to her
chest, lest she be judged on the quality of her penmanship. One
task she'd never be put in charge of was calligraphing place cards
or invitations. Speaking of... "Have invitations been sent?"

"Yes, but we've decided to change the venue," Greg explained. "Frost Greeting Cards is in the business of holidays, you
could say, so the annual Christmas party is a big deal. People

don't tend to miss it, especially when this is the VIP list only. It was originally set for a hotel in Boston, but we, uh, had a change of plans." His frown returned.

Frost Greeting Cards? Her lips parted in realization. Frost. Of course. Misty Point was home to many big-name families who fled to the rocky shores and sandy beaches for their summers.

Charlotte feigned a blasé smile even though her heart had started to pound. She suddenly felt hot and flushed, and she unwrapped her wool scarf from her neck, wishing she could shed her coat. A corporate Christmas party for Frost Greeting Cards. In twelve days.

She stared at the notebook, pretending to write something important when all she was really writing was "two hundred guests, Frost Greeting Cards," over and over. Her handwriting had grown illegible, even to her.

"So tell me, Gregory," she said in her most assertive tone. She'd heard Kate use it many times when she tagged along for meetings with brides or business owners; it was the first time she was adopting it as her own, though, and it didn't come naturally. "What do you envision?"

He smiled. "Please call me Greg. Gregory is what my mother calls me. It makes me feel like I'm in trouble or something."

"Oh? Do you find yourself in trouble often, Greg?" She stiffened, catching the flirtatious insinuation of her question, wondering if he'd caught it, too.

To her relief, he just gave a good-natured shrug. "I've been known for my share, I suppose." He paused, his eyes falling flat. "Lately, though, I think trouble has found me."

Interesting. She pushed back the flicker of curiosity and tapped her pen against her notebook. "Well, Greg, normally a party of this size requires a bit more planning, if I'm being honest."

He looked her up and down. "You look like you could handle it."

"I do?" Charlotte exclaimed joyfully, and then stopped herself, feeling a horrifying heat wash over her cheeks at the startled surprise in Greg's expression. "I mean, I do. I can, I mean. I can *certainly* handle this."

She glanced down at her outfit, from the wide-leg trousers, which she supposed were fashionable when she'd purchased them two years ago, to the patent leather ballet flats that were completely inappropriate for this weather. She'd tossed on a black sweater, which fit a little snugger than it used to, but it was chicly covered in a charcoal wool trench coat that grazed her knees. Yes, she supposed she did look the part, even if she didn't feel it.

She bit down on her lip, trying to temper the joyful grin that was widening with newfound confidence, and suddenly caught herself. It was a typical tactic, one she'd seen so many times before, and fool that she was, she managed to fall right into the trap yet again. Greg was just another one of *them*—a rich bachelor, too handsome for his own good, who had mastered the art of flirtation. A typical cad who knew how to get what he wanted with a slow grin and a few meaningless compliments.

She narrowed her gaze. In many ways, he was really no different than Audrey's father. And look how that had turned out.

"If you'll follow me into my study, we can go over the details," Greg said.

More determined than ever to keep this strictly professional, she followed him down a long hallway, past dim rooms with drawn curtains and furniture covered in tarps. She kept her eye on her surroundings, trying her best to ignore how perfectly his shoulders filled that navy cashmere sweater, the way his dark hair curled ever so slightly at the neck. He walked with confidence, a man assured in his position in life. A man who didn't have to worry about anything more than securing a table at the newest five-star restaurant on opening night, she presumed. She knew the type. She knew it all too well. They were all the same, these rich city guys who grew up with a silver spoon, vacationing in summer homes in Misty Point. Nothing was permanent to them—they flitted from city house to beach house, from woman to woman. You couldn't tie them down. Even if you tried.

And oh, she had tried.

"Please, sit," Greg said once they entered a small study with cherrywood wainscoting and built-in bookshelves containing coffee table books and vases of various shapes and sizes. A faded picture of an older man and a young boy hung on the wall between the two sconces that lit the room. Greg indicated a leather chair across from a large antique-looking desk, and she sat down, unbuttoning her coat and shrugging it from her shoulders.

Greg watched her impassively and then, catching her eye, looked away and adjusted himself in his seat. On his desk was a framed photo—the only other personal touch in the room from what she could tell. From the difficult angle, Charlotte could barely make out the face of a smiling woman holding on to Greg's arm. She tugged her coat free of her arm and leaned forward, deflation sinking in when she realized he was probably taken—not that it mattered, of course—until Greg casually reached over and turned the frame facedown on the desk.

He cleared his throat. "I just drove in from Boston late last night, so you'll have to forgive the state of the house. It's been locked up since I was here in September."

Charlotte waved a hand through the air, dismissing his concerns with a friendly smile. If he thought this place was a mess, she couldn't imagine what he would think of her apartment. Or Bree's house.

She smiled and calmly folded her hands in her lap. This was another trick Kate had taught her. Always put your clients' worries at ease. Show them their concerns are valid, but manageable. Show them you can handle things they feel they cannot. Show them nothing overwhelms you, not even the most daunting of tasks. Like a party for two hundred guests. In twelve days.

Charlotte pressed her lips together. Perhaps she should try the same tactic on herself. God knew she could use someone to ease her ever-growing anxiety—someone who would smile benignly as she fretted and who would tell her hey, it was no problem, they'd organize her disaster of a life and tie it up with a pretty little ribbon to boot.

"Are you planning on staying in town for a while?" she inquired.

"I'm not sure yet," Greg said, leaning back in his chair. "I'm in a bit of flux at the moment. I can't really plan much beyond this party, honestly."

Charlotte nodded and glanced down to skim the email Greg had set on the desk. Two hundred guests, cases of the finest Champagne, heavy passed hors d'oeurves, a dessert buffet, a pianist… "Do you have a piano?" she asked, and then realized that of course he would. It was probably a Steinway.

"Yes, but I'm afraid I don't play." He paused. "Do you?"

"Only if you count 'Chopsticks.'" They shared a smile as the room went silent. She cleared her throat. Right. Back to business. "What about the decorations?" She glanced down at the paper, pretending to find it more interesting than terrifying. "Did you, um, have any preference?"

Greg tossed his hands in the air. "I suppose the usual Christmas garb."

She dipped her chin as her eyes held his. "Christmas *garb?*"

"Do whatever it takes. Trees, wreaths. Lights, I suppose." He scowled.

She wrote this down quickly in her notebook. "Not feeling the Christmas spirit this year?" She arched a brow, and he gave her a wry grin.

"That noticeable?"

She smiled. "Just a bit."

"Let's just say it's been a rough couple of months, and it looks like it's not going to get easier any time soon."

She frowned. "I'm sorry to hear that."

"It is what it is." He smiled tightly, but his eyes seemed sad. "Besides, Christmas is just a commercial holiday anyway."

Charlotte looked down at her notes, hoping her expression gave nothing away. That was another piece of advice that Kate had given her. The client was always right. Even when they were dead wrong. "Well, this information is a great starting point, but were there any questions you had for me?"

She waited, knowing he wouldn't ask about fees—for a party of this level of extravagance, thrown together on such a short time frame, budget would not be a factor. Besides, Greg seemed to have far more on his mind than the planning of this party. It was a nuisance to him, she could tell. A task he wanted to outsource, something he didn't want to be bothered with. Something he would hand over to someone he could trust to handle it. Kate would have called him a dream client, a client with big pockets who didn't hover or micromanage. The realization made Charlotte's heart begin to race. She couldn't let this slip through her fingers.

She held her breath, feeling uneasy as she realized he was still staring at her. Oh, God. Was he really considering not hiring her? Had she messed up, been too late? Had she been wrong to inform him a party of this size usually required months of planning, not weeks? Did she look as inexperienced as she sort of was?

She thought of Kate, of how miserable it would feel to let her down again, to see the disappointment in her eyes. Her sister had taken her under her wing, despite their tainted history, and now she was finally in a position to make things up to her, to prove to her that she had turned her life around. But that wasn't all that was on her mind. Selfishly, she couldn't stop thinking of the fee for this type of party, the commission she could collect, the bills she could finally pay . . .

She stared back at Greg, arranging her features in a calm expression with a gentle tilt of her head, hoping she didn't look as desperate as she felt, waiting for him to give a response.

"Just one question, actually," he said, leaning back in his chair and tenting his fingers thoughtfully.

"Yes?" she managed.

"Tell me," he said. "Are you by any chance, single?"

★ ★ ★

As soon as the question slipped from his lips, Greg knew he had made a mistake. He'd sent her the wrong message, indicated that he was interested in her, when he most certainly was not. He wasn't in the market for a girlfriend right now. He supposed, he thought humorlessly, rubbing a hand over his jaw and a day's worth of stubble, he *was* in the market for a fiancée. Or someone to at least play the part.

Charlotte's sharp green eyes widened, and with a flicker of amusement, Greg noticed she was wearing mascara on only one eye. "Are you asking me on a date?" It was more of an accusation than a question.

"Not exactly," he began, and then stopped when he saw the flush of pink rise up her cheeks. He opened his mouth to explain, but Charlotte pressed her lips together, giving him a hard look. "I'm sorry. You're probably involved with someone."

"I'm here to plan your party, not discuss my personal life."

He watched her carefully, suddenly finding her personal life forefront on his mind. There was something about her that intrigued him. Nervous, he realized, watching her eyes dart from him to the window and back again. For some reason, she was nervous, and something told him it wasn't because he'd inquired into her relationship status.

He leaned his jaw into his hand, listening to the sound of her heel tapping against the wood floor. She toyed with the ballpoint pen in her hand, drawing his attention to the chipped purple paint on her nails.

He felt himself smile. None of the women he'd dated in Boston would have even walked their dogs without a fresh manicure or perfectly applied face.

"I wasn't clear," he said. "I'm not looking for anything *romantic*."

Her eyes flashed, telling him he'd misspoken again. "And just what are you looking for then? A one-night stand? A good-time girl to keep you company during your stay in Misty Point?"

"I'm afraid you've misunderstood," he said, frowning.

"Oh, I don't believe I have." She shook her head as she reached for her handbag.

"Please," he said, holding up his hand as she started to stand. "I didn't mean to offend you. I can explain."

After a significant hesitation, she sat back down, her eyes hooded and entirely unimpressed. "Go on."

He cleared his throat, suddenly realizing how ridiculous this was. He wondered if there was another way around this, if he might ring up one of his female friends back in the city, but knowing them their social calendars would be booked through the New Year, and too many of them had started calling to check if he was interested in "lunch" or "drinks" once he and Rebecca called things off anyway. He wasn't interested now any more than he'd been interested then.

Right. Better to keep this strictly professional. No personal connection at all. No false pretenses. No one would get hurt.

"It would seem I'm in need of a date for the party." There. He'd said it.

Her expression gave nothing away. Finally, she spoke. "And you thought *I* could be your date?"

Well, when you put it like that . . . "Something like that."

"I'm sure a guy like you has no problems finding a date."

"You sound like you've already got me figured out," he said mildly, but he struggled not to frown.

"I know your type," she said with a shrug.

He raised his eyebrows. "My type?"

She gave him a withering smile and hooked her bag over her shoulder. "Sorry, but I work for an event planning company, not an escort service."

"I don't need an escort. Just a date."

"As you said," she remarked. "So why me?"

"Well, you'd already be at the party. And you seem nice . . ."

"Nice?" She snorted. "That the best you can do?"

"And . . . normal."

Here she grinned a little. "You really know how to charm the ladies. Now I see why you're in need of a date."

"So you'll do it?"

"No. Sorry." She pinched her lips, as if that was that.

"Well, if you change your mind—"

"I won't." She stood once more, shutting down the conversation.

He stood, feeling like an ass. "I shouldn't have asked—"

He expected her to nod, to say something rude, to turn on her heel and walk out the door without another glance his way. Instead, a shadow of something close to fear flickered over her face. She glanced down to the notes for the party he'd printed, bringing her hand close to the papers on the desk.

He pulled out a business card and pressed it into her palm. "In case you change your mind." He led her back into the hall and opened the front door, allowing a gust of winter wind to fill the room. "Well, thank you for coming by."

She hesitated again, and then, with a simple goodbye, walked through the door and out into the cold December afternoon, leaving Greg standing in the hall, no better off than where he'd started the day.

Chapter Six

Kate was in her office when Charlotte walked in twenty minutes later, still reeling from the audacity of that man. The nerve! The arrogance! The...the gall! She dropped onto the pale-blue tufted satin visitor chair across from her sister's desk and dropped her bag to the floor.

"How was the meeting?" Kate asked hopefully, closing her laptop to give Charlotte her full attention.

"Oh!" Charlotte crossed her arms tightly across her chest, her eyes blaring a hole in the floral pattern of the soft gray area rug beneath her feet as she recalled her meeting with Gregory Frost. What a cocky bastard. She'd gone there to work, to put forth a respectable effort, and all he'd wanted to do was play, have a little fun with her. Well, she was damn sick of being a passing amusement to the likes of him. Just because she was a townie didn't make her a port of call.

"Charlotte?" Her sister's tone had turned worried. "Is this about Mom and Dad? I know. I keep telling myself that this is just temporary, but, well, it's weird to think of someone else living in our house. Still, I guess we're adults now. And it is only temporary."

Charlotte eyed her sister. She could speak for herself. Kate had her life together, a fiancé, a dog, a house of her own. But then, Charlotte had a child. A child who depended on her for so much more than she could have prepared herself for.

"It's not about Mom and Dad," Charlotte said. Well, maybe it was, a little bit. After all, if she could have moved back home for a while, she wouldn't have to worry about stretching her next paycheck or getting her landlord off her back. She wouldn't be thinking of Jake again, which she had, the entire drive here, and how much easier her life would be if he would just own up, take responsibility, share the duties of parenthood. She opened her mouth to explain what had happened, how she had let an event for Frost Greeting Cards slip away, but the worried look on Kate's face stopped her.

Kate had given her this meeting so Charlotte could help, not to add to her sister's stress level. What good would complaining do? Now, when it was supposed to be such a special time for her sister? A time she deserved, after Charlotte had ruined her first go-round.

"You seem distressed," Kate observed, and Charlotte nodded gratefully, sitting straighter in her chair as she steeled herself for the moment. She opened her mouth to speak, but Kate pulled a sympathetic face. "I suppose you've seen the paper, then."

Charlotte frowned. "The paper?"

Kate raised her eyebrows and pulled the *Misty Point Gazette* from the top of a stack of papers. Charlotte knew her sister made it a point to read the society column each Sunday, scouring for business opportunities in the forms of engagement parties or weddings, or even silver anniversary celebrations. Now she flipped through the pages, stopping halfway through. After a slight hesitation, she turned the paper and set it on the desk. "Well, you were bound to find out anyway." She sighed.

Curious, Charlotte leaned forward, her eyes barely scanning the newsprint before her heart dropped into her stomach. She stared at the center image, too stunned to speak. There he was. The man who had ruined her life, or come damn close to it, smiling back at her—smirking, really—just as handsome as ever. Beside him was a blonde Charlotte had never seen before, her grin syrupy, boasting a dimple on each cheek, her arm possessively wrapped around Jake's waist, calculated, no doubt, to show off the ridiculous rock on her ring finger.

Jake Lambert—Audrey's father—was getting married.

"I wasn't sure if you knew," Kate hedged.

"No," Charlotte murmured. But then, she would be the last to know, wouldn't she? And it certainly wouldn't be directly from the source. She hadn't seen Jake since before Audrey was born, and any attempts to get through to him had resulted in voice mails left unreturned. He couldn't even be bothered with his own child; he hardly felt he owed her any explanation when it came to the rest of his personal life.

"I'm sorry," Kate said quietly.

"Are you all right?" Charlotte asked her sister, nervous to tread on such a touchy topic, but Kate just smiled sadly in return.

"I've moved on, and for the better. Though I have to admit I was surprised..." The space between Kate's eyebrows pinched with concern. "Are *you* okay?"

"What? Of course!" Charlotte's voice was alarmingly shrill.

She balled a fist, wishing her heart wasn't aching, that she didn't feel like she might burst into tears. Quickly she pulled up every horrible, terrible memory of Jake (which wasn't hard to do), settling miserably on the last time she'd seen him, when he wouldn't even meet her eye as he wrote her a check for ten grand, as if by not looking at her made her—and the baby growing inside her—somehow less real. "The guy's a snake, Kate. We both know that."

She pulled back from the desk, forcing a bright smile that felt frozen on her face, hating the awkward tension laced with pity she saw pass over her sister's expression. She had no right to show emotion about Jake in front of Kate, even if he was Audrey's father—if you could even call him that.

"I'm surprised he didn't tell you himself," Kate said, and Charlotte had to bite her lip to keep from blurting out that she didn't see Jake, didn't speak to him, didn't hear from him at all. That there was no arrangement, no child support. No acknowledgment.

"Well, we both know how forthcoming with the truth he is," Charlotte replied. Even though Jake had lied to her, told her Kate had broken his heart, that it was over between them, finished, that had never been true. And if Charlotte had known that, she never would have accepted a second round of drinks, or a third, not listened to him tell her how much better she was making him feel, how pretty she was...

But then, there never would have been Audrey, she reminded herself firmly. It always came back to that one wonderful grounding thought.

"We're both better off without him," Kate said firmly, but even though Charlotte nodded, she couldn't wholeheartedly agree.

Charlotte looked away, toward the wall of framed photos Kate had hung on the far edge of the addition that now housed her event planning company. A radiant bride was cutting her cake, and the groom looking on with an adoring grin, his hand placed carefully over hers.

To think she'd once dreamed of a day like that for herself. The white wedding, the honeymoon to an exotic destination . . . Instead she was hunkered down with a baby who didn't sleep through the night, overwhelmed by the reality of practicality, not romantic frivolity. Forget fantasizing about a wedding dress. Now she was dreaming of the day she might fit into her wardrobe again, since God knew she couldn't exactly swing a new one right now.

She eyed her sister carefully. At least one of them had come out of this mess in a good place. Kate had found a better man, that much was certain, and she'd settled into her cozy life with her new business and sweet little dog named Henry. Charlotte couldn't have wished for a better outcome for her sister. But she secretly wished for an equally tidy outcome for herself.

Kate folded the paper and set it to the side, a subtle indication that the topic of Jake and his bright future was over. "So the meeting went well?"

Charlotte nodded and gave a grim smile. She felt weary, and her head had started to ache. Jake was getting married. He didn't have a care in the world. No responsibilities. No mouths to feed. Her landlord had called twice more since she'd left the meeting with Greg—make that *Gregory*—Frost and she couldn't dodge the calls much longer. November's rent was now thirty days late, and December's payment was technically due today. And she couldn't cover any of it.

"Do you think Mr. Frost wants our services?" Kate continued.

Charlotte snorted. He wanted it, all right. In the form of some arm candy for the night. "Oh, I think so," Charlotte said bitterly.

"That's wonderful, Charlotte! I knew you could do it!"

Charlotte blinked. Rattled.

"Well, he hasn't made a decision just yet," Charlotte said quickly, thinking of the business card tucked safely inside her coat pocket. She had planned to rip it up and chuck it in the nearest bin, but now she wasn't so sure that was the best idea.

The sisters lapsed into silence, and Charlotte picked at the remnants of her purple nail polish, grimacing at how unprofessional it must have looked. Before Audrey, she never would imagined leaving the house like this—she'd had a standing weekly appointment with Maria at the nail salon. But then, before Audrey, a lot of things were different. Before Audrey, she didn't go to the grocery store with wet hair and sweatpants that were a little snug in the hips, either.

Before Audrey, she cared about her appearance. Now all she cared about was her little girl.

"What else is planned?" she ventured. "Any other promising leads?" Maybe she could trade the Frost party for something else. Usually her responsibilities around here consisted of coordinating with vendors or checking on the status of various orders, a little paperwork, some light scheduling, but a client all of her own was a big step up.

"Not really. Everything for Christmas and New Year's is already well in the works, and it usually slows down after the holidays for a while. But things should pick up again in the spring and summer, of course." Kate offered her a small smile. "At least you're getting child support to keep you going. And it must be a hefty sum, considering what Jake's worth."

"Hmm." Charlotte looked away, but her fingers had started to shake. Not a penny. Not for food. Not for clothes. He'd written her one check in all the months since she'd first told him she was pregnant. Hush money after she'd gone to his office and all but demanded he step up. And because it was all that he'd ever offered and probably ever would, she'd taken it.

"Although, why he lets you live in that apartment—"

"Oh, it's just temporary!" Charlotte said. How temporary, she didn't want to know. While clean, it was small, with only one bedroom, and the few furnishings that hadn't come with the property had come from their parents' basement. The first time Kate had come over, Charlotte had explained she was saving for a house, and having trouble finding exactly what she wanted, and of course Kate knew that in a resort town like Misty Point rents were naturally inflated. Besides, it was cozy, she'd pointed out, and already partially furnished. It was a stepping stone, she'd said with false cheer, but Kate hadn't looked convinced—Charlotte had always liked the finer things in life, and they both knew it: the fashionable clothes, the expensive beauty treatments, the dashing yet completely unavailable men who drove flashy cars and knew how to show a girl a really good time and make her feel special for about five minutes before they were on to the next. A place like hers was a reality check. A harsh reminder of the consequences of her choices. Since then Charlotte exclusively met Kate at her perfectly pretty little house or somewhere in town. And Kate always brought a gift for her niece.

Her parents understood. Said she was being responsible with her money, rather than wasteful, the way she might have been just a short year or two ago. But they, too, were quick to shower Audrey with everything they could. Not a week went by that a bag of items her mother "simply couldn't resist" was waiting for her at their house when she stopped by for dinner.

"Well, hopefully you'll hear back from Mr. Frost soon! Since you'd be doing the bulk of the work, it seems only fitting to give you the full commission."

"Full commission?" Charlotte sat up a little straighter, thinking of how hastily she'd exited the meeting.

Kate nodded. "It's only fair. That would be a nice little Christmas bonus!" Kate smiled and opened her laptop as Charlotte gingerly lifted a bridal magazine. She flicked through the pages without absorbing any of the images.

Christmas bonus. Kate didn't have a clue. Not about the state of Charlotte's affairs, not about the commission she had walked away from. Not even about the size of the Frost account.

Full commission.

She slid her hand into her pocket until her fingers found the crisp cardstock. Then she pulled her hand free and tapped her pocket flat, just in case.

★ ★ ★

Even though it was half past two, Bree had yet to take a lunch break. One of the nice things about running your own business was the flexibility of turning the sign whenever you wanted to. The downside, however, was never having the time to do that.

Back when Gran was still alive, Bree would help out in the

shop every Sunday. It had been a highlight of her week, getting alone time with her grandmother, working side by side in a
room filled with so many pretty things, away from her brother,
who had a habit of leaving dirty socks on the floor of his room,
or belching when he walked past her in the hallway, just to get
a rise out of her. He loved nothing more than sinking his teeth
into a juicy burger, calling it a delicious "cow" and making her
weep for the innocent animal's life that was suddenly and selfishly cut short.

Men. She rolled her eyes to the ceiling. She'd been surrounded by them for all of her life. So how was it that she was
so clueless about them as a whole?

She'd been the favorite grandchild. She'd always known it.
And wasn't that her destiny, perhaps? She was the first female
Callahan to grace this earth in five generations. Her mother had
resigned herself to having only boys, as all the women who married Callahan men did, including poor Gran, who longed for a
little girl she could dress up and take shopping with her. Bree's
mother had every intention of calling her second son Brian, and
when Bree was born and it was determined that she was most
definitely not a boy, her mother had been too shocked to even
think about a proper girl's name, never having dared to tempt
fate by entertaining the possibility.

Bree was the family princess. And as much as her mother
adored her, no one loved her more than Gran. It was Gran
who tucked saltwater taffies into her apron pocket and discreetly
slipped them into Bree's hands. It was Gran who taught her the
way of the world, told her stories about her days dating Bree's
grandfather, about the many men who asked her out after his
early death. And it was Gran who Bree turned to when she was

a teenager and lovesick, and it was Gran who would talk her down from the clouds and tell her which boy was worth her time and which one wasn't.

Gran would have said that Simon was not worth her time. She would have said this the very first time that a weekend went by that Simon didn't make plans to go to dinner or a movie or even out for coffee. And even after Bree broke down and called (something she never could have admitted to Gran), and Simon all too happily answered and was forthcoming with details of his time at Nolan's Pub with the guys, Gran still would have given Bree that long, knowing look. Maybe even a little *tsk*.

It was too bad that Gran had passed away before Simon had come along, Bree thought with a sigh. She could have spared her a lot of heartache.

She rang up the last order of the postlunch afternoon rush and carefully wrapped the embellished pine wreath in brown paper. It smelled sweet and woodsy, but oh, if her nose didn't twitch from all the fragrances in the room.

As soon as the customer disappeared out onto the snow-covered sidewalk, Bree counted to five and then power-walked to the glass-paned front door, her pulse quickening in satisfaction as she turned the sign to CLOSED.

She spun around, her mind spinning with possibilities. She'd had a busy morning. She could afford to take a full hour. Besides, she wouldn't see another rush until four o'clock, when school let out and mothers took their youngsters into town for Christmas shopping.

She took her coat from the back room and shrugged into it. A full hour. She could go to Murphy's, have a sandwich and coffee and read a book. Except she didn't really like the one she was reading these days. She could go to the hardware store, pick up some paint swatches for the kitchen. She still hadn't found the exact shade of taupe she had in mind. Or she could walk by Simon's office, just in case he happened to be heading out on his way to meet a client, as he sometimes did.

Her heart quickened at the thought of a chance encounter.

But no, if and when she ran into Simon again, she wanted to be looking her best. And today, her fingers smelled like a forest, her hair probably did the same, and her skin was dry from this cold streak. And she'd forgotten her lip gloss at home. And she wasn't even going to think about the completely practical wool turtleneck sweater she was wearing, which hardly screamed sex appeal.

No, best to save that run-in for a better day.

She locked the front door behind her and hurried down Harbor Street toward Murphy's, the best lunch spot in town, dodging shoppers and puddles of icy water, even though she was sporting her red knee-high rubber boots. She grabbed a spot at the counter that gave her a view of the window and placed an order for clam chowder. An indulgence, perhaps, but what did it matter these days. No one had seen her bare thighs since August.

The carols were playing, but she decided not to let them remind her of her lonely little Christmas. Instead, she focused on the cheerful decorations—Patrick Murphy, the owner, had a thing for toy trains, and Christmas was his chance to go all out—and the wintry view out the window. There was a light dusting of snow on the branches and store awnings, and shoppers were huddled in scarves, clutching red paper shopping bags.

Misty Point might be known as a seaside summer destination, but Bree much preferred it in the off season, especially winter, when mostly just the residents were in town, free to enjoy the snow-flocked trees and quaint town square, and the candles that seemed to light every window, starting at four on the dot.

The waitress slid her clam chowder over the counter, along with a few packets of crackers. Bree took her first bite, savoring it. Another reason she loved this town. Fresh seafood.

Really, there might be a bigger pool of men in nearby Providence or certainly Boston, but this was where she'd set her roots. This was where she wanted to stay.

And besides, could she really leave behind Gran's shop, or her house, now when it was finally starting to feel like her own?

Grinning, Bree thought of how proud her grandmother would be that her only granddaughter was holding it all together so well. That everything she had worked so hard for could carry on. It had been an adjustment, but now Bree had purpose. An entire life of her own.

And that wasn't such a bad thing, was it?

She took another bite of her chowder and mentally worked out her Christmas shopping list as she ate. A scarf for her mother. A tie (she hated herself for her lack of originality sometimes) for her father. God knows what she'd get Matt. A cloth doll for Audrey—she loved spoiling that child.

Something other than a tie this year for Dad, she thought. She could do better. And thanks to the recent uptick in sales from the store, she had the funds, too.

Her stomach full and spirits slightly lifted, she paid the bill, leaving a generous tip, and buttoned up her coat. She was just reaching for the door handle when she saw him.

Simon. She had somehow managed to avoid never crossing his path or running into him in the three months since they'd broken up. And now, here he was. With his nut-brown hair and wire-framed glasses, loping down Harbor Street with that long, lanky stride. His coat wasn't buttoned, but then, it never was. Something about this bothered her. Caused a little pang in her chest. Made her realize that in so many ways he was still exactly the same person. The only difference was that his life was going on without her in it.

She wondered where he was going. It was a strange hour to be walking through town. Maybe he was seeking her out. Heading toward the flower shop. But no. She watched as he passed it, feeling that bitter sting of regret that she knew had no place there anymore.

She could follow him. Keep a safe distance. But then she risked the chance of him suddenly turning around, noticing her. And then what? She was wearing a chunky sweater that added a solid ten pounds to the ten she'd already put on since they parted ways. And she'd just eaten clam chowder. So instead of smelling like a forest, she risked smelling like a fish tank.

No. She'd just stand here and wonder and watch, until he was once again out of sight.

He ducked into Mulligan's Pub at the corner of Oak Street. Probably meeting a client for a late lunch, then. She pressed a hand to her stomach, realizing how easily he could have chosen Murphy's instead.

Right. It was time to get back to the shop. Sell some

damn poinsettias. And go home to her lonely, empty, dark house. But a house that was still hers. And couldn't be taken away.

Maybe she'd knock out a wall tonight. She grinned at the thought.

Chapter Seven

Charlotte relieved the sitter before making her last stop of the day to pick up some wedding cake designs for one of their favorite clients—a young bride with an overbearing mother-in-law who had too many opinions and would no doubt make trouble in the long term. Still. It wasn't her responsibility to point that out any more than her sister could, and so they bit their lips and did what they could to help. And made silent promises to themselves never to wind up in the same situation.

Kate nearly had ended up in that situation, after all. The Lamberts were notorious snobs. Jake's parents hadn't been any more accepting of Kate than they would be of their unknown grandchild. Charlotte had fantasized about showing up at their house, informing them of their change in status, but she didn't need another door closed in her face. And now...Jake was getting married. No doubt to a girl they approved of. From a family who had as much or more money than they did.

For the tenth time in as many minutes, she told herself that it would all be okay.

So Jake was getting married. So he'd have new children, without ever claiming the one he already had. No one needed to know the details. If they did, it would stir up all that dirty stuff that had no business in any of their lives.

Charlotte glanced up into the rearview mirror as she pulled the car to a stop in front of the bakery. Catching her eye, Audrey gurgled something incoherently and flashed a gummy smile.

"Ready to go see Auntie Colleen?" she asked the baby as she unfastened her from the car seat and hoisted her onto her hip. Colleen McKay wasn't a relative, and more of Kate's friend than her own growing up, but it seemed that everyone was an "auntie" of some sort in Misty Point, and Charlotte wasn't about to complain. The way she saw it, Audrey needed as much family and love in her life as a girl could get.

They both did.

She'd managed to get a spot right outside the front door of Colleen's Cakes, and she hurried to the sidewalk and stepped inside the bakery, grinning as the smell of vanilla and sugar filled the warm air.

"Smell that, Audrey? That's called cake. It's absolutely delicious. And in about five months, you will have your very first taste of it."

"I hope that means you'll allow me the honor of making her first birthday cake," Colleen said, stepping out from behind the counter to lift the baby from Charlotte's arms.

"You might have to wrestle my mother for that duty," Charlotte replied honestly, feeling confident that her parents would be back in Misty Point for the occasion.

Colleen looked confused. "I thought your mother didn't bake."

Charlotte raised an eyebrow. "Ever heard of a boxed mix?"

The two women chuckled softly. "Well, there's still time. And I already have such a sweet design in mind for it. Don't worry. I'll let your mom think it was all her idea, and I can just be the one to execute the design."

"What would I do without you?" Charlotte asked, knowing there was much more in that statement than the promise of a delicious first birthday cake for her daughter. She'd been so apprehensive about her return to Misty Point, but Colleen had shown no judgment, made no mention of the past, and instead had gradually turned into a close friend and someone she could wallow with on the days where it seemed that more and more people other than the unlucky few had found their happily-ever-after.

Make that their traditional happy-ever-afters, Charlotte thought, glancing at Audrey. Fairy-tale endings came in all packages, she now knew.

"Do you have time for a piece of cake or coffee?" Colleen asked as she led Charlotte to the back of the room, where her decorating workspace was. "Or are you just here on business?"

Charlotte considered the frustration she felt every time she tried to wiggle into her prebaby clothes and weighed it against the day she'd had. Stress won out.

"A slice of cake sounds delicious. Thank you."

Colleen's dimples quirked. "Good. I've been selling my spice cakes all day and I'm dying for a taste for myself. Settle in at a table near the window and I'll bring us two plates and some coffee. I have a feeling that baby still isn't giving you much rest."

"Nope." Charlotte flashed her daughter a rueful smirk. "But she's worth it."

Charlotte walked over to her favorite table and dropped into a chair that lent a pretty view of Misty Point's main road, Harbor Street. It looked particularly festive tonight, with a fresh dusting of snow that only lightly covered the cobblestone street. Shops had already switched over their decorations from fall to winter, and most of the display windows were etched in twinkling lights or garland. It was exactly the type of picture-perfect first Christmas experience she had hoped to offer Audrey. In her fantasy, though, she was a little more carefree and a little less heavy-hearted.

With Audrey still propped on her knee, she managed to unzip the tiny pink parka with one hand before pulling off the little knitted beanie her mother had included in the bag of clothes she'd given to Charlotte on Thanksgiving. Wisps of light brown hair stood on end from the static, and Colleen laughed as she joined Charlotte at the table, sliding one plate with a generously sized serving across the surface.

Charlotte picked up a fork. "I know I shouldn't, but..."

"It's the holidays," Colleen rationalized for her. "Besides, it's not like I have an excuse to deprive myself." With that, she sank her fork into the cake and brought an enormous dollop of frosting to her mouth.

"I take that to mean you still haven't worked up the nerve to ask Matt to be your date for Kate's wedding?" Poor Colleen had been pining after her cousin since middle school, and he seemed perfectly oblivious. Or not interested. But Charlotte struggled to imagine that. With her beautiful strawberry blond curls and bright blue eyes, Colleen was as beautiful on the outside as she was on the inside. "Don't give up hope just yet. The wedding is still eight weeks away."

"Meaning we both have no excuse to find a plus-one, right?"

"Wrong." Charlotte cut her fork through the frosting and brought it to her mouth. Forget the calories. For one blissful moment, her troubles were gone. "I have my date right here. Isn't that right, Audrey?"

Colleen gave Charlotte a long look. "I meant a date in the form of another adult. Preferably a tall, ruggedly built man with thick hair and deep-set eyes." She laughed, but her expression soon turned more serious. "Come on, Char, don't you ever think of getting out there again?"

"Nope."

"But you never had trouble finding dates. Unlike me." She helped herself to a larger bite this time.

"That doesn't mean I was dating anyone worth having me." Charlotte raised a knowing eyebrow. She hadn't directly mentioned Jake any more than anyone else had since she'd returned to town, and she wasn't about to start now. As far as she was concerned, he was a part of her past, and not one that she wanted to relive.

"Besides," she continued. "I have a baby to think about now. The last thing I need is to be dividing my attention, or worse, getting let down by someone who isn't interested in being a father."

At least, not to her child, Charlotte thought, feeling her eyes sting again. She took another bite of cake, but it lodged in her throat. No doubt that blonde in the society column photo was planning on having two point five perfect blue bloods, who would attend the best private schools and take up yachting at an early age. Jake might find he loved fatherhood. Or he might spend most of his time in the city while the blonde held down the Misty Point mansion. Either way, it didn't matter. Those children would be provided for. Acknowledged. While Audrey...

"I think I'll get some water." Charlotte stood and crossed the room to the counter, happy to have her back to her friend until she had collected herself. Really, nothing had changed. And did she think that Jake wouldn't someday find a woman who fit his family, pleased his parents, didn't jeopardize his hefty trust fund that they'd threatened to take away when he'd proposed to her sister?

Reality was tough. And she should know that by now.

"Do you want me to talk to my cousin?" Charlotte asked as she carried two glasses of water to the table, careful to set them out of Audrey's reach.

Colleen blanched. "Talk to Matt? About me? This isn't high school."

"I could just feel around. See if he's bringing anyone. Might be worth showing up alone if he's without a date." Charlotte grinned. "Besides, the singles table won't be so bad. Bree will be with us. We're quite the trio these days."

Colleen looked a little sad as she took another bite of her cake. "Well, it's easy for me to say when it isn't my life, but I have a feeling about you, Charlotte. In fact, I'm putting my money on the fact that by this time next year, things are going to be different for you."

"God, I hope so," Charlotte admitted. Catching her friend's sharp glance, she felt her cheeks heat. "It's not easy, doing this whole parenthood thing on my own. Sometimes I worry that I'm letting Audrey down."

Colleen looked at her quizzically. "Are you kidding me? Audrey?" To underscore her point, she tickled the little girl, who was already giggling and gurgling, just happy to be out with the ladies.

Charlotte managed a proud smile. "I suppose she does seem happy."

"She's happy. And you deserve to be happy, too. Sometimes I think you don't believe that."

Charlotte looked down at her plate. Colleen was right about that.

★ ★ ★

It took three storybooks and four lullabies to finally settle Audrey for the night—or at least for a few hours. Charlotte sighed heavily as she closed the bedroom door behind her, careful to turn the door handle slowly, so the latch wouldn't startle her, and then tiptoed across the creaky wooden floorboards to the kitchen. She opened the pantry, frowning at its contents, and pulled out of a box of cheddar-flavored crackers. Some dinner.

Charlotte leaned back against the counter in her galley kitchen and sank her hand into the box, woefully bringing a fistful to her mouth. Somehow, she had never imagined that when she was twenty-eight years old, much less a mother, that her nightly meal would consist of a cornucopia of random junk food. Oh, she supposed she could cook, but there seemed very little point in cooking for one; the ritual of it seemed alarmingly depressing to her, and the sheer amount of time it would take rendered it completely impossible.

In a fit of masochism, she had snagged a copy of Sunday's society section from the office, just so she could read the article in its entirety, without her sister present. Although Kate had moved on and found someone who treated her infinitely better than Jake had ever treated either one of them, it was still a sore point in their relationship, and not something Charlotte was proud of.

Everything had always come easily to her older sister. Grades, sports, and then boys. Just once Charlotte wanted to feel important. Well, now she was important, all right. To a seven-month-old who depended on her for everything: milk, food, clothing, shelter. Nothing could have prepared her for this level of responsibility. And she was doing it all on her own.

And making a fine mess of it, she feared.

She slammed the newspaper into the trash without reading it. Jake had taken up enough of her time. There was no use thinking about those days now. She'd always had poor discretion when it came to men. It was the reason she was in this predicament now. Even though when she held Audrey close to her chest, or rocked her to sleep and stared at her perfect little face, with those indescribably sweet lips or that impossibly small nose, she knew she wouldn't want it any other way.

Helping herself to one last mouthful crackers, Charlotte closed up the box and placed it back in the pantry, groaning when she saw the state of the living room through the doorway. Toys and picture books covered the entire floor space, and an overflowing laundry basket sat at the edge of the room, silently beckoning her. Shoulders slumping, she wandered into the living room, picked up two empty baby bottles, and carried them back to the kitchen, where she quietly washed them out and set them to dry upside down on a towel.

Often she enjoyed this time of evening, after Audrey had gone to bed and before she would wake up crying in another three hours, but tonight the apartment felt too still; there wasn't enough distraction from the noise in her head.

Worriedly, she sat down with the day's mail, her gut knotting with each bill, many angrily marked FINAL NOTICE. She closed her eyes and released a long breath before standing and retrieving her phone from the depths of her coat pocket, cringing when she saw the flashing light in the corner. Yet another missed call from her landlord. This wasn't good.

With shaking hands, she began dialing the phone. She would just explain the situation and ask for an extension, just as she had last month. She'd eventually paid October, surely that was good for something, even if it had make it impossible to pay for November. And now December...

She rubbed her forehead. Tomorrow she would have a talk with Kate and explain she needed more work, or why she might have to start looking for another job elsewhere. The thought of leaving her sister in a lurch when she was hoping to spend some time planning her wedding made Charlotte have the uneasy sensation that she alone could be responsible for tarnishing both of Kate's chances at happiness. But telling Kate the reason why would almost be worse—her sister shouldn't have to clean up her mess, not when she had already suffered so much for it.

Charlotte chewed her fingernail, then frowned when she realized the damage she had done to the nail polish. As much as it killed her to find another job and leave the event planning company, she was starting to think there wasn't much of a choice.

Except... Maybe Greg wasn't the cocky, arrogant cad she had taken him for. Maybe he was—*Stop it, Charlotte.* He was just like all the other seasonal residents, just like all the other rich, handsome, sun-slicked guys who stopped by in the summer. He was just like Jake.

But unlike Jake, he was offering help, however indirectly, when she needed it the most. She might have been a fool in love in the past, but she wasn't too big a fool to pass up an opportunity when she saw one.

Pushing her chair back from the table, Charlotte walked to her coat and fished in the pocket until she found the card. She stared at the name and rubbed the pad of her thumb over the embossed letters. With the other hand she dialed the mobile number listed. She reached the sixth digit and stopped. What the hell had she been thinking? What would she even say? Groveling didn't suit her, and it certainly did little to endear one to men. Another sad life lesson she'd learned the hard way if Jake's silence proved anything. Besides, it was what he wanted, wasn't it? It was what he expected when he'd slipped her the card after she'd turned him down.

Well, she'd had her share of giving men their way. She was done feeding egos.

Miserably, Charlotte walked back into the living room and collapsed onto the couch, pulling a stuffed bunny from under her back and tossing it to the side with the rest of the toys she'd received as gifts or purchased at the secondhand store. She averted her gaze from the laundry and leaned back to close her eyes. Just for a minute. Just until Audrey woke up wanting to be fed. Again.

Guilt waged strong, as it always did when she started feeling this way. Was it normal to be this tired? According to most of her family, they seemed to think that she had it easy, had plenty of sleep. She could hardly complain, hardly vocalize the mixed feelings that plagued her every day. The elation when Audrey giggled, the frustration when Charlotte could finally doze off, only to be woken again. Needed.

A sudden pounding pulled her upright. She glanced at her watch, surprised to discover that only ten minutes had passed, even though it felt like the dead of night. She'd fallen asleep, deep and quick, and now . . . Now someone was beating on her door.

She stood, frozen in fear, and then inched to the door as the pounding resumed, wondering if she should run for a kitchen knife, and then realizing that none of them were even clean. But did that matter? she thought wildly. The pounding resumed and she pressed a hand to her stomach, feeling the hard knot under the surface. Tears welled hot in her eyes. She was tired of living alone. Tired of having no other adult to share her problems or make them a little easier.

She walked closer to the door and pressed her nose to the surface, an eye to the peephole, and felt what was left of hope escape her.

Her shoulders sinking with dread, she turned the locks and opened the door, coming face-to-face with her scowling landlord.

"Hi there, Mr. Livingston," she said with forced brightness. A cold gust of air rushed in and she wrapped her arms around her chest, feeling vulnerable in her long-sleeved T-shirt and flannel pajama pants. She reached over to grab her thick wool cardigan from the back of the armchair.

"I'm here to discuss November's rent check." Mr. Livingston didn't waste any time cutting to the point of his visit.

Charlotte stepped onto the porch, shivering as a cold wind

blew right through her sweater. She pulled the door closed behind her and looked squarely at the older man. There was no use lying. "I don't have it."

"You don't have it." His jaw seemed to tense, and Charlotte thought of all the unanswered calls he had made. Shame filled her. This wasn't like her. And she was trying. She was genuinely trying.

She looked down at her socked feet and shifted the weight of her body, gripping the doorknob tightly in her palm. "Not right now. No."

"You have left me no choice, Charlotte!" the man said, and Charlotte winced at the genuine distress in his voice. He smacked the side of his rod-straight hand into his palm, causing her to flinch. "I've given you *chance* after *chance*."

"I promise it won't happen again," she pleaded, panic setting in. "I just need a few more days."

He shook his head sadly. "I'm sorry, Charlotte, but I have given you enough extensions. If I don't have the money for November *and* December's rent tomorrow, then you will have to leave."

"But I have nowhere to go!" she cried. "And my baby—"

Her baby. Just the thought of Audrey, asleep inside, unaware of the fact that her mother—her only parent—was a giant screwup.

He frowned at her. "You have family in town."

Charlotte's response fell quiet on her lips. This was the downside of living in a town like Misty Point. Everyone knew you and your circumstances. And what they didn't know for certain, they surmised.

"Move in with your parents. Or your sister."

Charlotte held back a response to that. She didn't even want to explain why neither option was possible.

"Look, Charlotte." Mr. Livingston's voice softened. "This is business. Put yourself in my position. I need the money. I have to cover the property tax, the maintenance. You think that sidewalk gets salted for free? I have bills and expenses, too. I have kids, too. Joey's starting college next year. You know what that costs these days?"

College. Another hurdle to think about. At least she had eighteen years to solve that problem.

Charlotte nodded her understanding and muttered a promise she wasn't sure she would ever keep before she closed the door behind her. She leaned back against it, feeling her shoulder blades press into the wood as she sank to the floor. What the heck was she going to do?

She checked her watch. Seven fifteen. Only a matter of hours since she'd stormed out of Gregory Frost's house. Surely the chances of him finding another event planner by now were slim. Especially in Misty Point.

Hurrying to her phone, she called Bree to see if she wouldn't mind coming over to sit with Audrey for a bit, and then went to her room to primp.

Chapter Eight

———∞∞∞———

Bree had been in the messy, strangely unpleasant, and down-right frustrating process of retiling the master bathroom wall when Charlotte's call came. More like *trying* to retile the wall. The videos she'd watched made it all look so easy! So why then did some tiles jut out more than the others, and nothing exactly lined up, and certainly not without a fair bit of effort.

She closed her eyes. She'd think about all this another day. Right now, she was being asked to babysit her sweet little cousin once removed, as the family had discovered was the formal name for the connection. She'd read her books and rock her in that old, rickety chair, and she'd stop thinking about what a disaster she would be coming home to.

Bree quickly cleaned up her supplies, washed her hands, and changed. She didn't bother with makeup tonight, and she kept her hair swept up in a ponytail. Less chance of Audrey pulling on it, and she so liked the finest strands, the ones that had maximum pain impact.

Charlotte's apartment wasn't far from the house, and Bree

happily followed a snowplow most of the way there, only having to turn onto snowy, slick pavement when she pulled onto Charlotte's side street. Her cousin's apartment was on the ground floor of a two-flat, a former single-family home back in the day, no doubt, and in much need of loving care.

Maybe once she tackled her own home she could fix up Charlotte's place a bit, Bree mused. If she ever finished, that was. What had once been a clear image in her mind of exquisite restoration was now turning into a physical mess.

A mess she wouldn't think about just yet.

She hopped out of her car before she could think any more about that and hurried up the steps to Charlotte's front door. She could hear Audrey wailing through the glass pane. Huh. So much for her fantasy of a nice, quiet, domestic evening with a cuddly little baby.

The door flung open, and Charlotte stood before her, Audrey red-faced and openmouthed on her hip, her nose running so profusely, Bree felt herself flinch. Suddenly arranging perfectly spaced subway tile seemed far easier than settling this crying baby.

"She's teething," Charlotte explained in lieu of a greeting, and opened the door wider to reveal black leggings, knee-high boots, and a cream-colored tunic. A sparkly necklace graced her neck, and . . . was that perfume Bree smelled?

Charlotte had told her she had a last-minute appointment. From the looks of things, it was more like a date.

The living room was, as usual, sprinkled with stuffed animals and building blocks and various plastic toys that lit up or played music. Some might call it a mess, but Bree didn't mind. To her it felt lived in, homey. It was modest, with a mixture of furniture that came with the apartment or had been pulled out of Charlotte's parents' basement. But it was filled with love.

Filled with a lot more than Bree's house was.

That heavy lump in her chest returned when she thought of what it must be like to have something to come home to other than some power tools.

"Do you want to go to Auntie Bree?" The question was clearly rhetoric. Charlotte wasted no time in handing the baby over, not that Bree minded.

She loved the soft feel of her. She never stopped marveling at how light she was, how easy to hold and maneuver.

The baby sneezed in her face. Bree blinked. Then froze. She could set the baby down, run for a tissue, but where would she put her? And she was sort of afraid to open her eyes for fear of what might seep in.

"Oh. Oh dear." Charlotte muttered to herself as she hurried across the room to the bathroom, quickly returning with some tissue. "She sneezes if she's cried too much."

"Just one of her many funny habits," Bree said, wiping first her face and then Audrey's. The child seemed to brighten, startled by the gesture, and her sobbing faded into a hiccup. Bree laughed.

"I'm sorry to leave you with such a mess. She was asleep, but then when I got out the hair dryer, she woke up..."

Bree walked over to the couch and settled Audrey on her knee. She bounced it lightly, just enough to keep Audrey entertained, but not enough to jostle her stomach. (A lesson she'd learned the hard way the time Audrey deposited an entire bottle's worth of milk onto her favorite silk top.) "You said you had an appointment?"

Charlotte didn't meet her eye as she opened the closet door and pulled her coat from the hanger. "I shouldn't be long."

Interesting. So she was dressed up, and she'd dodged the question. Bree narrowed her eyes. "Where's the appointment?"

"What?" Charlotte stopped buttoning her coat for a moment. "Oh. Um. Client's house."

"At this hour?" Bree whistled, not buying a word of it. It was nearly eight. This was beginning to sound more and more like a dinner date.

"Well, he works, and this was the best time..."

Ah. So it was a he. Of course it was.

"Well, it's very accommodating of you."

Charlotte wrapped a scarf around her neck. Not the chunky, handknit scarf that she'd made in their monthly knitting club, mind you. No, she pulled out her pashmina. The hunter-green one she always wore for special occasions.

"Customer service comes first," Charlotte laughed. "Kate drilled that into me on day one."

"It's my motto, too," Bree said. She bounced her knee a little harder, wondering how to get the information out of Charlotte. "So, this client. Dating material?"

At this, Charlotte gave her a long look. "You know I don't have any interest in dating."

Bree gave a small smile. "If you say so."

Charlotte pulled her handbag out of the closet—her good leather handbag, not the canvas tote she used to keep her files or Audrey's diaper supplies—and hooked it over her arm before closing the closet door. "Well, I'm off. There's a bottle in the fridge if she gets fussy. Just heat it for sixty seconds and do the wrist check. But she'll probably fall back to sleep soon. And I won't be long."

"Good luck!" Bree called, grinning mischievously.

Charlotte paused as she reached for the door handle. "Thanks. I have a feeling I'll need it."

★ ★ ★

It was past eight when Greg turned off his computer for the day, only the darkness through the windows and the rumble of his stomach confirming the time. He'd always had an ability to focus, to sit down and lose himself in his work. It was a trait he'd inherited from his mother, he supposed. Even if that was one of the few things they had in common.

The picture of Rebecca was still facedown on his desk. He turned it over and studied the picture impassively, before opening a drawer and tucking it under some papers. He'd come here for a quiet Christmas. In fact, he'd come here to forget about Christmas. Didn't he have to deal with it enough, ten hours a day from the day after Mother's Day through December 26?

Christmas had always been important in their house, but not in the traditional sense. It was the busiest time of the year for the company, and by the time it wrapped up on December twenty-fifth, his mother could do little but sit beside the crackling fire with a glass of sherry in her hand, smiling from a distance as he unwrapped the gifts her assistant or the nanny had purchased for him and had professionally wrapped in company paper. Christmas was an industry, a moneymaker. People wanted a magical holiday? Frost Greeting Cards could give them one, from the greeting cards to the wrapping paper to the ornaments they collected year after year. Frost was a part of every home at Christmas, a part of every memory, a part of a thousand feel-good moments.

Greg dragged out a breath. And now, for the first time in his thirty-four years, Christmas was invading his home.

He slammed the drawer shut. Marlene had stocked the pantry and fridge with food, but Greg didn't feel like cooking. He was too hungry to weigh his options, too anxious to focus on another task. The proposal for the Burke's Christmas display was coming along well, and tomorrow he'd go into the office to meet with the research and marketing teams. He knew that Frost Greeting Cards had what it took to beat out Darling Cards, but his mother's earlier words haunted him, flitting back to the forefront of his mind any time he took a step back from his computer screen.

Would his mother really hand the company to Drew instead of her own son? No matter how many times he asked himself the question, Greg always came back to the same bitter realization: Yes.

Flicking off the lights to his office, Greg was nearly to the kitchen to scrounge up some cheese and crackers and a full bottle of wine when the doorbell chimed. Frowning, he walked back to the front of the house. A delivery, perhaps? He checked his watch. Highly unlikely at this hour.

But not, he thought as he flung open the door, as unlikely as the person standing before him.

"Well, isn't this a surprise." Greg grinned at Charlotte, but she barely returned the gesture.

She skirted her gaze to her left.

"I'm not here for long. I was just, uh, passing by, and I wanted to see if I'd left my portfolio here by any chance."

Greg raised an eyebrow. So she wanted to dance around the issue. Well, he didn't have time for games. He didn't have time for much, as she herself had been so keen to point out. Not when his entire career was hanging on a damn Christmas party scheduled for less than two weeks from tonight.

Two weeks. Maybe he'd forgo the wine. Grab the whiskey instead.

He didn't bother to feed into her excuse. "And here I was thinking you'd reconsidered my offer."

"And which part would that be?" Charlotte asked. "The part about planning your party or the part about moonlighting as your date?"

"You said yourself that planning a party on this short of notice is a challenge. You were right."

"So you still want my help?" Her voice seemed to lift at the end. A note of hope, perhaps?

He decided to hedge his bets, even though he'd spent an hour this afternoon calling event planners with no luck. "I do. For the party and the date."

She narrowed her gaze on him. "You're not going to let that go."

"Look, I wouldn't have asked if I wasn't desperate." He'd said it to make her sympathize with him, to make her think she was helping a poor guy out, but as the word came out he realized it was true. He was desperate, damn it.

"Desperate?"

"I mean—" *Shoot.* "I can't show up to the party alone. It's that simple."

She looked at him thoughtfully. "So, what would I have to do? Just hold on to your arm and smile sweetly?" She batted her eyelashes and curled her lips into a smile that revealed a dimple. "Pretend I'm your girlfriend?"

He shoved his hands into his pockets and studied the grooves in the wooden floorboards beneath his feet as he considered his next words. His ridiculous predicament. "I don't need you to pretend to be my girlfriend."

A quizzical expression crossed her face. "Then what would I be?"

He sucked in a breath, holding her stare. For not the first time, he regretted ever asking Rebecca to marry him. Had he not, his mother might never have latched on to this idea. "My fiancée."

Her jaw slacked. "No one would believe that!"

"Why not?" He was coming around to the idea. It could all be very simple, really. "I see half these people once a year, the rest I work with, but we don't discuss our personal lives. They'll believe it." They had to believe it.

Sensing her hesitation, he said, "We met at a party in Boston. We've been dating for two years, and I popped the question over the summer. See? Easy. I took you to a little Italian place for our first date. We don't have a wedding date set yet, but we're thinking spring. That's all anyone would care to know."

"Where'd you propose?"

Greg thought back to the night he had gotten down on one knee, placed the ring Rebecca had picked out on her finger. He thought she'd be impressed, but something told him she expected something more lavish.

"Right here in this house." How ironic.

Charlotte inspected him, frowning. "And then what? Are they going to think we broke up or something?"

Greg hadn't thought that far ahead yet. He told himself it wouldn't matter. If he landed the business, it would be good enough. It had to be. It should be. "You let me figure that part out. All I need is a party and a date."

"I'll need full payment for the event up front," she dared to say.

He let out a half laugh. She was quick, he'd give her that, but he was no dummy. "Half up front, half on delivery. *Full* delivery," he added. "And I want to see receipts from the vendors."

She lifted an eyebrow. "You run a tough bargain for someone so desperate."

"Take it or leave it," he said. But he knew she would take it. He knew when she'd hesitated in his office. She wanted the job. She just hadn't wanted to admit it.

"I want a good reference for our company," she continued.

"If the party's a success, of course."

"Oh, it will be a success," she said.

"Do we have a deal, then?"

Her brief hesitation felt long. "You've got yourself a deal, all right." She held out a hand. *"Honey."*

Chapter Nine

For the first time in months, Charlotte had a plan. Okay, so it wasn't necessarily a great one, but it was better than nothing. With the first check from the Frost party, she would pay off November's rent, her cell phone bill, and the minimum payments on both her credit cards, even though the one had been cruelly canceled this morning, right in the midst of the holidays. The second payment would go to January and February's rent—wherever that would be—and by then, fingers crossed, the buzz from the Frost party would have opened more doors.

For now, she had a month without rent. And a month without a home, technically. Her stomach churned as it did every time she remembered that tidbit.

Still... it was a fresh start, Charlotte decided, forcing those optimistic feelings to push through. She smiled into the sunshine. Come the New Year, all would be right again. The mess of this past year would be behind her, soon a dark, distant memory. She'd find a new place—a better place—and she'd take control of things again. She was going to make smarter choices, starting today. All she had to do was get through December, and they'd be on their way.

First stop: the Frost mansion.

Snow had fallen overnight, covering the tree branches and sidewalks with a fresh blanket of dusty powder. With Audrey strapped into her car seat, snuggled in a soft pink flannel blanket, Charlotte finished scraping the windshield, wincing at the freezing wind that burned her cheeks.

She glanced up at the apartment house that had been her home for the last few months and set her jaw. No use dwelling on another failed attempt of getting her life in order.

She tossed the scraper into the trunk on top of Audrey's disassembled crib, three trash bags of toys and clothes, and the half of the rest of her belongings that weren't already packed into the passenger seats. The apartment had come mostly furnished, allowing for an easy exit. She let out a shaky sigh as she wrestled to shut the trunk. When she arrived at the Frost house, she had to maintain a sense of control; that was first and foremost. The last thing she needed was for Greg to think she was the desperate one, that she needed him more than he needed her. No, she knew what happened in that type of situation, and it usually didn't work out in her favor. There was no greater disservice a woman could do to herself than to let a man think you needed him. Look how far and fast Audrey's father had run when she'd turned to him for help.

Pressing her lips together, Charlotte banished all thoughts of Jake with a steely determination and climbed into the driver's seat. There would be no thinking about him right now. She was getting her life back. She was setting an example for her daughter. And it was starting today.

"It's the start of a new life, Audrey," she called to the backseat, but of course, her words fell on uncomprehending ears. Charlotte flicked on the radio, aching for the sound of an adult voice. Lately she'd been talking to herself when she was at home. Oh, she'd start with talking to Audrey, but a baby could only give so much reaction, and eventually the need to fill the silence had transformed into conversations with herself in front of the mirror, in the shower, or even in front of the television. She threw hours of energy into trying to get Audrey to talk to her, even though she knew it was pointless. She was too young, of course. She started dreaming of the day her little girl was older, when they could walk hand in hand down the street, chatting and laughing. And oh, wouldn't Jake be sorry then. Wouldn't he have missed out.

She frowned at the road. That dream didn't include coming back to a run-down one-bedroom apartment, and it sure as heck didn't include maxed-out credit cards and the inability to independently provide Audrey with all the things she deserved in this world. Especially when her father was flitting between his eight-bedroom Misty Point "cottage" and his Beacon Hill brownstone.

She cranked the volume to drown out the thought, just as the radio announcer said, "It's December second, folks, and you know what that means!"

"It means only twenty-three more days until Christmas!" Charlotte replied. She grinned at Audrey's reflection in the rearview mirror.

"So tell me, what do you have planned for Christmas? Twenty-fifth caller wins a holiday compilation CD, and the lines are going wild. What's your plan for the holiday? Will the Wake-Up Guy here. I'm listening."

Charlotte gripped the steering wheel and pressed her foot on the gas, anticipation fueling her with sudden energy. "So here's the plan, Will. I'm out of an apartment, and I won't have cash for a new one until the start of the year. I could ask my sister for an advance on my paycheck, but for about a thousand reasons, the least of which is that I am tired of looking like a screwup in her eyes, I can't do that. I can't ask my parents, either, because they have done enough. So instead, I'm thinking of asking my fake fiancée to let me crash in his mansion. That's right. My fake fiancée, Will. I mean, most of my high school friends are married and have moved away by now, and the best I can do is play house..." She blew out a breath and flicked off the radio as the twenty-fifth caller screamed with joy over their free CD.

Charlotte rolled her eyes. If only life could be that simple. If only her problems consisted of what to make for dinner that night, chicken or pasta *again*, or whether the Saturday night movie would be a romantic comedy or, sigh, another action flick. She longed for mundane. For a routine, dull, humdrum domestic life. Once she had wished for pomp and flash, for designer clothes and a lifestyle she only watched from afar. The sparkle that shimmered off the surface of the yachts down at the marina, the glitz that filled Main Street each summer season. Now she wished for someone to just sit across from her at the breakfast table. A manageable dream, but one nonetheless unfulfilled.

Instead, she was whipping through town in a car she'd had since she shared it with her sister in high school, her meager possessions packed into every nook of its interior, en route to a bona fide stranger's house where she hoped to spend Christmas. She was living the life.

Audrey's first Christmas. She hadn't even bought her any presents yet. She had meant to, but then that credit card had unexpectedly reached its limit. She knew her parents would shower Audrey with gifts, but it wasn't the same as something from her. Still... A first Christmas should be a special time, captured forever in the form of dozens of photographs, spent nestled around a tree with an ornament that said BABY'S FIRST CHRISTMAS. It should be spent in the comfort of home, not at the whim of whoever was willing to take them in for the month.

Next year would be better. She had a year to make sure of it.

With that promise made, she turned into the long driveway of the Frost house and pulled to a stop.

Perhaps sensing that the mood in the car had suddenly shifted, or perhaps just expressing her feelings over the fact that the car had stopped moving, Audrey began to wail. *My sentiments exactly,* Charlotte thought miserably as she stared up at the large stone house through the windshield. It felt just as intimidating today as it had yesterday.

She had half a mind to shift gears and floor it back onto the main road, but one proper glance back at that sweet little face and those eyes that held hers so earnestly made her pause. She closed her eyes, only for a second. She'd do anything for Audrey, and this had to be done.

"Here goes nothing," she muttered, releasing her seat belt and pushing open the door.

She hesitated with the car seat, wondering if she should remove it from the base or carry Audrey on her own. It would be easier to make a quick getaway if she didn't have to deal with that three-point harness. She stared at the contraption, one of so many large plastic items that had come into her life in the past seven months, and unhooked Audrey with a click.

She hurried up the winding path to the front door, sheltering Audrey's face in her neck against the biting wind, and pressed the doorbell with a determined finger. It had seemed like such a good idea this morning. Now, however, her stomach rolled over as the latch clicked and the door swung open.

"Charlotte." Greg stood in the open doorway, his feet bare and his hair wet. She could smell the fresh soap on his skin. He glanced from her to Audrey and back again, his expression crumbling with confusion. "I didn't expect you so early."

Charlotte gave her most confident smile and said, "I figured I'd get an early start on the project."

Greg didn't reply; his focus had drifted to Audrey, his eyes watchful, his expression alarmed.

Charlotte cleared her throat and continued. "I've had a bit of a problem with my apartment. There's an issue with the heating system," she repeated the story she'd created last night when she had rocked Audrey back to sleep, knowing she wouldn't find any sleep and that the baby's schedule for once had nothing to do with it. "I, um, had to move out for a bit. I figured it might make sense for me to stay here. It might lend some credibility to our . . . situation."

Now she had his attention. Greg tilted his head toward her, his brow growing to a point. "Here?" he repeated. "You want to stay *here*?"

She hadn't expected him to be overjoyed, but the bewilderment in his tone rattled her.

"Why not?" Charlotte shrugged. "You need a fiancée, and I need a place to crash." She gave a breezy smile, but her heart was doing jumping jacks. Why had she ever thought he would agree to this?

Greg inhaled deeply, his brow drawing to a point.

"My stuff's in the car," Charlotte prompted when he said nothing more, realizing Greg was barely registering anything she was saying.

"Who's that?" Greg interrupted abruptly, his stern gaze trained on Audrey.

Charlotte hesitated and then plastered on her biggest grin yet. "This is my daughter," she said casually. She could feel her smile waver as Greg's eyes widened. "Her name is Audrey. Isn't that pretty?" she added quickly, hoisting the baby higher on her hip. "I have a thing for old movies, watched way too many of them when I was pregnant, and..." And she was blabbering. And bringing more attention to the fact that she had a child. A child that he didn't seem very thrilled by.

If he turned them away, they'd be back where they started, only worse. She'd have to go live with Kate, make up an excuse for why she was out on the street, claim a pipe had burst at her apartment or some other temporary problem, until she figured out next steps. The thought of lying to Kate made her queasy— but the thought of telling her the truth...Having to drag her into yet another problem sparked by Jake, and right before her wedding nonetheless...So much worse.

"You never said you had a baby," Greg finally said. Though he was speaking to her, his eyes never left Audrey, who, Charlotte noticed in a rush of relief, had decided to smile, proudly revealing all four of her tiny teeth.

"Well, we just met yesterday," Charlotte said brightly, determined not to go down without a fight. "It didn't come up."

Charlotte clutched her daughter closer to her chest. The last thing she needed was another man who couldn't handle her child, even if this was just a temporary situation. If Greg was going to have a problem with Audrey, she'd leave. No looking back. It had been hard the first time around, when Jake had made it clear where he stood, but it had become easier in time. Audrey needed Charlotte. She was her mother. And she didn't have room in her life for anyone who couldn't understand that. Client or not, she wasn't going to let anything make Audrey's first Christmas worse than it already was.

"Hmm." Greg frowned and then looked at Charlotte with sudden curiosity. "What about her father?"

"What about him?" she asked simply, but her chest had grown tight.

"The deal was that you'd pretend to be my fiancée. How can you expect this to be convincing if another man is in the picture?"

Charlotte looked him squarely in the eye. "You don't need to worry about that. There's no other man in my life. Or Audrey's life, for that matter."

The furrow in Greg's forehead deepened. "Don't you have family you can stay with?"

Charlotte saw no other choice. It was time to double down, go all in. "Do we have a deal or not, Mr. Frost?"

"We shook on that deal last night, from what I recall."

"Fair enough." Charlotte shrugged and started to turn away. "I guess I'll see you on the thirteenth then. For the party. You can reach me by phone, of course, and I'll be in touch about menus and flowers." She waved her hand dismissively through the cold morning air. "Party details."

"Wait." His voice was gruff, but there was resignation in his deep brown eyes.

Charlotte bit back a smile. She knew she'd win him over. She'd never struggled to attract men. Keeping them was the issue, she thought bitterly. But in this case, she needn't worry about that. Greg was a business deal, a paycheck. He was good for what he was offering, and he wasn't offering anything real.

He stepped back from the door after a heavy pause and made a grand sweeping gesture with his arm. "Come in, then. *Both* of you."

★ ★ ★

A woman with chin-length gray hair stopped dusting a lamp base and blinked several times at Charlotte before shooting a discreet look at Greg.

"Marlene, this is Charlotte, the, um, friend I was telling you about."

Marlene didn't look fazed, Charlotte was quick to note. Clearly, she'd been let it on the ruse.

"Marlene has been taking care of the house for years," Greg explained. "She looks after the place and, well...she's like family."

"A pleasure to meet you," Charlotte said, thrusting out her left hand, given that her right hand was busy holding Audrey.

Marlene's smile was warm as she skirted her gaze to the baby. "All mine, of course."

"Charlotte is actually going to be staying here through the party. Would it be possible to have the carriage house ready by this evening?"

To Charlotte's disappointment, Marlene shook her head. "The furnace is out, and since I didn't know you were coming back ... I'll make a call," she said quickly. "But the room next to mine is made up."

Greg's jaw set as he looked at Charlotte. "Would that suit you?"

Not seeing much of a choice and comforted by the other woman's presence, Charlotte nodded.

"I'll give Charlotte a quick tour before I leave for the office," Greg told Marlene, who nodded silently, her gray eyes now so large Charlotte wondered if the poor woman would ever blink again.

Dutifully, she followed Greg through the maze of halls, knowing that as soon as the tour was over, she would be completely lost. They made their way through formal rooms and narrow hallways and eventually up the stairs to where Charlotte and Audrey would be sleeping for at least one night.

Greg paused outside the bedroom door. "I hope this will do," he said, holding back as she went inside.

Charlotte sucked in a breath as she wandered through the large bedroom, where a row of tall windows lent a beautiful view of the front garden, now covered in a blanket of glistening snow. The walls were painted a pale robin's-egg blue, with silk drapes in a darker shade skimming the floorboards and extending all the way to the high ceiling. A white desk and armoire each anchored one wall, while a four-poster bed with the most pillow-soft duvet Charlotte had ever seen centered the far wall. A huge, all-white bathroom was tucked behind a door, with a tub that could fit at least two—not that she'd be inviting anyone to join her, thank you very much.

"This is beautiful." She shook her head, biting her lip to hide her grin so Greg wouldn't catch on to just how much it all meant to her. She hadn't been in a room this lovely since a family vacation to a ski resort when she was a teenager, and then she'd had to share with Kate, who was a restless sleeper and kept kicking her in the shins. In return, Charlotte had skimmed her ice-cold feet over Kate's bare legs until her sister squealed.

"I'll put fresh towels in the bathroom," Marlene said as she appeared in the doorway. She seemed to hover next to Greg, unsure of what to do next.

"The crib is in my car. I had to take it apart..." And very oddly positioned the mattress to fit in the backseat, Charlotte didn't bother to mention.

"I suppose I'll need to assemble that, then." Greg said it matter-of-factly, as if it were the obvious conclusion, but Charlotte couldn't help but smile.

"I'll get it out of the car, then." Charlotte looked around the room, wondering where to set Audrey, knowing there was no safe place now that she was crawling and curious. "I have a playpen I use during the day. It takes a while to set up the crib."

"Tonight then. But you'll need help unpacking before I leave for the office. Marlene, can you assist Charlotte while she and I go to the car?" Greg said briskly.

Marlene blinked up at him. "You mean..."

"That's right, Marlene. We need you to hold the baby."

★ ★ ★

A baby! Greg gripped the steering wheel as he swerved into his reserved parking spot at Frost Greeting Cards and screeched to a halt. A baby had never been in the cards, never hinted at—what the hell was he going to do with a baby?

He didn't do babies. He didn't hold them, didn't coo to them, nothing. They weren't in his nature. Babies were one thing to him and one thing only: a deal breaker.

His mind reeled as Rebecca's last words came back to him. *If you love me* . . . And then, the ultimatum. He'd seen it coming, sensed the change in her, ignored the not-so-subtle comments, hoping they would go away. Hoped that the woman who loved her career as much as he loved his, who rolled her eyes at the sound of a fussy child in a restaurant, who preferred to blow through her paycheck on designer clothes and spa treatments would come back to him. Because that's the kind of woman he needed. A woman who looked after herself, while he took care of himself.

And then Rebecca's best friend, Amanda, had to go and have that baby. Suddenly, the cool, breezy woman at his side was talking about children—*their* children—and that's when the night sweats had started. Children were never part of the deal. She knew it; she wanted it that way, too. They were a power couple, they valued their freedom, and neither one of them had any interest in that sort of thing. Until Rebecca suddenly changed her mind.

He closed his eyes and drew a long breath, repeating the yoga exercises he had witnessed his mother practice on the rare occasions they saw one another outside of a business meeting. Calm. He needed to be calm. Six hundred employees in that glass tower were watching him, expecting him to lead them on the path, to show up with a confident stride and a friendly grin. To never sweat. He couldn't fall apart now over a baby, of all things, especially not a temporary one, and certainly not one that wasn't even his.

He blew out of a breath and counted to ten.

By the time he had counted to thirty, he knew he couldn't give it any more time. He climbed out of the car and darted to the revolving doors of Frost Greeting Cards, deflation setting in when he saw the lobby's transformation. Every year on December first it happened. A huge tree stood in the center of the atrium, wrapped in lights and garland, with hundreds of Frost Greeting Cards ornaments hanging from the spiky branches. The usual blue carpet runner that led to the reception area had been replaced with red, and the soft sound of carols came over the speaker system. Greg's lip curled. It was December all right, and that meant they had a matter of weeks to land the biggest account of the year. Having the Burke's department store spotlight on the books before year end would be a big boost to their revenue, but more so, it would ensure his promotion to CEO upon his mother's retirement. Fiancée or not, he was sure of it. Almost.

Greg stepped into the private elevator that led to his top-floor offices, and when he arrived on his floor, he handed his coat to the assistant who stood to greet him.

"Coffee?"

He gave a tight nod, his stride long and determined as he moved to his office. He closed the glass doors behind him and flipped through his messages. Two already, from his mother. He glanced at his watch and gave a wry smile. Technically, being located on the East Coast gave him a three-hour head start, but somehow his mother still managed to start her day before him.

Greg picked up the phone and dialed. "Good morning, Mother," he said after her curt greeting.

"How's the Burke's proposal coming along?" Rita inquired, and Greg felt his temper stir. When he was a kid, he loved watching reruns of those cheesy family sitcoms, even the ones filmed in black and white. His nanny would sit and play solitaire on the coffee table while he sat on the rug, mesmerized. The shows were more or less the same, usually focusing on some problem one of the kids had at school or with a friend, but it was always made right at the end, by the time the mother pulled the roast out of the oven and the family gathered at the table, just after the father strolled in from work, dropped his briefcase, gave his wife a peck on the cheek, and collected the evening newspaper from the family dog's mouth. His favorite episodes were the seasonal ones, where the families would gather around the tree they had decorated together, and eat cookies and sip cocoa and write up lists for Santa.

One time Greg had made the mistake of asking his mother why their life couldn't be more like the ones on television. His mother had offered to buy him a dog; the nanny claimed she was allergic. Eventually he had given up telling her about the shows, and not long after that, he gave up watching them altogether. Later he learned the people on television were actors, playing a part that wasn't real. Their lives were just as fake as this Christmas sham the Frosts were selling to everyone.

Greg accepted the coffee from his assistant and took a sip, leaning back in his chair. "I have a meeting in half an hour with the research department to go over some last-minute details about projected sales. Marketing is finishing the proposal today."

"Well, for damage control I went ahead and booked a lunch meeting with the Burke's team for tomorrow at the office," she continued. "It would be the perfect opportunity for us to lay the groundwork for the party."

"You're flying in?" Greg asked.

"Just for the meeting," Rita cut in. Without pausing for breath, she asked, "How's the party coming along?"

Greg placed the mug on his desk, his fingers still wrapped around the handle. "I hired an event planner yesterday. A local company in Misty Point."

There was a pause at the other end of the line. "A *local* company? Are they any good? I was rather hoping you would have hired a big company in Boston, Gregory." She *tsk*ed her disappointment.

Greg lifted his eyes to the ceiling and took another measured breath. "Well, our usual company wasn't willing to travel to Misty Point, and no one else was available on such short notice. She seems quite competent," he said, realizing that he wasn't so sure of that, actually. Charlotte had been bit . . . *frazzled* in their meeting, and he had been so distracted with this other silly matter that he hadn't even bothered to ask for a portfolio or resume. He'd assumed the information on the website was representative and she would be able to handle the event. He cleared his throat. "Besides, there's no time to hire anyone else. The party's a week from Saturday. You should just be happy it's happening at all given the sudden change of plan."

"Well, if you're sure . . ."

"I am," he said.

"And your fiancée *will* be there, right?"

Greg picked up the mug, boasting a corporate logo in black ink, and took a long swig of coffee. He could tell her right now, call her bluff on yesterday's threat. She'd never hand the company over to Drew. Family was important to her—or at least the image of it was—and as her only son, he knew that held more weight than any engagement. Deep down his mother couldn't care less about his personal life. Some of his friends longed for the lack of intrusion, but they hadn't grown up as a Frost. They took things like home-baked cookies and family meals for granted.

"About that, Mother—"

"Oh, don't even tell me!" His mother's voice was shrill. "Don't even *tell* me she can't make it, Gregory! My nerves are already shot, just thinking of this impending retirement. I'm already stepping down against my will; the last thing I need is to walk away without the Burke's campaign. If I'm being forced to retire, I want to go out on a high note."

Greg tapped his finger on his desk. This wasn't the first time his mother had made such a passionate proclamation when it came to her retirement. If it was up to Rita Frost, she'd continue on as CEO until the day she expired, but company policy mandated no CEO could serve for longer than thirty years—it was his grandfather's way of keeping things "fresh."

"You know I think we can get that campaign regardless of our . . . family situation." He waited as silence fell on the other end of the line. He'd unintentionally hit a nerve, reminding his mother of their less-than-conventional circumstances.

The rumor Rita had started just over thirty-four years ago was that Greg's father had died in a car crash, leaving her a widow who preferred to take back her maiden name, given its esteem and her active role in the company. The truth of the matter was that the man had bailed with no intention of ever getting down on one knee, much less being a father to her child. It was a sore spot in his mother's past—something she never discussed, and something Greg had learned only by overhearing conversation between his grandparents when he was too young to fully understand. She busied herself in covering her feelings, he'd realized when he was older, looking back, but eventually she had given in to herself and hardened.

Greg's own holiday card from Darling Cards had arrived, presumably opened by his assistant yesterday when he'd been out of the office, and was now propped on the credenza near the window, taunting him. He leaned forward on his desk with sudden interest. He studied the image, noticing the way it stood out from the dozens on either side of it, and he knew it represented more to his mother than stiff competition. The Darling family sprawled the width of the letter-envelope-sized card. They were attractive, even if they were dressed in those ridiculous Christmas plaids, and their smiles were nothing short of smug. There were dozens of them, all brought together for one perfect photograph, indicating that such moments were a casual, common thing. Greg clamped a hand over his mouth when he spotted Edgar Darling wearing that jaunty little cap his mother was so put out by, but he knew she would have swapped places for a minute. Cap and all.

He thought of their own family photo and what it would look like in comparison. Rita Frost. And her son. Gregory. Two people side by side, sitting in corporate attire in one of their bicoastal corner suites, or perhaps standing in front of the corporate tree down in the lobby, possibly trying to pass it off as their own. She'd probably be sitting in a chair. Maybe he'd be standing just behind her, slightly off to the side. Perhaps he'd rest a hand on her shoulder, while her hands were folded primly in her lap and her ankles were crossed. He sputtered out a mirthless chuckle at the thought and covered the receiver with his palm so his mother didn't hear.

There was nothing funny about it, though. For him, it was all he ever knew, and he was fine with it—most of the time. But his mother always felt a void, always longed for something— or someone, he supposed bitterly—who wasn't there. It was the reason the company meant so much to her, the reason why the looming retirement sent her into a tailspin. There was too much time, too many days to be filled. With what? With whom?

Greg tried to adjust how their family photo would look, knowing as well as his mother that it could never be deemed as impressive as the Darling family from first glance. His mother's cousin could join in, to fill things out, along with her husband; her son, Drew, and his wife; and of course Drew's three strapping sons.

Greg's jaw began to ache. Drew wasn't even a Frost. He was a Richardson. There was no way his mother could seriously entertain the possibility of letting Drew take over instead of her own son. Her only son. Her only true family other than her sister, who had never even worked at Frost Greeting Cards a day in her life.

Disgusted, he looked away from the photo, making a mental note to toss it in the trash as soon as this phone conversation was over.

"We're a prestigious company, Mother. Our Christmas card sales have beat Darling for the last ten years running, as have our ornaments and the new holiday décor and craft lines. We produce goods that people buy. I think we have this in the bag."

"I'm not willing to take any risks," his mother said evenly. "Now, what is it you have to tell me about your fiancée? Please don't even think of telling me she isn't coming."

Greg rubbed his index finger over his forehead, feeling the

onset of a migraine. "She's coming," he said. "Charlotte is coming." He winced, waiting for the inevitable pause.

"Charlotte?" His mother sounded understandably confused.
"I thought her name was Rebecca."

Damn. Though he rarely discussed his personal life with his
mother, he'd overlooked her razor-sharp memory.

"That's the name of the woman I dated before Charlotte," he
said, hating himself.

"Oh." His mother paused. "Oh—another call coming in.
Must run! Bye now!" And with that, without further question,
she disconnected the call.

Another call. A more important call was more like it.

Greg held the phone for a moment before finally setting it
down. He should be relieved, he knew. Not disappointed.

Chapter Ten

W hat had she gotten herself into?

By the time Charlotte dropped Audrey off with the sitter and pulled into Kate's driveway, she was already regretting her decision to go along with this charade. She took the brick-paved path to the addition behind Kate's garage that housed their office, biding her time as she considered her next step.

She knew she was prone to being impulsive, it just came far too easily for her, but she had to tread carefully here. She couldn't get Kate's hopes up yet about this client, not if the entire plan could blow up by tonight.

Kate was tapping on her computer when Charlotte walked into the open office, hoping the worry didn't show in her expression. Greg was not exactly thrilled by the discovery of Audrey, that much was clear, and she supposed she *had* sprung that bit on him. There was a very strong chance that he would find other arrangements today at the office.

She stopped, grinning a little easier. It was one thing to find another event planner. But another fake fiancée? One would have to be a complete idiot to go along with something like that!

Her brow pinched only slightly as she dropped her handbag straps onto the hook.

"There you are!" Kate said, looking more excited than usual. "If you have time this morning, I was hoping you might come with me over to the flower shop. Bree put together a few samples for my arrangements and I want your opinion."

Charlotte blinked in surprise. Her sister wanted her input on her wedding? "I would *love* that!"

Kate scooted back her chair. "Great. We could leave now and grab a coffee on the way, if you'd like."

Charlotte hadn't removed her coat yet, and with a grin, she pulled her handbag off the hook and slung it back over her shoulder. "Your car or mine?"

They ended up in Kate's car, with the plan that she could drop Charlotte back at the office on her way to a lunch meeting with a high-maintenance bride who called Kate at least twice a day in tears over some new crisis.

"Her latest is the concern over her maid of honor's back tattoo. It seems she had no idea her friend had gotten one until she'd already decided on the dress."

"Halter?" Charlotte ventured.

Kate looked at her sidelong. "Strapless. I told her no one would care, that all eyes would be on the bride and all that."

The sisters exchanged a meaningful stare. Both knew that was a lame excuse, but what other hope was there?

"What did she say to that?" Charlotte asked as they approached the center of town, and the roads turned to cobblestone. Even though it was midmorning, the clouds were dense and the lampposts still glowed.

"She said that *she* cared. And from what I can tell, her feelings are the only ones that matter right now." Kate pulled to a stop at the intersection. "Please don't let me become one of those brides."

"Oh, I won't." Charlotte laughed. "But I think you've dealt with enough bridezillas to know better." She grew quiet, thinking of Kate's upcoming wedding. Kate was yet to announce her maid of honor yet, but Charlotte could only assume that her best friend, Elizabeth, would be the chosen one. And that would be fine. Really it would. It would be . . . expected.

Of course, for Kate's first wedding, Charlotte had been chosen as the maid of honor, but seeing how she'd handled that duty, she knew better than to hope for a second chance. But that didn't stop it from happening every once in a while.

The sign for Rose in Bloom was still turned to CLOSED, but Bree was ready to greet them at the door, all smiles and excitement as she turned the lock and ushered them into the fragrant room.

Charlotte could still remember coming here every Valentine's Day growing up. Her father made it a tradition to order their mother a dozen pink roses. "From the girls." He'd wink, and Bree's grandmother would smile back.

"Find a husband like this one day, dear," she'd always say to Charlotte, and Charlotte would just nod politely, not understanding what she was agreeing to.

But now she understood. Now it was crystal clear. Find a good, solid, loving man. A man who thinks of his wife on Valentine's Day. A man who takes his daughters on outings.

A man that Jake could never be. A father figure that Audrey would never have.

"Thanks for letting us come by early," Kate said as she unwrapped her scarf. "I know you don't open until ten."

"I wanted to give you my undivided attention," Bree said as she leaned over the counter and minimized her computer screen. Charlotte couldn't be sure, but she could have sworn she'd seen Simon's face in the top right corner. Catching her stare, Bree asked, "How's our sweet Audrey?"

Charlotte felt her heart swell at the mere mention of her daughter. "I think she's really close to saying her first word. I hope it's *Mama*."

Bree tipped her head. "Don't be disappointed if that's not the case. From what I've heard, the first word out of baby's mouth is usually—" She stopped herself, her cheeks reddening, and Charlotte looked uneasily at Kate, who was giving her a pitying look.

"I'm sorry, Charlotte," Bree said pleadingly, and Charlotte brushed away the concern. She didn't want anyone to feel sorry for her. She'd felt sorry for herself for long enough, and she only wanted to focus on the good things now.

"If Audrey wants to say *Dada* before *Mama*, that's just fine," she managed to say, but her pulse flickered when she considered the new man she was living with. Something told her Greg wouldn't find that type of thing so cute. "She happens to have a toy dolphin called Dodo. And she loves him dearly."

"The one I got for her?" Bree beamed with pride. "I must have an eye."

"That's what your grandmother always said." Kate leaned over to smell a particularly beautiful Christmas arrangement. "Now, let's see what you've come up with!"

Bree winked and disappeared into the back room. Beside her, Kate let out a nervous breath. Charlotte knew that Kate had chosen roses for her primary flower, but she had been torn between staying simple or going for something a little more elaborate this time, with a mixed winter bouquet.

As soon as Bree reappeared holding two arrangements, Charlotte knew exactly which one she would pick if it were her wedding. The one on the left was simple and modern, with a subtle mix of tightly packed white flowers. But the one on the right was breathtaking—with creamy ivory roses, winter greenery, and beautiful red berries.

"I have an opinion, naturally, but this is your wedding, your decision." Bree winked at Charlotte and stared patiently at Kate.

Kate looked wistfully at both options, and for a moment, Charlotte wondered if she'd start getting picky and ask for a third, even though from what she knew, this was the final round on decision making.

"The winter bouquet," she said with a smile.

Bree looked delighted. "Exactly what I would have picked!"

"Me too," Charlotte chimed in. She made a mental note to call Bree later about the Frost party, if it wasn't too late to get on the schedule. She'd have loved to talk to her now while she had her, but this was Kate's moment, and besides, she still needed to see how the evening played out. There was still a possibility that Greg might reconsider things while he was at work. She swallowed back the nerves that threatened to ruin this moment and forced her attention back on the two women.

"These will look stunning against your dress." Bree tucked a sprig of berries back into place. "Have you decided on the color for the wedding party?"

"Oh, that reminds me!" Kate set a hand to her forehead, but she was smiling excitedly as she turned to Charlotte. "I've been meaning to ask you something—"

"Yes?" Charlotte's heart began to race as she waited for her sister to continue. Being asked to be maid of honor again would mean that everything was truly right between them, that all was officially forgiven and forgotten, and that they could in fact go back to the place they had been, before things went off track. She licked her lips, barely able to contain her emotions.

"Would Audrey like to be my flower girl? I was thinking we could put her in a wagon lined with flowers. She wouldn't have to do anything, but I wanted to include her in the ceremony."

Charlotte felt her smile slip before she bravely mustered one of the biggest grins she could offer. "She'd be honored."

"Oh, I'm so excited," Kate gushed. "Every last detail is finally coming together."

Every detail, Charlotte thought. Except one.

★ ★ ★

Bree offered to drive Charlotte back to the office so Kate could go straight to her appointment. Her motive was purely ulterior, of course. They needed to go over some last-minute details for Kate's shower this Saturday. And Bree was yet to get the details of Charlotte's mysterious outing.

She hadn't been gone long, just as she'd promised, but Bree wasn't buying it. The pashmina. The boots. The sparkle in her eye. She was up to something.

"Should we go to Fiona's for a quick lunch?" she asked, knowing that Charlotte could never turn down a trip to the tea shop.

"So long as it's only an hour," Charlotte said. "I have a lot of paperwork to do, and I don't want Kate to think I'm slacking off."

"Isn't that one of the perks of working for a family member?" Bree joked, but the look Charlotte flashed her was stone serious.

"I wouldn't take advantage of Kate like that."

Bree was momentarily startled. "No. Of course not. I meant... It was just a joke."

"I can't joke about things like that. Not with everything that's happened." Charlotte was frowning now, and Bree felt like a heel.

"You don't mean you still worry about things? Seems to me you guys are just fine. You've both moved on. Kate's getting married..."

"This wedding has to be perfect," Charlotte said.

Bree hesitated. That sounded like more than just wedding planner talk. "It will be perfect. And so will the shower. Let's go have some food and discuss it."

She grabbed her coat from the back room and locked the door behind her. The girls walked in silence for the four blocks to Fiona's Tea Shop. Bree decided she would wait until the order had been placed and the tea served (the owner, Fiona, could be a little too chatty, usually when you least wanted her to) before digging for information.

But as they opened the door to the shop, Bree spotted her friend Colleen standing near the hostess stand. Colleen's face transformed into one of sheer relief at the sight of her friends, and she quickly joined them.

"I was just talking with my mother." She gave them a meaningful stare, and Bree could tell that through her smile, her teeth were gritted. "She has a *delightful* young man she'd like me to meet."

"Cute as a button, he is," Fiona said from behind her daughter. "Redhead with freckles. Skin as white as snow."

"You hear that?" Colleen quipped, her eyes sparking.

"I'd marry him myself if I could," Fiona finished.

Beside her, Bree could feel Charlotte's shoulders begin to shake.

"Maybe you should pursue him yourself then, Mother," Colleen said, brightening. "You've been on your own for ten years now. As you always say, time's a tickin'!"

Bree tried to think about something terrible, like puppy mills or Simon having lunch with the gossipy receptionist at his office, but it was no use. She felt her laughter release through her nose in a strange, strangled snort. "Let's get the table by the window," she said hurriedly, grabbing Charlotte by the elbow.

"I'll join you!" Colleen announced, following close at their heels. She waited until they were settled at their favorite table near the window, the one that lent a perfect view of Harbor Street and had high, velvety soft wing-backed chairs clustered around a pedestal table, to whisper, "Thank you for coming along and saving me. She was just about to pull out her phone and call him herself when you came in."

"Maybe he's cute," Charlotte offered. She unbuttoned her coat and shrugged it from her shoulders.

Colleen raised an eyebrow. "Red hair and freckles. I suspect he has a brogue, too."

"Your mother just misses Ireland," Bree told her.

"Well, she's welcome to move back!" Colleen said.

"Aw, now, you'd miss her if she left," Charlotte said with a knowing smile.

After a beat Colleen picked up her menu. "Fine. You're right. I would. But that doesn't mean she doesn't drive me crazy."

"Don't worry. Someday you'll be married and then she'll be off your back," Bree said as she studied her options.

"More like then she'll be after me for grandchildren. She's not shy with that as it is, you know. And I'm not even married!" Suddenly Colleen's face flushed. "I'm sorry, Charlotte. I didn't mean it like that. I just—"

Charlotte slanted her a glance. "No apology needed."

The girls decided on their order—forgoing traditional lunch fare for the standard tea tray of scones and finger sandwiches.

"So, what's new with everyone?" Colleen asked, and Charlotte seemed especially evasive, Bree noticed.

"Nothing new here," Bree offered. "How about with you, Charlotte? You're working full-time for Kate now, right?"

"Only for the month," Charlotte said. "I'd love to keep the hours, but I know things slow down after the holidays."

"Well, she'll need you to cover for her while she goes on her honeymoon, right?" Colleen asked.

Charlotte seemed to brighten at this. "We haven't discussed that yet, but yes, maybe."

"Speaking of her wedding, do we have any more details on the guest list?" Now it was Colleen's turn to look evasive. She took her time stirring her spoon around her tea.

Charlotte shot Bree a knowing look. Bree bit back a sigh. Colleen could do a lot better than Matt, not that she wouldn't love to see her brother settle down with someone as wonderful as her friend. But Matt wasn't the settling-down type. And Colleen needed to accept that.

"I think Kate is still waiting for the rest of her RSVPs to

come in." Changing topics, she asked, "When is Kate going to decide on her bridesmaid dresses? She's cutting it close, even for a rush order." She hoped that Kate knew better than to put them in something poufy or peach. "It's not like Kate not to have everything on schedule." But then, she was so busy handling other people's big events right now that she was letting Charlotte handle an account as big as Frost, after all...

"She hasn't even decided on the wedding party yet," Colleen pointed out. She looked at Charlotte. "Has she?"

Charlotte seemed to wither in her chair. "Not that I know of."

"Well, we can ask her on Saturday," Colleen said with a shrug. "She probably just forgot to mention anything until she decides on the dresses, and I saw the J.Crew wedding catalog peeking out of her handbag the other day—maybe she's going for something we can all wear again. Wouldn't that be nice? Of course, I'm sure we're all in the party."

Like last time, came the unspoken thought in the group.

Fiona came around to the table, a beautiful silver, three-tiered tray in her hands. Bree immediately felt her spirits perk when she noticed the cookie selection at the very top—something Fiona put out only during the month of December.

"I added extra scones for you girls. And clotted cream." Fiona winked.

"Thanks, Mom," Colleen said.

"Of course when I was single, I watched every morsel that touched my lips," Fiona continued, patting her apron patiently as silence fell over the table. "Wanted to look my best. Never knew when Mr. Right was going to walk through the door."

She pursed her lips and glanced at her daughter for what felt like eternity before giving them all a warm smile and turning to greet the customers who had just come through the door.

The girls stared at each other for a few seconds before bursting into a fit of laughter.

Colleen applied a liberal amount of clotted cream to her scone and took a hearty bite. "I like my food. I'm a baker, for crying out loud. And I am not going to apologize for that."

"Good for you. And I like your curves," Bree said, sometimes feeling like she resembled a teenage boy when she stood next to Colleen.

"And Mr. Right will like your curves, too," Charlotte said.

Colleen's expression turned wistful, and Bree knew what she was thinking. She was wondering if Matt liked curvy women. Well, the answer to that was that Matt liked all women. And he would have made the moves on Colleen long ago, if he wasn't afraid that Bree would murder him.

Suddenly, Bree had an idea. "Charlotte, is that client you met with single?"

Charlotte added an extra lump of sugar to her tea. "I don't know."

"What's he like?" Okay, it was an odd question, a random question really, but Charlotte was up to something. Bree was sure of it.

"Oh, corporate guy. Corporate party." Charlotte shrugged, but she struggled to make eye contact.

Interesting.

"A boring suit then," Bree said, watching Charlotte thoughtfully.

"No, he's not—" Charlotte stopped, catching herself. She rearranged the silverware a few times, adjusted the napkin in her lap.

"Perhaps he might be a good match for Colleen," Bree pressed.

"Oh, no. Contrary to what my mother wishes, my career is coming first these days," Colleen said, but Bree just ignored her and gave Charlotte a patient stare. The girl was hiding something, and just like when they were little and Charlotte had managed to stuff two brownies she didn't intend to share into the pockets of her overalls, Bree was determined to get it out of her.

"Oh. I don't think he's looking to date just now." Charlotte frowned at her plate. "But before I forget, I might need your opinion on some arrangements for a party he's planning."

"Anytime," Bree said casually as she reached for a cucumber sandwich. She'd let things drop for now, but something told her she'd be learning more soon enough.

Chapter Eleven

⸺⁂⸺

Later that night, Charlotte glanced up from her laptop as the glare of headlights appeared in the window. Her heart skipped a beat as she hurried to finish her phone call with the only caterer available on such short notice. Not her first choice, but it would have to be good enough.

Charlotte bent down to where Audrey was sitting on the carpet, playing with her stacking blocks, and swooped her daughter into her arms. She glanced down to the floor in dismay; toys were littered all over the large Oriental rug, extending from the windows to the giant Christmas tree that Audrey was especially curious about. More than once, Charlotte had needed to put the caterer on hold to keep Audrey from tugging too hard on the branches.

Charlotte swept the toys and books to a corner of the rug with her toe and hoisted her daughter higher on her hip, rolling back her shoulders as she waited for Greg to come inside. She glanced to her laptop, wondering if he should find her working instead, and then, hearing footsteps from somewhere deep in the house, decided it was too late. She stood in the living room—at least, she thought it was the living room, but it was hard to tell with so many rooms to the house—and waited.

Moments later, Greg emerged in the arched entranceway, looking almost comically casual in comparison with the grandeur of the room. He'd loosened the knot to his tie and his striped shirt was untucked. His nut-brown hair was still slick with melted snow from his walk from the garage to the house, and it stuck up in tousled peaks, as if he had carelessly combed his fingers through it. He paused when he saw her, his expression blank before slowly allowing a semblance of a smile.

Charlotte released a pent-up breath. "Welcome home!" she said with decided cheer. Nope, nothing weird about this. Nothing weird at all. She gripped Audrey's pudgy thigh, hoping he wouldn't wonder why Audrey was here and not still with a sitter, and said brightly, "How was your day?"

Greg looked momentarily disoriented. "Okay, I guess. How about yours?"

Charlotte smiled a little easier. This wasn't so bad! After all, it could have been worse. He could have walked in the doors and sent her packing. So it was a little weird, being in this strange home and all that. She'd get over it. She had to. And really, maybe it wasn't all that weird. They were two adults, each fulfilling their end of a bargain. An arrangement, if you will.

Still. It was weird.

"Great, great actually!" She turned and grabbed her notebook and as best she could with one free arm, flipped it open. "I found a caterer, and they're sending me the menu options. I also jotted down some ideas for the flowers. I was thinking we go with poinsettias based on the physical scale of the rooms here, but that we limit the table arrangements to black magic roses—those are red—and greenery. That is, if we're even doing tables. I know we hadn't discussed that yet." She paused, but his eyes had glazed over. "Well, if not, arrangements would be nice for the buffet and end tables, something to add color to the room. Although, bar tables might be nice in the foyer, over near the bar. Oh! And I spoke to the caterers about the bar menu, and they're sending that over, too. And—"

"My goodness!" Greg chuckled as Charlotte looked up, startled. "I can see you've been busy."

"Time is of the essence, of course. And I want the party to be a success."

He gave her an appraising nod. "Too bad everyone that works for me doesn't have your...um, enthusiasm."

Charlotte felt her confidence rise on his words. "I suggest we go with heavy appetizers and desserts, set up buffet-style."

Greg shrugged and glanced down at a stack of mail in his hands.

Charlotte tried again. "Passed flutes of Champagne or a signature drink might be a nice addition. Especially since this is a formal event. I was thinking we can play on the word Frost...maybe some kind of white martini with a frosted garnish."

Greg frowned at an envelope in his hand, tore it open, and then, catching the silence, glanced up to her. "What? Sorry." He fluttered his hands in her direction. "Whatever you think is best." He began reading the letter.

Kate had warned Charlotte about clients like this. At first it seemed ideal—they took a hands-off approach and let you design the event—but in the end, it almost always led to issues.

Just because a client didn't voice an opinion didn't mean they didn't have one. And then it usually came too late. The last thing Charlotte needed was more trouble.

She decided not to press her luck just now. She'd wait until he was in a better mood, less distracted. That was the thing with men, she'd learned. It was all about timing. Though no amount of timing ever seemed to work when it came to Audrey's father.

"Why don't we discuss this later? I should assemble the crib anyway." There was no sense in looking overly eager after all...

Quickly, she shoved her notes into her bag, which was propped on the large, polished coffee table that Marlene had scrubbed at least twice today in Charlotte's presence, no doubt eager to banish any fingerprints that Audrey left as she cruised around the room. It was an awkward, one-armed movement as she clung to Audrey, who had taken a painful grip of the fine hairs around her face into her tiny fist.

Greg dropped the mail onto the table. "I'll set up the crib."

He seemed so confident, so sure in his ability, but she knew it was trickier than it looked. "Have you ever set up a crib before?"

Greg shrugged. "How hard can it be?"

Charlotte just bit back a smile.

★ ★ ★

Twenty minutes later, Greg sat gripping a drill in his sweaty palm, all too aware of Charlotte hovering behind him near the bed, where she was trying to keep the baby entertained.

"You sure you don't need any assistance?" she asked.

"Nope," he said, even though the answer really should have

been *Hell, yeah*. He knew the basics, how to use a drill and a wrench, how to unclog a drain, but he was far from handy, and times like this, he was reminded of the fact that he'd grown up without a father. Sure, nothing could have stopped a mother from teaching him how to use tools and fix things around the house, but she'd been too busy at the office. His grandfather had taught him a few things. How to cast a fishing line. How to dock a boat. Most of his time at this house was spent trailing the man from room to room, observing what he was doing, feigning interest in television shows he liked. Enjoying his company. If he'd known he was only going to get a few years, he might have asked for more.

He set down the directions and stared at the pieces of the crib that were still facedown on the floor, despite his efforts. He had a Harvard MBA, for Christ's sake. And he couldn't figure out how to assemble a crib. If that wasn't proof that babies weren't his thing, he wasn't sure what was.

"Here." Charlotte appeared next to him, her palm open. Reluctantly, he handed over the drill. "There's a trick to it. It took me a while to figure out, too." She grinned as she crouched beside him on the floor.

Aw, now, great. She was dancing around his ego. Trying not to come flat out and tell him he didn't know what the hell he was doing and her patience had expired.

"Where's the, um..." He looked around, and noticed that the child was sitting at the edge of the room, flipping pages in a cardboard picture book.

"Just let me know if she starts to move," Charlotte said as she dropped down to her knees and began expertly maneuvering the parts of the crib.

Greg's eyes hooded when he realized he'd had three pieces upside down the entire time. And that she'd known it. It must have taken everything in her to say nothing for the last thirty minutes. He glanced back over to where the baby was awkwardly holding the small book. "She seems happy for now."

Charlotte grinned as she pulled an elastic band from her wrist and swept her hands through her hair until she'd made a ponytail. "She is happy. At least I hope so."

Greg opened his mouth to inquire about her circumstances, then stopped himself. It wasn't his business, he decided. And he wasn't inclined to make this arrangement personal.

"Mind passing me those two bolts over there near your foot?" Charlotte asked as she quickly set to work. "The long ones."

He did as told and handed over the metal hardware, blinking in surprise as she promptly fitted both and triumphantly secured the two large pieces of the crib together.

"You're an expert at this," he remarked.

"Oh, it's easy. Anyone could—" Her cheeks flushed a dark red and she licked her lips, not able to meet his eye as she reached across his knee for a few more screws. She drilled two more before saying, "I didn't have much of a choice but to learn how to do things like this."

He frowned. He supposed she didn't. Being on her own with a kid.

In no time at all, Charlotte had finished the crib, and Greg insisted on moving the mattress into the frame, even though it was fairly obvious by now that Charlotte could have managed it herself. And had before, no doubt.

Charlotte pulled a fresh sheet out of her suitcase and made up the crib before setting the baby inside with her books. One of them he recognized.

He smiled, reaching into the crib to take out the old book about the babysitter bunny. "My grandmother used to read me this book," he remarked. He shook his head as he turned the pages, the images coming back to him now. "I hadn't thought of this book in more than twenty years."

"It's one of Audrey's favorites," Charlotte said.

"I wouldn't have even thought it would still be in print."

"Oh." Charlotte seemed nervous. "I picked it up at a rummage sale." She opened another book for Audrey, not meeting his eye.

No doubt she bought a lot of things at rummage sales, Greg thought, feeling embarrassed by the grandeur of this house. It wasn't a reflection of him. His apartment back in Boston was minimal. Devoid of showy material possessions.

Devoid of a lot of things, he considered.

But this house was his grandparents' home, filled with their things. Their memories.

"You know, this makes me think of something," he said. "Do you have a few minutes? I'd like to show you something downstairs."

"Sure. Audrey will be content for a bit. Once the books start hitting the floors, we'll know she's ready to start wailing, though."

She must have read the panic in his face, because she started backpedaling. "Oh, I mean . . . "

He held up a hand. He knew what she meant. Babies threw things. And they cried. A lot.

Just two reasons why he wasn't interested.

Greg led her down the stairs and into one of the less formal rooms at the back of the house, where he liked to watch television. There were some old photo albums in here that might be worth setting out at the party, just to drive home that family feeling his mother was intent on showing.

The television was blaring, no doubt left on by Marlene, who liked to catch up on her soap operas while she dusted. He found the remote control wedged between two suede sofa cushions and directed the device at the television just as Charlotte blurted, "Wait."

Greg paused, noticing the warmth in her smile, the adoration in her eyes as she stared at the screen. Following her gaze, he gave an inward groan. A Frost Greeting Cards Christmas commercial. The extra sappy one where the little girl with two pigtails and red bows bakes gingerbread cookies with her mother and then sends them to her deployed father, who forgoes the crumbling cookies at the end to read the card, emblazoned with the Frost Greeting Cards logo just below the little girl's crude signature.

Greg stifled a yawn as the commercial finally faded. He turned to Charlotte, a wry grin already spreading over his face, when his breath caught. Were those *tears* in her eyes? They were. They most certainly were.

Oh, good grief. She was one of *them*. He should have pegged her. She was one of the millions of people who lapped up Christmas, loved everything about it, from the tinsel to the flashing light on Rudolph's nose.

Catching his wide eyes, Charlotte gave a watery smile. "Sorry. That one gets me every time."

"You and about a million others." He flicked off the television and the room fell dim. "It's our most successful commercial three years running."

"I never really noticed it until this year." Charlotte shrugged. "Now that I have Audrey, I don't know, everything's changed. When I see that little girl on the commercial, it makes me imagine how Audrey will be a few years from now. It'll be so fun. Baking Christmas cookies with her..."

Greg just stared at her, then back to the screen. He'd seen this commercial a hundred times, maybe more, and never thought anything about it.

"I'll let the market research team know they hit the sweet spot with this one, then."

This seemed to please Charlotte, because she grinned until her dimple quirked.

Right. Back to business. Clearing his throat, he opened the lower cabinet of the built-in shelves and pulled out the photo albums his grandmother had kept over the years. He ran a hand over the cover, almost afraid to look at what was inside, at the years of his life he'd tried to push aside, at the part of himself he'd tried to deny.

This was his grandparents' house, yes, but it was the closest thing to a real home he'd ever had. It was a big home, far from modest, but it was built through innovation, hard work, and a vision.

A vision he intended to see through.

"Tomorrow you should call Stacy at my office. She'll set you up with a bunch of products from the warehouse. The more Frost Greeting Card items we can have included—subtly, of course—the better this party will be."

"I'll get on that first thing." Charlotte nodded firmly. "This party's going to be a great success."

"It'd better be," Greg mumbled, and a flicker of something that looked an awful lot like panic fell over Charlotte's face.

"Perhaps in the morning we can go over some of the details," she suggested.

"I have an early meeting tomorrow," he informed her. Just thinking of lunch with the Burke's executives and his mother made his stomach burn. He swallowed the sour taste in his mouth. "A very important meeting."

Charlotte blew out a sigh and looked him squarely in the eye. "Well, last I checked this party was important, too. To both of us. You need it to go smoothly, and I'm counting on the second half of that commission."

"Don't forget the other part of our deal," Greg reminded her, even though he practically cringed at bringing attention to it again. It had been a nice evening, surprisingly. Until now.

"Oh, I haven't," she said haughtily. "But I'm more than just your fake fiancée. This party needs to be planned, and I meant it when I said that something like this usually takes considerably longer to pull together."

"And I meant it when I hired you to plan it," he said tersely. "So plan it."

Charlotte huffed. "I intend to plan it. I've been working hard all day, and I'll be doing the same tomorrow. But I expect you to cooperate; otherwise, you've lost your say."

Greg turned back to her, frowning. "What does that mean?"

"It means that if you don't want to give me your opinion, then you've waived your rights to complain when I do things my way."

Now wait a minute here. Too much was riding on this party for him to relinquish complete control to a total stranger, regardless of her background or what he was paying her. "I'll review your notes tonight and give you my thoughts tomorrow," he said.

She gave a smug smile. "Good."

From somewhere upstairs, he heard a loud thump, followed by another. And for the first time that day, he was happy there was a baby in the house. It was the only sobering reminder that Charlotte was just around for another two weeks and that he had no business wishing it might be a little more.

★ ★ ★

Charlotte stared at the crib, positioned sweetly near the window. It looked right at home there, not that she'd be saying that part aloud. The books she'd given Audrey to read were on the floor, and the little girl was holding on to the rail, grinning.

Greg picked up the toolbox and stood near the doorway. "So...that's it then? No...bolts need tightening?"

Charlotte considered how closely he'd dodged an innuendo and bit the inside of her cheek. "I think it's all good. Thank you again," she said, wondering if she should say something more. She eyed him carefully, noticing that from this distance he seemed more like a guy she might have met at a party or down at one of the hangouts near the marina, not like her client.

"Have you eaten yet?" Greg asked abruptly.

Charlotte startled, and quickly scanned his face, looking for a hidden meaning. Was she expected to cook dinner? That would be...a disaster, frankly. "No," she said, and then, still unsure, ventured, "Have you?"

"No, and I missed lunch, too." He tipped his head, giving

a shrug that bordered on casual but was probably anything but. "How about dinner? Then we can go over more of the party details, and uh . . . the other thing."

Thing meaning fake date. Fake fiancée.

She'd stick with *thing*.

"Might give us a chance to get to know each other a little better. If we're going to pull this off, we can't appear like strangers, can we?" He grinned.

Charlotte transferred Audrey to her other hip to keep her mind from getting the better of her. This is how it always began. A smooth invitation that led to a fling and, later, heartbreak. But not this time, she reminded herself. This was business. Nothing more. So what if Greg was mildly good-looking in a Patrick Dempsey sort of way? Even if he was interested in her, which he most certainly was not, she knew better.

Men like Greg just didn't take women like Charlotte seriously. They took blond blue bloods seriously. Girls with country club memberships and private tennis coaches.

"Why don't we try that place down on Harbor Street?" Greg suggested. "You know, the small one on the corner, with the red bistro tables in the summer?"

Charlotte felt her back teeth graze. "Bistro Rouge." Her chest was thumping with bad memories.

Catching her expression, Greg asked, "You don't like it?"

"What?" She quickly arranged her features back into a smile. "No, I like it. The food is delicious," she admitted with a weakening smile.

"Perfect, then," he said, clapping his hands together as if that settled it. Audrey, noticing his gesture, began clapping her chubby hands together, giggling with satisfaction. Startled, Greg watched her from under his furrowed brow and then gave a slow, reluctant grin. Finally returning his gaze to Charlotte, he said, "I'll make reservations."

Charlotte swallowed, wondering if he had thought the logistics through, and decided he hadn't. "I'll call the babysitter, then." She'd give her an excuse, tell her Greg was a client and it would be easier to watch Audrey here in case the meeting ran late after dinner. She frowned, wondering just how suspicious that sounded. Deeply, she decided.

Relief seemed to sweep Greg's face when he said, "Oh good. I was wondering if you had anyone lined up. For the party," he added.

Charlotte nodded assertively. "Of course. I work, after all. It's not like I carry my baby with me on the job." Well, not every job. She paused, suddenly remembering she only had fourteen dollars in her wallet. She supposed she could have Greg drive her past an ATM machine on their way to the restaurant; there was at least a little something in there, though not much. Although Lisa had been babysitting Audrey for months, she insisted on cash payment, no checks, no promises of adding it to the weekly tab on goodwill. Smart girl, Charlotte thought bitterly, thinking of her shameful track record. It wasn't supposed to be this way. She was an adult now. A mother. She had to get her life in order.

Charlotte walked over to the bedside table where she'd left her phone. "I'll just need to stop by a bank, if that's okay."

Greg waved a hand through the air. "Don't worry about it. I have cash. How much are sitters these days? Four, five bucks an hour?"

Charlotte glanced up from her phone. "Try fifteen to twenty."

To her satisfaction, Greg's eyes burst open. *"Twenty?"*

"Isn't that awful?" No wonder she was struggling with money! The damn sitter was bleeding her dry. "And half the time the baby is asleep and they're just watching television."

Greg shook his head. "I might have to switch careers."

"Oh, so you like babies?" Charlotte asked, and then stopped herself as the color drained from Greg's face. "Oh, but then, who wouldn't for twenty bucks an hour to sit around and watch television? Ha-ha." Her cheeks were burning, Charlotte scrolled blindly through her phone until she came to Lisa's number.

"Marlene's here. I can ask her to watch Audrey. That is, if you'd be comfortable with that arrangement." Sensing her hesitation, he added, "Marlene has three children and four grandchildren in Providence."

Charlotte frowned, thinking of the panic in the woman's eyes that morning, how more than once she'd felt the weight of someone's gaze on her and turned to find Marlene hovering in a doorway, her mouth slightly agape.

"I didn't know she . . . Well, she seemed so . . . surprised."

Greg's mouth drew into a line. "There haven't been any children in this house since I was little, and that was a long time ago. Trust me, she's good with children. I speak from personal experience." His smile turned fond, but there was a sadness in his eyes.

"Okay then," Charlotte said, a little reluctantly. "I'll get Audrey settled for the night. She might not even wake up while we're gone."

Fat chance of that, she didn't bother to say. Audrey was a professional catnapper. Every two or three hours she was roused from her sweet sleep for no apparent reason. Numerous parenting manuals that Charlotte had checked out from the library advised on sleep training. Some were of the firm stance to let the child scream it out, see that they weren't going to get your attention. Charlotte had tried that for all of two nights and caved. She'd slept less than ever, for starters, and she'd never felt more selfish in her life, either. Even more selfish than she did around her sister, which was really saying something.

Lately she was following the advice of comforting the child in the dark. Keeping the lights off, not talking, and adhering strictly to the baby's needs sent the message that you cared but that it wasn't playtime.

Or so the book said . . .

"I'll freshen up. It shouldn't take more than ten minutes."

"*Ten* minutes?" Greg parroted. "You're quick."

He sounded like her cousin Bree. In other words: clueless. Charlotte gave him a watery smile as he walked out of the bedroom, and then she locked the door firmly behind him, just in case he got any notions.

Chapter Twelve

Bistro Rouge was decked out for the holidays, just like every other establishment on Harbor Street. The entire town was transformed since he'd been here in the late summer. Garlands and lights wrapped every lamppost. Wreaths adorned every window. Snow covered the sidewalks in a serene blanket. It was like something out of a postcard. Or something off the cover of a Frost greeting card.

Greg curled his lip at the tree in the corner of the restaurant, the fake presents tucked underneath wrapped, he noticed, in a print Frost had discontinued four years ago.

"Something wrong?" Charlotte asked.

Greg reached for his glass of wine, indulged in a long sip, and slid his eyes over the rim to his dinner date. Dinner companion, he reminded himself. Fake date, nothing more.

"Christmas at the office. Christmas at home." He gestured to the garland hanging from the mahogany bar at the corner of the room. "Christmas everywhere."

"I think it looks pretty," Charlotte replied, giving him a sweet smile.

Greg cleared his throat and picked up the menu, scanning it quickly before deciding on the heaviest meal on the list. He was ravenous—that was it. He never could think clearly on an empty stomach.

"Yes, well. When Christmas is your business more than nine months of the year, you look forward to escaping it every now and then."

"Well, I'm looking especially forward to Christmas this year." Charlotte set her menu to the side of the table and reached for her wineglass. "It's Audrey's first Christmas. I want it to be special."

Ah yes, Audrey. Greg closed his menu with a heavy slap and slid his wineglass along the thick white tablecloth. "I apologize for my reaction this morning. I was...surprised."

Charlotte shrugged. "I probably should have told you I had a daughter before I came to the house this morning," she said, and then, after opening her mouth to say something, she closed it firmly.

"When you said you were single, I hadn't realized you had been married."

Charlotte's cheeks flushed. "Oh, I've never been married."

Greg frowned at his rudeness and then perked up as the waiter approached, happy for the brief distraction. When their orders were given, he said, "I apologize. I shouldn't have jumped to conclusions."

Charlotte deftly sidestepped the apology. "Speaking of marriage, you still haven't told me why you need a fiancée so badly."

Greg supposed she had a right to know, even if he didn't feel like talking about his current predicament. Or why he was in it. "My mother has it in her head that we'll stand a better chance of landing an account with Burke's department stores if we give the impression that we're a family-focused company. Which we are," he added. "And they will be in attendance at the party."

"So she knows this isn't real then?"

Greg hesitated. "Not exactly."

Charlotte looked at him quizzically. "What would give her the impression you were really engaged?"

"Because I used to be engaged. And my mother doesn't know that it ended."

If this was startling news to her, she didn't show it. "What happened?"

Greg took a long swig of his drink. "We didn't want the same things." Wasn't that how it usually went?

Charlotte rearranged her silverware with the tips of her fingers, the fading, chipped paint on her nails clear for all to see. Greg smiled. Rebecca wouldn't be caught dead showing her nails like that. She would have dealt with it at the first ding.

"My mother never met her," Greg continued. "So it shouldn't be very difficult to convince her you're my fiancée."

"Never met her?" Charlotte stared at him.

"My mother doesn't have much time for things like family dinners." His smile felt strained when he said, "I suppose I should be grateful. I have friends whose mothers never get off their backs about finding a nice girl to settle down with. My mother is more interested in asking for the latest sales projections than the status of my personal life."

Charlotte frowned, and Greg reached for his glass, refusing to feed into that pity in her eyes, into the uneasy stir of his gut.

"Couldn't you have just asked a date?"

"Could have." But a date implied a promise of something

with more potential, not a clear-cut arrangement. "I didn't want to make things messy, you could say. I've had my share."

Charlotte gave a small smile. One that told him she could relate.

She reached for her wineglass and then set it back down again. "Shouldn't I know some things about you? Where you were born, that type of thing? I mean, I am marrying you, after all." She grinned, and Greg leaned back in his chair, feeling more relaxed.

"I was born and raised in Boston. My birthday is April fifth. The Misty Point home belonged to my maternal grandparents and later my mother. We would summer here on and off, before my grandparents passed away. Then after they died, my mother bought a place on the West Coast, where she now resides, and so we spent the season there." Greg drew a breath, thinking of anything else that might come up in conversation. "I went to Phillips Exeter for high school, graduated from Tufts after that, followed by Harvard for business school, and then immediately went to work for the family company. My mother's name is Rita, and she's the CEO of Frost Greeting Cards, scheduled to retire at the end of the year. I have no siblings. No pets, either," he added as an afterthought. He took a sip of his drink. His whole life could be summed up in a matter of sentences. It didn't sit well.

Charlotte nodded slowly. "And who will take over then? As CEO? Should I know this?"

"You should absolutely know this." Greg grinned, feeling his spirits rise. "Because that person would be me." And it would be. So help him, it most certainly would be.

That position was rightfully his. He had worked for it. Earned it. Fought for it. Even when he wasn't old enough to work, he had supported the company from afar, sitting at home, night after lonely night, while his mother expanded the empire. And now it was coming down to something outside of his control. It was coming down to Charlotte. The lovely, quirky woman sitting across from him held his future in her hands.

He made a mental note to make an appointment for her to have a proper manicure before his mother stormed into town.

★ ★ ★

By the time their entrees had arrived, Charlotte had learned that Greg had broken his arm in the third grade, then again in the fifth, and that he had broken his nose skiing at the age of seventeen on a ski weekend in Vermont. She knew he played soccer in grade school and lacrosse in high school and that he hated mushrooms. She knew the names of his extended family members and his favorite teachers, and she knew that he always asked for pepperoni pizza and chocolate cake on his birthday, which infuriated his mother, who tried for years to insist on keeping reservations at a Zagat-rated French restaurant in Cambridge, and who always had to cancel them at the last minute.

"Enough about me," Greg finally said. "What do I need to know about you?"

"Will it really matter?" she asked. "I can be anyone, so long as I'm there, right? No one will know me. They'll take your word. You can make up any story you'd like about me."

"I'm more interested in fact than fiction," Greg said. "You

have me at a disadvantage. At the very least, you could tell me your most embarrassing childhood memory."

Charlotte laughed. "There are probably too many to remember. My sister was the perfect daughter. I was always trying to live up to her, always falling short."

"Ah, so you have a sister." He gave her a slow grin. "See, that wasn't so bad, was it?"

"No," she admitted. Still, she didn't want to reveal too much. It was better that way. Made her feel less vulnerable.

"So what else?" He seemed so earnest, so...nice, that she didn't really know how to react. When she'd agreed to this arrangement, she hadn't expected there would be dinners or outings or conversation. She hadn't expected to let someone in.

Charlotte reached up to fiddle with her earring—an old nervous habit—and then realized she wasn't wearing any. It had been so long since she had a reason to wear them, and there had been that terrible time when Audrey had yanked one of her chandelier earrings a bit too hard, that she had given up and eventually stopped to think about it altogether.

"My life's not very exciting," she said. "I plan parties by day and take care of my daughter by night. Riveting." She plastered a brave smile on her face, but Greg's hooded stare unnerved her. He wasn't buying it any more than she was, and he didn't seem like the type to let things drop when he wanted his way. Or an answer.

She twisted the napkin in her lap and looked around the room, her eyes immediately landing on the table near the window. It was empty, save a flickering votive candle and a small bouquet of flowers, but Charlotte could almost see herself sitting there, waiting for him to meet her, wondering how she would frame it, what he would say. *I'm pregnant, Jake.* Or perhaps, more optimistically, *Jake, I have good news.* When he'd finally arrived, twenty minutes late, looking bored and impatient, she'd lost her nerve. She'd barely waited for the waitress to bring him his drink before blurting it out, and the shell-shocked look on his face that never did transform into a smile confirmed her worst fears.

She pulled her gaze away. Her hands were shaking and Greg was watching her carefully.

"So you grew up in Misty Point?" He tore off a piece of baguette and offered her the rest, but she shook her head. She'd be lucky to squeeze into that black sheath she hoped to wear for the party as it was.

"A townie." She gave a thin smile, knowing how that went over with men like Greg.

"And you met Audrey's father in town?" He set his wrists on the table and leaned forward. "I'm sorry, but if we're going to pull this off, I need to know what I'm dealing with here."

Charlotte met his eye. "Audrey's father and I aren't on speaking terms at the moment. I imagine he'll be back in town for the holidays, but I wouldn't know for certain." She pressed her lips together and refolded the napkin on her lap. Her explanation was an understatement, but it was better than the truth. If she told him any more, there would be questions, and she didn't feel like defending her decision to let things be the way they were. She knew she could have gone to a lawyer and demanded child support, but lawyers cost money. She could have gone to Kate but... that was yet another subject matter better left alone.

"He mostly lives in Boston, but he has family here." She paused, careful with her words. "I just moved back from Boston over the summer, actually."

She decided to omit the part about how she'd chased Jake to Boston to begin with, in the hopes that he would change his mind, grow a heart, want to be a family. Instead he'd paid her ten grand to go away. Money that she'd accepted, because it was all he was offering her. Money that was all too quickly gone.

"Boston's a good city," Greg said amicably. "But I like the change of pace in Misty Point."

Charlotte nodded eagerly, grateful for the shift in conversation. If she never went back to Boston, that was fine with her. Once she'd dreamed of getting out of her small hometown, of living a life more glamorous and exciting. But she'd tried that road. And it was hard and lonely.

Greg lifted the bottle of wine from its bucket and refilled their glasses. "Do you get back to Boston often?" When Charlotte gave what she hoped was a vague shrug, Greg frowned at her. "So Audrey's father visits her here?"

"No," she said simply, and the look on Greg's face indicated that he was far from surprised.

His jaw was tight as he cut into his steak. "Anyone can father a child, but it takes a real man to be a dad."

Charlotte frowned at the hurt in his voice. "Sounds like you're speaking from experience."

"I never knew my father." Greg took a large bite of his food.

Charlotte shifted in her chair. "I'm sorry. I . . . hope I didn't hit a nerve."

Greg shrugged. "I guess you could say I have little tolerance when it comes to men skirting the responsibilities of fatherhood."

"Of course." Charlotte paused. "Have you ever thought of looking for him?" she asked, selfish curiosity causing her to sit straighter in her chair as she waited for his response. It had been something she'd wondered about for months, but especially now with Jake's recent wedding announcement. When would Audrey begin to ask questions about her father? What would she tell her? How could she protect her daughter from the pain of finding out her father might love his other future children, but not her? It pained her, caused a physical ache in her chest every time she thought of it. How could anyone not love such a beautiful little girl like Audrey? So sweet and happy, with those big bright eyes and that smile!

She pressed her lips together. Look at her! Her one night out in months and here she was missing her daughter. She should be enjoying the chance to be her own person again, even if she had become a shadow of her former self.

Greg set his fork and knife on the edge of the plate. "I've never thought to look for my father, actually. I guess I just figured there was no reason. He chose not to be a part of my life, so what point would there be in chasing him down? I can't force the man to want to know me. You can't force a parent to genuinely care," he added.

"No," Charlotte said softly, knowing exactly what he meant. You couldn't force anyone to care. "No, you can't."

"It's his loss, I suppose," he replied. "Whoever he is." Greg shrugged and resumed his dinner, and after one last wrenching glance in the direction of that fateful reminder, Charlotte did, too.

★ ★ ★

The bell above the door of Tony's Pizzeria chimed as Bree pushed inside, happy to be in the overly heated room. She brushed the snow from her shoulders and scooted to the right side of the reception vestibule, cursing to herself when she saw Sonny poke his head around the kitchen door.

"Ah, Miss Callahan! Here for your usual pickup!"

Bree winced. It wasn't *that* usual. It was just something she did on the nights she watched *Dancing with the Stars*. And *Bachelor in Paradise*. And fine, *The Real Housewives*. "That's right."

Sonny studied the line of brown paper bags, neatly stacked and waiting, and pulled the receipt from one.

"Garden salad for one, extra chickpeas, no chicken." Sonny started to laugh, as if this was a new joke, even though he said it every time she came in to get her dinner. Every. Single. Time.

"Ha-ha." She smiled through gritted teeth. As she did. Every. Single. Time. "The life of a vegetarian."

"I can't tempt you with a delicious pepperoni calzone this evening?"

Bree wrinkled her nose. Last time it had been a sausage and peppers grinder. "Just the salad."

Sonny gave her a rueful smile as he rang up her order, even though she knew what it cost, down to the penny. "Ah, Miss Callahan, you don't know what you're missing."

A man to share dinner with, perhaps? The hope of a family of her own, dwindling by the day? The promise of something other than reality television at the end of a long day?

With her takeout bag in hand, Bree pushed through the door, vowing, as she did every time she had the same exchange with Sonny, that she would stop ordering from Tony's. She just needed to get her kitchen back to functioning order and then she'd make her own damn salad.

Right. Tonight. She would get to work on that kitchen. She'd already given up on the bathroom tile...

She rounded the corner back toward flower the shop, where her car was parked in the alley, groaning when she considered the snow that had no doubt accumulated on its roof, when she saw a flash of green material just ahead. Charlotte's scarf.

Brightening at the sight of her cousin, she raised an arm, grinning as she opened her mouth to call out, and then clamped it shut again when she saw the tall, masculine figure appear at her side.

She blinked, wondering for a moment if she should turn and walk back, feeling for some reason like she was stumbling upon something she wasn't supposed to know. Something that Charlotte had clearly chosen to keep quiet about.

Charlotte was talking, her hands tucked into her pockets, no body contact being made. It could just be a friend...But she wouldn't hide a friend. And since when did Charlotte hide anything?

They were coming closer now, and there was no avoiding it. "Charlotte?" Bree's voice seemed to get lost in the icy wind, but Charlotte looked up, her expression turning from one of surprise to one that could only be labeled as guilt.

"Bree." She flitted her eyes to the man beside her, who had stopped walking as they approached. "This is...This..."

The man thrust his palm out. Bree looked up, got a good long look at him. Definitely not a friend.

"I'm Greg."

"I'm Bree," she said.

"My cousin," Charlotte offered.

My, she wasn't being very forthcoming with words tonight,

was she? Normally, Charlotte was chatty and impulsive, not one for measured or controlled conversation.

Interesting. Very interesting.

"Greg is a client," Charlotte said quickly, lest there be any misunderstanding, no doubt.

Still, Bree wasn't entirely convinced. A client. The client Charlotte had dressed up to meet, perhaps?

"I see the family resemblance," Greg said, grinning. "It's the eyes."

Yes, the eyes. Charlotte and Bree had both inherited green eyes from their mothers. When they were younger, people had assumed they were sisters, and Bree had willingly gone along with that. Being stuck with a brother and a slew of male Callahan cousins was a burden on a deep level for a girl who loved making daisy chains and rearranging her dollhouse furniture. She loved nothing more than the holidays and outings she shared with the Daniels girls. Well, that and her time with Gran, of course.

"Where are you two off to at this hour?" Not exactly subtle, but Bree was feeling bold. She liked Greg. He was tall and handsome and had a smile that put her at ease. There wasn't a suspicious glint in his eye. Unlike Charlotte...Her cousin was practically twitching.

"We just came from dinner," Greg said affably.

We? "Anywhere good?" Bree directed her question at Greg. It was obvious that Charlotte wasn't going to be handing over any information.

"Bistro Rouge," Greg offered, and Bree met Charlotte's eye. Even in the dim lighting, she could see the flush spread across her cheeks.

"Fancy," Bree said, shivering against the icy wind that cut through her coat. She held up her takeout bag. "Well, I suppose I should get this home before it gets cold." They didn't need to know that it was a salad. With extra chickpeas, no chicken.

"Well, have a good night," Charlotte said, already inching away.

"Nice meeting you," Greg added. His smile was warm and easy and just like that, an evening with a glass of wine in front the season finale of *Dancing with the Stars* felt lonelier than ever. And she'd been looking so forward to it...

Chapter Thirteen

Audrey was crying before the sun had even poked its light through the thick gray clouds. Charlotte sighed and flicked on the bedside light, blinking into the dim room as she tried to catch her bearings.

It amazed her how quickly she could be roused from slumber. Before Audrey, it would take more than an alarm to pull her awake, and usually several swats at the snooze button, too. Now she was up in a flash, feet on the floor, groggy mind growing quickly clear, on duty.

Still...it would be nice to have another set of hands once in a while. Someone would take shifts, offer to let her sleep in, or just help get a full six hours for once.

Or someone who would remember the special moments—the first smile, the first tooth, the first time Audrey learned to ride a bike.

Charlotte's father had taught her to ride a bike. Her mother hid in the kitchen, biting her fist, apparently waiting for the sound of a crash, the wail that followed skinned knees. But her father had been patient, running behind at a quick pace, his hand clutching the back of her banana seat until he quietly let go. Charlotte could still remember the squeal of delight she'd given when she made it all the way to the end of the street, the pride in her father's eyes when he gave her first a high five and then pulled her in for a long hug.

There would be no moment like that for Audrey. Oh, she'd learn to ride a bike of course, and Charlotte would be right there watching every moment. But it would have been nice to have someone else share in watching her grow.

It would have been nice for both of them, Charlotte thought, staring at the baby who was now smiling up at her.

She pulled Audrey from her crib and unrolled the changing mat on the floor. One glance at the clock on the desk confirmed her suspicions: It was only five o'clock. The house was quiet, most likely because it was built so soundly, but just to be sure, Charlotte was careful not to take any risks of waking anyone.

She popped Audrey's pacifier in her mouth and unlocked her door, her eyes darting down the long hallway as they hurried to the stairs. The kitchen was at the back of the house, that much she could remember, but it seemed that she made several loops back through some living rooms before she finally found it.

"Oh." Charlotte stopped in surprise when she saw Marlene standing at the center island counter, already dressed, a sleek-looking coffee machine percolating behind her.

The older woman looked at her suspiciously, and then, with a smile that revealed two dimples, fixed her eyes on Audrey. "May I?" she asked, already coming around the counter with her arms extended.

Charlotte felt her shoulders relax. "Of course." While she'd mastered the art of heating a bottle with one hand, she couldn't deny how much easier it was with two.

She set her diaper bag on the counter—well, it was really just an old beach bag that she used for a new and practical purpose—and found the box of baby oatmeal and a container of formula.

"Looks like she's getting some new teeth!" Marlene remarked, cooing at Audrey until the little girl squealed in delight.

Charlotte winced as she heated water in the microwave. "Quiet, sweetheart," she whispered. She pulled an apologetic face at Marlene. "I don't want to wake Greg."

Marlene just ran a hand through the air. "No need to worry about that! Greg left at least an hour ago."

The microwave beeped, and Charlotte didn't even worry about the sound. "Really? And here I thought I was the only one up at this house."

"He often goes to his gym before the office. A hard worker that one, and a nice young man, too." She seemed to give Charlotte a coy look.

Unsure of what to make of that comment, Charlotte smiled politely and focused on mixing the bottle. Audrey might seem amused now, but if experience had taught her anything, it was only a matter of seconds before she would remember she was hungry again and start wailing.

Without asking for permission, Marlene took the bottle from Charlotte's hand and expertly adjusted Audrey in her arms. "Greg told me about this arrangement you two have."

Charlotte felt her cheeks heat. "I'm not—I mean, I don't—" She stopped. What was there to even say? She wasn't this type of girl? She didn't normally go along with things like this?

But to her surprise, Marlene just started to laugh. "That Greg will do anything for that company."

Would he? Charlotte wasn't so sure she liked the sound of that. It sounded an awful lot like Jake. Jake, who was willing to break her sister's heart and use her as bait in one fell swoop, all so he wouldn't be cut out of his father's commercial real estate business. Jake, who was too busy staying good with the family to acknowledge the other one he had right here . . .

"He's just like his mother in that respect, but don't go telling him that! At heart, he's more like his grandfather."

"You knew Greg's grandfather?" Charlotte helped herself to a cup of coffee. It was rich and smooth and even more delicious since she was able to relax and enjoy it.

"Oh, he was a fine man. A warm, caring man. Now don't get me wrong, he had an eye for business. He built that company from nothing. A hard worker. Much like Greg."

Charlotte thought about this as she sipped her coffee. Warm. Caring. A side of Greg she'd seen more than once already. Maybe she'd misjudged him. Or maybe she just couldn't believe that good men existed anymore.

"Greg is doing me a favor by letting me stay here," she admitted, thinking of how rotten it would have felt to go begging to Kate, when she was in no position to be calling on favors. "It is unconventional, though."

Marlene just laughed as she gave Audrey a little bounce. "A little unconventional, yes. The way I see it, what's the harm?"

Charlotte smiled uneasily as she set down her coffee mug

and began mixing the ingredients for Audrey's oatmeal. Exactly. What was the harm indeed?

★ ★ ★

Charlotte had already been hard at work for over an hour when her sister's figure appeared in the doorway. Kate set a hand to her chest and closed her eyes for a moment.

"My God, Charlotte!" she breathed. "I thought we had a break-in."

There wasn't a hint of sarcasm in her words, and it was true that Charlotte was never the first person in the office, even on the days she worked a full eight hours.

"I woke up early and thought I'd get some stuff done before I drop Audrey off with the sitter," she said.

Kate hung her coat and handbag on a hook against the wall and walked over to Audrey, who was snuggled in her carrier, sound asleep. "Isn't she a sweetheart."

Charlotte felt a familiar twinge of anxiety. She told herself she was being ridiculous. Kate was Audrey's aunt after all; of course her sister loved her daughter. It didn't matter that Jake was her father and that Kate had once loved him. Once planned an entire life with him. Imagined children with him, no doubt. Children who would have looked an awful lot like Audrey.

Someday she'd find a way to make it up to her. For now, the best she could do was to show Kate how much it meant to her to have this job. She had to take it seriously and prove she could handle it. Kate had given her so much. What had she ever given in return?

"How did you even get in?" Kate asked.

Charlotte regarded her quizzically. "I have a key, Kate." Her sister had given it to her the day she'd opened the business; Charlotte just hadn't had the occasion to use it before.

"I suppose you do." Kate shrugged off the statement and sat down at her desk, powering up her computer with a press of the button.

Charlotte sent a document to the printer and rose to collect it, crossing the open-floor-plan office with a confident stride. As nonchalantly as she could, she plucked the papers from the tray and skimmed through them, aware of Kate's watchful gaze on her the entire time.

"What are those?" Kate asked, and Charlotte smiled at the hint of curiosity in her tone.

"Oh," she said. She pinched her lips to keep from smiling. "Just some menu options for the Frost party."

Oh, had the wait been worth it! Kate's lips parted on the statement, and her blue eyes turned to wide circles. "So you got the account? Well done, Charlotte!"

Charlotte beamed. "But that's not all."

Kate looked at her with interest. "Oh?"

"This is *the* Frost. Frost Greeting Cards. It's their corporate holiday party."

Kate's mouth fell open. After a beat, she said, "When is it? How many people?"

"On the thirteenth. Two hundred guests."

"Two hundred!" Kate's smile faded quickly. "But that's less than a week and a half from now!"

Charlotte felt her heart sink. She knew what was coming next. Kate would want to take over, drop everything, work herself to the bone. She shouldn't have made it sound like such a big deal. But she'd wanted that approval. So badly. "I have it under control, Kate."

Kate didn't look convinced. "Yes, but, Charlotte, come on. I've been doing this for years, and no offense, but you've only assisted me for a matter of months. On a part-time basis."

"I can do this, Kate!" Charlotte cried, coming around to sit in the chair opposite Kate's desk. "You told me you wanted me to take over more responsibilities so you could focus on your wedding, remember?"

Kate sighed. "That's true, I did. But I thought this was some small house party. Not a corporate event."

"I've already hired a caterer and the client and I have really...connected." She swallowed. That was all Kate needed to know about that.

Kate hesitated. Charlotte could almost see the wheels turning in her head. No doubt she was calculating her risks, deciding if she could even take on the workload now, and what would happen if she didn't.

"Do you promise to keep me updated on everything?"

"Yes!" Charlotte leaned forward eagerly, biting back her smile.

"I mean it, Charlotte. If you run into something that you aren't sure about, you'll come to me right away?" Kate eyed her warily.

"Cross my heart." Charlotte went through the motion of swiping her hands across her chest and crossing her fingers, the way they used to do when they were little and still shared secrets, not hid them. She stared at her sister imploringly, holding her gaze, willing her to give her a fighting chance again.

Trust me, Kate, she thought pleadingly. *Trust me again.*

"Okay, then." Kate shrugged. "You landed the business; you can see it through. But remember what's at stake here, Charlotte."

The company's reputation was what Kate meant, but Charlotte just nodded her head. She knew what was at stake, all right. And it was a hell of a lot more than the bottom line.

Chapter Fourteen

Bree adjusted a stem of amaryllis and slid the round vase toward her, ready to begin the last of the arrangements for the annual Ladies League luncheon at Misty Point Marina, an event that Rose in Bloom had been part of since its inauguration seventeen years ago. Back then, her grandmother had been a member of the Ladies League, no doubt as eager for the company as she was the business, and the annual holiday lunch was one she looked forward to. She never made the same arrangements twice, and each year she challenged herself to outshine the last.

Last year had been Bree's first year handling the order on her own. This year she intended to follow in Gran's footsteps and outdo herself.

With the last flower tucked into place, she wasted no time in grabbing her coat, fluffing her hair from the collar, and quickly loading each vase into the trunk of her car. They were packed in cardboard, so they wouldn't slide around, but Bree was still extra careful as she rounded the curvy and often bumpy roads toward the marina.

She was wearing her best black wool coat and her favorite scarf—a winter-white wool that was dotted with gold sparkles—and just the right touch of matte red lipstick that was acceptable for both daytime and a formal event such as this.

Not like she was invited. No, the Ladies League was a bit... How could she put it? Stuffy? Old? Antiquated?

She walked into the sea of gray hair and bit back a smile. There was no polite way too put it. She was just too young for this crowd.

"Bree Callahan!" A woman Bree vaguely recognized as a customer in her store came teetering over to her on heels that really didn't work well on such plush carpeting. Her fingers seemed to wiggle as she eyed the arrangements Bree was holding in the box, and Bree reflexively pulled back before the woman could manhandle the delicate petals. "These are even better than last year! Aren't they, Flo? Margaret, come look at these!"

The event didn't start for another thirty minutes, just enough time to allow for a quick setup, but that didn't seem to stop the women from filtering through the doors.

Bree noticed Colleen across the room, setting up some white, glittery cupcakes on a stand, and gave her a wink. Her friend just widened her eyes in response and mouthed something Bree couldn't make out. Colleen jabbed at the air, making faces and mouthing something urgent, but it was no use. Bree was surrounded by a sea of white and gray and, okay, even a tinge of blue hair. And way too much perfume.

"I need to get these set up and grab the next batch from the car," she explained. She managed to scoot to the nearest table, but for some reason, the group of women accompanied her.

"How's the flower shop, Bree?" Margaret Miller, town librarian and former boss of her aunt Maura, inquired pertly.

"Wonderful," Bree said as she fluffed up the petals on the centerpiece. She really had made Gran proud. The white freesia and amaryllis were a perfect contrast to the bright red berries she'd tucked into the silver-plated vases.

"And the house? I heard you moved into your grandmother's old house."

Ah, yes. Margaret was nosy, and not just when it came to research. Had she not been a librarian, she would have made an excellent detective.

"That's right. I'm having fun putting some personal touches on it." Bree smiled politely as she grabbed another arrangement from her box of four and sailed over to the next table.

Unfortunately, Margaret beat her to it.

"Any fun plans for the holidays?"

Actually, yes, she was thinking of suggesting a girls' weekend away with Colleen, maybe to Stowe or Killington—God knew they both deserved a few days off and their shops would somehow survive without them—and she had been looking forward to finally tackling the first-floor powder room, but the eager sheen to Margaret's eyes made her pause.

Something was up, and she didn't like where this was headed. She glanced over at Colleen, who from across the room was violently shaking her head, causing her strawberry blond curls to rustle.

Crap. She'd been warned. But she hadn't gotten the clue in time.

She set the vase down. "Just the usual traditions, I suppose. How about you?"

But Margaret wasn't interested in talking about herself, it would seem. She licked her bottom lip, batted her eyelashes a few times, and said, "So no young man in your life, then?"

Bree felt her eyelids droop. "Not at the moment. No."

"Yes, I heard about you and Simon Johnson." Margaret clucked her tongue. "You're better off. He was so lanky. And those glasses!"

Bree felt her defenses prickle. She liked those glasses. And so his posture was a bit tall and thin. He looked so nice in a suit, and his abs were surprisingly ripped...

Flick. Flick. Flick.

She snapped the rubber band on her wrist over and over, all the while staring at Margaret and willing her to go away. But the woman was saying something, and Bree wasn't listening. She'd been too busy remembering that smile...

Flick.

Flick. Flick.

She glanced over at the dessert buffet in desperation, but to her dismay, Colleen had vanished.

Stifling a sigh, she turned back to Margaret Miller. "Well, I should really get the rest of the flowers set up."

"You know," Margaret said as she followed Bree to the next table. "You might want to give online dating a try. I was opposed to it at first, figured it was just a bunch of weirdos and creeps looking to murder someone." She laughed. Bree did not. Instead she thought of Simon. Sweet, lanky, bespectacled Simon. If she had just tolerated his... crap a little longer, she wouldn't have to be standing here listening to this unsolicited advice.

And really, had he been so bad? So he'd stood her up a few times. And he didn't call very often in between their dates, which involved spending less and less time at nice restaurants and more and more time sitting around watching sports. He took up the whole couch when they watched TV, spreading out, leaving her to sit on an armchair that was really too stiff. He left his socks on the living room floor, but then so did her brother. He was a man. He wasn't perfect. Maybe she had expected too much.

Flick.

Flick, flick, flick.

"My niece Victoria, you remember her, of course." Of course. Victoria. Victoria had been a recent client of Bree's. Her garden-style fall bouquet had been exquisite, if Bree said so herself, and everyone had commented on the centerpieces. Victoria's wedding was everything Bree had dreamed of for herself. She'd had a backyard ceremony, complete with a trellis, a string quartet, and live doves, and her groom had even teared up as she walked down the aisle.

Bree had gone home and helped herself to a pint of Chunky Monkey after that wedding.

"Well, I know I'm not supposed to share this, but you know she met her husband online." Margaret pursed her mouth, waiting for this tidbit to soak in.

Bree hoped her expression didn't register her surprise. Victoria had told everyone they'd met on the beach, that she'd just been walking along, collecting shells, and she'd stumbled over a sandcastle, and then...Oh, for God's sake! Of course she met him online.

"They seem like a very happy couple," Bree remarked, not willing to commit just yet to putting up a profile and shopping for a husband. She was only just finally starting to build a life for herself. A lot had happened in the past year: inheriting a business and a house, and of course, losing Simon. Now wasn't the time for any more upheaval.

With that, she explained that she really did need to finish setting up and hurried away to fetch the rest of the arrangements.

Honestly, who had time for dating? Who had a desire? She had a business to run and a house to renovate. And a DVR filled with her favorite programs.

Still, she couldn't help but consider it. An online profile. What picture would she put up? The one of her and Colleen taken at Victoria's wedding had been lovely, but she'd have to crop her friend out of the photo, and that didn't sit right. She supposed she could ask one of her cousins or friends to snap a few photos of her, but they'd wonder what they were for, and then no doubt be thrilled that she was finally moving on.

Moving on. Was that what she was doing?

She blinked rapidly at the crowded parking lot while fishing in her pocket for her car keys. Yes. She was moving on. She was young—well, youngish. Was she going to sit around and sulk, or was she going to gussy up and get out there?

She'd crop Colleen out of the photo. Her friend would understand.

She was smiling to herself as she hurried across the parking lot, her trunk already popped from the remote keychain, when she heard his voice.

Simon. He was calling her name.

She froze, then turned, oh so slowly. And God help her, there he was. And he was smiling. And he looked friendly. After the whole flower-sending debacle, she could never be quite sure how he would react if they ever bumped into each other again.

Oh God, the flowers. She had sent this man a bouquet!

Was he laughing at her? She could no longer detect if that was merriment or happiness in those soft brown eyes. His glasses needed cleaning. They always needed cleaning. How many times would she slide them off his nose and rub them on the hem of her shirt? "What would I do without you, baby?" he'd ask.

So many times she'd wondered just what he was doing without her, and now he was here. Standing in front of her. Smiling at her.

"How've you been?" he asked.

No mention of the flowers. Good.

"Great! Never better!" Was it just her, or did she detect a slight knitting of his brow? "I moved into Gran's house, finally."

"Ah, so you took the plunge!" He grinned. She swooned a little.

"I'm fixing it up. It needs a lot of work, but...it's fun." It wasn't fun. It was messy and frustrating and eye-wateringly expensive, but no need to get into that. She hesitated before daring to ask, "How about you?"

He shrugged. "Same old, same old. We have a corporate lunch here. Annual thing."

Of course. They had a holiday lunch here every year. She'd been so focused on getting the flowers to the meeting room that she hadn't even looked at the signs in the lobby to see what else was taking place.

"I'm dropping off flowers for the Ladies League lunch. Christmastime in Misty Point..." She trailed off, unsure of where she was going with that statement.

"You sticking around town for the holidays?" he asked, and Bree felt a stab of disappointment. She always stayed in Misty Point for the holidays. How didn't he know that?

"Of course." Her smile felt a little strained. She could feel Gran watching her, tutting. "Wouldn't miss the tree lighting."

"Remember last year?" He grinned, almost wistfully, she realized with a jolt.

She narrowed her eyes on him suspiciously. Of course she remembered. Not that she'd be telling him as much.

He continued. "After we went to Nolan's, had a bottle of wine, and split a lobster."

"You let me have both claws," she remembered, thawing a little.

"That was a fun night," Simon said after a beat. He held her gaze a second too long. Enough to make her heart tug a little. "Maybe . . . maybe we can do something like that again this year. For old time's sake?"

His grin was wider, downright hopeful, and Bree could only blink in response.

It was this easy? All these months, she'd avoided a run-in almost as much as she fantasized about one, and he had the nerve to casually ask her out? Because that's what he was doing, right? Asking her out?

Or perhaps, feeling her out.

Well.

"Maybe." She took a step back.

"Tree lighting is at five-thirty," he said, as if she could forget. As if anyone who had grown up in Misty Point didn't know this fact.

"Five-thirty," she said, nodding.

"Well." Simon nodded, grinning, then jutted his chin to the left. "I should probably get inside before the shrimp cocktail's gone."

Bree laughed—a little too loudly, damn it—and said, "Bye."

Simon shoved his hands in his pockets, giving her one last smile before he walked away.

Her hands were shaking as she opened the trunk and stared at her arrangements. She needed to get the rest of them into the building, and soon, but first she needed to clear her head. Process what had just happened.

She looked up at the sky just as the snowflakes began to fall, swirling down around her, landing on her nose. She grinned. It might just be a magical Christmas after all.

★ ★ ★

Charlotte glanced at her watch and then back to the door of Murphy's again. It wasn't like Bree to be late. She reached into her pocket and pulled out her phone. No missed calls. Not even from her landlord, she thought wryly.

Still, it didn't change the fact that a week from Sunday, she had nowhere to go. She planned to ask Colleen if she could camp out at her apartment, just until the end of the month. The burst pipe scenario worked perfectly, and once she got her bonus from the Frost party, she'd be able to put a deposit down on a place for January.

She knew just the building. A quaint converted mansion just parallel to Harbor Street, right in the center of town. They had a two-bedroom unit with a balcony and in-unit laundry available for the first of the year, and Charlotte intended to call the property management company today. The cost was dear. But if she had the deposit, first month's rent, and a letter of recommendation from her employer, it could be hers. Certainly her sister would happy to give a reference, and the burst pipe story would make the transition during the holidays all that much more plausible.

The bell above the door jingled, and Charlotte looked up to see Bree walk in the room. She held up her hand to catch her cousin's attention.

"Sorry I'm late." Bree was breathless as she pulled out a chair and unwound her scarf, but there was nothing apologetic in her tone. If anything, she seemed a little distracted, and not in an entirely bad way.

Charlotte frowned. The last few times she'd seen her cousin, she'd been a bit lost. But today her eyes were sparkling and there was a bouncy energy to her as she flipped over her coffee mug and waited for a passing waiter to fill it.

"I was just dropping off the flowers for the Ladies League," she said. She licked her lips before saying, "You'll never guess who I ran into."

Charlotte felt her heart skip a beat. "Jake?"

Bree shook her head. "Simon."

"Simon?" Charlotte repeated. She didn't like that dreamy smile on her cousin's face. "As in the Simon who strung you along for a year and then broke your heart?"

"I wouldn't say he strung me along." Bree sniffed.

Charlotte knew when to hold her tongue. Simon had most definitely strung Bree along, if you call waiting a week between dates and canceling plans at the last minute as stringing someone along.

"So you were happy to see him then?" She posed this question delicately.

Now Bree was frowning. "I wouldn't say happy. Just...caught off guard. I mean, I've always wondered what would happen if I ran into Simon again. I'm sort of surprised that I haven't yet. Not that I've been trying to..."

"You seem happy. Or you did, when you first came in," Charlotte pointed out.

"I sound like a fool, don't I? Simon broke up with me, and here I am happy to see him." She shook her head. "What's wrong with me?"

"There's nothing wrong with you," Charlotte said, wondering if she would have had the same reaction if it had been Jake. "You cared about Simon. He hurt you. It's complicated."

Bree nodded. "Enough about me. It was nice seeing you last night." She raised an eyebrow suggestively.

"I know what you're going to say, and I'm going to stop you right there," Charlotte said. "Greg is a client."

Bree said nothing. She just stared. It was one of her tricks, something she'd done since they were kids. It worked remarkably well, especially on Matt. But Charlotte wouldn't cave. Not on this one.

"I promise you, Bree. Greg is a client." And he was a client.

"So that was a business dinner?" Bree didn't sound convinced.

"It was just a business dinner," Charlotte assured her . . . and herself. It was just a business dinner. A meal where they discussed their arrangement. So why did she suddenly feel as if she was keeping something from her cousin?

She picked up her menu and studied it intensely, even though she had already decided on the Caesar salad while she was waiting for Bree. "We should order next time the waitress walks by. I have a meeting to get to."

"A meeting?" Bree repeated with a knowing smile. "Why do I suddenly feel like *meeting* and *client* are code words for something?"

Charlotte had to laugh. "If something develops between Greg

and me, you will be the first to know. But don't expect that conversation to happen."

"Why? He's cute!"

Was he cute? Okay, yes, he was cute. And hearing another woman point that out made her realize just how cute he was.

She was getting off track.

"It doesn't matter if he's cute. My life isn't my own anymore. Every mistake I make has bigger consequences now."

Bree set down her menu and folded her hands over it. "And getting involved with this adorable and charming and seemingly interested man would be a mistake?"

A mistake was one thing it could never be.

But even as she thought it, a part of her couldn't help but wonder why her cousin felt the need to press the issue, why it seemed so important that Charlotte settle down, find someone.

Was it really that bad to be a single mom? Was she somehow doing her child a disservice? Did Bree—and maybe everyone else—think Audrey would be better with a father in her life? With a traditional family?

"He's a client," she stressed. An unconventional one, but a client all the same.

But Bree just shrugged. "Does that matter?"

Charlotte didn't bother replying, even though the question was no doubt rhetorical. Right now, a lot of things mattered. But her love life was far from one of them.

Chapter Fifteen

⊶⊷⊶

One of Greg's most vivid childhood memories was the year of the Frost Greeting Cards televised Christmas special. It was the only year his mother had indulged in conventional holiday traditions since his grandparents had passed away, embracing things such as hanging stockings from the mantel, stringing popcorn, and baking cookies in the shapes of little trees and candy canes. She'd dressed in a festive red sweater dress, gracefully pulling her shoulder-length brown hair into a low ponytail, and Greg had been trussed up in beige corduroy pants, a white button-down shirt, and a hunter-green sweater. It had been Rita's idea that they look "smart yet casual." After all, they needed to appeal to the masses; they needed to invite the television audience into their home, to show them how warm and cozy the Frost lifestyle was—no different than the brand they built, the cards they created that were meant to be shared with loved ones, meant to soothe in a hour of need and comfort in a time of loneliness.

And so Greg stood next to his mother in their gleaming, underused kitchen at the Misty Point house, smiling but not looking directly into the camera as advised, happily slamming the cookie cutter onto the dough his nanny had rolled out earlier—Rita had explained to the camera crew ahead of time, grinning apologetically, that it would be better for her not to get too messy and have to take breaks to clean up or wash hands. Greg sprinkled the sugar as a holiday soundtrack played in the background, and then Rita made a grand show of bending over and removing the tray from the oven and carefully arranging the prebaked cookies on a large ivory platter edged in red ribbon and holly, before sailing into their magically transformed living room where they would string popcorn and strategically hang a collection of Frost's most expensive ornaments from the twelve-foot spruce.

Greg would never forget that last Christmas in the family home, or the fleeting sense of hope it gave him. It was a side of his mother he'd never seen before. And a side he hadn't seen again. Until today.

"Cookie, gentlemen?" Rita gave her most generous smile and motioned to the tray in the middle of the conference room table. "They're an old family recipe passed down from my mother, and her mother before that. I bake them every year. Just one of our many *family* traditions."

Darren Burke helped himself to a large sugar cookie in the shape of a tree and inhaled it in three large bites before reaching for another. From the corner of his eye, Greg could sense his mother's watchful gaze. *They're falling for it, Gregory,* it said. He cleared his throat. Too much was on the line to get caught up in old family resentments. His mother was trying to make this deal work, and so he'd play along, too. He had too much riding on this.

"Oh, what can I say?" Greg said, sliding a rueful smile in his mother's direction. "I never could resist one of your sugar cookies, Mom." He popped one in his mouth. Soft, buttery, with just the right amount of sweetness. The bakery over on Hill Street never disappointed.

"These are almost as good as the ones my daughter makes," Darren said, slurping his coffee. "She was up at the house over the weekend with her two little girls, baking dozens and dozens of cookies with my wife." He smiled fondly. "What a sight that was."

Darren Burke's son and current chief marketing officer, Jimmy, took the opportunity to take two more cookies, which obviously pleased Rita to no end.

"Christmas traditions are such a *wonderful* gift we can pass down through the generations, don't you think, gentlemen?" Not waiting for a response to her question, Rita pressed, "That's really the message we like to send here at the company. It's not about giving a card or hanging an ornament. It's about creating a tradition. Making a memory." She beamed.

Greg looked at Darren, who was sitting back in his chair, his two big hands splayed on the edge of the table. He was lapping this up, just as his mother knew he would. She proffered one more cookie in his direction before flashing Greg a stern message with her eyes. He opened his leather portfolio. It was time to get to business.

"As you'll see from the numbers our research team has put together, Frost continues to be the leader in holiday goods. Our card sales have continued to rise over the years, and wrapping paper sales are at an all-time high."

Greg showed them the mock-up for the display the marketing team had created, and examples of similar setups they had done over the years at other retailers. It was good work, just as good as Darling Cards—and better in his opinion—but it might not be enough in the end.

Darren Burke turned to him. "Will a portion of these proceeds go to any specific cause?"

Greg didn't dare look at his mother. As with many large companies, they supported a variety of charitable organizations, but nothing in particular when it came to their holiday items. "Excuse me?"

"Darling Cards is giving a portion of their seasonal proceeds to help underprivileged children at Christmas. Children in foster care, group homes, even hospitals." Darren looked at him expectantly.

"How *lovely*," Rita crooned from the end of the table. Her eyes were unnaturally bright, her smile too large. Too frozen.

"It's their way of making the holiday special for those who can't be home to enjoy it."

"Yes. I *see*. Of *course*. How *special*." Rita was nodding her head now. Buying time, Greg observed. Even from the five-foot distance, he could see the wheels turning, the gleam in her expression as an idea took hold. "Family is the most important thing at the holidays, of course. No card or ornament or gift can match the simple pleasure of being home, surrounded by the ones you love the most." She settled back in her chair, her expression turning wistful.

Greg's mouth went dry as he waited for her to continue. He took a sip of water to curb his mounting anxiety. Rita could be ruthless when she thought an opportunity was slipping away.

"I'll never forget when Gregory went away to college, and

how hard that was for me. I just wanted him with me every day, you know?"

The Burke father and son exchanged a knowing glance, nodding in understanding. Greg didn't bother to mention that he was the one who had stuck around the Boston area. His mother was the one who spent more and more time on the West Coast.

"I remember I sent him a box of my famous chocolate chip cookies and I scribbled a little card. *A taste of home,* that's what I wrote. Well, Gregory would probably be embarrassed to admit it, but he kept that card. It wasn't just about the cookies, and the hours I spent over that hot oven. After all, once they're eaten, they're gone. But a card, a card lasts forever. It captures a moment in time, a sentiment however brief. It keeps family together, even across the greatest distance."

Greg managed not to roll his eyes as his mother sighed softly and gazed out the window for effect. The Burkes sat perfectly still in their seats, absorbing the story, before finally turning to each other with a nod.

"Well, unfortunately we've got to be in New York tonight for a dinner meeting. We've got someone driving in from Long Island." Darren pushed his chair back from the table and stood, adjusting his tie.

For a moment, Rita looked stricken, but she quickly composed herself. There were a hundred different people Darren could be dining with tonight, but the Darlings were based on Long Island, and Rita knew it.

"We'll see you in Misty Point next week, then?" she confirmed, standing to lead them out of the conference room. "We're so thrilled you'll be joining us in our *family* home for the holidays."

"Looking forward to it," Jimmy said. "We'll be in touch sooner with any questions."

Satisfied, Rita flung open the door and led them in to the waiting area, just as Charlotte rounded the corner with Stacy. Greg stiffened at the sight of her, forgetting for a moment that he'd asked her to meet with the marketing and public relations department. Never one to miss a trick, Rita looked from Charlotte to Greg with a confused frown.

A dozen excuses ran through his mind, but it was useless. His mother had seen her. And she would see her again at the holiday party, just as Darren and Jimmy would, too. There was no opportunity to turn and run, no chance of pretending he didn't know her.

As of this moment, Charlotte was officially his fiancée. Just for the holidays, that was.

* * *

Honestly, Charlotte didn't know what the big deal was! From the look in Greg's eyes, you would think she'd messed up or something, and this time she was sure: She had not. She was on top of her to-do list; she was getting things done. She was *on time*. Greg had told her to get in touch with Stacy about the decorations and she had done just that. And yet he had the nerve to look unhappy to see her.

"Stacy," Greg said. "I'm glad to run into you. I need you to go over to the warehouse and check on our inventory of the new Build Your Own Christmas villages. We need to be sure the last shipment arrived."

An older woman next to Greg said to the two men with

them, "Our DIY line is very popular. It really gives an opportunity for a family to sit down and spend time together, the old-fashioned way."

Charlotte knew for a fact that they had just seen this exact item in the warehouse only an hour earlier. Charlotte had thought they might make a nice centerpiece item for the dessert stand.

Greg waited until Stacy had left before turning to her, his smile wide. "Isn't this a surprise?" She stiffened as he put a hand around her shoulder. "*Mother*, you remember *Charlotte*," Greg said. He gave her arm another tight squeeze, but Charlotte didn't need his less-than-subtle message. She got it now. This was his mother. Rita Frost. Who these other people were, she wasn't sure, but one thing was clear. She was officially the blushing bride-to-be.

And she wasn't wearing an engagement ring.

She pushed her left hand behind her back, and then, on second thought, around Greg's waist. He felt solid and thick and warm beneath her arm. And good. Too good.

"It's so nice to see you again," Rita suddenly blurted, and catching on quick, Charlotte nodded her agreement. She yanked free of Greg's death grip to give the petite woman in front of her a good hard hug. Instantly, she was engulfed with heavy perfume, the scent of expensive shampoo, the smooth fabric of clothes that did little to soften her stance.

Greg's mother's body stiffened on impact, and then Charlotte felt a light pat on her back, barely enough to be felt through her sweater. Despite the charade, Charlotte couldn't help but indulge in a brief frown.

Rita quickly released her. "So wonderful to see you..." She

glanced up at Greg, blinking rapidly. *"Charlotte."* She gave a smile that didn't quite meet her eyes, and from their close proximity Charlotte was able to discern a resemblance she hadn't noticed initially. Both mother and son had the same shade of brown hair, the same dark, deep-set eyes.

"Charlotte, this is Darren and Jimmy Burke of Burke's department stores." Greg's voice was tense. "I'd like to introduce you to my fiancée, gentlemen."

At this, both men's expressions transformed into large smiles, and handshakes were given all around. Amid the clatter of congratulations and questions about the wedding date, Charlotte felt Rita's eyes boring through her. Charlotte smiled, but the gesture wasn't reciprocated.

"We look forward to seeing you next week at the house," Greg concluded. He draped his arm around her waist again. It had been a long time since she'd felt the warm reassurance of a body close to hers. It felt good to belong to someone. Even if it was just pretend. "Charlotte's been working night and day to get it ready."

"Christmas is my favorite holiday," Charlotte admitted. "I suppose I'm getting a bit swept away this year with—"

Greg's eyes blazed. "With the party! And the engagement, of course." His smile tightened. "The party is a great excuse to go over the top this year."

Charlotte nodded quickly. She'd almost slipped. "I love decorating my future home for Christmas." She felt Greg exhale.

"We're looking forward to it," Darren said, pressing the elevator button. "And I have to say I'm impressed that you would host a company event in your family home."

"Our company is family run," Rita purred. "We try not to draw a line between home and office."

The elevator doors slid open and the two men stepped inside, nodding their goodbyes. Only once the doors had quietly closed shut and the lights above the elevator bank indicated the car was moving toward the first floor did Rita turn to fix Greg with a look that sent a shiver down Charlotte's spine.

"Well, the cat's out of the bag now. So much for announcing your engagement at the party and really making a moment of it," Rita said, giving a brittle laugh.

"My engagement isn't a party trick, Mother," Greg said firmly, and for a moment, Charlotte had to remind herself this engagement wasn't even real. It was too easy to be swept up in the momentousness of a man actually standing up for her, defending their relationship.

Something Jake had never done.

Rita ran a dismissive hand through the air. "Ah, well. Maybe it was better to let them know now. It will give them something to think about tonight when they're dining with old Edgar and his little *chapeau*." She turned her sharp eyes on Charlotte, saying coolly, "Tell me, Charlotte, do you make it a habit of coming to Gregory's office unannounced?"

"Today was my first time here, actually," Charlotte said evenly. She looked up at Greg, who was looking straight ahead in the distance, frowning. "I just came to pick up a few last-minute items for the holiday party."

Rita's brow pinched tight. "The party! That's what the event planner is for." She pinched her lips and stared at Greg with naked disappointment. "But then, I suppose that's what you get when you insist on hiring someone from *Misty Point*."

Charlotte stood rooted to the floor as Rita stormed into a nearby office. Her own temper was starting to prickle. The old

Charlotte would have said something snappy, acted on emotion and said that she was out of here. No fake engagement, no party. Nothing. But the new Charlotte...She drew a long breath. She'd come too far to have someone like Rita Frost put her in her place again, belittle her as a person, judge her on social rank. She knew the type all too well. Greg's mother was no different than Jake's, and just like the Lamberts, Rita Frost clearly thought someone like Charlotte could never be good enough for her son.

But then she didn't know the real Charlotte. She had no idea that Charlotte was a single, unwed mother. A townie from Misty Point. An event planner.

Charlotte frowned. A woman like Rita would never welcome her with open arms. And a man like Greg probably couldn't, either.

Greg gave Charlotte an apologetic smile, one that lifted the right corner of his mouth into a lopsided grin. His eyes looked sad and resigned, and Charlotte felt herself waver.

It was just for the holidays, she reminded herself, even though the reminder suddenly disappointed her a bit.

Greg tipped his head in the direction of the office—a silent invitation she begrudgingly accepted with a lift of her chin. After a sigh so heavy she could see it roll through his shoulders, he followed his mother into the room, with Charlotte close behind.

This was Greg's office, she realized at once. She recognized his navy wool scarf hanging on the back of his leather chair. It was a small thing, of little significance really, but somehow the observation made her feel connected to him.

"Well, that was a success," Greg was saying as he swiveled

his chair and sank into it. Charlotte hovered at the edge of the room, sweeping her gaze around the minimal décor, trying her best to avoid direct eye contact with Rita.

Rita gave a noncommittal sound and plucked a dead leaf from a plant at the corner of Greg's desk. "The holiday party will have to be an even bigger success. Tell me, what's going on with the event planner you hired?"

Greg hesitated. "The usual party planning, Mother. I hired her, and I'm staying out of it."

Charlotte managed not to roll her eyes. She'd spent the better part of the early afternoon trolling the Frost warehouse with Stacy, picking out wrapping paper for the fake gifts that would circle the base of the tree, garland and ornaments from their latest line, and even the latest compilation of Christmas music they put out each year, branded with the Frost logo, redesigned for the holidays in a shimmery white font, overlaying a perfect snowflake.

She'd hoped Greg could give her a little more insight into his vision, into what he really wanted the party to look like, the feeling he hoped to convey. Well, she'd have to strap him down tonight. At the very least, she needed his thoughts on the menu.

"I just hope this event planner knows how much is riding on this party," Rita said, then thinned her lips. Turning to Charlotte, she gave a tight smile. "I'm being rude, please forgive me. As you can see, we are under quite a bit of pressure today."

"I'm sure that Charlotte understands," Greg said mildly. "You two can talk more at the party."

Charlotte noticed how carefully he'd worded this suggestion. He didn't offer anything that would imply the two women getting to know each other better. For a brief moment Charlotte remembered that to Rita, at least, she was truly Greg's fiancée, the woman her son was going to marry.

Pity the girl who ever really fell into that role.

"Nonsense," Rita huffed. "If there's one thing I don't like, Gregory, it's being caught by surprise, with my guard down. No, we can't risk any more awkward situations in front of the Burke's team." She smiled at Charlotte. "Charlotte and I will just have to have a nice little *tête-á-tête* beforehand. Tonight."

"But your flight—"

Rita tutted away his concern. "I took the company jet. I'm sure the flight can be pushed back for a few hours. And I can think of nothing more wonderful than a cozy winter dinner with my wonderful son and his...charming fiancée. Besides, I want to see how the house is coming along for the party."

Chapter Sixteen

⊖⊖⊖

The winter sky was already turning to dusk as Greg, his mother, and his *fiancée* approached the revolving glass doors in the lobby.

"Am I driving with you?" Rita inquired, pausing at the sidewalk just before the reserved parking section, where Greg's black sedan was seated in its usual spot.

Greg hesitated. He needed time with Charlotte: time to prepare her, time to get facts straight. "If you wouldn't mind taking my car, I'd like to ride with Charlotte."

Rita frowned. "Why don't I just call a driver?"

"Because I need my car back at the house tonight, and Charlotte and I took separate cars here," Greg explained. "If I had known you were going to change your travel plans, I would have personally picked you up from the airport this morning."

Rita smiled and patted his arm, and for a moment, Greg felt shaken. When she wanted to be, his mother could be sweet, even a little nurturing. But those moments were sporadic, usually leaving him unnerved when she reverted back to her hard self so quickly.

"Give me the keys." Rita sighed as Greg handed them over. "I suppose I should let you two lovebirds have some time alone," she added, but something in her tone seemed forced, reminding him his mother didn't really care if he was engaged or not. All she cared about was appearance. And Greg being engaged was convenient for her.

Idly, he wondered if she would be okay with the fake engagement, the pretense of something real for show. So long as it met the end goal, he couldn't see her having an issue...He stopped himself. This was not a time to be taking risks. His mother was fired up, frazzled over her impending retirement and likely to do something rash on her way out the door. On the off chance they didn't land the Burke's account, his last hope of taking over as CEO was having Charlotte at his side until it was safe to let her go.

Let her go. He didn't like the sound of that.

Greg continued to watch his mother until she slipped into the car and turned on the headlights. He turned to Charlotte. "Where's your car?"

They hurried over the pavement, still slick despite the dusting of salt, in silence. Only the tapping of Charlotte's heels against the concrete could be heard echoing through the darkening evening, or the occasional beep of a car lock in the distance. Finally they slowed, and Charlotte stopped in front of her car.

Her car. Greg closed his eyes and counted to five. He had completely forgotten in the chaos of everything that Charlotte drove a beat-up navy sedan that was at least twenty years old and looked it.

He dragged his hands over his face and held them there. This couldn't be happening. A fiancée was one thing. A fiancée his mother didn't approve of was another. Charlotte was a middle-class Misty Point local. He could just imagine how his mother would respond to that.

Luckily for him, she wouldn't have a chance. This was a fake engagement, he reminded himself. And his mother didn't have to know anything about the real Charlotte.

Not that she would have any interest, anyway.

"What's wrong?" Charlotte asked, unlocking the driver's side with a turn of her key.

"Nothing. Let's just get in."

Charlotte frowned but didn't argue as she slid into the driver's seat and reached over to pop the lock on his side. Greg rolled back on his heels and began wandering around the back of the car to the passenger door when he spotted it. Amongst the over-flowing loot from the Frost warehouse was the car seat, sitting proud and confident, as brazen as a throne.

His breath caught. The baby!

Greg quickly swept his eyes over the parking lot, past the people straggling from the office, shoulders slumped, wearily walking to their cars. There was no sign of his car or his mother. She'd probably already pulled out and was on her way. Hopefully.

But just in case . . .

Greg opened the back door and reached over the wrapping paper rolls to the car seat, clutching it in two hands. He tugged hard, but it didn't budge. He gave it a little shake. Still nothing.

"What the hell are you doing?" Charlotte cried from the front seat.

"We can't let my mother see this," he said firmly. He jostled the giant plastic thing a little more. Still nothing.

He had started to sweat. Little beads of perspiration dotted his forehead, and the air in the car suddenly felt stale and thick, despite the cold temperature. He pulled back, straightening his back. He had to get a grip. This was his mother, after all. His *mother*. He should be able to have an honest relationship with her. He should be able to appeal to the side of her that loved him and cared for him and had raised him.

But then, she had barely raised him. The nanny had.

He slammed the back door shut and opened the front, sliding into the passenger seat. "Sorry," he said.

After a pause, Charlotte said, "Here. We'll cover it with this blanket." She leaned over the armrest and, from the floor on the backseat, retrieved a purple baby blanket that she draped over the car seat like a tarp. Greg watched all of this with an increasing level of doubt, but there was nothing more he could say. His mother had seen her. The Burke's team had seen her. She was it. His future wife.

He grinned. He could have done a hell of a lot worse.

Charlotte turned to him, her green eyes sharp as she reached for her seat belt. "Better?"

Greg glanced in the direction of his reserved parking spot. It was empty. "We need to beat my mother to the house," he said. "Take the back roads instead of the highway."

"Yes, boss," she replied, but she was grinning.

Greg settled back against the headrest as Charlotte pulled out of the parking lot, both hands gripping the steering wheel as she peered straight ahead. It had started to snow, and she flicked on the windshield wipers. Christmas music bleated through the speakers.

"So, that was a surprise," Charlotte finally spoke. She chuckled softly, but there was an undercurrent of tension in her voice. "I assumed I was just going to the warehouse, picking out decorations. I had no idea Stacy would bring me into the office to show me photos from last year's party."

He would have to talk to Stacy immediately. She was discreet—everyone at the company was—but there was no doubt that gossip this juicy would fly through the office like a swarm of bees in a hive. He didn't think she'd overheard the conversation between Charlotte, his mother, and the Burke's team, but one could never be too careful, and the last thing he needed was his mother discovering through casual conversation that Charlotte had been introduced to Stacy as the event planner. One misstep and the entire plan would be a bust.

"Fair enough. I had no idea my mother would invite herself over to the house. She doesn't like to come there."

"Bad memories?"

Greg had never thought of it that way. "Perhaps," he mused.

"I take it you two don't get along?"

Greg considered this statement carefully. "It isn't that we don't get along. More that we aren't very close."

Silence fell over the car as they joined the traffic nearing the next set of lights. Greg shifted in his seat, agitated. At this rate, they would never get back to the house first. And it would be just his luck if Rita was standing at the garage, shivering in the cold, greeting them when they pulled up the driveway. Hopefully she brought her keys or Marlene was there to let her in.

"We need to talk about tonight. Where's Audrey right now?"

"With the sitter," Charlotte explained.

"Good. Hopefully she can stay a few extra hours, through

dinner. Let's call ahead and make sure there isn't any evidence when we walk in."

There was a long pause. "She stayed at the sitter's apartment today, so she didn't make a mess in your home. I'm sorry that my daughter is such a problem for you."

Aw, damn. He hadn't meant it like that. "I'm sorry," he said firmly, hoping she believed the truth in his words. "Right now all I can think about is pulling this charade off. I'd rather not complicate things or bring your daughter into it. That's all."

Charlotte nodded. "I understand. Frankly, I'd rather my daughter not be used as a pawn in this scheme."

"Then we're in agreement."

"So what do you need me to say?" Charlotte asked. She took a right turn at the light. They'd be in Misty Point in twenty-five minutes if they didn't hit more traffic.

"As little as possible," Greg said. His mother would have just as little personal interest in his fiancée as a person as she did her own son; chances were high that conversation could be controlled. "Just stick to the story we agreed on."

"Did your mother ever meet your last fiancée?" Charlotte asked. "The real one?"

Greg felt his jaw tighten. "Maybe once. When we were dating. I doubt she gave it much thought, though."

"But you told her when you proposed?"

Greg didn't like talking about Rebecca. "In passing. I don't think she connected the details."

"I'm sorry," Charlotte said softly.

"Don't be. It's just the way my mother is." In a way, he was fortunate she hadn't cared to get to know Rebecca. If she had, he'd be in more trouble now than he already was.

Charlotte turned up the music and tapped her thumb against the steering wheel as a Christmas carol blared over the speaker, and with a flicker of panic, Greg glanced at her nails, relieved to see that she had finally scraped off the remnants of that purple polish. One less thing to worry about, at least.

His mother had to like Charlotte. Or, better put, she had to not dislike her.

Rebecca, he knew, would have immediately impressed his mother. She was cool as a cat, tall and blond with ice-blue eyes and professionally maintained hair. She dressed and spoke impeccably, and more than that, she knew how to hold her own with the likes of Rita Frost.

Maybe it was because she was so much like her, he realized, chagrined.

But Charlotte was different. Charlotte was beautiful in a more wholesome, natural way. Her appearance wasn't store-bought or artificial, and when she talked, she said what she meant.

Charlotte was almost exactly the kind of woman he would have proposed to, if a few circumstances, like the fact that she had a baby, were different.

Strange then, how the person who until recently had truly been his fiancée wasn't anything like Charlotte. At least, not in any way that mattered.

Chapter Seventeen

Rita Frost arrived at the house ten minutes after Charlotte and Greg had hurried from the garage. Charlotte had barely enough time to remove what little trace of a baby there was from the house, but she did notice that Marlene had washed Audrey's breakfast bottle and oatmeal bowl and left them to air-dry on a towel in the kitchen.

She looked around, wondering if Marlene was around now, but there seemed to be no trace of her. Too bad. She was warm and friendly, which was much more than she could say for Greg's mother.

The doorbell rang as she reached the top landing of the staircase. Charlotte had to smile to herself. The chime was loud, a sound one might expect to hear in an old monastery, not a home. To think she had been concerned no one would be aware of her presence on the front steps that first day. Now she walked over to her guest bedroom and closed the door, looking forward to returning to it later tonight, with Audrey sleeping quietly in the nearby crib...for at least a few hours.

Gliding her hand on the rail as she skipped down the sweeping, curved staircase, she froze at the sight of Greg standing in the large foyer, staring up at her. His smile was pleasant, but his expression was tense. She paused, and then resumed her step at a more dignified speed.

"I was just telling my mother how much you love to cook," Greg said carefully, his gaze locked on hers. "Marlene is a part of the Misty Point Christmas decorating committee and apparently won't be back until after nine."

"As if this town isn't already decorated enough," Rita commented.

Charlotte refrained from mentioning that this weekend was the annual tree-lighting ceremony and festival of lights. She looked forward to it every year, especially the party in the town square, and she was especially looking forward to bringing Audrey this year.

Instead, she focused on the unspoken question being asked of her. She tried not to panic when she thought of the Thanksgiving cheesecake that had set off the smoke alarm and braced herself for where this conversation was headed.

"Cooking is one of my favorite pastimes," she said with a sweet smile.

Rita pinched her lips. "How odd. Now, let me see what's been going on here. Charlotte, have you met this event planner? Gregory's insisted on hiring someone local." She pulled a face. "Why, I'll never know . . . There is so much more talent in the city."

Charlotte's mouth fell open, but Greg quickly stepped forward. He motioned in the direction of the living room. "Why don't you go relax, Mother? I'll get you a glass of wine while Charlotte gets dinner started."

Well, crap.

She glanced nervously at Greg, who looked pasty in complexion.

"Charlotte is a real gourmet," Greg said eagerly, and Charlotte nodded her enthusiasm, even as her head began to spin. "It's one of the things I love most about her."

Love. When was the last time anyone had told her they loved her, or referenced that emotion toward her? Her body tingled at the thought of it, but she shook her head clear when she remembered that it was just all part of the act, that he didn't really love her.

That she couldn't even cook.

Rita Frost was a woman of high standards. She walked around with an air of disappointment, her mouth a thin line, her eyes narrowed and darting. If the party wasn't a success, there was no telling what it would do to Kate's company's reputation. How could her sister forgive her then? And what would it mean for the deal she had cut with Greg?

Rita patted her flat stomach. "Nothing too heavy, please. I don't want to look bloated for the party next week. It's too important."

"Of course!" As if she needed another reminder.

Charlotte headed quickly to the back of the house and stood in the spotless kitchen. The rack hanging above the large center island boasted at least a dozen shining pots that looked fresh out of the box, and the granite counters appeared untouched. Charlotte started opening various cabinets, looking for the pantry, which she finally found and noted with relief was as well stocked as the fridge.

If only she knew what to do next.

She thought of the meals she had prepared for herself lately. Boxes of crackers or pretzels or toast with peanut butter usually made up her dinner. Back in Boston she could make a box of dried pasta and a stick of butter stretch for three days. Audrey wasn't even eating much solid food yet, so there seemed to be little point in wasting her precious free time cooking...and cleaning. She closed her eyes. Unless Greg knew what he was doing, they were in trouble.

"Please tell me you know your way around a kitchen," a deep voice behind her whispered.

Charlotte turned to face Greg, standing sheepishly in the doorway. Still in his work clothes, he managed to look completely rumpled. His crisp shirt seemed to have wrinkled since they left the office, and his dark brown hair was haphazardly slicked from his forehead.

"Well, not this kitchen. I can cook, of course. I mean, *obviously*. Who can't?"

He slid his gaze to hers as he flung open the pantry door. "I can't. Unless you count using the microwave or the coffee maker." He grinned.

Charlotte eyed the gleaming contraption that was no doubt imported from Europe. "Then you have one over me. I don't plan to touch that thing. So don't even think about asking for coffee for dessert." She closed her eyes. Sweet Mother. Did she have to make dessert, too? Her recent track record was far from successful.

As if reading her mind, Greg volunteered, "My mother doesn't eat dessert."

She smiled with relief. "Good."

"I know this wasn't part of the plan, Charlotte, but do you

mind? Just for tonight?" His eyes were so hopefully, his smile so boyish.

Well, now she'd done it.

Wound up playing house with a handsome and increasingly likeable man. And it was getting far too cozy for comfort.

"Sure." She turned to the sink and began washing her hands with a pounding heart. What was that dish her mother always used to make when they had a neighbor or friend over for dinner? Her mother always claimed it was so easy... She supposed she could call and ask, but it would be rude to not chat for a bit about the new condo in Florida, and Granny's health. She hardly had time for that at the moment.

Kate. Kate would know what to do, of course. But then, Kate always knew what to do.

What was she thinking? She couldn't call Kate. She'd just have to go off memory.

"I'll need potatoes, chicken, balsamic vinegar, and rosemary," she said, recalling as many of the ingredients as she could. She was missing a few, she was sure, but it would have to do. "And cream and butter if you have any." Charlotte tied on an apron, pulled two pans from the rack, and after blowing out a long breath, got to work.

"Thanks for doing this, Charlotte," Greg said as he poured a glass of wine to bring back to his mother. "I have to admit I wasn't sure this arrangement would work at first."

Charlotte stopped peeling the potatoes and looked at him, trying to ignore the tightening in her chest when her eyes locked with his. "Well, I didn't come this far just to let it fall apart now. You're not the only one who needs to pull this off, you know."

His brow creased for the briefest of moments. "Well. I'd better get out there. Good luck."

Good luck with the meal or good luck with his mother? Or good luck pulling this whole thing off and not losing the business and her sister's respect? She busied herself with preparing the food. She couldn't think about that right now.

★ ★ ★

Half an hour later, Charlotte swept into the dining room, carrying a platter of rosemary chicken and mashed potatoes that seemed only the slightest bit lumpy. The kitchen was a disaster, but she doubted Rita would even go in there, and really, she'd done the darn best she could if she did say so herself. She set the plates on the center of the table, atop iron trivets, and gave Greg a wink.

"Well, dig in," Charlotte said when Rita and Greg sat staring at their plates. She couldn't help but notice the pointed glance Rita gave her son. Oops. She probably could have said something a little more fitting. Like *bon appétit*.

The chicken was slightly overcooked but no one seemed to care. Rita pecked at her food like a small bird with those pinched lips; she didn't strike Charlotte as a woman who enjoyed a big meal. Greg ate as if he hadn't been fed in months, visibly enjoying every last bite and helping himself to seconds.

Conversation revolved around the company and, of course, the holiday party. "They only have a week to decorate this entire house! I want that exterior sparkling! And the drive should be lit up, welcoming everyone. Oh. Have they thought about parking?"

Charlotte made as many mental notes as her spinning mind would allow, wishing she could subtly keep a notepad under the table. Parking. Of course. And lights for the trim of the house. She'd call a company first thing in the morning. Time was running out, and things were booking quickly.

"At least there's a tree in the front room. That's a start, even if it's not decorated," Rita continued. "Let's just hope the food is good. I wish you would at least consult with someone from Boston. They could easily drive the food down in vans."

"There's no time," Greg said sharply. "Besides, Misty Point is a resort town, full of wealthy people throwing parties and events. I'm sure there are plenty of local businesses to accommodate your fine tastes, Mother."

Lifting her eyebrows, Rita lowered her gaze to her plate, and the subject dropped. Within seconds, conversation resumed, the main subject this time being the dissection of the afternoon meeting and lunch with the people from Burke's department stores.

By the time they had finished the meal, Charlotte had almost completely relaxed. Nothing had been asked of her. Rita seemed to have no interest in Charlotte's life or interests or background. If the party went this smoothly, there was no doubt she'd be receiving the rest of her payment from Gregory. She could give Audrey a wonderful first Christmas, Kate would surely give her more accounts of her own, and Charlotte would finally feel she was making things up to her sister, in the only way she knew how. The New Year would be the beginning of a great new life. She smiled as she sipped her wine.

Greg, however, was not smiling.

"Is something wrong, Gregory?" Rita inquired tersely.

"I'm surprised you'd notice," he replied evenly.

"Well, of course I'd notice. You're sitting there with a scowl on your face. It's the same look you used to get as a little boy when you didn't get your way. Which seemed more often than not, despite all I did for you," she muttered.

Uh-oh. Charlotte shot Greg a pleading look. It had all been going so smoothly!

"I'm just tired of discussing work," Greg said tightly.

"Well, what do you want to talk about then? The weather? Christmas?" Rita gave a laugh as if the mere mention of the holiday was silly and quaint. "You and I both know we're not like that, Gregory. We don't sit around the dinner table discussing trivial things."

"I didn't know my life was trivial. This is the first time you're meeting Charlotte, after all. Aren't you curious about the woman I'm marrying?"

Charlotte was positively glaring at Greg now, but he didn't make eye contact with her. She stared longer, hoping he would pick up on it, that he would remember what they were doing here, but still he just stared levelly at his mother at the opposite end of the long table. There was hurt in his eyes, she realized.

"Well, I'm sorry, Gregory," Rita huffed after a long silence. "Obviously the Burke's account is foremost on my mind at the moment. Here we have a perfect opportunity to continue discussing our strategy, our last in-person meeting before the holiday party next week, which will truly be our last chance to seal this. Don't tell me you're getting sentimental on me." She turned to Charlotte. "Charlotte and I will have plenty of time to get to know one another after all this other business is settled. I'm sure she understands that this takes precedence, of course."

Charlotte twisted the thick cloth napkin in her lap. Tension hung in the silence like a heavy blanket. She was holding up her end of the bargain, right down to even making the damn dinner. It hadn't occurred to her that he might be the one to toss his hands up in the air, back down on their deal, and throw away any chance she had of making a better life for her daughter and proving herself in her sister's eyes.

"Never mind," Greg finally said. He slid his chair back from the table and stood. "Charlotte, dinner was delicious. As usual." At this, Charlotte stifled a laugh.

"Shall we take a walk of the house so we can confirm the details for the party?" Rita suggested.

Charlotte nodded eagerly, but she couldn't shake the impact of the moment. In all the time she had known Jake, he had never tried to defend her, never tried to put her first or demand that she be given respect. He'd let his family be his guide, let their haughty ways and social ranking take precedence over how he treated first Kate, and then her. And then their daughter.

But Greg had been different.

And even as she told herself that this engagement wasn't real, her connection to Greg was becoming a lot more real than she had prepared herself for.

Chapter Eighteen

Three more days. Three more days until the tree-lighting ceremony and then...And then what? This was where Bree always reached a dead end.

After their breakup talk in August—which was supposed to be a relationship conversation and ended up taking a disappointing turn—she'd only dared to think she and Simon might ever find a way back to each other. The flowers...a major error in judgment, and one she hoped would never be referenced again. But time. Yes, maybe time was what Simon had needed. She'd given him his space. She'd let him miss her. And now...now there were only three more days until the tree lighting.

She could always skip it. Let him have a taste of his own medicine. But that wasn't her style—never had been. She would go, expecting nothing, wanting (hopefully) even less, and use this as an opportunity for some much-needed closure.

Either way, one thing was certain: She'd be looking her damn best. Let him see what he'd been missing.

She shivered as she walked down Harbor Street, her cousin

Kate at her side. Caroline was manning the shop. The extra deliveries and holiday orders made it impossible to cover alone, but one of the true perks of seasonal help was that she could step out for a long lunch break without having to worry about the sign being turned. Today she was accompanying her cousin to the bridal salon to check out some of the final touches that had been made to Kate's dress.

"Is Charlotte joining us today?" Bree asked.

Kate shook her head as she reached for the door handle of the shop. "She's covering the office so I can be here at all. I need to bring her by, soon, though. We need to decide on Audrey's flower girl dress. I thought she could come in on a wagon edged in greenery." She cut her a sharp glance. "You can do that, right?"

Bree laughed. "Of course. And it's a sweet idea. Any more thoughts on the bridesmaids?"

"Honestly, I've been so busy with work that I let that slide. Hopefully this weekend Alec and I can put together the wedding party list and let everyone know." She grinned at Bree. "Of course you're a bridesmaid. I assumed you knew that."

"But of course! I am, after all, your only female cousin. And I look ravishing in tulle."

"Oh, I'm not going for tulle," Kate said to Bree's extreme relief. She crossed the room and held up a stunning A-line strapless gown in a thick taffeta. "I had my eye on this. And luckily, it's one of the ones they can get on short notice." She clucked her tongue. "I don't know how I let this go for so long."

"I love it!" Bree exclaimed, gently touching the material. But as happy as she was not to be sporting some one-shoulder pouffy affair, another part of her couldn't help thinking what a shame it would be that she would be without a date.

Unless... She knew she shouldn't tempt fate, but the wedding wasn't until after Christmas, and who knew, maybe she and Simon would get back together over the holidays.

Flick, flick. The poor rubber band was about to snap.

Kate started chatting with Sofia, the owner of the shop. It was the only bridal salon in town, and Bree knew that most brides came to Sofia for their dresses. She'd probably do the same someday.

My, wasn't she feeling optimistic today! She walked to the rack where the veils were kept, all so frothy and delicate, like some sort of candy confection. Her fingers were just itching to take one from the hook, place it on her head, and imagine what it would be like...

She backed away from the rack carefully and took a seat in the center of the room on the tufted sofa she'd sat on last time she was here. And the time before, when Kate was planning her wedding to Jake. They never talked about it anymore, but Bree knew from firsthand experience how hard it could be to let go.

"You okay?" she asked Kate as Sofia slipped into the back room.

Kate nodded. "It used to be hard for me to come here with my brides, but now that I have Alec, it's different. Everything happened for a reason. Besides, it's Charlotte I'm worried about. Have you heard that Jake is getting married?"

This was news to Bree, and she wondered why Charlotte hadn't mentioned it. "Is Charlotte upset?"

"I can't be sure," Kate said. "But unlike me, she can't just move on. They have a child together."

Bree had been wondering whether to broach the topic of her recent suspicions to Kate, and now she couldn't resist. She shifted on the sofa, until she was looking right at her cousin. "I wouldn't be so concerned about her moving on. I have a feeling she's met someone."

Kate's eyes were round. "Really? But...she never said anything." She looked a little wounded.

"She never told me, either," Bree said quickly. "But I saw her with a very handsome man the other night, and something tells me they were more than just friends." Or clients, as Charlotte would wish her to believe.

Kate gave a little smile. "I wonder who the mystery man is."

★ ★ ★

Greg poured himself a whiskey from the decanter that Marlene had kept refreshed on the bar cart since back when his grandfather was still alive and sank onto the couch. The Christmas tree blazed before him. Charlotte must have put up the lights today, he realized. No doubt his mother's observations on its lack of decorations had prompted some action.

He sat forward, noticing another addition to the room. The leather-bound photo albums he'd given to Charlotte her first day here were stacked on the center. He reached forward, turning the cover on one, feeling all at once sad and happy at the image staring back. It was taken on his grandfather's boat, when he was only four or five. He was holding a fishing pole, smiling proudly at the camera. His grandfather had one hand shielding his eyes from the sun, the other draped over Greg's shoulder. It was one of their favorite pastimes. The two of them, on the water, or just tinkering down at the dock. There would be fresh lemonade when he came back to the house. He could picture his mother sitting on the back veranda with his grandmother, smiling.

Smiling. He frowned, wondering if time had distorted his memory. But, no, he was certain of it. Those were happy times. The happiest ever, perhaps.

"Mind if I come in?" a soft voice behind him asked. Charlotte stood in the doorway holding a small speaker in her hand. "Baby monitor," she explained, setting it on the coffee table as she sat down at the opposite end of the couch.

"I owe you an apology for last night," Greg said, closing the photo album.

Her grin was rueful. "For a minute there, I thought you were going to blow our cover."

Greg settled his head back against a cushion and looked up at the ceiling. "Maybe I should have," he said.

"Don't say that!" Charlotte snapped, jarring his attention.

He turned to her. "You really want to pull this off, don't you?" When she didn't reply, he pressed, "Why?"

Charlotte stared at the tree. "I told you," she said. "When I set my mind to something, I don't back down."

"Ever?"

She slanted him a look. "Not easily."

"I like that quality in a woman," he said, and then sat upright, quickly draining the rest of his whiskey. He'd overstepped with that comment. Even if he meant it. "But you didn't answer my question. Why did you even agree to this?" He'd seen the way she'd wavered that first day in his office, the way she'd hesitated when he'd called her bluff. "Is it because of the party? Does your company really need the business that badly?"

"No!" Charlotte insisted hotly. She settled back against a throw pillow. "My sister owns the company, and she does quite well. If you must know, this is the first account she's let me handle on my own. I didn't want to let her down."

Her first account. Greg inwardly groaned, hoping his expression didn't betray his true feelings. "So you'd rather go along with pretending to be my fiancée than lose out on the opportunity to plan my party," he summarized.

Charlotte hesitated. "More or less." She tucked her feet under her and adjusted a pile of pillows behind her back. "My sister and I aren't on the best of terms. We've...been through some things. Personally, not professionally. I...I just don't want to let her down again."

"Again?"

"It's complicated," Charlotte said.

Greg stood and crossed to the bar cart, allowing himself a refill. "Can I get you anything?" he asked, but Charlotte shook her head.

"Audrey will probably wake up in a few hours."

Of course. Greg measured himself a generous pour and placed the cap back on the etched glass decanter. "So you really don't mind doing this on your own, then? Raising Audrey, I mean."

He walked slowly back to the couch and resumed his seat, perhaps an inch or two closer to her than he had been. If she cared, she didn't show it either way. He swallowed back his disappointment and then quickly snuffed it out completely when he realized what it was. She was a pretty woman sitting on his couch in a tight blue T-shirt and gray sweatpants. And he was a man. A normal, healthy man who would of course react to such a thing.

But it didn't mean anything more than that.

As discreetly as he could, he inched back to the side of the couch, setting his elbow on the armrest.

"She's my daughter. Of course I don't mind raising her," Charlotte said, and for a moment, Greg felt like a jerk for asking such a thing, until she continued. "But I won't deny that it's hard. Harder than I could have expected. Still, I wouldn't trade it for the world."

Greg lowered his eyes to his glass and heaved a long breath. He set it to the side, unfinished. It didn't help. It couldn't dull the pain that always came after he saw his mother. Nothing could.

"You're still upset about your mother," she observed.

"That obvious?"

"Is she always like that? I mean—"

He felt his mouth pull to a thin line as he replayed the dinner. "You know, the thing is that she actually thought you were my fiancée. It was her first time meeting the woman I'm supposedly marrying, and she didn't ask you a thing about yourself."

Charlotte gave a small smile. "It sort of took the pressure off. We don't have to worry about her poking holes in our story."

Fair enough. He was losing focus, something he rarely did, especially when it came to the business. His grandfather's business. The thought of it going to Drew...He took a sip of his drink, feeling it burn all the way down his throat. "I'm too old to be getting upset over it, I suppose."

"I don't think so," Charlotte said. "You want her approval. Everyone wants that from the people they love. It's why you're doing so much to succeed in the company."

"Frost Greeting Cards is all I have ever known. It was as big a part of my life as my own parent." He gave a bitter laugh. "It was like the sibling I was always competing with. At a certain point, I couldn't imagine my life without it."

"That's why this party is so important to you," Charlotte said, nodding.

"It's more than that." Greg hated even thinking about this. "If things don't go well with Burke, my mother threatened to give the company to my cousin Drew when she retires. My distant cousin."

He couldn't imagine sitting back and watching his distant cousin take control of the company. Drew hadn't lived and breathed Frost the way he had. He hadn't been invested in it, lived it, or breathed it. It wasn't a part of his daily life. It was just a job he took when he graduated college. An easy transition into the family company.

"Could she really do that?" Charlotte frowned.

"She could."

Charlotte hesitated. "Well, could and would are two very different things. She's anxious."

He wished he could believe that, but he wasn't so sure.

"Don't worry," Charlotte said, patting his hand. "The party will be great. Just the thing you need to land that account." She smiled at him, letting him almost relax, when a cry crackled through the monitor, startling them both. Charlotte leaned across the couch, closing the distance between their bodies until he could smell the faint sweetness of her shampoo. Catching his stare, she locked eyes with him, and for a moment, everything around them went still. Her lips were parted in expectation, her green irises soft and warm. There was a dusting of freckles on her nose he hadn't noticed before. He could lean in, just an inch, maybe two, and see if she'd do the same.

Quickly, he stood up, ignoring the startled expression that passed over Charlotte's face. "I should probably let you tend to Audrey," he said, noticing that the crying had increased in volume. Had it been going on that entire time? Somehow he hadn't even noticed.

Charlotte flicked off the speaker and the noise stopped. She stood up, a small smile playing at her lips.

He wondered if she had felt it, too. The connection. Or possibly just chemistry. Just before he could get lost in the fantasy he had created, she turned to him and said, "Speaking of the party. I really need your decision about the menu by the morning, or I'll have to place the order myself."

He frowned. "Oh. Of course. Yes."

"Both of us need this event to be a success, Greg. We're a team in this." Charlotte held up the monitor and began backing out of the room, her smile the last thing he saw as she disappeared from the room. "See you tomorrow, then."

He nodded, just once. Tomorrow.

★　★　★

Charlotte woke to Audrey's familiar cry, as she did every night. She had it down pat by now—the middle of the night wake-up was just for a change, not a feeding. She glanced at the bedside clock, noting that it was only midnight; she'd felt like she'd been asleep for hours somehow.

She changed Audrey quickly and rocked her in her arms as she softly sang the same lullaby her father had once sung to her, nestled in his arms in the big old rocking chair that was still in her childhood room. She tried not to think about the fact that Audrey would never have a memory like that to cherish. She told herself that no father at all was better than a lousy one, but when she dared to wish, dared to dream, she knew she wanted her child to have two parents who loved her.

"I'll just have to give you double the love," she said as she set Audrey back in the crib and backed away slowly.

She walked through the dark room and sat on the edge of the bed, knowing that she wouldn't fall asleep again soon. She had no books with her, and there was no television in the room, not that she could turn it on anyway with Audrey sleeping soundly nearby.

The way she saw it, she could stare at the ceiling until Audrey woke again, or she could venture downstairs to that cozy study Greg had shown her last night. With its soft leather couch and built-in bookshelves full of movies, she was bound to find something that would hold her interest. And it was tucked far enough away that she didn't see how she could disturb anyone, either.

She tossed a sweater over her T-shirt and grabbed the baby monitor. Soon she was closing the French doors behind her, alone in the study. She turned on a table lamp and studied her choices, grinning when she saw one of her old favorites: a holiday movie she hadn't watched in years.

She was just snuggling up with a thick chenille blanket when the door creaked open, causing her to jump.

Greg stared at her in amusement, one eyebrow lifted in silent surprise as he stared at her from the doorway. He'd changed since she'd left him a few hours ago, but only into jeans and a sweater. From the looks of it, he hadn't gone to bed yet.

She looked down at her flannel pajama pants, suddenly wondering if she'd overstepped.

"I'm sorry. I thought I wouldn't bother anyone here. I couldn't sleep."

He shrugged. "That makes two of us. And it's no bother. I'm usually awake at this hour."

"Oh." Charlotte glanced at the television, where the opening credits were starting to play.

"So, what are we watching?" Greg walked casually into the room and dropped onto the sofa next to Charlotte.

She moved over an inch, even though she could have stayed exactly where she was, just close enough to feel the heat of his skin.

She moved over another inch. No good would come from thinking that way.

"A Christmas movie," she told him.

He curled his lip. "A Christmas movie?"

She balked at him. "You don't even like Christmas *movies*?"

He shrugged, but his grin was rueful. "Overexposure."

She considered this. Being surrounded by Christmas cards and decorations for the better part of a year might be a bit too much of a good thing, she supposed. Still, she wasn't about to back down, not now that she had her heart set on watching it.

She pointed out the double set of French doors against the far wall, where a view of a snow-covered stone terrace shone in the moonlight. "Look at that. It's a winter wonderland out there. It's the perfect night for a holiday movie."

He didn't look convinced. "If you say so."

"I do." Charlotte settled back against a pillow. "Besides, this one is really terrific—"

"Wait. You've seen it before?"

"At least a dozen times! We watch it every Christmas. It's sort of a family tradition."

Greg's brow furrowed. "That sounds nice."

Charlotte grinned, imagining how wonderful it would be when Audrey was old enough to partake in the event. "Usually we make a big bowl of popcorn, have some hot chocolate. We can recite all the lines, of course, but that's just part of the fun. Whenever I think of this movie, well, it just feels like coming home."

Greg glanced at her. "I can make some popcorn if you'd like."

Charlotte considered the holiday dress she'd hoped to squeeze herself into for the party, and then decided the diet could wait. She grinned. "I'll pause it. You don't want to miss the opening scene."

"Oh, I wouldn't want to do that," Greg teased, but she could sense that he was pleased.

Charlotte couldn't wipe the smile from her face as she snuggled deeper under the chenille blanket and waited for Greg to return with the popcorn. Despite the size of the house, she could soon make out the sound of popping—she glanced sharply at the baby monitor, silently willing Audrey to be unaware of the noise. She was enjoying herself, maybe more than she should, and she wasn't ready to be on mom duty again just yet. For a few moments she wanted to just be Charlotte.

And somehow, with Greg, she was. Greg, who didn't know her past. Greg, who had no hold on her future. Greg, who knew her just as she was. Today. Present moment only. No mistakes. No slipups.

She stared at the frozen television screen. A year ago she had watched this movie alone, with tears streaming down her face as she worked her way through a family-sized bag of potato chips, wondering if her sister and parents were watching it together, if they were happy she wasn't with them.

Little did she know at the time just how different this year would be. Better. Or at least on the up-and-up.

Greg came into the room with a bowl of popcorn, his grin sheepish. "I won't lie. It's microwaved."

"The best kind," Charlotte remarked. Her eyes widened slightly as he slid onto the couch beside her again. Was it just her imagination, or was he coming a little closer this time?

She looked to her right. There wasn't much more space left for her to move. "Ready to start the movie?" she asked, gripping the remote.

He passed her the bowl of popcorn, and she helped herself to a few kernels. "This isn't one of those feel-good movies, is it?"

She raised an eyebrow. "It's a holiday movie. What do you think?"

He shook his head, but she could tell by his faint smile that he liked her response. "Oh, boy. Let's get it over with then."

"I have a feeling you're going to enjoy it. Trust me."

He gave her a strange look. "I do trust you."

She rearranged herself on the couch, unsure of what to make of that remark, and fighting back the strange feeling that she just might be able to trust him, too. If she let herself.

The fell into silence as the movie started, and a few glances at Greg told her that he was fully engrossed within minutes. She smiled in satisfaction and decided to enjoy herself and put her troubles from her mind for a bit. But the next thing she knew the television screen was quiet. There was popcorn sprinkled all over the leather couch, and the baby monitor crackled somewhere behind her.

She tried to remember the last scene in the movie she'd watched and realized with a sinking feeling that she'd fallen asleep well over an hour ago. Her eyes sprang open. She wasn't in her bedroom, and the pillow under her cheek wasn't a pillow at all. It was a chest. A very hard, very sturdy, very manly chest. She blinked in panic. Staying as still as she could under the tense circumstances, she listened to the steady drum of Greg's heartbeat through his sweater, felt the rhythm of his breath as his chest moved softly up and down, moving her with it, almost lulling her into a state of tranquility.

He was asleep. And so help her, she intended for him to remain that way.

Inch by inch, she eased herself off the couch, grabbed the baby monitor by the handle, and made her way to the half-open French doors.

"Hey."

She winced, and closed her eyes before turning to face the owner of the smooth, groggy voice that was much too deep and husky for her own good. "I think we fell asleep."

She didn't bother mentioning just what position they'd ended up in, or how that might have happened. She felt the blood drain from her cheeks when she considered that while she had dozed off somewhere around the scene where the young boy goes to the mall with his wish list, meaning somewhere in the first third of the movie, it was entirely possible that Greg hadn't nodded off until a few minutes ago.

"Too bad. That was a pretty good movie."

She nudged him with her elbow. "Told you so."

He arched an eyebrow. "Rain check then?"

That sounded an awful lot like an invitation she should probably resist, but with that friendly grin and those warm eyes,
really, what was a girl to do? "Can't wait."

And she realized as she turned from the room and hurried
back upstairs that she couldn't wait. And that was really quite a
problem.

Chapter Nineteen

Charlotte looked up from the pile of invoices Kate had asked her to review and checked her watch. She still had four hours of the afternoon left before businesses started to close, and with the party only a little more than a week away now, she needed to make use of all the time she had left, even though she would love nothing more than to take a break and go soak in that glorious tub in her en suite bathroom. But that would be irresponsible. Grounds for being fired, really. After all, she was technically working on the jobsite, right now. Even if it was starting to feel a bit too much like home...

She had decided to work in the living room, next to the Christmas tree. Already it was looking better in here. The tree was lit with more than a thousand lights, and she'd spent the better part of the morning carefully hanging hundreds of Frost ornaments Stacy had loaded into her trunk on her visit to the warehouse. She'd opened each ornament box as if it were a gift, wondering what would be tucked inside, and then taken a moment to study the charming ceramic objects before finding just the right spot for them on the enormous branches. There was just one ornament she had hoped to find and hadn't, but she told herself that didn't matter. This wasn't their home, and this wasn't even where they would be spending Christmas.

It was baby's first Christmas, and she didn't even know where they would be.

No use worrying about that now when she still had to get through the Frost party. If she indulged in fretting over all the uncertainties of her future, she'd never be able to focus on the present, and right now, she had too much work to do for the party. Greg might be an easy enough client, but Rita Frost was not, and there was no telling what the Burke family expected. This party had to be top-notch. No hitches. No mistakes.

Charlotte crossed a few items off her list and moved on to the next task. She frowned. The flowers! She had meant to visit Bree yesterday to discuss her options in person—a detail Kate had always stressed was of utmost importance. But of course, Bree had the honor of going to the dress fitting with Kate, while Charlotte was left to hold down the office, in case a bride called in tears. And three had, of course. One over the five pounds she'd gained since Thanksgiving that threatened to ruin the cut of her dress. Another over a backorder on the favors. And of course... another meltdown over the maid of honor's back tattoo.

Charlotte wondered if her sister had decided on the bridesmaid dresses yet. She'd ask Bree today. See if Kate had hinted about the maid of honor. It was better to know than to live in false hope.

She closed her folder and set it to the side. It was time to get Audrey from her nap. If she slept any later, she'd never fall asleep tonight, and there was no way that Charlotte was going to risk another interrupted evening. Last night had been a one-off. And it couldn't happen again.

In their room, Audrey was sleeping on her back in the crib, just as Charlotte had left her more than an hour before. Her little hands were balled into tight fists, her round cheek pressed to the cool sheet. Her chest rose and fell softly with each tiny breath. Charlotte smiled. She could watch her all day like this.

Reaching down to scoop the baby, Charlotte let Audrey's head fall back against her shoulder as she carried her down the stairs, covering her with a blanket as they stepped outside and hurried to the car. With any luck, Bree would be free for a few minutes to chat, and if not, Charlotte would have to just look around the room for inspiration. Poinsettias would be an obvious choice, of course, but Charlotte wanted this party to be unique and memorable. Not just to prove herself to Kate, but because she was starting to realize just how important this event was to Greg, too.

And she was starting to suspect that it had a lot less to do with winning the Burke account than he believed.

Despite having taken an almost two-hour nap, Audrey slept through the drive, and she was still deep in slumber when Charlotte pulled her car to the front of the flower shop. She sat in the warm car for a few minutes enjoying the silence, while all around her the winter chill was made up for by the beautiful decorations on Harbor Street.

Not bothering to unhook the sleeping baby, Charlotte balanced the carrier on her forearm and proudly walked through the front door of Rose in Bloom, the bells above the door announcing her arrival and thankfully not waking Audrey. If she could get through this without Audrey stirring, that was all she could really ask for today. She needed to concentrate, and that was a mighty tough thing to do with a baby wailing in your ear, muddling your thoughts, leaving you feeling so frazzled at times, so completely overwhelmed, you didn't know where to start with the long list of things that needed to be done every day in life. Much less in work.

More than once, when she'd taken Audrey shopping, she'd abandoned her cart halfway through. Between a crying baby and the lack of sleep and the thought of having to load up the car and then unload it all—plus a baby, who needed to be fed and changed, ASAP—it was sometimes just too overwhelming. Each time she'd gone out to the car, face flushed from frustration, and then realized that if she didn't finish her shopping now, she'd have to come back tomorrow, because there was no one else to buy the diapers. Quitting wasn't an option.

Charlotte sighed as she transferred the carrier to her other arm, careful to dodge one of Bree's Christmas displays. The thing was heavy, and her arm was already tired, and was it just her or was it really hot in here? She knew Bree complained about the refrigeration, but honestly! She unzipped her coat with her free hand, feeling slightly better, and returned to her task. The flowers had to be perfect, or no doubt Rita Frost would have something to say, and Charlotte didn't want to give her anything to say. For Greg's sake, as much as her own, she wanted this party to be perfect.

She had just stopped to admire some of the beautiful red roses when she heard his voice. Her heart dropped into her stomach as her breath seemed to stop. Ever so slowly, she shifted her gaze to the left, searching through the sea of green and red plants until her worst suspicion was confirmed.

There he stood, at the counter, his back to her, his arm resting casually on the waist of a woman who, even from this angle, looked perfectly coiffed and manicured. And blond.

Jake.

Charlotte's heart began to pound. She looked around for Bree, knowing how quick her cousin would be to back her up. She hitched the carrier higher on her arm and turned, coming face-to-face with a surprised but smiling middle-aged store clerk she had never seen before. Of course, she thought. Bree had hired seasonal help. "Can I help you with something?" the woman asked a little too loudly.

Charlotte could feel the blood rushing in her ears. She couldn't see him. Not like this. Not here. Not without a lick of makeup on her face and hair that still needed to be washed. God help her, she wasn't even sure she had put on a bra that morning. Greg was already gone when she'd woken up, and the day had just slipped away...

She shook her head at the woman and pressed a finger to her lips, sliding her eyes back to Audrey in what she hoped was a pointed message. The woman's face immediately melted, and in a stage whisper, she crooned, "My, what an angel. Let me know if I can help you with something."

Charlotte nodded and darted behind the large Christmas tree Bree had set up in the center of her shop. She should leave. Right now. She should turn and go while she had the chance. She knew she should, but she couldn't.

He was Audrey's father. Her father! And he was standing in this very room, breathing the same air. Charlotte set her free hand to her chest. She could feel it pounding through her coat. She looked down at Audrey, still asleep, still unaware of the mess of her mother's life, the circumstances of her existence, and felt her resolve tighten.

For Audrey's sake, she wouldn't give up on Jake.

Maybe...maybe if she let him know she wasn't interested in him romantically, that she wanted nothing more from him than to just acknowledge his own child, he would step up.

On shaking knees, she stepped forward. The room seemed to close in on her, the voices at the counter swarming together. She took another step, and then one more, until soon she was too close to turn and run. For Audrey, she reminded herself. She owed her daughter this.

"Jake."

He turned at the sound of his name. His eyebrows rose in question, an expectant half smile on his lips. At the sight of her, his brow shot down into a thick, firm line. His eyes darkened, and any trace of a smile disappeared.

"Charlotte." His voice was tight and gruff, attracting the attention of the woman at his side. Charlotte swept her eyes over the woman, noting with some small satisfaction that the photo in the paper had clearly been her best moment, and then turned fully back to Jake. She looked him straight in the eye, wondering what this woman knew, what he had told her. Frankly, she didn't care.

Audrey was his child. And it was time Jake admitted that.

"I hear congratulations are in order," she said pleasantly. She plastered on her best and biggest smile, even though she was practically baring her teeth.

Jake frowned, clearly guarded, and shrugged his response.

"I've had some wonderful changes in my life, too, recently. Have you met Audrey?" Of course he hadn't. The last time she'd seen him she'd been eight months pregnant. With a trembling hand, she pulled down the soft blanket to reveal Jake's daughter.

She stared at him, boring her eyes through his, challenging him to look down, to feed into his curiosity, to recognize his own features in this small child. She had his chin. Maybe his nose, too.

Jake's gaze never strayed from hers. He didn't look down.

She stared at him in disbelief. Waiting. Hoping. But still, he refused to look down.

The bastard. The callous, coldhearted bastard.

"We have to get going." He turned to the woman at his side, who had lost interest in being social and was flicking through an album of bridal bouquets.

"So soon?" Her voice was sweet, but her jaw was starting to ache from clenching her teeth so hard.

His eyes were stony as they locked hers. "We have an early reservation at the club."

The club. Of course. It was Friday night after all. The Lamberts always ate at the county club on Fridays when they were in town. Not that she'd ever been invited. Or her sister.

"Well, hopefully we'll be seeing a bit more of you while you're in Misty Point," Charlotte continued. "I know Audrey would love to know her daddy."

Jake's face went white as his fiancée whipped around, eyes wide in horror, starting at Charlotte, then Audrey, and finally at Jake. Her expression said everything. Jake's resistance to accept his role ran deep.

Tears stung the back of her eyes, but she swallowed hard, determined not to let it show.

"Oh, he didn't tell you?" Charlotte asked, tipping her head. She shifted her eyes back to Jake, narrowing them, wishing there was something more, something bigger she could do to express her outrage. Instead, she said coldly, "Well, I can't say I'm surprised, given this is the first time he's met the child he refuses to admit is his."

"Is this true?" The blonde was gaping at Jake now. Charlotte half wondered if she'd toss the ring at him. And she realized that she didn't care. Let Jake get married. Let some other woman have him.

She deserved better. So did her sister.

So did Audrey.

She shook her head in disgust. Even now, with his own child close enough to touch, he stood there, like the coward he was. "Can't say it yet, huh, Jake? Even now, when your daughter is right here in front of you, you still can't even look at her." When Jake said nothing more, she finished, "You don't know what you're missing, Jake. And you don't deserve her, either." Heart still racing, she protectively angled the carrier closer to her chest and turned from the counter as if in a fog. She walked straight to the door, past the poinsettias and roses and holiday wreaths and the tree that grazed the ceiling, its ornaments sparkling with the promise of a magical Christmas.

She took great care in settling Audrey into the backseat and backing the car out of its space. The decorations were hung through the town, and the lights were already lit around every lamppost, but this time, it didn't fill her with joy the way it usually did. Hot tears began to blur her vision, and she wiped them quickly away, turning up the music to cut the all-consuming silence of the car.

"I tried, Audrey," she whispered. She had tried. She was still trying. But no matter how much she did, or sacrificed, or worried, it still came back to the glaring fact that Audrey didn't have a father and that nothing could make up for that. She could hug her and hold her and feed her and wipe her tears, but she was only one person.

And somehow, it would just have to be enough.

Jake or no Jake, she had to focus on the positive. It was Christmastime, after all, her daughter's first. No matter what it took, it would be memorable—even if there weren't many presents under the tree, and even if they didn't have a home of her own, Charlotte was more determined than ever to make it special for the two of them. And no matter what, Audrey would never know that her father had turned his back on her. Twice. Without another glance in her direction.

★ ★ ★

Greg frowned as he swerved into the garage and then killed the engine. It had been another stressful day, and he was ready for the weekend. He sighed as he dialed the security code at the back door, shedding the weight of the afternoon, determined to leave his troubles behind him for the evening. He could think of nothing better than a cold beer, a giant pizza, and—

A screaming baby.

An ear-piercing wail seemed to ricochet off the walls as he closed the door behind him. For a brief moment, he had half a mind to turn and run, get back into his car and drive into town.

But then he saw her, Charlotte, standing in the distance, in the kitchen. And wasn't she a sight.

"Welcome home!" She smiled and bent down to lift a screeching Audrey. She flashed him an apologetic grin, and then laughed softly.

Greg hesitated and then strode down the hall and straight into the kitchen. He'd never thought of this place as anything more than a house since his early childhood days when his grandparents still lived here, but he had to say that in the past few days since Charlotte had come to stay, it really did feel like a home, and it wasn't because of all the Christmas decorations. For the first time in too long there was life, and warmth, and chaos. The usual impeccable order of this place had been destroyed with plastic blocks and thick cardboard books with colorful pictures.

Somehow he couldn't imagine how empty this old house would be when they left. Solitude was what he'd come here for, what he'd sought out, but now . . .

"Sorry about this," Charlotte was saying, talking quickly. "Audrey's hungry; I was on the phone with the caterers and I didn't get her dinner ready in time, and well." She shrugged. In her arms, Audrey's face was red as a beet, her eyes squeezed tight as hot angry tears fell steadily. She threw her head back as her mouth flung open, and Greg leaned forward, frowning. Was she holding her breath?

Audrey took that opportunity to release her energy. Right into his ear. He heard bells before he forcefully pulled back, and Charlotte's laughter overrode the Richter-scale-breaking level of that child's cries.

"I'm sorry, I'm sorry," Charlotte said, seemingly to calm

herself, but when she finally stopped laughing, another ripple sputtered from her lips. "It's just . . . your face!"

Greg straightened himself. Audrey had quieted to a mere sob, having gotten the worst of it out of her system, he hoped, and now appeared to taking her frustration out on Charlotte's hair, which she clung to with two chubby fists. If Charlotte minded, she didn't show it.

Greg raked a hand through his own hair, just to make sure it was still intact. Was this . . . normal?

Maybe normal for others, he decided, but not for him. His mind trailed back to Rebecca. As much as she claimed she suddenly wanted children, she would never have been able to tolerate something like this. Her perfect hair and clothes would have been ruined. It would only have been a matter of time before she enlisted a full-time nanny and suggested they go off on a European vacation to have some adult time.

He looked at Charlotte. "I've been meaning to ask if you've had an update on your apartment."

For a moment, Charlotte looked startled. She finished wiping up the baby food that had splattered on the counter and tossed a jar into the bin. "It looks like I won't be able to move back in," she said, focusing on Audrey.

Greg paused. "Never?"

Charlotte shrugged. Her cheeks had grown pink. "I'll get a new place in January. I'm going to tour an apartment next week if I can break away long enough."

"But for this month?"

"Oh!" Charlotte trilled. "I'll probably just crash at a friend's house for a few weeks. So long as Audrey's first Christmas is special, it doesn't really matter where we are." She smiled bravely, but her eyes flitted around the room.

Greg narrowed his gaze, recalling her words last night, the way she'd taken on this ludicrous proposition to begin with, the fact that she'd shown up on his doorstep the next morning.

"Well, if you need to stay here until you find a new apartment, that's fine with me."

"That might work out," she said casually, and Greg bit back a smile. "It might help us keep up this pretense until everything is certain on your end. Your mother doesn't officially retire until the end of the year, right?"

"Right. And we wouldn't want to look like we suddenly broke up after the party," Greg said, careful to have a reasonable excuse, even though that had been the furthest thing from his mind when he'd suggested she stay. His mother wouldn't know, wouldn't care. So long as Burke's signed them for next year's Christmas display, she'd be content. Besides, it wasn't like she'd bother to ask about his wedding plans again anytime soon. He could easily keep things going with a casual mention here or there until one day he was inexplicably single again. And by then, it wouldn't even matter to her.

"No, no, we wouldn't." Charlotte hooked her gaze with his, and Greg felt the air lock in his chest. She was his for the holidays, he reminded himself. Just for the holidays. Come January first, she'd move on with her life and he with his.

And somehow, he was already missing her.

Chapter Twenty

Charlotte stared at her phone screen in disbelief. The one time her sitter had dared to cancel on her in all these months just had to be an hour before her sister's surprise wedding shower.

She groaned as she looked at Audrey, who was sitting in her car seat on the kitchen counter, her face covered in oatmeal. At the sight of Charlotte's distress, the baby started giggling in glee, revealing a mouth full of the food, which soon was dispensed all over her bib.

Great. Now Charlotte would have to bathe her before she figured out what to do next. Kate wouldn't mind if Audrey was a guest. It wasn't that big of a deal. Except that Charlotte had been really looking forward to just one night out with the girls. Just one.

Her mind went darkly back to Jake again. Jake, who was never on duty, but before she dwelled on that too much, she grabbed a paper towel and began wiping Audrey's face. It was a privilege to be able to spend time with her daughter, after all. One that Jake could never understand.

There was that maternal guilt again. Maybe it was for the best if Audrey came along to the shower. Then she wouldn't have to feel guilty over being happy to leave her for a few hours.

"Everything okay in here?"

Other than for the fact that yet again, I'm wondering how fit I am to be a mother? Charlotte turned to see Greg standing in the doorway of the kitchen, looking a little too handsome for a guy who had been holed up in his office working all day. She averted her gaze, lest she get any ideas, and continued cleaning up Audrey, who was started to squirm in protest.

"Oh, fine, fine. You know that party I mentioned I had tonight?" She'd been sure to mention it when she saw him for the five minutes that morning before he shut himself off in the den. "Well, my sitter canceled. But it's fine, really. No big deal. I'll just bring Audrey with me."

"But isn't it your sister's wedding shower?" he asked.

Now Audrey was really fighting her. Moving her head and scrunching up her nose and...It was no use. Charlotte stopped wiping her face, closed her eyes for three calming breaths, and turned to Greg with an overly bright smile. She had a bad feeling she looked as deranged as she was starting to feel. Audrey had been fussy all day, and she hadn't napped. No doubt those teeth were finally about to poke through...And the only thing that kept her patience from snapping was the thought of putting on a pretty outfit and enjoying some girl time tonight.

So much for that.

"It's fine," she told Greg. "My sister won't mind."

"Well, let me see if Marlene can help—"

"She went Christmas shopping," Charlotte replied. She'd thought of that, too.

"Huh." Greg's face was pulled into a frown, and he seemed to hover behind her as she cleaned up the oatmeal and rinsed the bowl out in the sink. "You know, I can always watch her while you go."

Charlotte's gasp was audible. "You?"

"What? Is that such a crazy idea?" Greg's grin was a little bashful. Or maybe just uncertain.

Still...he was a grown adult. He was successful. Capable. Functioning. And Audrey would probably fall asleep as soon as Charlotte left anyway, considering she hadn't napped all day.

"Are you sure?" she asked, eyeing him warily.

"Sure. You already fed her, and if you write down what I need to do, I'm sure I can handle it."

"You'd just need to give her a bedtime bottle. I'll get it ready. She goes to bed at seven, and she might even be asleep before that. I'll try to only stay out for three or four hours in case she wakes up needing a change."

"A change?" Greg asked.

Charlotte gave a little smile. "A diaper change."

She thought she saw Greg gulp.

"Are you sure you can handle this?"

"Of course. She's what...about one?"

"Seven months."

"Seven months." Greg looked slightly perplexed, but then gave an affable shrug. "It's just a few hours. What's the big deal?"

★ ★ ★

What had he gotten himself into?

Charlotte hadn't even gotten out of the driveway before the

smell filled the room. Greg turned in desperation to the back door, but he knew he couldn't chase her down even if he wanted to, and really, what kind of man would that make him? Afraid of an infant!

The child's face was a strange shade of red that was starting to border on purple and the smell . . . Greg covered his nose with the sleeve of his shirt, taking breaths through his mouth.

He stared at her, wondering if she could sit there like that, in her car seat, which was all buckled over her fresh pajamas, as if she could fall out at any minute, even though it was sitting on the floor of the back den, where he had planned to watch a little football and maybe even enjoy a beer. So much for that.

Deciding he couldn't avoid the inevitable much longer, he grabbed the car seat by the handle and carried the baby up to Charlotte's guest room. There, in the corner of the en suite bathroom, was a changing mat set out on top of an Egyptian cotton bath mat, a stack of all sorts of creams and diapers stacked beside it.

He hadn't felt such dread since he was in the ninth grade and working up the courage to ask Nina Catanzariti to the spring dance.

The baby was starting to cry now. He eyed her, and she seemed to sober up for a moment, as if understanding that this wasn't easy for him, either, that they were sort of in this mess together.

It was bizarre that those little eyes could see the world, sense things, just like he could. As he continued to watch her, she blinked at him, her crying subsided now, until her chin began to quiver and then her lower lip and then . . .

A door slammed.

Marlene!

He burst out into the hall, leaving Audrey in the car seat in the bathroom and called out to her, his voice almost strangled in panic.

"My God!" she exclaimed, hurrying up the stairs with her coat and shoes still on. "What is going on? Greg? Is everything okay?"

He pointed, into the guest room, and Marlene stared at him in brief confusion before pushing past him into the room. She swung her head around the empty room but it didn't take her long to follow the trail of the baby's wails.

The next thing Greg heard was a burst of laughter.

"Afraid of a little baby, are you, Greg?" She was shaking her head when he came back into the room. The baby was already out of her car seat, cuddled in Marlene's arms, who was cooing soothing words to her as she bounced her on her hip. "I think she needs a change."

"Yes, I'm aware of that." Greg rubbed a hand over his forehead. He was getting a headache from all this noise.

"Where's her mother?" Marlene asked.

"At her sister's wedding shower," Greg replied. Or on her way there, perhaps. It was going to be a long night.

"Well, why don't I get this little girl settled, and then maybe you can read her a story?"

Greg stared at Marlene, wondering if she had hit her head on her outing. The child wasn't even one. What could she understand of a story? But fine. Okay, he would read her a story.

"Go on, now. I think Charlotte has a stack of books on the desk chair near the crib."

Greg closed the bathroom door behind him and went off in

search of the books. Sure enough, a bunch of colorful cardboard options were stacked on the antique writing chair. He decided on one about a snowman and hurried downstairs.

Marlene came down a few minutes later, the child on her hip rather than buckled into the car seat. Before he could protest, she set the child on his lap. "There now. Uncle Greg is going to read you a nice bedtime story."

Uncle Greg? Greg picked up the book, surprised that the child could sit up on her own, and rather impressed by it, in fact. Stiffly, he set a hand on the armrest, just in case she fell backward. Wouldn't want her hurting her head or anything.

"Well." He turned uneasily to the first page, slanting a glance at Marlene, who seemed to be suppressing a smile as she slipped out of the room.

He stared at the page. There were three words to the sole sentence on the page. He read them quickly, then turned to the next page, realizing with a start there were only two more page turns to go before the ending.

Read the child the book? He'd be finished in less than fourteen seconds!

He heard Marlene clear her throat from the doorway. "Just a hint? Improvise. Talk about what's on the page."

Greg suppressed a groan. If they expected the parents to elaborate the story, why didn't they just add more to it?

"There's a little white fluffy snowman. See the snowman?" God, he felt like a fool. No doubt Marlene was around the corner, wishing she had her video camera handy.

He startled when the baby let out a gurgle of sounds that seemed something like a giggle and began slapping at the snowman excitedly.

He stared at her, a smile creeping over his own face. She was actually enjoying this!

"See his hat?" He touched it, noticing that it had a felty feel. Sure enough, the child touched the hat.

Amazing!

He turned to the next page, where the snowman was dancing. When you pressed a button at the bottom of the page, music played. And did it play! For fifteen minutes straight, thanks to Audrey's endless enthusiasm for pressing the button.

He read the story to her five times over, amazed at how much she... understood it. There was a personality in there. A little girl whose zest and smile sort of reminded him a bit of Charlotte.

When she fell asleep in his arms twenty minutes later, he found himself strangely disappointed. They were just starting to have fun!

"It's awfully quiet in here," Marlene said, appearing in the doorway. She reached out her hands. "Want me to bring her up?"

"No," Greg surprised himself by saying. "I can do it."

He slid his arms under the baby and carefully stood. She was light, requiring little effort to hold, but he walked up the stairs as if treading on glass. He didn't breathe until she was set down in her crib—safe and sound.

He stood for a moment, watching her eyelids flutter with sleep, before he finally turned off the lamp and closed the door.

★ ★ ★

Charlotte pushed through the swinging door into Elizabeth's

kitchen, her arms laden with the ingredients she planned to use to make tonight's signature drink. White cranberry juice, vodka, and simple syrup. She'd also picked up some cranberries and mint leaves for a garnish.

Kate was setting out martini glasses, while Colleen put the finishing touches on her contribution for the evening: a stunning white cake that glittered as if it had been dusted with fresh snow.

Charlotte set out her ingredients, determined to make her effort match everyone else's. It was her sister's shower, after all. No one else could say as much. But still, she couldn't overlook how good they had all been to her sister. Especially back when Kate needed it the most.

Right. She would make it up to Kate one step at a time, and tonight's way was through her Winter White Cocktail, as she was calling it. She'd only be having one herself, and nursing it, considering she still had to drive back to the Frost house and no doubt Audrey would have her up throughout the night.

Frowning, she pulled her phone from her pocket and checked the screen. No missed calls. No text. Nothing. Was this a good sign or a bad one?

She'd sneak away and call to check on Audrey. Once she'd made her cocktail.

"I think my cake is ready to go to the buffet table," Colleen announced. She stepped back to wave her hands game show host–style over the dessert and Kate and Charlotte both dutifully clapped. Clapping was indeed warranted.

Charlotte felt glum. Even though Colleen was a trained pastry chef and had gone to school to learn things like cake decorating, she couldn't help but wish she was good for something more than bringing the alcohol tonight.

She sprinkled some sugar onto a plate. So help her, this garnish would look like it did in the picture in that magazine she'd skimmed in the grocery store checkout line. The cranberries and mint would sparkle just as bright as Colleen's cake. And it would be the drink they would all be talking about, not about how Charlotte had gone and mucked up her sister's first engagement.

Colleen carried her cake through the swing door, leaving the sisters alone.

"You shouldn't worry about setting out the glasses," Charlotte scolded gently. "This is your party. Go out there and relax."

"I will in a bit," Kate said. She snagged a mini quiche from a tray and leaned a hip against the counter. "This was really sweet of you guys to surprise me with the shower. Makes it all feel so real!"

"It is real," Charlotte said. She frowned at the not-so-sugary cranberries on the plate. What was she doing wrong?

"Bree hasn't said anything about the flowers for the Frost party," Kate suddenly said.

Charlotte dropped the cranberries onto the plate and stared at her sister in dismay. "You're checking up on me?"

"What? No." Kate shook her head. "I stopped by there on my way here to check on the flowers for the Loren wedding and she mentioned it to me."

Ah. Charlotte again felt silly. She grinned, thinking of what a bridezilla Hannah Loren was. "Now that's one wedding where I wouldn't want to try to catch the bouquet. No doubt by the end of the night, she'll be slamming it into the crowd!"

Kate laughed and popped the rest of the mini quiche into her mouth. "I have to admit I'll be happy when this one is over. And I think her fiancé will, too."

"If he doesn't jilt her first," Charlotte murmured, thinking of how many times she'd overheard Hannah snapping at the poor guy every time he offered up a suggestion.

She looked up at her sister, panicking. She'd done it. She'd put her foot in her mouth. Ruined what was the promise of a nice party by stirring up the past.

She opened her mouth to apologize, but Kate just reached for her wineglass and said, "I forgot to tell you Hannah's latest request!"

Charlotte blinked, momentarily caught off guard. "Oh?" She turned uneasily back to the cranberries and mint leaves. What was the point of a signature drink without the garnish?

"She wants an ice sculpture for the cake topping."

Now even Charlotte had to laugh. "But won't it be rather . . . tiny?"

"That's what I said!" Kate laughed. "I had to conference poor Colleen into the call to explain that either the entire cake would have to be kept frozen or the ice sculpture topping would melt in about ten minutes flat. Hannah threatened to find a cake baker who would accommodate her wishes, until Colleen was nice enough to offer up a solution."

"Which was?"

"She'd going to make something out of sugar that will resemble ice."

Charlotte whimpered at her not-so-sugary cranberries. Wait! She needed to make them stick. Duh. She wasn't thinking clearly. This was her first night out with the girls since Audrey had been born and her head was in two places at once. But her heart...her heart was still with Audrey.

Was she crying right now? Hungry? Would Greg remember to drop the milk on his wrist, check the temperature before popping it into her mouth? And what if he dropped her? What if he was carrying her down the stairs and his heel slipped and...She shuddered and brought the colander over to the sink and turned on the faucet. Greg hadn't called her. Or the police. And this was her sister's engagement party. She tried to keep things light. "Was Hannah satisfied with that?"

"Once we pointed out that she'd have trouble finding a baker to take an order on such short notice, she was." Kate clucked her tongue. "Please don't let me ever become this crazy over my wedding."

"How are the plans coming along?" Charlotte asked, feeling that familiar sensation twist inside her gut. It was bad enough that Elizabeth was hosting tonight's shower and not her—wasn't the sister the obvious choice, and wasn't her role as a guest especially glaring? Weddings felt like such a touchy subject between them—even if it was their business.

"I just have a few more things to decide on, really," Kate said, and Charlotte couldn't help but think of the bridal party. Had her sister already decided and just chosen not to mention it? Perhaps Kate was tiptoeing around their relationship as much as she was.

It wasn't like Kate to cut things so close. Maybe she'd already made the calls. Maybe Charlotte just hadn't made the cut.

Could she blame her?

The familiar sense of shame weighed heavy, reminding her why she wouldn't mention her run-in with Jake any more than she would mention that he was never involved in Audrey's life. The past was a fact; there was no dismissing it, and maybe, no forgetting it.

Kate set down her wineglass carefully. It was clear from her hesitation that she had something to say. "If you'd like to invite someone as your guest, you know you're more than welcome to."

"What?" Charlotte laughed, but then immediately frowned. First Bree and now Kate! Was it this important to them that she find a man?

"I'm just saying...you don't have to let me know yet. I can always leave a spot open, just in case."

Charlotte shook her head firmly. "I have no intention of bringing a date. Besides, who would I invite?" Greg, she considered, but that would be a conflict of interest, considering he was technically a client. Besides, come January their agreement would be over. She'd be on her own again. Just her and Audrey.

She frowned deeper, even though she knew it was for the best.

Kate gave a smile. "No pressure. But if someone comes along..."

Charlotte turned back to her garnish. She'd already had one man disappoint her daughter; why should she give another the same opportunity? Still, everyone—except her—seemed to think that a man in her life was exactly what she needed.

Or did they just mean a traditional family, a father under the same roof?

"I have more important things to worry about than dating,"

she said firmly. *Like protecting my child from further pain and rejection.* "Like the flowers for the Frost party."

And some other unmentionable details her sister need not know...

Chapter Twenty-One

⊙⊙⊙

Twenty-four hours to go.

Twenty-four hours until Misty Point's annual tradition arrived—from the parade to the hot chocolate stands to the tree lighting.

Sometimes she considered that she had imagined it. After all, Simon had been on her mind far too much these past few months. But no, it was real. Simon had broached the subject of the tree lighting. She had replayed the conversation enough times, while staring at the ceiling, a customer who had just asked a question, or a green stoplight until only the sound of honking horns could snap her back to the present moment. No, she was certain that Simon had suggested it. She had simply nodded, agreed to it, something like that.

Regardless of the murky details no doubt brought on by a complete emotional meltdown that had rendered her unable to fully process what was happening during the conversation in the parking lot, she was certain that Simon was looking forward to seeing her. Tomorrow.

Tomorrow...Her heart began to soar, and just to keep from completely drifting away for the rest of the party, she gave the rubber band on her wrist a particularly hard snap.

She winced. Well, that was a good sign. It meant she hadn't had to snap it in a while.

More like she had stopped thinking there was anything wrong with thinking about Simon again...

Simon. Just the name made her smile—she couldn't help it. He wasn't perfect, and things had certainly unraveled by the end, what with her looking for more of a commitment and him, well, looking for more space.

And space was what he'd had. And now maybe he realized that he didn't like that space.

She plucked a truffle from the tray. She couldn't decide which was sweeter—the chocolate or the satisfaction of knowing that Simon had missed her.

She'd wear her red cashmere Christmas scarf and her good black coat that hit just above her knee, right near her best black boots. So she might be a little cold. She'd live! She'd wear that red sweater that everyone always complimented her on, too...Just in case he suggested they go for a drink afterward. Or back to his place...

Flick. Flick.

Now Elizabeth was raising her wineglass—one of the set of ten that Bree had given Elizabeth for her bridal shower last summer—and the room fell quiet. Everyone stared at Elizabeth, positioned in front of her mantel, just to the side of the beautiful fir tree that stood proudly in the bay window, glistening with lights and silver ornaments.

Maybe Bree would get a Christmas tree after all. Maybe Simon would help her decorate it! They'd done that last year. Sort of. She'd been all excited about sharing the experience, but he'd hung one ornament and let her do the rest while he turned on the television and kicked off his socks.

Her mouth thinned. Well. No use thinking like that. He'd grown up a bit. Learned from the errors of his ways.

"I just wanted to make a toast," Elizabeth was saying. She turned to Kate, smiling proudly, as only a best friend could. "Kate, you made my special day the wedding of my dreams, and I hope that your day is every bit as magical. You deserve it, honey."

The guests started to clap, and even Bree felt herself begin to tear up, until she noticed Charlotte. Charlotte was not clapping. Charlotte did, however, look like she was blinking back tears, just perhaps not the happy kind.

She scooted down on the couch until she was within earshot of her cousin. Kate was starting to open gifts now, and everyone was oohing and aahing over the loot.

"Everything okay?" she asked.

"What?" Charlotte felt her cheeks heat. "Of course."

"I liked your cocktail," Bree offered, even though it was a little hard to drink with those cranberries floating around in it.

"The cranberries were supposed to be sugared. They were supposed to glisten, like they were covered in snow." Charlotte looked tense.

"Well. They look pretty just as they are." Bree patted her knee. "Are you sure everything is okay?"

"Of course, it's my sister's bridal shower," Charlotte replied, turning away.

Bree sank back in the couch. Something told her there was a

lot more going on than Charlotte was saying. About the shower. And about a whole lot more.

* * *

She had forgotten to call Greg. Imagine that, a mother had clear forgotten to call and check on her child. Whom she had left with a man who seemed to know nothing about babies.

What kind of parent did that make her? One night off duty, and it was like she was single again, without a care in the world!

Charlotte's hand gripped the steering wheel as she hovered five miles over the speed limit, hugging the winding roads back to the Frost house.

It was the shower. And Kate's hints about finding a date. And Elizabeth's speech. And those damn cranberries.

She should have been the one to tap on her glass, make a toast. And she'd considered it. She'd thought she might stand, say something, but then her mind had gone blank and all she could think about was the drink. Her lone contribution to the event.

And then her sister was opening gifts. And then...the moment was lost.

Elizabeth would probably be chosen as maid of honor, and really, Charlotte just needed to accept that. Elizabeth had stood by Kate when Charlotte had failed her. And now Kate and Elizabeth were going to be sisters-in-law.

Kate hadn't seemed disappointed by Charlotte's lack of toast, or by the fact that she hadn't hosted the shower. Had she preferred it this way, that Charlotte take a backseat, hover in the background, where she couldn't make any more trouble?

Tears wetted her eyes, but she didn't cry. She was on a mission. To get home. To see her baby. To get her life back under control again.

The snow was picking up, and she flicked on her windshield wipers, grateful when the iron gates appeared just ahead.

She practically ran across the cobblestone path to the back door she now preferred to use, saying a silent prayer that the reason Greg had never called was because everything was under control.

She breathed a sigh of relief when she saw Marlene in the kitchen, making herself a cup of tea.

"Oh thank God," she said, and caught the glimmer of amusement in Marlene's eye. "Is...everything okay?"

"More than okay, I should say," Marlene said with a slow smile. "Audrey is sound asleep. She woke up about twenty minutes ago, and I gave her a quick change before she dozed off again."

"And Greg?" Charlotte frowned.

"I think your little girl won him over," Marlene said. "And wore him out. He's been asleep for hours, started snoring in front of the television. I didn't have the heart to wake him."

Charlotte could barely believe what she was hearing. "So...it went well. He didn't mind?"

Marlene took a sip from her mug. "I think he was a little uncertain at first, but if you ask me, I think he enjoyed himself."

"Well, good!" Charlotte still couldn't wrap her head around it. Greg had seemed so skittish around Audrey. Competent, yes. But comfortable? No.

"Did you have a good night?" Marlene asked as she slid a plate of cookies over to Charlotte.

Charlotte pushed them away and unwrapped her scarf. "I did have a good night," she said, though she wasn't sure that was entirely true.

Chapter Twenty-Two

⋘≺∙≻⋙

The next morning, Greg had just finished the last sip of his coffee when Charlotte appeared in the doorway. He looked up, surprised to see her and, he realized, more pleased than he should be.

"Good morning!" she said, marching farther into the room and depositing Audrey into that car seat she seemed to bring with her everywhere.

"Good morning," Greg replied. He folded the newspaper and leaned back in his chair, noticing that Charlotte was already dressed for the day in those tight-fitting jeans and a soft gray cowl-neck sweater. "I wasn't sure you were awake yet."

Charlotte glanced up and gave him a hard look. "I have a seven-month-old. It's nine thirty. I've been up for four hours."

Greg watched as she settled Audrey with a rubbery toy giraffe and then stood to prepare a bottle. She hummed to herself as she worked, seemingly comfortable with his presence. She seemed at home here in this kitchen, and Greg had a strange feeling that he was the guest in the room and not the other way around.

Since Charlotte's arrival, the entire feel of the house was different. It had sprung to life, and not just with garland and greenery. The house felt filled—with noise, with laughter, with the things that glued a family together.

A family. Greg frowned and ran his hand through his hair, looking back to the paper. What the hell was he thinking? Greg didn't do family. He had no experience with that—at least not since his grandparents had died. He wouldn't know what to do with a family.

He busied himself with the next headline, frowning deeply.

"What do you have planned for the day?" Charlotte asked pleasantly, interrupting his thoughts.

Greg looked up from the paper and shrugged. It was Sunday, and he usually liked to linger over his newspaper for a few hours with a pot of coffee. He and Rebecca would rarely get moving before nine, and then spend their mornings in silence, companionably reading their favorite news sections before heading out to a casual brunch in the neighborhood. There was always a social event on the calendar, some charity fundraiser or opera to attend that filled their weekend evenings. But not this weekend. He had the entire day to himself. And he wasn't so sure he liked the thought of it after all.

Not that he wanted to go back to the ways things were, though. He'd never really enjoyed those fundraisers, and he would have preferred to attend a few meaningful events a year to support a cause that really meant something to him, not just to see and be seen, as Rebecca liked. At first, he'd been grateful for an opportunity to stop going, but as the weekends wore on and the silence and loneliness began to sink in, he grew restless.

"I'm going into town for a bit, if you're interested," Charlotte continued.

An invitation, was it? Might be a good chance to get to know her a bit better...in time for the party, of course. "What did you have in mind? Christmas shopping?"

Charlotte seemed surprised at the suggestion. "Oh. No...I'm going to take Audrey to see Santa. It's her first time, and, well, I've been really looking forward to this." Her smile widened.

Greg studied her for a long moment, following her movements as she prepared two bottles and stowed them in a large bag and then counted out small jars of baby food in various colors. Something inside him softened at the sincerity of her gesture, at the care she took preparing her daughter's things.

"A trip into town sounds good. I should probably get a Christmas gift for my mother while I'm there." It didn't matter what he bought her. She'd look at it with disinterest before pushing it aside, never to be thought of again. Still, the gesture needed to be made. Especially this year.

"Perfect. Then it's settled," Charlotte announced, and with an eyebrow raised in expectation, she pulled the keys from her pocket and said, "Let's go!"

Half an hour later, they were settled into the car, heat blasting from the vents as they circled downtown Misty Point in search of a parking spot. The town was already bustling, and shoppers filled the salt-covered sidewalks edged with snowbanks, clutching shopping bags as they weaved their way through the crowds. Carts on each corner filled the air with steam and the fragrant aroma of roasted chestnuts and hot chocolate.

"The Christmas market is set up!" Charlotte was grinning

ear to ear as she clutched the steering wheel. Greg sat cramped in the passenger seat, taking in the garland wrapped around the iron lampposts, the cobblestone streets that seemed to be almost designed for this Christmas backdrop with far less enthusiasm. He couldn't let it get to him, all this so-called magic of the holiday. He had to focus on the bottom line. Every person he saw on the sidewalk or in a store was most likely a Frost customer, especially at this time of year. They bought into Christmas, which meant they bought Frost products.

"I used to love this day. First Sunday of December. We'd get hot cocoa, walk around the stands..." Charlotte had lost herself somehow. Her eyes were sparkling and her smile was wide, and Greg wasn't even sure if she was talking to him or to thin air.

Or Audrey. He frowned. He hadn't considered that.

Finally, Charlotte pulled into a parking spot, screeching to a halt so dangerously close to a large bank of plowed snow that Greg reflexively shot his hand to the ceiling of the car to brace himself. If Charlotte noticed, she showed no reaction, instead nearly squealing with glee as she unhooked her seat belt with a flourish.

"We're going to see Santa, Audrey!" she cried joyfully, and Greg found himself feeling downright confused. Audrey was practically an infant. Was it common for people to talk to babies as if they could actually understand?

Climbing out of the car, Greg pulled his collar against the sharp wind and stared down the street. Even from this distance, he could hear the Christmas carols streaming from the speakers in the town square. Children ran excitedly along the snow-packed sidewalks, jabbering about toys they wanted, and young couples strolled hand in hand, leisurely stopping to look in shop windows and admire the holiday displays.

He wondered where he fit in all this, what an onlooker would make of their situation. Stepping onto the sidewalk, with Charlotte pushing the stroller, he had to assume that to anyone who didn't know better they might look like a family. A regular family out for a weekend stroll and some holiday shopping.

And wasn't that what he wanted? What he needed, he corrected himself. A family? He needed to portray himself as a family man. He needed to fit the image people had of Frost Greeting Cards. But he didn't need to like it. Or aspire to it. Or want it so badly he suddenly felt his chest knot when he thought of the day he would walk these streets alone again.

A little girl in pigtails skipped past him clutching a candy cane, and he suddenly flashed forward a few years. Maybe someday he'd see Charlotte again, with a little girl holding her hand, and he'd remember today, and he'd remember this year, when— just for the holidays—they were his.

He pulled back sharply as a man pushed into him and then hurried by without so much as an apology. Greg turned and watched the offender hurry down the street, his arms laden with shopping bags, before disappearing into yet another store.

"You see, this is what I hate about Christmas," he said, pointing down the sidewalk.

Charlotte just grinned and bent down to adjust Audrey's hat. "I don't think there's anything to hate about Christmas."

He gave her a long look. Was she serious? "All the pushing and shoving and greed. They say it's about family and friends, but from where I stand, the holidays bring out the worst in people."

"It brings out the best in people, too," Charlotte said, smiling.

"You're too optimistic," he replied.

She just shrugged. "You should try it sometime. If you let yourself enjoy the holidays, you might end up having a little fun."

He doubted that. "Christmas is an industry." At least it was in his household, he thought, thinking back on the way his mother had discussed the holiday, for as long as he could remember, always in reference to sales or profits or margins. "A fantasy." He pointed to a window display of Santa and his elves to underscore his point.

Charlotte refused to be ruffled as she began walking down the sidewalk. "Sometimes it's nice to have a little fantasy in our lives. Even it's only once a year. It's nice to have a reason to be hopeful."

Greg considered her words as they turned the corner. He opened his mouth to say something, to grudgingly agree that maybe she had a point. A small one. Even if it was all some sham that people bought into, no harm was really done. And maybe it would be nice to have an excuse to believe in magic once a year. If you bought into that type of thing, that is.

The words were just about to slip from his mouth when a little boy down the street began to wail, soon throwing himself onto the ground, where he rolled around on the coarse salt, icy water seeping into his blue jacket. His legs flailed, nearly kicking passersby, and even from a distance, Greg could count all the kid's molars, practically see his tonsils. His mother stood above him, face red, warning loudly that all Santa would bring him was a lump of nice hard coal if he kept this up.

Yeah, this is what he hated about Christmas. It was all a commercial event. A way for the retailers, like Frost, to earn a profit. Not that he was complaining. But there was no way he was ever going to see the holiday as anything more than it was. As much as they preached the message that Christmas was about family and being together, he knew what it was really about.

But right now, he thought, glancing to Charlotte as she happily steered that giant stroller through the crowds, he didn't mind being one of the crowd, and just for today, he'd pretend he didn't know the real meaning of Christmas and feed into the fantasy. But just for today.

★ ★ ★

Charlotte inched forward in the long, winding line that seemed to barely move. Children dressed in their Sunday best were growing antsy, and just in the time they'd been there, a few frustrated mothers had called it quits. She supposed she should have known the line would be worse on a weekend, but there was only so much she could squeeze into a single day, especially with the Frost party less than a week away.

Greg stood at her side, waiting out the experience. If he was annoyed or impatient, he didn't show it, and something inside her tugged. She couldn't help it. This was how it was supposed to be. Audrey's first Christmas was supposed to be spent as a family, with two parents excitedly bringing her for a first photo with Santa. As much as Charlotte had been looking forward to this, her chest had felt a bit heavy as she dressed Audrey in the little red dress Kate had bought for her last month. She didn't like the thought of having no one to share this moment with, no one to reminisce with about it later.

But thanks to Greg, she supposed she didn't have to.

"No personal cameras!" a bored-looking man dressed as an

elf called out, and Charlotte felt her stomach knot with anxiety.

She frowned and took the brochure he thrust into her hand, her heart sinking when she saw the list of photograph prices. The packages started at twenty-five dollars, and that was just for one copy! She would have loved two. Even better, she would have loved a digital copy to be able to send to her parents.

"Typical Christmas ploy to get people to spend more money," Greg grumbled.

"I would think in your business you'd be pleased that everyone's happy to open their purse strings at this time of year," Charlotte commented.

"It just goes back to what I said. Christmas lines the retail industry's pockets. Do you think all these people think about the supposed real meaning of Christmas?"

"I know I do," Charlotte said quietly. All she wanted was a special first Christmas for her little girl. It didn't have to be much. It just had to be memorable. "I don't really care about the gifts," she added. *Not too much, at least,* she thought. It would be nice to have the money to buy Audrey the things she wanted to give her, but at the end of the day, a few heartfelt tokens mattered just as much. "All I want is to be able to give my daughter one magical day each year. I want her to look back on these memories and know she was loved. That's the real meaning of Christmas for me."

She looked down at the price list again and pressed her lips together. Just because she couldn't afford everything she wished to be able to give her daughter didn't make what she could offer any less meaningful. Or so she kept reminding herself. But times like this, when she thought of how much Audrey deserved to have a keepsake picture with Santa, she couldn't help her thoughts from wandering back to Jake. He probably spent cash like this on a round of drinks for his friends. Daily. And there was no telling what that engagement ring had cost. How could his own daughter not be worth a dime, much less a second of his time?

She steeled herself against her darkening mood. She had looked too forward to this event too long to let Jake ruin it for her now.

"Everything okay?" Greg asked as they approached the front of the line.

Santa was visible, sitting plump and jolly with his forearms rested on the oversized velvet armchair. He was a good one, Charlotte thought, with a real beard, pink cheeks, and a kind face. For a fleeting moment, she felt her spirits lift.

"Of course!" She beamed at Greg, but she could tell by the slight squint in his gaze that she hadn't convinced him. There was hurt in her voice, disappointment. Her chest had started to ache. "It's just . . . sometimes I feel sad for Audrey that her father chooses not to care about any of this."

A shadow darkened Greg's face. "No child should have to grow up feeling that way."

Charlotte swallowed hard, thinking of the pain that Greg seemed to still carry with him, wondering if Audrey would do the same. But then she thought of Greg's mother, the ice queen, and she knew things would be better for her own child. She'd make sure of it. Audrey would look back on her childhood and want for nothing. There was nothing a disinterested father could give Audrey that she, as her mother, couldn't.

At least she hoped not.

She bent down to unbuckle Audrey from her stroller and lifted the baby into her arms so she could smooth down the dress. Oh, it was pretty. Red velvet with smocking and tiny puffed sleeves edged in a satin ribbon. There was a matching bow attached to an elastic ribbon that Charlotte had put on her head, and little patent leather Mary Janes, indescribably small and sure to be a lifelong keepsake. This would probably be her only child, after all. Regardless of the circumstances, she intended to make the most of it.

"Which photo package would you like, ma'am?" the elf asked her.

Charlotte frowned. Since when did people start calling her *ma'am*? Only a mere matter of months before Audrey was born, when she still had the time to doll herself up, no one had thought to call her *ma'am*. Back then she was a *miss*! She was sometimes still carded. What had happened to that young, carefree girl she once was?

Audrey, she realized with a small smile. That's what had happened.

She deposited Audrey onto Santa's lap and stood back to admire the scene. She clapped her hands and sang a little song until Audrey flashed her biggest smile, and Charlotte nearly burst with pride. She felt Greg's eyes on hers, but didn't look his way. She was sure she looked like a clown, but she didn't care. And she didn't need anyone sobering this moment for her.

"Just the single photo," she replied as she leaned forward to pick up Audrey, who burst into wailing tears in her arms.

"How about the disc?" Greg cut in. Charlotte turned to him sharply. She could feel the heat working its way up her cheeks. She opened her mouth to protest, but before she could, Greg reached into his pocket and smoothly pulled out his wallet. "A photo like this only happens once."

Charlotte didn't know if he saw how much the gesture meant to her. She hoisted Audrey higher on her hip, barely able to suppress the smile that formed on her lips as Greg pushed the empty stroller to the front desk and, after paying, handed her three large copies of the photo and the disc.

"I figured you'd want to give a copy to your sister and your parents," he said.

She stared at him, trying to find the words that showed her full gratitude.

"Thank you," she whispered.

He shrugged and began pushing the stroller out of the crowd. "Consider it an early Christmas gift."

She gave him a knowing smile. "I thought you didn't buy into all this Christmas stuff."

He was still smiling when he turned to her, but his dark eyes were anything but amused. "What can I say? If you keep it up, you might end up turning me into a believer."

★ ★ ★

Greg took the small red paper bag from the store clerk. That completed his Christmas shopping. A bracelet for his mother that she would be sure to toss in a drawer and forget. What a relief that was taken care of.

"Oh, look." Charlotte stopped walking and turned her attention to a Christmas tree decked out with ornaments of every shape and size. She was holding a small pink one, with writing he could barely make out. "Isn't that sweet?"

He didn't think much of it but decided it was best to play along. "Should we get it?"

"Oh. No." She shook her head and backed away. "Next year. When I have my own tree."

He leaned in for a better look. "But it's a baby's first Christmas ornament."

"That's okay. She won't know the difference." Charlotte grabbed the stroller and pushed it forward.

Something about this situation was starting to nag him. Charlotte didn't appear to have two dimes to rub together, and she clearly had nowhere to spend the month. "Do you mind if I ask about Audrey's father?"

Charlotte didn't look at him as she maneuvered the stroller through the open door and onto the crowded sidewalk. "There's nothing to tell. Audrey was...a surprise. And Jake—her father—never wanted to take responsibility. When I said he wasn't involved, that was a bit of an understatement. He's never even met Audrey. Well. He sort of did. Once."

"A deadbeat then. As suspected." He closed his eyes. Held up a hand. "I'm sorry. That was rude."

Charlotte laughed at this. "It's the truth. He is a deadbeat. He's also getting married. And he also has more money than God."

"Then why not sue him?" It seemed so obvious.

Charlotte shook her head, her cheeks turning pink. "No." Her voice seemed to shake with certainty. "I don't want to make things worse."

He didn't know how they could be much worse, but she clearly felt strongly about this, so he let her be. He lowered his gaze to the cobblestone sidewalk, wet from snow, and lazily glanced up to the street. The sky was gray and overcast, and the streetlamps cast a warm glow that reflected off the garland-draped store windows. It would probably snow soon. If it kept up like this for the next few weeks, they'd be sure to have a white Christmas. Not that he particularly cared.

"I've tried reaching out to him," Charlotte continued, "but nothing seems to work. Audrey doesn't even have his last name."

"But you have rights," Greg said. They were nearing her car now, and he pressed his lips together. It was rusted on the side, around the wheels, and one of the tires looked low. The thing must have a hundred and fifty thousand miles on it. He doubted it even had air bags. "You shouldn't have to be doing this alone, Charlotte. At the very least, you should be getting child support."

She said nothing as she lifted Audrey from the stroller and placed her in the car seat. She quickly hooked her in the harness, closed the door, and then with an expert flick of her toe and move of her hands, collapsed the stroller flat. "I wanted Jake to come around on his own. I wanted him to *want* to be a father." She lifted the stroller into the trunk before he could help and slammed the lid shut.

"Yes, but you said he had money. The child support would at least make your life easier," Greg pointed out.

"Money isn't everything," she said firmly, silencing him with those words.

Anything else he might have said stopped there. Money wasn't everything, and that was a lesson he had learned growing up. Even without his unknown father's input, his mother might have been able to buy him the best gifts and send him to the best schools, but money didn't buy someone's love. There had been times over the years when he had thought of his father, especially as he grew older, and watched his friends become fathers themselves, but he never missed him. He couldn't miss someone he never knew, an experience he never had. And he didn't long for it, either.

He looked down at Audrey through the window, noticing the way her chubby hands gripped the edge of her soft pink blanket. What kind of man would deny this child and leave Charlotte to fend for herself? No man at all, he decided.

"It's getting cold. Let's go home," Charlotte said. *Home.* She said it casually, without apology or even explanation after the words were out, perhaps not even realizing what she had said. But Greg didn't mind.

In fact, he rather liked it. And he decided not to read into that sentiment any further.

"I have a better idea," he said. He pointed to the crowd that was gathering along the sidewalk. "Don't you think Audrey would like to see the Christmas parade instead?"

Chapter Twenty-Three

⊶⊶⊶

The Christmas parade?" Charlotte gave Greg the once-over. "I didn't think this was your type of thing."

"It's not," he admitted. He shrugged. "My grandfather used to bring me every year. We did the whole cocoa and Christmas market bit, too, believe it or not. I haven't been back to it since he passed away."

Charlotte frowned. She knew better than to ask if his mother had brought him. "I didn't realize you ever spent holidays in Misty Point."

"We didn't really. We were always in Boston. But we'd come to town for weekends throughout the year, and this event was usually timed with that visit." He frowned. "I wonder if my grandfather planned it that way. My grandfather loved Christmas. I think that's why he started the company."

"But your mother—" Charlotte looked confused.

"Hates Christmas?" Greg finished for her.

"Maybe it makes her sad," Charlotte said. "Christmas is a

tough time of year for some people." It had been miserable for her last year, spending it alone.

"My mom never really talks about her parents. Heck, she rarely speaks of anything but the business anymore. Guess somewhere along the way, I gave up trying."

"Don't give up," Charlotte said, grabbing him by the arm. He seemed puzzled by the firmness in her voice, but she didn't care. "You don't ever give up on family. You just... keep trying."

He stared at her, and finally nodded. Something in his eyes told her he might just follow her advice.

They put Audrey back in the stroller and walked back down Harbor Street toward the town square, where crowds had already gathered around the large tree set up in the center. Greg stopped to get them each a hot cider while Charlotte added another blanket to Audrey, who was fast asleep in her stroller.

"She'll miss the show," Greg pointed out.

"That's okay." Charlotte sipped her cider while she pushed the stroller with one hand. "She needs her rest and... it's nice having a little peace and quiet for a moment." She grinned, and Greg did, too.

"You know," Charlotte said. "I wonder if I ever saw you here. I used to come every year to this event with my family."

And she'd be looking oh so forward to sharing it with Audrey once she was a little older. Audrey might not remember this experience, but Charlotte would, and she would tell Audrey all about it someday...

Omitting the part about the fake family and all that, of course.

Instead she'd just refer to him as a friend. And he was a friend, in a strange sort of way. Who knew... maybe they'd even keep in touch after the month was over. She was starting to hope they would.

Oh no, she thought, setting a hand to her stomach. She was falling for him. For the good looks and the easy charm.

Just like she'd fallen for Jake. And she knew how that had turned out.

She chewed her lip. She felt unsteady, unsure. She was in too deep. She'd let herself slip. And she'd promised herself never to do that again. She'd promised Audrey.

"Charlotte?"

At the sound of her name, Charlotte turned, feeling herself blanch when she saw her sister waving at her through the heavy crowd.

Before she could process what was happening, Kate and Alec were pushing their way through the people toward her, their smiles turning to expressions of confusion when they noticed Greg standing beside her.

"This is a surprise!" Charlotte chuckled nervously and leaned in to give her sister a quick peck on the cheek. She stepped back, hoping that somehow Greg had magically disappeared, but nope, he was still right at her side.

"You know I never miss the parade or the tree lighting!" Kate explained. "I was going to call you to join us, but..." Her eyes skirted to Greg and Charlotte sighed heavily. There was no avoiding it.

"Kate, this is Greg." She could only hope that was vague enough.

Her sister smiled as if nothing was amiss, and Charlotte breathed a little easier. "Nice to meet you. I'm Charlotte's older sister."

"Ah, yes, Charlotte has told me all about you."

Kate raised an eyebrow, and Charlotte said hurriedly, "He knows I work for your company." Immediately, she regretted mentioning the business. Quickly, she said, "Have you seen Audrey? She'd wearing that pretty red dress you gave her."

Distraction successful, Charlotte watched as Kate leaned down to coo over the baby. "Greg, this is my sister's fiancé, Alec Montgomery." With any luck, they'd have a little guy talk. Hopefully that didn't involve what people did for a living.

"So this is how Misty Point celebrates the holidays?" Alec grinned. "Charming."

"It is!" Charlotte nodded with too much enthusiasm for the remark, eager to avoid looking in Kate's direction. She turned to Greg, hoping to keep the conversation on track. "Alec is from Boston."

Greg perked up at this. "Oh, really? Which part?"

And…that backfired. Before long the men were engrossed in memory lane, reliving all of Alec's old favorite haunts, and Kate used the opportunity to slide between Alec and Charlotte and nudge her to the side, out of earshot of the men.

"So, why is this the first time I'm meeting this guy?" Her blue eyes homed in on Charlotte, and she knew there was no way she was getting out of this anytime soon.

"We're just friends." And friends is how they would stay.

"Friends?" Kate didn't seem to buy it. "You two look pretty cozy to me."

"It's not like that," Charlotte insisted, but she couldn't help but brighten a little at her sister's observation. They did look cozy. They looked…like the family Charlotte had always hoped to have.

But couldn't, she reminded herself. She couldn't have that

family. She'd tried, and failed. And she wasn't about to try again. Fool me once, as the saying went.

Kate just shrugged. "If you say so..." Her grin was mischievous as she turned back to Alec. "I hate to run off, but William and Elizabeth are waiting for us over near Paddy's. They claim it's the best view of the parade." She glanced at Charlotte. "You're welcome to join us, unless..."

Unless she and Greg wanted to be alone, presumably. Seeing no choice but to go along with this idea so as to get away from her sister and protect the arrangement she and Greg had in place, Charlotte shook her head.

"I think we'll hold our spot here. I haven't had lunch and you know how much I love those German pretzels they sell in the stalls." She relaxed as her sister and Alec disappeared.

That had been too close.

"I wasn't sure if our cover was going to be blown," she muttered to Greg.

"I decided to follow your lead. I take it she isn't in on the plan, yet?"

"Are you kidding me? If she had any idea I was mixing business with pleasure, she'd fire me." But that wasn't the worst of it. She'd lose faith in Charlotte. Again. And Charlotte couldn't bear the thought. Her sister was finally trusting her again. Giving her a small opportunity to make things right, make things up to her in the only way she could.

Greg's mouth twitched. "Mixing business with pleasure, eh?"

Charlotte felt her face heat. "That's not what I—Oh, you know what I—"

He set a hand on her shoulder. God, it felt good. Sturdy and warm. And safe. "Relax. I'm just kidding."

Only something in his eyes told her he wasn't.

Now her stomach felt all fluttery. Uh-oh. This wasn't good.

"Come on," she said, pulling out her phone. "If we're going to pull this off, we'd better start by making it look real."

She tapped the camera setting and held up the screen. Lights glittered in the background, almost as bright as her own smile. And just for a moment, she dared to pretend that all of this wouldn't disappear as soon as you could say Merry Christmas.

★ ★ ★

Bree checked her watch again, even though only a minute had passed, and then thrust her hands back into her pockets. The hot cider stand was in her line of sight, and it would go far in keeping her warm, but she didn't dare leave her post. The crowds were thickening now that the sun had set. Everyone was filtering into the square, ready for the carolers to lead them in song before the tree lit up.

Surely Simon was among them.

She craned her neck when a tall, broad-shouldered man blocked her view of the street. She supposed Simon might have slipped past. Maybe he was closer to the tree. She pulled her phone out of her pocket and checked for missed calls. The screen was blank.

She should call him. For all she knew he could be standing on the other side of the square, which, while unlikely, wasn't completely outside the realm of possibility. He might have walked past in the crowd, not seen her, and tried to find a quieter place to stand.

Without giving it another thought, she scrolled through her list of contacts to his name. She tapped the screen, held the phone to her ear, and listened to it ring. Three. Four. Maybe he couldn't hear it with the carolers.

The carolers! They were starting.

His voice came on the line. Voice mail. But that didn't stop her from closing her eyes, listening to that deep, smooth voice, savoring it right up until the final beep. She hesitated, wondering if she should say something, and decided to hang up. He'd see the missed call. And if he hadn't deleted her name from his contacts list, he'd know who to call back.

There were fewer people coming in from the street now. Most of the town was gathered around the tree in the center of the square, watching quietly as the carolers dressed in old-timey clothes sang from fake caroling books. Usually Bree found this tradition extremely charming, but today she had no patience for it. She waited a few more minutes at the opening to the green. The rest of the square had been closed off by a fence of makeshift stands in the form of an old-fashioned Christmas market. Really, this was the only place one could enter. So where was Simon?

And why hadn't he called back?

She waited, searching the empty street and finally crowds, searching for a face that might be searching for her. And as the music reached a high point and the lights suddenly turned on, the entire crowd let out of a cry of delight. There was a cheer, and the carolers sang their final song of the night, "O Christmas Tree." That was her favorite part, and she was missing it!

But she didn't even care. Once the sound of the carolers

standing against the beautiful twinkling lights would send a shiver down her spine. It would fill her with hope and possibility.

But tonight, she didn't feel the magic. Tonight, she felt nothing at all but a heavy heart of disappointment.

Chapter Twenty-Four

⁎⁎⁎

Charlotte stared at the picture they'd taken yesterday at the Christmas parade. Greg had suggested she get it printed. They could frame it, stick it on the mantel. Make it look like they were a real couple.

The only thing was, in this photo, they did look like a real couple. They didn't look like two actors playing a part, or two strangers posing for the lens. They looked...happy, she supposed. They looked...right.

"Here you go, a vanilla latte with extra foam."

Charlotte hurried to turn off her phone as her sister approached the table. They were sitting at a window table of Jojo's Café, after just returning from a spectacularly disastrous meeting with the bridezilla of the bridesmaid's back tattoo.

"Should we wait for Bree?" Charlotte asked as she emptied two packets of sweetener into her drink.

"She said to start without her." Kate looked over Charlotte's shoulder and grinned. "Never mind. There she is."

Charlotte did a double take as her cousin approached. Her

usually rosy skin was pale and sallow, and there were dark circles under her eyes. Her hair was pulled back in a haphazard bun, and she seemed to be on the verge of tears.

"Is everything all right?" she asked worriedly. She exchanged a glance with Kate, who seemed to share her concern.

Bree waved a hand through the air. "Just tired is all. Busy time of year and all that. Let me get a drink, and I'll be right back."

Charlotte waited until Bree was out of earshot before saying, "Something is up."

Kate nodded once. "Absolutely. And I have a bad feeling it has something to do with Simon."

"Did she mention to you that she ran into him the other day?"

Kate frowned. "No. But I saw him at the tree lighting ceremony with another girl last night. I just assumed that Bree saw and this is what upset her."

"Hmm." Charlotte blew on her coffee. "Did they look like more than friends?"

"More than friends?" Bree interrupted as she slid into her seat. She lifted an eyebrow at Charlotte, her mouth curving mischievously. "Are we talking about you and Greg?"

Kate grinned. "I met the mystery man yesterday. He was quite handsome."

Yeah. He was handsome. And kind. And funny. Every time she thought of the way he bought those photos of Audrey and Santa, her heart warmed. She'd decided to use the photos to make gifts for her family. It wasn't much, she knew, but it meant something.

"He's just a friend," Charlotte stressed. Friend. Client. She hoped that Bree wouldn't correct her. Quickly, she said, "I didn't see you yesterday, Bree. Where were you standing?"

"I came home later," Bree said. "Just for the tree lighting."

"Did you go alone? You should have called me," Kate said.

Bree unwrapped her scarf. She looked positively miserable. "It's fine. I didn't stay long. I don't feel very well, actually."

Charlotte scooted her chair away. The last thing she needed was to get sick right before the Frost party. "Hopefully the tea helps," she said.

Bree just nodded. "A bit."

Hmm. It seemed to Charlotte that Bree wasn't so much as physically sick as she was heartsick. She knew all the signs by now. Lack of sleep. Lack of appetite. Crestfallen expression. Broken spirit.

She smiled to herself. Somewhere along the way she'd stopped feeling that way. Even now, when she should be panicking, she was feeling perky and excited about life again. Even the knowledge of Jake getting married didn't bother her so much anymore.

Bree dragged out a long sigh and frowned into her mug.

Okay, she had it bad. Charlotte could only assume that her sister was right. It was clear that Bree wasn't over Simon, and seeing him with another girl would be devastating. Why couldn't Bree just find a nice, solid, responsible guy? Someone who treated her like she deserved to be treated. Like how Greg treated her.

Charlotte stopped herself right there. Greg might be nice now, but she knew all too well how these things ended up. Besides, how did she know he wasn't just being sweet to keep her on his good side? God knew he needed her right now.

About as much as she needed him, she thought, frowning.

"Well, right now I need to recover from my meeting with Crazy Bride." Kate took a sip of her drink. There was Crazy Bride and Neurotic Bride and Mean Mother-in-Law and Green Bridesmaid. Oh, there were nice clients, too. Sweet, friendly women who they were sad to see go off onto their happily-ever-afters. But weddings brought out big emotions, and Kate and now Charlotte often had a front row seat to every meltdown along the way.

"She actually asked her maid of honor to have her tattoo removed before the wedding. She offered to pay and everything."

At this, Bree managed a laugh. "I'm sorry, but that's just so . . ."

"Selfish?" Charlotte shook her head.

"I'm glad we're having this conversation," Kate said. "If either of you dare to accuse me of being unreasonable over an ugly bridesmaid dress, I will remind you that I am not asking you to undergo a medical procedure for my personal happiness."

Bridesmaid dress? So she was on the list then? Charlotte's chest began to pound and she felt her cheeks go hot. So there it was then. A bridesmaid. Not a maid of honor. Just a bridesmaid. One of the crowd.

Why had she ever dared to hope for anything more given the circumstances?

"Hey, I liked those bridesmaid dresses," Bree said.

Charlotte blinked. "You've already picked them out then?" Her voice was tight, and she hated the note of disappointment that crept in.

"She showed them to me the other day," Bree said, nodding. "You should see what she has in mind for Audrey, too."

Of course. Audrey. The flower girl. She knew she had needed to work that day, stay back at the office and help of course, but it stung that so much had been discussed in her absence. When Kate was planning her first wedding, she'd included Charlotte in all her plans. But then, that was before...

Tears stung the back of her eyes and she knew it was time to leave. She had no one to be upset with but herself, but that didn't make the pain any less. She glanced at her watch. It was half past four, and there was little reason to drive back to the office now. She'd pick up Audrey a few minutes early, even if she did have to pay the sitter for the full day.

She gave a shaky smile. "Better get home." Home. If they had any idea what home was to her these days... Well, she'd be in very big trouble. Again.

* * *

Greg was in his home office, catching up on emails, when he heard the crash.

He jumped from his chair and hurried out of the room, his mind beginning to run through every worst-case scenario that might have happened, all of them involving Audrey.

This house wasn't baby-proofed. Wasn't protected from small, curious hands. Christ, one of his grandmother's antique Chinese vases alone could probably do lethal damage.

Charlotte looked up at him with wide eyes as he darted into the living room, the Christmas tree at her feet.

"Oh my God, is—" The child. He couldn't even think about it.

"I'm sorry. I was trying to get this ornament on a high branch and my sleeve caught something, and, well..." She cringed.

"So no one was hurt?" he clarified. "You're not hurt."

She shook her head, but a pleased smile seemed to pull at her mouth. "I'm afraid the only thing that suffered the fall were a few of the ornaments. She bent down and picked up the pieces of Star in the Sky, 2005's ornament of the year. "I'm sorry."

"Don't be," he said. "I'm just happy no one was hurt. When I heard the crash, I thought maybe something had happened to Audrey." He ground his teeth, hating just how easy that scenario could play out. Tomorrow he'd ask Marlene to look for anything that might be a danger and place it elsewhere.

"Audrey has been asleep for an hour," Charlotte said. "I thought I'd use the time to make more headway on the party decorations, but given the noise...I wouldn't be surprised if she's awake up there, bawling her head off. "

"Why don't you go check on her while I get a broom?" Greg suggested. Shards of porcelain were far too close to Charlotte's toes for his comfort. He reached out a hand to help guide her over the rubble, surprised at how small and light it felt in his own.

"Thanks," she said, her mouth quirking.

Before he could reply, she'd released his hold on her and dashed out of the room. He watched her go, trailing the sound of her feet on the steps, and then went to fetch a broom from the closet in the kitchen.

By the time Charlotte returned fifteen minutes later, he'd cleared up every last piece of broken ornament and righted the tree.

"Oh no." He could hear the dread in her voice before she'd even come into the room. "It's worse than I thought!"

Greg slid his gaze back to the tree, taking in the picture with amusement. At least half the ornaments had suffered from the fall, if not more.

"I think I have some other ornaments somewhere," he offered, recalling the boxes his grandparents had kept in the attic. "Some might even be original Frost ornaments."

Charlotte's eyes lit up. "Really? Wow, that would be perfect. It would really underscore the tradition of the family company, which is exactly what you wanted, right?"

Greg didn't like the sudden shift in topics. It was easy to get caught up in the fantasy, to forget that at the end of the day, this was all about the company. The family company.

So why then, only now, did he suddenly feel like he was a part of a family for the first time?

He left the room, went to the attic, and found a few boxes he recalled seeing up there. The room was full and dusty, and he made a promise to himself to revisit it again after the party, see what he might uncover under all the tarps and blankets that covered his grandparents' belongings.

When he returned to the living room, Charlotte was standing at the base of the tree, rubbing her hands together.

"It's chilly in here."

"This house always gets drafty," he agreed. "It's one of the reasons my mother hates coming here."

Charlotte lifted an eyebrow. "Then why have the party here?"

"For show," Greg told her. The entire party hinged on reputation, after all. "Why else?"

"Maybe there's more to it," Charlotte volunteered.

Greg thought about the photos in the album, the memory of his mother sipping lemonade, laughing as he came up the lawn, his pant legs wet and sandy. "Maybe." He paused, not wanting to think about his mother any more tonight. Already thoughts of the Burke's campaign were swimming to the surface of his mind, settling in heavy, like a weight he couldn't shrug. He shouldn't have brought up his mother. "I can light a fire if you'd like."

She nodded and walked over to the tree as he crossed the room and set about tenting the logs. At his place in Boston he had a gas fireplace. A mere flick of the switch created an instant glow, but this old house had been modernized in pieces, and he liked that some of its charm remained untouched.

"There," he said after a few minutes. He rolled back on his heels and stood, admiring his handiwork.

Charlotte stood beside him, a tired smile on her face as she stared into the hearth. He watched as the curling flames reflected in her eyes. She looked so pretty. Soft and sweet. He had a sudden urge to stand and kiss her.

Instead he cleared his throat and looked sharply at the tree behind her. "You've done a nice job with this," he said.

"All these Frost ornaments are so beautiful," she said, reaching into the box and holding up a small porcelain snowman he vaguely remembered from his childhood.

She went on to talk about another, but Greg's mind was already wandering, his attention on anything but the tree. His gaze followed the length of her hair, which hung loosely over her shoulders, cascading down her back. Her voice was soothing, a sound that he'd come to enjoy filling these rooms almost as much as the sound of that crackling baby monitor that was propped on an end table.

He suddenly realized she was staring at him expectantly.

"What was that?" he asked, realizing she'd said something to him.

"I was just asking if you had a favorite ornament," she said.

Greg couldn't care less about these ornaments, at least not the newer ones. Oh, he knew some people collected them, slapped down twenty bucks or more for each perfectly packaged parcel. It had been his grandfather who started the idea of creating a limited keepsake ornament each year, and Rita had kept up with the tradition. It was the best way to home in on the collectors, while the rest of the market just bought on whim or for gifts. The annual keepsake ornament was produced in limited quantities and usually sold out within a weekend before hitting the online auction boards for sometimes fifty times the price. Without fail, some poor fools who thought a trinket that cost fifty cents to produce was worth a few hundred bucks snatched them up. "It makes their Christmas feel complete," Rita had told him briskly when he mentioned it. Greg had suspected that once or twice Rita herself had listed a keepsake ornament at online auction under an alias, just to see how much it would go for. It was all about the bottom line with her.

"Oh, I don't know," he said, exhaling deeply as he scanned his eyes over the heavily decorated tree. Charlotte had added ribbon and lights and tiny little bells that made the entire thing jingle if touched. But he had to admit it was beautiful, and the guests for the party would be impressed.

"I just love those little baby's first Christmas ornaments," Charlotte went on.

It wasn't the first time she'd mentioned it. Greg considered this and shrugged, slightly perplexed that something like a baby's first Christmas ornament actually meant something to people. But it did. To millions of people each year. Not that he would know. Their tree growing up only had the keepsake ornaments. The expensive stuff. Rita wouldn't think of adding any personal touches to a tree that was in her home. It wouldn't fit the Frost image.

"This one is interesting," he said, reaching out to touch a crystal icicle that reflected the light, but at the same moment, her hands shot up, touching his. He felt the spark, the intensity of her touch, however soft it might be. She gave an embarrassed laugh, but he didn't find any of it funny. He found it...surprising, he supposed. Her lips were pulled into a pretty smile and the lights were twinkling behind her and he inched toward her, leaned in. Her lashes fluttered for one brief, startled second, and her lips parted and he could have kissed her. Then and there.

Instead he pulled back, cleared his throat. She was a single mother. And he was...well, a Frost. And all he should be thinking about right now was this party that could transition him to his birthright as head of the company. He reached over to adjust an ornament that didn't even need adjusting, but the ringing of his phone in his pocket interrupted his task. It was probably something to do with work. Some last-minute crisis with the Burke's pitch. Some latest hiccup with the party.

He gave Charlotte an apologetic smile and slid his hand into his pocket to retrieve the device, his brow immediately furrowing when he looked down at the screen.

It was Rebecca.

Chapter Twenty-Five

⊶⊷

Charlotte made a stop by Rose in Bloom on her lunch break, hoping to catch Bree and not one of her seasonal employees, who, while friendly enough, didn't lend the same personal touch she was looking for right now.

Bree had impeccable taste—she'd know exactly what to choose for the event. Even if she did lecture Charlotte for waiting a matter of days before the event to place her order.

"This Saturday?" Bree said, as expected, when Charlotte timidly—and quickly—mentioned the date. "Why are you just coming in now?"

Charlotte opened her mouth to explain that she had stopped by last week, and then decided not to mention it.

"I'm sorry," she said instead, wincing. "I've had less than two weeks to pull this entire event off myself, and well...this was one detail that fell through the cracks."

Bree pursed her lips. "Let's see what I can do. Luckily this is a holiday party and I have plenty of items in stock. Run through your ideas and we'll figure it out."

"Oh, thank you," Charlotte gushed, still not completely recovered from the reality that she had come dangerously close to not having any professional flowers for the event at all. She was all too aware that any other florist would have turned her away. But Bree, being a cousin, wouldn't do that.

"I was going to bring it up yesterday at the café, but I didn't want to upset Kate. You know how twitchy she gets about these things. She'd have my head if she knew I didn't already place the order."

"And rightfully so!" Bree gave her a wink. "Let's see what we can do."

Within a few minutes, the women decided on winter greenery with berries and Sahara roses for the arrangements. "Red is tradition for this season, but between you and me, I'm sick of it. And I'll be seeing enough of that color through Valentine's Day. Not that I wouldn't mind if a handsome man decided to bring me red roses for the occasion."

A handsome man like Simon, no doubt.

Bree jotted down the order and asked for the address. "These are for your client Greg?"

Charlotte nodded. "Yep."

"The cute one." Bree grinned.

"Stop."

"Well, if you're not interested . . . Is he single?"

Charlotte knew Bree was only joking, at least she thought she was, but she didn't like the thought of Greg with another woman. It was a good thing Colleen hadn't seen him yet, or she'd be asking the same question.

"Not at the moment," she replied. Greg was otherwise engaged until this Saturday night.

This Saturday night. She put a hand to her stomach when she thought of how important this night was.

"Charlotte?" Bree was staring at her.

Charlotte gave an embarrassed smile. "Sorry. I was just starting to think of everything I have to do for this party. I want to get it just right. It's the first time that Kate has entrusted me with a project of my own. I don't want to let her down."

Bree patted her hand. "You two will work through this. It might not seem like it just yet, but everything will work out the way it's supposed to. In the end."

Will it? Charlotte thought of Audrey, her sweet little baby whose own father couldn't even deign to look into her eyes, and felt her chest tighten.

"I don't know if you've heard that Kate isn't the only one planning a wedding," she said.

Bree set down her pen and sighed. "I've heard about Jake. His poor fiancée came in here to get a quote for the flowers one day when I was on break. The man has some nerve coming in here, if you ask me."

"He sure does," Charlotte agreed. She didn't see the reason to explain that she had also been in the store at the time.

"Well, at least he's helping you out with child support," Bree commented. "And you'll find someone better. Maybe you already have."

"Is it so bad for Audrey to be stuck with just me?" she asked, her emotions getting the better of her.

"What?" Bree looked so surprised by Charlotte's question that Charlotte immediately felt guilty. "That's not what I'm saying at all. You're a wonderful mother, Charlotte!"

Don't cry, Charlotte warned herself. *Do not cry.* She pushed back the lump in her throat. "I'm trying to give her a full life. I know she'll never have a house with a picket fence, or a dad who holds her on his shoulders, or a sister..."

"Hey, I never had a sister, either," Bree pointed out, grinning. "But you're young, Charlotte. You have a whole life ahead of you yet to live. That's all I'm saying. And Greg..." She wiggled her eyebrows.

Charlotte shook her head. These comments about Greg weren't going to stop unless she put an end to them and she didn't need her cousin filling her with hope she shouldn't have, or desire for something that would only lead to disappointment. "Greg is a client, Bree. I promise you that." A client who had almost kissed her, she was sure of it, not that she would be admitting as much.

"Uh-huh. Sure he is." Bree laughed under her breath as she began typing the order into her computer.

"He is," Charlotte insisted. "And if it looks like more is going on it's because...it's because that's part of the deal."

Bree stopped typing. She slid Charlotte a long, hard look. "Part of the deal."

Charlotte huffed out a breath and leaned over the counter. "The only way he let me have the gig was if I agreed to pose as his date for the event." Really, when you said it like that, it wasn't such a big deal at all. "Just please don't tell Kate. Something tells me she wouldn't understand."

"Wait a minute. You mean to tell me that you are pretending to date that man? A man who is, in fact, your client."

Well, when you put it like that... "Yes." Charlotte hesitated. "Look. This is a big client. And this is a big opportunity for me!"

"And how often are you seeing this man?"

Charlotte couldn't lie now. The truth was out, at least to Bree, and she may as well tell her everything. "I'm sort of staying with him."

Bree's eyes bulged. "At his house?"

Charlotte shifted on her feet. She muttered something that sounded affirmative.

"Well." Bree sighed. "I guess he doesn't seem like a serial killer."

Charlotte grinned. "Of course—"

Bree tipped her head. "Although, serial killers are notoriously charming. And often attractive."

Charlotte narrowed her eyes. "Says who?

Bree bristled. "You know I love watching *Dateline.*"

Charlotte shook her head. "Look, if he kills me, don't you think he'd be the first suspect on the list? You know my arrangement with him." She stopped. What was she even saying? Of course Greg wasn't going to kill her. He wasn't a serial killer or axe murderer. He was... well, he was sort of perfect really.

Perfect on paper, she reminded herself. So many men were perfect on paper. Like Jake.

Except Jake was cold and calculating and self-serving. And Greg was warm and sweet and thoughtful.

And she was officially going to stop reminding herself of all his wonderful qualities. He was her client. And as she'd just told Bree, this was nothing more than an arrangement.

"And there's nothing else going on between the two of you?" Bree didn't sound convinced.

"He's a nice guy," Charlotte said. "And he's smart. But he wouldn't be doing this if he didn't have to."

She frowned at that thought, wondering just how true that really was anymore.

"Promise you won't tell Kate?" she asked.

Bree nodded. "It's not my place to tell her. But who said she isn't going to find out on her own?"

★ ★ ★

Charlotte rolled to a stop in her sister's driveway and indulged in a long, heavy sigh. It felt good coming clean with Bree, but she couldn't overlook the suspicion in her cousin's eyes. Bree wasn't buying this arrangement, not completely at least.

Was it that obvious her own judgment was becoming cloudy?

Greg had almost kissed her last night. And she'd almost let him! And what if he had? What then?

She released her seat belt. No use thinking about that right now. She had to put together a parking plan for the party and finalize the catering menu since Greg still hadn't given any thoughts on the matter. Something told her that he'd be fine with whatever she decided on. Still, she'd run it all by Kate, just to be sure.

The path to the office was salted. Alec always made sure to clear it and salt it first thing after a snowfall. The driveway, too. Charlotte smiled wistfully. Even her old landlord hadn't bothered with that much.

The next place she lived would be better. She'd tour the building on Monday, after the party. Once her check was in hand...

She was smiling by the time she reached the door, but it faded when she saw the note posted to the paned frame. She plucked the Post-it from the glass and read it with a racing heart. "I'm in the house. We need to talk."

Well, this wasn't good. In fact, it was probably downright bad. Nothing good came from a conversation that started with the words *We need to talk*. And since when did they have meetings in the house?

She glanced desperately at her car. She could get in, drive off, never come back.

She wanted to. She really, really wanted to. The old Charlotte would have done just that. Fled. But the new Charlotte... The new Charlotte had responsibilities. And even though she longed to get behind the wheel, peel off, maybe hide out at Paddy's for a few hours and turn off her phone, she couldn't.

Maybe Kate just wanted to talk about the status of the rapidly approaching Frost Greeting Cards party. Charlotte could handle the inquisition, especially now that she had finally ordered the flowers. There were workers at the house now, hanging wreaths and lights from every window and branch available. The menu—She had gone with option A. There. It was settled. If Kate asked, they were having fifteen different passed hors d'oeuvres and a dessert buffet that included a chocolate fountain. The decision was made. She'd send off the email the moment she got in front of her computer.

Slowly, she walked to the back door, where a light was on in the kitchen. She paused before reaching for the handle, and took a calming breath. This was her sister.

Besides, they'd been through much worse.

Kate was in the kitchen, baking cookies, when Charlotte pushed open the door. Odd, but definitely not unpleasant.

"Don't we have work to do?" she joked as she unzipped her boots and set them on the mat.

"I needed a break, so I thought I would get a head start for the cookie swap this Friday." Kate floured the surface of her counter and slapped a roll of dough onto it. Unnecessarily hard, Charlotte felt, but maybe she was reading into things.

"I forgot about that," Charlotte said. Colleen's mother hosted a cookie swap every year at the tea shop. She set everything out on the tiered trays, and everyone sipped tea. Seeing how she'd missed last year's party, she wasn't inclined to miss this year's.

"What kind of cookies are you bringing?" she asked, sliding onto one of the counter stools.

Kate didn't reply. Instead, she handed Charlotte a copy of the newspaper.

Great. So they were officially off the wonderfully safe subject of cookies.

Charlotte stared at the paper blankly. "I don't understand."

Kate set down her rolling pin and flipped the paper over. There, on the bottom right corner of the front page was a picture of Greg in front of the Christmas tree she remembered seeing in his office lobby.

"I can explain," she blurted.

"Can you? Bree told me she saw you on a date last week. Then we run into you and Greg Frost at the parade. What is going on, Charlotte?"

"I'm not dating him," Charlotte said. Well, not really. "We're just...spending time together." Yes, that's exactly what they were doing. She felt relieved at once until she saw how round Kate's eyes were.

"Charlotte, this is a client!"

"I know that," Charlotte said defensively. And she did. Most of the time. "Is it forbidden to be friends with clients?"

"So now you're *friends*." Kate locked her eyes for an uncomfortably long time. "He's an attractive man, Charlotte."

As if she needed the reminder. "And?"

"And...I know how you are."

Charlotte felt her jaw set. There it was. All that work. All these attempts to change her ways. None of it mattered. "I'm not that person anymore."

Kate looked at her miserably. "You know how I feel about mixing business with pleasure."

"That's not what I'm doing, Kate. I'm just keeping the client happy. I promise."

Kate looked uncertain. "You really promise that's all it is?"

"The guy doesn't know many people here. He wanted some company. Is that really so bad?"

Kate raised her eyebrows and picked up the rolling pin. "Just be careful, Charlotte. And..."

She knew what was coming. She couldn't bear to hear it. "I wouldn't do anything to jeopardize the success of this party, Kate. Trust me."

Kate frowned. She didn't look convinced. Charlotte noticed the worried line that tightened the center of her forehead and knew she had made the right decision. If she told Kate what was really going on, Kate would put a stop to it. She'd take over the party herself, and then everything would be lost. The money she so badly needed. The opportunity to prove herself to her sister. And, of course, Greg would be gone, too.

She had to remember to keep her eye on the prize. The party

was only four days away, and once the night was over, she'd have a check in hand, a client for the firm, and finally, finally, finally, a fresh start at a relationship with Kate.

Yes, everything would be better after Saturday. She just had to get through the rest of the week first.

Chapter Twenty-Six

There were many ways Charlotte could spend the three hours between when Audrey drifted off to sleep after her last warm bottle of milk and when she would wake up again, hungry for more. She could read a book, but she had started one right before Audrey was born, and more than seven months later, was still inexplicably only on the fourth chapter. She could go over her plans for the party again—but she felt strangely on top of things there. The tight schedule had forced her into action nearly as much as her desire to make everything a success. She could take a hot bubble bath in that luxurious clawfoot tub in her en suite. But Greg could arrive home at any minute.

Instead, she decided to bake. Cookies were the one thing she was good at. Well, maybe not *good*, but she could roll out a tube of premade dough just as well as anyone else, and besides, the decorations were the fun part. If they came out especially bad, she wouldn't admit who had brought them. Besides, Fiona packed that tea shop on cookie swap day. Dozens of women from town stopped by for the fun. Her contribution could fade into the crowd, and there were always a few tins that went untouched, like poor Caroline Owens's rock-hard rugelach.

Marlene was out again, Christmas shopping, she'd said as she tucked her red-knitted hat over her ears not long after Charlotte had come home, still a little shaken up from her interaction with Kate. There was no sign of Greg, but Marlene had left a stew in the slow cooker, and so, after settling the baby, Charlotte had helped herself to a bowl, even though her appetite had dissipated considerably since yesterday. Was it her sister or was it the memory of that near kiss? Or was it expectation of what would happen when Greg came back tonight?

Right. The cookies. She rolled out the dough and cut the shapes with the cutters Kate had lent her. She watched them for the entire twelve minutes they were in the oven, lest she set off a fire alarm again. Once they were cooled, she set to work, decorating each as best she could with the icing and sanding sugar she had picked up at the grocery store in town.

She was just starting a second batch when she heard the back door open and Greg's tread on the floorboards. She couldn't help it. Her stomach began to flutter, and she had to set a hand to it to settle herself.

This was really not good at all. In fact, this was exactly what Kate had warned her about. And wasn't Kate always right?

★ ★ ★

Greg had driven fast—faster than he should with the slick roads and the fresh dusting of snow that had accumulated since he'd left for Boston that morning—but he couldn't help it. Rebecca wanted to work through things, said she'd drop the baby conversation for now, that she'd been swept up in what her friends had, not what she really wanted.

But what did he want? Not Rebecca, not what they'd had. He realized that now. Their life was all about parties and boats and the newest restaurant opening. There were no quiet nights at home. His apartment in Boston was sleek and industrious.

And every second in it, every moment with Rebecca, every thought of going back to the way things were, made him that much more eager to get back to what he had now.

More Christmas lights had been added to the trees that lined the driveway since he'd left early this morning. Clearly, Charlotte had heeded his mother's advice, and quickly. Garland was now draped over the front door, and a wreath hung from every window by a red ribbon. The kitchen light was on, and he took the back door, puzzled at the smell of sugar and vanilla.

Marlene didn't bake, not often, and she knew how he felt about the holidays.

But it wasn't Marlene at all, he realized, as he rounded the corner into the kitchen. Charlotte was standing at the center island, a piping bag full of bright green frosting in her hand, a dusting of flour on her cheeks and the tip of her nose.

He grinned. "I thought you didn't know how to cook."

She held up the packaging of premade cookie dough. "I can work an oven. Sometimes." She motioned to the tray. "Care to join me, or does your dislike of the holiday extend to the treats?"

"I think I'll just eat one instead," he said, reaching over to help himself, but she gave him a light slap on his hand.

"You can eat what you decorate. Otherwise, these are for a cookie swap."

"Cookie swap?" He vaguely remembered a Frost commercial

about such a thing at one point in time. "Is that like a potluck with cookies?"

Charlotte grinned. "Exactly!"

Greg looked down at the cookies. They were messy and uneven and some were burnt around the edges. The different colors of icing were bleeding into each other. "You're bringing these?"

"Yes." Charlotte stopped icing a cookie and looked up at him. There was challenge in her eyes when she asked, "Why?"

He didn't have the heart to comment on her efforts. He shrugged. "Just want to be sure I don't mess any of them up for you."

"Ah. So you're helping!" She seemed so pleased by this that he didn't quite know what to do. He'd almost kissed her last night. He'd almost thought she wanted him to.

He'd convinced himself otherwise the whole drive to Boston. But now . . . Now he had the urge to try again.

"Show me what to do," he said, coming around the corner to stand next to her. He was so close, he could feel her hip brush against his, feel the heat of her body. He waited to see if she'd inch away, but she stayed put, happily walking him through the instructions and demonstrating how to use the piping bag.

"You're quite an expert on this," he remarked.

She blushed. "My sister and I always made Christmas cookies. We liked decorating them best."

He tried to trace a white edge of icing along a cookie shaped like a star. Not great. But not terrible, either. "My grandmother used to have me make cookies with her. I was happy to help because then she let me eat them."

Charlotte laughed. "I can just picture it. I'm sure Audrey will be the same way soon enough."

Greg studied her smile, felt the pull he couldn't resist any longer.

She reached across his arm, leaning toward the second tray, and his hand slipped around her waist as his mouth came down to hers. She stiffened in surprise, but he didn't stop. And soon they were kissing. A long, slow, deep kiss, right against the counter.

Her eyes were bright when they broke apart, and her cheeks were pinker than usual.

He looked down at her hand, which was covered in red frosting and some sprinkles, and the cookies she'd managed to smash without probably realizing it. Maybe not even caring.

She licked the remains off her thumb before quickly grabbing a towel. "So much for that batch."

"We'll make another," he said, eager for an excuse to drag out the evening. "Do you have anoth er tube of dough?"

She laughed. "I bought extra just in case. Clearly, you know me well."

He was starting to, he realized. And it had been a long time since he'd really gotten to know anyone. And that was a scary thought.

Chapter Twenty-Seven

It was time to move on, put herself out there, get back in the saddle, as they say. Not to find a boyfriend per se, but just something to get her over this hump and the disappointment that Simon had once again let her down, stood her up, and that she'd let it happen.

She should just call it what it was: a rebound.

Bree poured herself a fresh mug of coffee and escaped to the back room of her shop. Caroline was covering the storefront for a few minutes while Bree was supposedly working on some orders. And she would. Once she'd created a dating profile.

She typed in the site name and all at once her screen lit up with pictures of happy couples and the promise that she, too, could find what they had! All she had to do was fill in her bio and upload the photo of herself taken at Victoria's wedding. Colleen had been carefully cropped from the photo, and everything was ready to go.

So why was she sitting here, hands hovering over the keyboard, second-guessing herself?

Right. She'd just take a little look-see first. Remind herself why she was doing this. She wanted a boyfriend. Eventually. Wanted a family someday more than she wanted to even admit. And as Gran used to say, they didn't just come to you when you were sitting home alone. You had to put yourself out there. And she was putting herself out there. Starting now.

She clicked on the Search tab and studied the fields. Age. Easy. She was now thirty-two (God help her), so she would be open-minded and say thirty to forty. Location? She wasn't willing to move anytime soon, if ever, but she doubted very much that this site would uncover a trove of available men in Misty Point, so she generously included a twenty-mile radius. With the press of a button, her screen filled with pictures of smiling men.

God, this was almost too easy. She took a sip of her coffee, starting to enjoy herself.

The first guy was cute, but he lived twenty miles away and he was only looking for a casual relationship. Good to know from the get-go. My, how refreshing! She quickly clicked out of his profile and moved on to the next. This guy lived a bit closer, just two towns over, really, and he was a doctor. My! Wouldn't Gran be proud.

And...he was separated. Not divorced. Separated. She flagged him for a later date.

She scrolled through a few more, then clicked to the next page. And the next. And then her body froze when she saw the image in the top left corner. A face she had come to memorize, one she saw every time she closed her eyes. It was Simon.

And worse was that it was a picture of Simon she knew all too well. A picture she still kept in her nightstand drawer for those especially lonely nights when she couldn't sleep and was thinking about how old she was getting and fretting over her eggs drying out before she found everlasting happiness. When she was too tired to paint the cabinets or figure out how to install a medicine cabinet in the gaping hole where the old one had been. When even the worry over those loose wires in the powder room couldn't stop her from thinking of how uncertain her future felt while everyone else seemed to have theirs locked in and figured out.

It was a picture not just of Simon, but of her and Simon, taken last June at the lighthouse. There was no denying, and as she leaned in to be sure, she could see a hint of her pink shirt where the image stopped.

The bastard had cropped her out of the photo!

Well. She was really shaking now. Trembling was more like it. She hesitated, afraid to open his profile, wondering if he would somehow find out. But then she thought of the drive-bys and the flowers and she thought, *Why stop now?* Here it was. All the masochistic information she felt so compelled to have. Right at her fingertips.

She opened his profile. Read his bio with a curl of her lip. He really did think highly of himself. Expert skier? Please. She could beat him down the slopes any day. Loved to cook? Unless he counted frozen pizza, that was a stretch.

She moved down to the bottom, clicked through a few photos, tried to ignore the pang in her chest at how handsome he still looked. And then she saw it.

Right there, black and white, clear as crystal. Simon was looking for a committed relationship.

And Simon had created his profile five months ago. Nearly two months before they'd broken up!

And Simon had been active online in the past twelve hours.

She closed her laptop and sat back in her chair. Her hands were shaking and her mind was spinning with too many thoughts, each one worse than the last.

But one thing was all too clear. Simon had never loved her. And no matter how much she thought that might someday change, he never would.

She stood up and reached down to her wrist, but instead of giving the rubber band a good hard flick, this time she slid it off.

★ ★ ★

Charlotte looked around the front hall and living room, which were coming together very nicely, and tried to imagine how everything would look Saturday night. She eyed the bare spot above the mantel and decided a swag of garland and lights would be fine. She'd get a matching wreath to hang on the mirror above. With the Christmas tree towering in the corner, already the room felt cozier and so much more lived in than it had on her first visit.

She stopped herself there. Christmas decorations had a way of transforming a space. It was easy to see it as more than that. To get caught up in the fantasy—the beautiful house, the perfect family, the memory of Greg's kiss long after his mouth had left hers.

But this wasn't her home. This was a venue, essentially.

Marlene came into the hall with Audrey on her hip. The sitter was sick and Marlene had gladly offered to help with child-care for the day.

"You can just tell that sitter of yours that I'll take over," she said as she bent down to pick up a rag doll that Audrey had dropped on the floor. Charlotte didn't have the heart to tell her it was a fruitless exercise. Audrey loved to throw that toy on the ground more than she enjoyed cuddling with it.

"I'd love to do just that, but I'm afraid she'd find another client and I'll be needing her again come the first of the year."

She frowned. Even after what had transpired between her and Greg, there was no denying the fact that she needed to find her own place to live soon.

"Just because you have a fake engagement doesn't mean you can't have a real marriage," Marlene teased, and Charlotte gave a hearty laugh to show just how ridiculous that joke was, but her cheeks flushed with heat at the thought. Marlene had tapped in on her one secret wish. A dream she hadn't even dared to admit to herself.

All this time she'd been happy enough on her own. Even convinced herself she was better off on her own. But now...now it would be hard to leave all this behind. And not just the house.

Would she ever have it again? And did Greg even want it?

The doorbell chimed, and Charlotte sighed. "That's probably my cousin Bree," she explained to Marlene. "She wanted to get a feel for the space before she commits to a vase. She's a florist," she explained, and then hesitated. "Well, she took over her grandmother's flower shop."

Marlene nodded. "I'll make some coffee."

Charlotte had mostly lost the taste for it after having Audrey, but she knew Bree would appreciate it. She smoothed her hair as she walked to the door and pulled it open. Bree stared at her with round eyes. "Here, I thought a butler would answer, not the lady of the manor!" She laughed, and after a beat Charlotte did, too.

Bree wasn't here to make trouble. Bree was here to help. Really, she needed to settle down and stop reading into every little thing, looking for problems that might not even be there.

"How does it look?"

Bree said nothing as she walked around the hall and into the adjacent living room, where Charlotte explained that the majority of the party would be taking place. Both rooms were huge and spacious, and with the furniture cleared out could easily accommodate the guests.

Bree frowned as she walked over to the tree. "Are these ornaments—"

"Frost originals," Charlotte said quickly, omitting the fact that she'd shattered half of them.

"My grandmother had this one! I found it in the attic the other day." Bree shook her head. "I just realized that I don't even have a tree this year. What does that say about me?"

"You can still put one up," Charlotte said.

"But why bother?" Bree frowned. "A tree just for me?"

Charlotte understood. Last year in Boston, she hadn't bothered. She couldn't have afforded one, and she hadn't wanted any reminders of all the joy and happiness she was missing. But this year... She looked around the room. This year was so different.

"Everyone will be back for Christmas," Charlotte said, thinking of her parents. "We always have fun."

"I know. It's just... sometimes I'm tired of being the single girl," Bree admitted, and to Charlotte's horror, her eyes filled with tears. "I can't help it. I want what Kate has. What Elizabeth has. Don't you?"

Charlotte considered this for a moment. Not long ago she would have stood firm, said she was fine on her own, that it was better this way. But was it better? Forget having someone there to help with midnight feedings or splitting the bills. What about sharing memories, holidays, keeping special moments alive forever? She'd tried to tell herself she'd be fine. Audrey would be fine. That they weren't missing out on anything at all. But she couldn't deny that wish anymore. She swallowed hard, and nodded. "I do. Of course I do."

★ ★ ★

After Bree left, Charlotte did another sweep of the front hall, envisioning where the bar table would go, and then paused to adjust the heavy garland that was wrapped around the banister. Outside, a crew was finishing attaching thousands of lights to the large stone house and the bare branches of the dozens of trees that lined the long stretch from the road. At the gate, two large wreaths had been hung by thick velvet ribbons, the very same that now anchored the front door from which guests would enter.

There were still so many more little details to attend to, and she should just continue to plow through her list—and she would—if she didn't have to keep stopping, and thinking, and smiling... It seemed no sooner did she finish a task and allow her focus to break than her mind was wandering, and all at once, Greg's lips were on hers, his hands skimming over her waist, touching her in a way she thought no man ever would again.

The doorbell chimed loudly, jarring her from her thoughts. Charlotte set down her notebook and quickened her pace to the door before the bell rang again. She needed Audrey to sleep for at least another hour so she could get a few last-minute things accomplished. The party was only three days away. It was a flat-out miracle she had even pulled together what she had in such a short period of time.

God, wouldn't Kate be impressed!

Unlocking the door and pulling it open, Charlotte was expecting to see one of the crew working on the lighting, but instead she came eye to eye with a tall blonde with ice-blue eyes.

"Oh," she said. She could feel her brow knit even as she mustered a pleasant smile. "Can I help you?"

The woman brought a hand up to a large diamond earring and stared at Charlotte stonily. "I'm Rebecca," she said coolly. "Greg's fiancée."

Charlotte felt her breath hitch. She knew it wasn't true. The relationship was over; Greg had told her so with no uncertainty. He wouldn't have lied...

Her heart began to pound when she considered the possibility of breaking up another engagement, of sleeping with another engaged man, falling for his charms. She pressed a hand to her stomach, thinking of Kate and the hurt she had caused her. The selfish, foolish act that had turned all their lives upside down.

But no, this was different. Rebecca was not wearing the ring. Greg had said it was over. And she believed him.

"Greg's at work," she replied evenly. She hadn't gotten this far in life by being intimidated by rich women like Rebecca. She wouldn't be stopped now.

"Are you the new help?" Rebecca asked with a delicate tip of her head, and Charlotte balled a fist to keep from reacting. "I don't remember seeing you here before."

"I'm...a friend of Greg's, actually," Charlotte replied. She hesitated, wondering why she hadn't just explained that she was the event planner.

Because she no longer saw herself in that role, did she? She'd crossed a line. The one she'd drawn for herself.

Uncertainty began to gnaw at her. Greg was charming and smooth, and he made her feel special. Wasn't that how it always was? A flirtation, a few gifts, a few amazing nights, and then...

Rebecca's eyes narrowed slightly as she gave Charlotte more notice. She swept her eyes casually over Charlotte, no doubt calculating the worth of Charlotte's clothes, and then rested her gaze on her hand.

"Greg had mentioned he had a new...*friend.*" Rebecca swept past her and into the hall, glancing around. She unbuttoned her camel cashmere coat and flung it on a nearby chair. Her neck was draped with a triple rope of pearls. She was taller than Charlotte, and the black pencil skirt she wore brought a curl to Charlotte's lip. Thinner, too.

Wait. She'd spoken with Greg?

"I didn't realize you two were still in touch."

"I just saw him yesterday," Rebecca replied.

Charlotte froze. There was nothing she could say to that without looking like a bigger fool. Heat warmed her cheeks as she stood facing the other woman. Greg had said he was going to Boston for a business meeting. And she'd believed him.

Charlotte glanced around the room, at the piles of paperwork she still needed to go through, the orders she needed to confirm, the invoices she needed to process. The living room, where the bulk of the party would take place, was in a state of disarray. Stacks of boxes filled with decorations waited to be opened. Extra seating was being brought in, and the front half of the massive room would be cleared out for the buffet table.

The deadline was pressing in on her, the enormity of the task she had taken on. Up until now, she felt she had a handle on it, but standing here, listening to this woman, she felt shaken and weary. Just this morning, her future had never felt so bright. But now, the heavyhearted feeling of dread was taking over, reminding her of all she stood to lose. And this time, it was more than she had gambled on.

Greg was never supposed to be part of the mix. This was supposed to be an opportunity to provide security, not uncertainty. She had Audrey to think about. First and foremost. Always.

"As you can see, we're in the middle of planning a party, and it's not the best time," Charlotte said firmly. "If you'd like to speak with Greg, he's at his office."

Rebecca cocked her head and plucked a leather glove from her hand, finger by finger. "Actually, I think I'm learning all I need to know by talking with you." She paused, holding the gloves in her hand, absentmindedly slapping them against her palm until Charlotte's teeth were set on edge. She hooked her gaze on Charlotte. "He mentioned his new friend." She pursed her lips. "And here I thought he was making you up as some . . . excuse."

She looked sharply away, and all at once Charlotte saw herself in the woman. As icy and cold as she may be, Charlotte recognized heartache when she saw it. And she could imagine that losing a man like Greg would be very hard to accept.

From the monitor on the table, she heard the rustling of fabric. She hoped Audrey was just stirring, that she would find her way back to a nice, deep sleep, but she knew it was useless. A soft whimper followed by a small cry pierced the silence. So much for getting much more done today. Though it was a convenient excuse to end this conversation.

Rebecca was looking at her in alarm, her gray eyes wide. "What's that sound?"

"It's my daughter, and I really must tend to her," Charlotte explained, walking toward the stairs.

"Your daughter?" Rebecca repeated, and Charlotte paused.

"Yes, my daughter." After a beat, she added, "Why?"

The expression of shock had not yet left Rebecca's face. She blinked twice and then, inexplicably, threw her head back in laughter.

Rebecca was still chuckling as she reached for her coat. She shrugged it on and, setting a hand on Charlotte's arm, said, "Enjoy it while it lasts. I might not know Greg as well as I thought these days, but I know one thing with him stands the test of time."

"And what's that?" Charlotte asked, pulling her arm free and folding her arms protectively against her chest.

Rebecca's heels clicked across the polished floorboards as she swayed to the door. She gripped the handle and whirled around, nailing Charlotte with a hundred-watt smile. "The man hates kids!" she said gaily, and with one last chuckle, slammed the door closed behind her.

Charlotte stood in the massive foyer, frozen to the spot. Her daughter's cries filled the room, as if she, too, were aching from those harsh words, begging to know how anyone could deny her. How yet another man could struggle to find a place for her in his heart.

Chapter Twenty-Eight

Twenty minutes after leaving the office, Greg could still feel the painful knots in his shoulders and upper back. He reached a hand behind his back and tried to rub out the tension, but it was no use. He was wound up, his mind still at work as he drove back to Misty Point on autopilot. Gripping the steering wheel with both hands, he maneuvered the car over a hill and down around a bend, noticing the ice that had gathered on the guardrail. He preferred the scenic route, even if the highway was sometimes faster. It usually calmed his nerves, grounded him. But not today.

It was already Wednesday, and Burke's would be making their decision Monday. Saturday night's event was the last chance Greg had to impress them, and the tension was especially high today. The proposal was in their hands, and the meetings were behind them, but the party could sway them in one direction or the other if they were on the fence. And Greg was starting to suspect they were.

His mind trailed to Charlotte as he neared the last few turns into the town of Misty Point. He'd been so focused on the job today, he hadn't allowed himself to even think about last night, but now as he pulled up to the house, he realized he couldn't wait to kiss her again.

Charlotte was disarming, with that magnetic smile and those bright green eyes. She was easy to talk to in a way that Rebecca and the host of women before her hadn't been. She wasn't about pretense or show.

She'd charm the pants off the Burke's team, he decided with a grin. She'd managed to win him over, hadn't she?

By the time Greg pulled up the long drive, under the arched glow of twinkling lights wrapped with precision around every branch and tree trunk, he was already feeling more relaxed. Hurrying to the door, he turned the key and let himself in. But as his eyes scanned the foyer and fell to the heap of Charlotte's things at the base of the stairs, his grin faded.

"What's this?" he asked Charlotte as she appeared in the doorway of the living room. That giant car seat was dangling from her arm. Audrey was already strapped in, sound asleep and tucked under a pale pink blanket.

"I'm leaving." She looked at him flatly, but the words were a punch to the gut.

He stepped toward her, but she held up a hand.

"Rebecca stopped by today."

Rebecca. Greg opened his mouth and closed it shut. He should have known she might stop by. Rebecca was used to having her way, and she hadn't reacted well when he told her their breakup was for the best. They weren't right for each other. He knew that now.

"If she upset you, I'm sorry. But you don't have to leave,"

Greg said. He pulled his phone from his pocket. "I'll call her. She shouldn't have come here. It's over with us. I told you that."

Charlotte folded her arms across her chest, and Greg realized with an uneasy stir that she was wearing her coat. Had he caught her just before she'd slipped out? Or had she been waiting for him to get home?

"This was a mistake, Greg," Charlotte said.

Now wait a minute. "Are you talking about our arrangement?"

Her look turned withering, and...wonderful. He'd messed up again.

"I should have known that's all you care about."

"It's not all I care about," he said firmly. He took a step toward her, but she took one back. He stopped. "I care...I care about you."

And he did. More than he wanted to. More than he cared to admit. She was a single mother with a baby. She loved Christmas. She was everything he wasn't, and God help him, he loved that about her.

Charlotte looked away. "We agreed to play a part, and we should have kept it that way. I don't know you at all, Greg. And you don't know me, either."

Now here Greg disagreed. "This isn't a fake relationship to me anymore, Charlotte. My feelings for you are real. You're the first person I've ever been myself around. The first person who cared to know the real me. You saw me as more than the heir to Frost Greeting Cards."

She pinched her lips, shaking her head. But there was hesitation in her eyes. He clung to it.

"No," she said. "No. You're passing through town, looking

for a little fun, and I was convenient. Once this ruse is over, you and I will be over."

He hadn't wanted to think that far ahead. Now he did. And he didn't like the empty future he saw. "I'm not like the men who hurt you before."

Charlotte was shaking her head. "You belong with a woman in your circle. A woman who doesn't need too much. A woman who is fine with a surface-level relationship and doesn't need anything more. You obviously saw something in Rebecca, and she and I couldn't be more different."

"Don't I know it!" he nearly shouted. He stepped toward her, but she stiffened. "I broke up with her for a reason. I'm with you now because—"

"*With* me?" Charlotte's eyes were wide. "We're pretending, Greg. We got caught up in . . . playing house."

"You're overthinking this," he countered. "We're two people who spent time together and who realized we had a true connection." He tipped his head, locking his gaze with hers, searching for understanding. "Didn't you feel something?"

She lifted her chin at that. "I liked who I was in your eyes. But I'm not that person any more than you're the person I thought you were. Don't you see? We fell for our own sham."

"You're exactly the person I think you are, Charlotte," he said softly.

She snorted and slid her eyes to his. "You think I'm someone you're not. You think I'm this great mother? I can't even buy my kid a Christmas gift. You think I'm some great cook? I usually eat crackers or toast for dinner," she added. "You wonder why I'm staying here and not with my sister? Because I stole her fiancé from her. I got pregnant, and the guy bailed on me. I broke my sister's heart. *That's* the person I am. And you know why I did it? Because I wanted to feel important. Just once, I wanted to feel special."

"I don't believe that," he said. There was more to it; he could sense the hesitation in her eyes.

"Look," she said. "You needed me to help you get this business deal. I needed you so I could make things up to my sister. That's all this was."

"There's more to it now."

She was shaking her head. "All of this...it wasn't supposed to go this far." A single tear rolled down her cheek and she pushed it away. "This became about me, and it was never supposed to. This was about my sister. Helping her out. About proving to her that I'm not the screwup she thinks I am."

"You're not a screwup," he said softly. He didn't care about her past or where she had been, what she had done. The woman standing before him was honest, real, and loyal. "You're special to me. You are exactly the person I think you are, Charlotte," he repeated, more certain this time. "You're passionate, and kind, and caring."

She was shaking her head now, a bitter smile playing at her lips. "I'm selfish, cold, and careless. And oh, of course...foolish. The family screwup, and here I go again..."

"No," he insisted. "No." He knew many cold and selfish people, but he refused to believe Charlotte was that way. He saw the light in her eyes, the sincerity in her smile many times. He knew the way he felt when he heard her welcoming him home, bringing a sense of comfort to him he had never known was possible.

"Oh yes, Greg." She chuckled mirthlessly. "I am *very* careless." She tossed her hands into the air. "Why else would I have gotten myself into this mess? Agreeing to pose as your fiancée was foolish enough. But falling for a man who could never accept my daughter...A man who...how did Rebecca put it? *Hates kids.*" She shook her head. "I have to go."

His mind was spinning as he watched her gather up a few bags and march toward the door. He wanted to shout something out, something that would stop her, but he knew there was nothing he could say. And he knew the only person he was angry with was himself.

She had a point, after all. A baby...a baby had never been in the cards. He didn't know how to be a father or a parent. And watching Charlotte with Audrey, the natural ease of her love, made him doubt any inkling he had.

Charlotte deserved better than the life she'd been living. And Audrey deserved a father.

They both deserved all those things and more. He just wasn't sure he was the man to give them what they needed.

★ ★ ★

The light above Bree's door was on, and through the glass windowpanes, Charlotte thought she could make out a light from the kitchen. With a shaking hand, she turned off the engine, released her seat belt, and plucked Audrey's carrier from its base. The crib was still at Greg's house—she'd realized this only once she'd pulled out of the driveway, but then, she hardly had time to dismantle it, and she didn't know where Greg kept his toolbox anyway. Besides, she wasn't going back to that house tonight. Maybe not even Saturday night.

Saturday night. So much for her grand plan.

Charlotte hurried across the front path and rang the doorbell. She pressed her nose to the glass, only relaxing when she saw Bree coming around the corner. Her cousin looked almost as bad as Charlotte felt. When she turned the lock and opened the door, Charlotte could see that her eyes were rimmed with red, and she was clutching a glass of wine as if it were a life vest.

Either Bree had seen another documentary on the meatpacking industry or something had happened with Simon.

Charlotte was placing her bets on Simon.

"I'm afraid I'm not the best company," Bree said, closing the door behind them.

"That makes two of us." Charlotte gestured to the wineglass. "Have any more of that?"

"If you don't mind that it came from a box," Bree said with a grin.

Charlotte set Audrey down in the living room and followed her cousin back to the kitchen, which looked a bit worse than the last time she'd been there, though she didn't see how this was possible.

"How's the renovating coming along?" She noticed that the light fixture had been removed since her last visit. That was it. It had been an old Tiffany-style affair, with stained glass. Pretty but hardly contemporary. Now the room was lit by a lamp that was perched on a chair seat, since the countertop was covered in paint cans and cabinet fronts.

"I'm going with a warm gray in here," Bree said as she filled a glass and handed it to her. She topped herself off. "I first need to figure out how to get all that wallpaper off."

She gestured to the far wall where strips of rooster-printed wallpaper had been torn off in jagged strips. Charlotte barely noticed anything but the enormous hole in the center of the wall.

"Oh. I thought I might open the floor space up, but then I realized I sort of need an engineer to tell me if that's a supporting wall." Bree's face crumbled before Charlotte realized what was happening. "It was just a really bad day and I...I needed to smash something."

Charlotte set her hand on her cousin's wrist. "Do you have something I might be able to smash?"

Five minutes later, they were in one of the spare bedrooms. A room that Bree tearfully explained she planned to turn into a reading nook, once she had successfully ripped out all the paneling that had been added when her grandmother redid the room in the seventies as a boys' hangout for all the grandsons.

Gripping the crowbar, Charlotte pried off the top corner of the wood and with all her might pulled. A moment later, a strip of wood had dislodged from the wall. Charlotte grinned. "This is addictive!"

She tried another piece, and another. "I could do this all night!"

"Be my guest," Bree said wearily, dropping onto an olive-green armchair that would no doubt be banished to the attic soon. She sank her head into her hands. "I'm just so tired."

"Well. I can have this room done in ten minutes at the rate I'm going!" Charlotte pried off another piece, wrangling it free.

"I thought this would be a fun project, that I could make this house my own, that it would be...enough. But it's not enough. And I don't think it ever will be. And now..." Bree sniffed loudly and then wailed, "Now it's all ripped up and ugly and I don't know how to put it all back together again!"

Charlotte stopped prying the paneling from the wall and stared at Bree. "I thought...I thought you were enjoying this home remodeling stuff."

"Are you kidding me?" Bree cried. "Look at my house! Gran...Gran would just die if she saw this. No pun intended." Bree sniffed again, wiped her nose on her sleeve. Charlotte noticed she had a chunk of plaster in her hair. There was no telling what project she'd been working on before Charlotte arrived.

"You'll get everything in place. It will be beautiful, I'm sure of it."

Bree looked at Charlotte doubtfully, but she stopped crying. "I thought it would make me feel better. Instead it just makes me feel worse."

"Is this about Simon?" Charlotte asked. She really hoped so. She didn't want another recap of *Fast Food Nation*. She'd never even seen the movie but had nearly stopped eating for three weeks after Bree had summarized it for her.

"Of course this is about Simon. The bastard," Bree added under her breath.

Charlotte tipped her head in sympathy. "Want to talk about it?"

"Nothing to talk about," Bree said. She set down her wineglass and pushed herself into a standing position. "The guy's a jerk. I don't know why it took me so long to see it."

"It's easy to see what you want to see. I'm guilty of that," Charlotte said bitterly.

Bree began peeling the orange plaid wallpaper from the top half of the wall. It came off in thin, random strips, but she didn't seem to care. "I'm not going to lie, I cried today, but not over Simon. Not really. I cried over the time I wasted on him, on someone who wasn't honest with me, who didn't deserve me. Guess you could say I'm mad at myself."

"I understand that feeling all too well," Charlotte said. "Time to stop giving people too much credit and start seeing them for what they really are."

Bree turned to her. "What has you so fired up tonight?" Before Charlotte could say anything, her eyes turned knowing. "Don't tell me. *Your client.*"

Now it was Charlotte's turn to drop onto an armchair. It smelled like sweat and teenage boy. "Is it that obvious?"

"I thought he was just a friend?" Bree asked pertly, but Charlotte saw the compassion in her eyes. "Go on," she said, lifting her wineglass from the table and taking a long sip. "Tell me everything."

And so Charlotte did. How she was broke. How Jake hadn't so much as looked at his daughter, much less taken any responsibility for her. How she was staying with Greg. How he'd kissed her. How he'd broken her heart.

"Oh, Charlotte." Bree stared at her, almost as if she didn't even know what to say.

"I'm a screwup. I make bad choices." Charlotte shrugged and took a long sip of wine.

"No, Charlotte. You are many things, but you are not a screwup. Jake—that snake—is the screwup. When I think that he had the opportunity to see that sweet baby...in my shop." She shook her head. "I'm so angry."

Uh-oh. Charlotte knew that look. It was the look Bree got when she was about to do something. Quickly, Charlotte reached down and grabbed the crowbar. "Here," she said, proffering it.

"Ripping out a wall won't help with this," Bree said, shaking her head. "What are you going to do, Charlotte?"

"I don't know," Charlotte replied. It didn't matter how much her heart ached. What mattered right now was that she didn't know what would happen tomorrow anymore. Where she would live. If she'd even have a job. What Kate would say . . . She groaned. Kate. "I suppose I have to go to the Frost party. Smile like the happy fiancée."

"No, you don't!"

"Yes," Charlotte said sheepishly. "I do. I need the money, Bree. And I don't want to make things worse with my sister."

"And how exactly would you be making things worse with your sister by being honest with her?" Bree asked pertly, and this time, she was sticking with that look.

Charlotte opened her mouth to speak, to explain, but no sound came out. She didn't know the answer to that anymore.

"Trust your sister, Charlotte. She loves you and that baby." Bree's eyes were pleading, and Charlotte's began to blur with tears.

She nodded silently. Bree was right. She'd spent so much time waiting for her sister to trust her again, she hadn't stopped to think that she needed to trust again, too.

Chapter Twenty-Nine

⸻⸻

The morning light filtered through the curtains of Kate's guest room long before Audrey's cries filled the room. Normally, Charlotte would feel nothing short of gleeful at a rare, luxurious morning to sleep in, but not today. Today she longed to be busy, preoccupied with something other than dread and regret.

So much for this being a fresh start and a new and improved, put-together Charlotte. She still hadn't learned her lesson, no matter how heavy the price.

Her chest felt heavy as she swung her legs over the bed. Kate and Alec were sitting at the kitchen table when she reached the last stair, her hand still lingering on the banister. They were sitting catty-corner, nestled in the bay window that overlooked the backyard, their voices low and hushed. They both looked up when they saw her in the entranceway, plastering almost identical smiles on their faces.

Charlotte pressed her lips together and forced a small smile as she walked to the coffee maker. "Audrey's still sleeping," she informed them as she filled her mug. She lifted the lid on the sugar bowl and helped herself to two heaping spoonfuls, knowing that if she kept this up she'd never get back into her prebaby clothes.

"We're not used to having a baby in the house," Alec said as Charlotte pulled out a chair at the table and dropped into it. He reached over and grinned at Kate. "Good practice."

Charlotte frowned at this. She couldn't help it. Of course Kate would find someone who wanted a family, someone who was committed to her and their future. While Charlotte...Well, she was still paying for her mistakes.

She stopped herself and took a sip of the coffee. It was wrong to be jealous of her sister's happiness like this. It was this kind of thinking—this need to feel just as important and special—that had led to her sleeping with Jake. And after what Charlotte had done, Kate deserved to be happy. And Charlotte wanted that for her, more than anything.

It was just...She wanted to have that for herself, too.

"I'll be out of here by January," she promised, as she had last night. It had been too late when she'd arrived to explain the whole truth. All they knew was that she had to move out of her apartment and would be finding a new one. The pipes, the heat...She couldn't even remember the excuse she'd given. But there would be no excuse today. Today she was telling Kate the truth.

"Don't rush on our account," Kate said. "Besides, Mom and Dad will be back soon and it will be fun to all be under the same roof for Christmas."

Charlotte was skeptical. "What about the stress of the wedding?"

"When am I not stressed about something?" Kate said with a wink, and Charlotte's guilt skyrocketed. Her sister was of course stressed about her wedding, and having houseguests was never easy, not when one cried for half the night. Unlike Greg's, Kate and Alec's home was of modest size, with three cozy bedrooms and a hallway bathroom.

"I'm here to help," Charlotte said. She noticed she'd spilled some sugar on the countertop and hastily brushed it into the sink.

"Just focus on the Frost party," Kate said. "That's most important right now."

Charlotte looked down into her mug, feeling the return of that hard knot in her stomach.

She had to face him sooner or later. She'd worked too hard to let another man stand in the way of a better life for her daughter or her relationship with her sister.

Charlotte sighed, not even caring that Alec and Kate were sitting in silence, observing her. All she wanted to do was bolt. From this town, from Kate, from Jake, and now from Greg. But she couldn't. She owed Kate more than that. And she owed Audrey a stable life.

And until she got the second half of her payment from Greg, there was no chance of either.

"I should probably get to the office," Alec said, pushing back from the table.

"Tell William I say hello." Kate smiled and lifted for a kiss.

Charlotte averted her eyes and slid into a chair at the opposite end of the table. She glanced at the clock on the far wall. Audrey would be up any minute, hungry and in need of all sorts of things. When Kate and Alec started a family, they'd be able to share the responsibility. Just once Charlotte thought it might be nice to have someone pat her shoulder and tell her, *You sit, I'll handle this.*

Kate waited until Alec had left before sliding into his chair, directly facing Charlotte. "I'm concerned about you."

Of course. When wasn't Kate concerned? When would she finally prove to Kate that she was fine, just fine? She didn't warrant special attention. And she sure as hell didn't deserve it, either.

"I told you. It's just the old furnace."

Kate frowned. "I thought you said the pipes froze."

Charlotte stiffened. "That too. I'm going to find a better place for a January lease. Too many problems at that place." Like being evicted. "The holidays are just slowing the work down. But honestly, you were right about that place, Kate. I think I'll start looking for something better next week." Her spirits rose a bit at the thought of that building in the center of town she'd been eyeing. If the party went well and Kate decided to give her more clients of her own, she could even stretch a bit, upgrade to a bigger apartment with in-unit laundry or a little balcony where she and Audrey could plant flowers...

Oh, who was she kidding? She could barely take care of herself or her kid. The plant wouldn't last a week.

"It's not the living situation I'm concerned about," Kate said. "You know you and Audrey are welcome here as long as you need to stay."

Charlotte felt hot tears spring to her eyes at that. She blinked and stared into her mug. "Then what has you so worried?" Unlike her, Kate was no fool. Even if Kate didn't know how far Charlotte had taken her fake engagement, she could sense something was amiss. No matter how much Charlotte tried to hide her pain.

"I want to know what's going on with Jake, Charlotte. I

know you don't bring his name up around me, but you don't have to worry about that. Honestly."

"What's there to discuss?" Charlotte asked, feeling tense.

"Well, I personally feel like he should have stepped up last night. His child was living in an apartment with no heat. Why didn't he help out?"

Charlotte hesitated. It was now or never. And she couldn't flat-out lie to her sister. Evading the truth had been hard enough.

"Jake has never helped out," Charlotte said quietly.

Kate frowned. "But...I thought we had that all straightened out. Over the summer, when you moved back. You said you were going to hire an attorney."

"I said I would. I did say that," Charlotte said wearily. "But then I started thinking about the things he'd done and the things he'd said. He doesn't want to be Audrey's father, Kate. And I don't want to force him to be. Audrey deserves more than that."

"But it's still his child. His responsibility. He owes her something."

"At what cost?" Charlotte said, shaking her head. She'd already thought this all through, a dozen times over. "So she can know this man and sense how much he doesn't care about her? I can't bear it. I can't bear the thought of my child feeling unloved by her parent." She drew a breath, energized by that terrible thought. "I won't do that to her, Kate. Jake doesn't want to be Audrey's father. So she has me. I can't provide everything for her, but...I'm trying."

Kate reached over the table and gripped Charlotte's hand. "Oh, Charlotte. I wish you'd told me sooner."

"I didn't know how. So much had happened, and...it's important to me that we get back to the way things used to be." She hesitated. "There's something else you should know."

Kate paused. "Something tells me I am not going to like this."

Charlotte couldn't agree more. She pulled her hands into her lap and started at the beginning, the very first time she rang Greg's doorbell, and finished with last night, wincing.

Silence fell over the room.

Finally, Kate spoke. "Thank you for letting me know. As for the Frost account, I will be taking over."

"But—"

Kate was already on her feet. She held up a hand. "I thought you and I were in a better place, Charlotte. But now I know I was wrong."

Charlotte sat in the empty kitchen long after her sister had left the room, staring out onto the snow-covered backyard, listening to Kate's little dog squeak his toy and scamper across the floorboards. She could have said a hundred things to try to defend her actions, but none of it mattered.

She'd messed up. Again.

★ ★ ★

Greg closed the door behind the deliverymen and stared at the boxes at his feet—dinnerware and glasses carefully packaged and sent over ahead of time by the catering company.

Greg wandered through the rooms, noting their transformation. The entranceway was stunning, heavily decorated with garland and lights and wreaths. A second tree had been set up in the arch of the stairs; high tables covered in crimson cloths dotted the space. Half the furniture in the living room had been cleared out, and the largest room in the house now seemed more spacious than ever. A buffet table stretched along the front wall, and the floor was cleared for mingling.

It would be a wonderful party, but did any of that matter without Charlotte here?

He knew he could call Rebecca. Get back together with her, as she so wanted. It would certainly clear up the predicament with his mother's need for a family image.

He sank down on the sofa facing the tree, remembering the night Charlotte had knocked it down. He smiled; then, feeling inexplicably nostalgic, he let his gaze drop to the albums that were still out on the coffee table. He pulled a different one onto his lap this time and opened it to the first page.

But what he saw wasn't a photo. It was a card. A Frost card. One he had forgotten about.

He picked it up carefully, turning it over in his hands as the memory came back to him.

He must have been seven, maybe eight years old, and it was the last week of school before summer break. The teacher had them make Father's Day cards, and when he refused to participate in the project, the teacher sent a letter home. He remembered being scared to hand the letter to his mother, wondering what she would say, refusing to make a card of all things, when he was a Frost! He was a greeting cards heir, as Rita liked to proclaim. Her frown deepened as she read the note and then set it on the counter with a heavy sigh. She didn't say a word about it, and that night she took him out for pizza and ice cream, and she didn't even care when he spilled the chocolate sauce down the front of his shirt. The next morning before she left for work, she handed him a five-by-seven envelope, embossed with the Frost logo, and told him to give it to his teacher. "She wants you to make a card?" Rita quipped. "Show her how we Frosts make cards."

Greg smiled now as he remembered how he felt that day, the confidence he felt handing in the card, among the construction paper junk the other kids had created. He felt like he had an ally. Like he and his mother were in cahoots. A two-person team that didn't need anyone else. Not even a father. But above all else, he felt loved.

He took the card from the envelope now, surprised at what he saw. It wasn't a Father's Day card at all. He'd been too young then to notice that. Maybe too distracted to care.

It was a card without words, but the picture said everything. An old man, his hair graying, his back hunched, and a young boy, looking up at him, holding his hand.

His grandfather.

Right. Greg stared at the card for several more minutes before tucking it back into the envelope and into the album.

He had a matter of days to get the Burke's proposal tightened up and win that holiday spot. And so help him, he would do it. Not just for himself. But for his mother. And for her father. And for the company they all represented.

★ ★ ★

The doorbell rang at three o'clock, when Greg was finishing up some paperwork. He'd decided to work from home that day. It was the best way to avoid distraction. At the office, he'd be called on for last-minute advice or thoughts on a project, but in the comfort of his home office—make that his grandfather's former home office—he could focus on the holiday party and how he intended to win the Burke account.

He waited for Marlene to answer it, but then a thought occurred to him. Charlotte.

Quickly, he pushed back his chair and hurried into the hall, but the woman Marlene had opened the door to was not Charlotte at all. It was her sister.

"We met at the tree lighting," he said uneasily.

Her smile was strictly professional as she held out a hand. "Kate Daniels."

He shook it, all at once wishing it was Charlotte's instead. Kate's eyes were blue, not green, and her smile wasn't quite as mischievous. But there was something about her, something familiar. Something he'd come to know.

"I'm taking over the account," she explained, before he could ask. She eyed him watchfully. "My sister told me about your arrangement."

"Did she tell you anything else?" Greg asked, detecting the hope in his tone.

Kate's expression remained neutral. "My sister made a mistake in agreeing to this . . . ruse."

"Don't blame her," Greg said. "I suggested it."

"And she took it to another level," Kate said, no doubt referring to Charlotte staying with him for the last week and a half. "As I'm sure you can understand, my company is very important to me."

"I understand that. And so does Charlotte." Sensing the doubt in her eyes, Greg said, "She did this for you."

Kate frowned. "I don't understand."

"The arrangement . . . It was my idea and she went along with it. But she didn't do it for herself. She did it because she wanted my business, and I guess I made it seem like there was no other way. And she wanted to make you proud of her." He motioned to the living room. "She's done an amazing job in a very short time."

"My sister doesn't always think things through," Kate replied, shaking her head.

"I'm not sure she made this choice with her head at all," Greg agreed. He gave her a pointed look. "I think she made it with her heart."

Kate's expression softened, and she nodded before turning her attention to the living room. "It really does look beautiful."

"She's not coming back, is she?" His stomach knotted every time he thought of the hurt in her eyes. He could have stopped her, could have called out or reached out and grabbed her, tried to explain, but instead, he had just let her go.

"I thought it best that I take over. As for your arrangement—"

"I don't care about the arrangement anymore," Greg replied, and Kate's eyes opened in surprise. "I just want Charlotte to be happy."

Kate gave a sad smile. "That makes two of us, then."

Chapter Thirty

⌒⊶⊷⊶⌒

Charlotte had managed to avoid Kate after she returned from her client meetings. She'd also managed not to think about the Frost party too much, because doing that only made her think of Greg. Really, she should be happy that Kate had insisted on taking over. It took the pressure off ever seeing him again.

And that should be a good thing. But for some reason, it didn't exactly feel that way.

Kate had met Alec after her meetings yesterday afternoon, and then the two of them had gone to the Harbor Inn to finalize their wedding plans, before no doubt going into town for a nice, romantic evening. Charlotte had stayed back at the house, indulged in an entire frozen pizza and the remains of some peppermint ice cream she'd found tucked in the back of the freezer, and read *Goodnight Moon* to Audrey exactly twenty-seven times. If she never saw that mouse again . . .

Now, though, there would be no avoiding her sister. The sun was up. She could hear Audrey stirring in her crib, and she could smell the coffee brewing downstairs. No doubt Kate had told

Alec all about her latest string of poor choices. No doubt she was only still employed because Kate was concerned about Audrey's welfare.

She should be grateful she still had a job. But having a job and deserving a job were two very different things.

She picked Audrey up from her crib and changed her diaper. Audrey was chewing her fingers with one hand, reaching up to grab Charlotte's hair with the other. She picked the baby up, set her on her hip, and pressed her cheek next to that sweet, smooth skin. No better feeling in the world, she thought. Right now, in this short, fleeting moment, all was right in the world.

She heard the front door slam.

Oh, no. Alec had left for the day. William always picked him up out front, and they carpooled into town, where they ran a financial advisory firm. That meant Kate and Charlotte and Audrey were alone. And Audrey couldn't take the pressure off by making small talk. Looking cute only did the job for so long.

Dread filled her as she crept into the hallway and began her descent down the stairs. Time to face the music.

In many ways, it would be easier to just be fired. She should probably start looking for a job. Maybe she'd see about staying with Bree, too. Surely at least one room in that large house could be baby-proofed.

"Good morning," she managed to force out as she turned into the white, spotless kitchen.

Kate was already dressed for the day and pouring food into Henry's bowl, who danced around her feet, yapping excitedly.

Charlotte couldn't help but laugh. "I don't know who's more excited for breakfast. Henry or Audrey."

Kate smoothed her skirt as she straightened, and Charlotte

looked away. She didn't want to face her sister. She didn't want to talk about anything again. Jake. Greg. All this was her problem.

Except for the fact that the Frost account was also Kate's problem now.

"I met with Greg yesterday," Kate offered, and Charlotte's hand stilled as she unscrewed the lid of the baby bottle. "The house looks great. You did a really good job, Charlotte."

A compliment? Charlotte licked her lip, forcing back a smile. No need to get ahead of herself here.

"I wanted to do a good job." Oh, crap. The back of her eyes stung and she fought to hold back the tears.

"I know," Kate said gently.

"I never meant to hurt you, Kate. I just...wanted to help." Now a single tear rolled down her cheek and she brushed it away quickly, but it was no use.

"Your heart was in the right place. I see that now. I just wish you could have known you could tell me. I'm sorry you didn't think you could."

Charlotte nodded, wanted to choose her words carefully. "I wanted you to be...proud of me," she finally managed.

Kate leaned forward in surprise. "Proud of you? Charlotte, I am in awe of you!"

Charlotte's eyes widened. "What?"

"My goodness, Charlotte, look at you. Look at how far you've come. You're a single mother, doing it all on your own, and now you've managed to land the biggest account this start-up has ever seen, however unconventional your tactics." Kate grinned. "When I see you with Audrey, it's almost hard to believe you're my little sister. I have a lot to learn from you, Charlotte."

"From me?" After everything she had done . . .

"You know I never really told you this before," Kate confided, "but I always sort of admired you."

Oh, now this was too much. "How?" Charlotte asked, gobsmacked.

"I was always so worried all my life. About grades, and activities, and then boys. I always struggled with everything being just right. I never felt like I was having much fun. But you . . . " She shook her head, smiling. "You just saw what you wanted, and you went for it. You were so carefree, and you rolled with life in a way I never could. I always wished I could be a little more like you."

Charlotte swallowed back the tears that threatened to form. First Greg and now Kate, both telling her that their opinions of her were vastly different than the one she had of herself. All this time, she'd been trying to prove to everyone around her that she was all right, that she could handle her life and live with her decisions. But maybe the person she was trying to convince the most was herself.

Her mind trailed to Greg, of the insistence in his eyes when he told her he knew her for who she really was, not the person he expected her to be. That he liked that person and wanted to be with that person. That he wanted *her*.

She pursed her lips to push back the sting. But not Audrey. He'd carefully left her out of things all along. And they were a package deal.

"I . . . feel really bad for everything that happened, Kate. I need you to know that—"

Kate set two hands on Charlotte's shoulders, stopping her midsentence. There was a softness in her sister's eyes that made

Charlotte's prickle. "I forgave you a long time ago, Char. Now you need to forgive yourself. And put on an apron, while you're at it. You have some cookies to bake if we're going to make it to the swap today. Remember our gingerbread sisters?"

Gingerbread sisters! She'd pushed that memory aside somehow. "Just like old times." She smiled as Kate plucked two cookie cutters from the drawer.

★ ★ ★

Bree eyed the bakery section of Harbor Street Foods with a critical eye, looking not for the most polished, pristine, perfect-looking cookies, but instead, the messiest, most unsymmetrical lot she could find. Yes, she was cheating. She had an empty tin in the car waiting to be filled with professionally made cookies. The way she saw it, it was better than showing up empty-handed, and who could really complain about a decent-tasting cookie? It wasn't like anyone had raved about her snickerdoodles last year. She'd seen more than one woman sniff them before setting them back on the tray.

No, this year, she was giving herself a much-needed break. She didn't have time to bake, and she didn't currently have a kitchen to bake in. Her eyes came to rest on some lumpy-looking oatmeal cookies. Not exactly festive, but they would do. Yes, they would do just fine.

She turned to go, hoping to check out and get to her car without bumping into one of the women who might rat her out, when she saw Simon push through the front glass door. She stood, perfectly still, knowing she could ditch the cookies and run, maybe hide out in the women's toiletries section for an unreasonably safe amount of time. Or she could carry on with her life.

She decided on the latter.

She walked to the cash registers, knowing he would see her as she did. Their eyes met for a brief, heart-flickering second before she put it back in check, and his eyes darted to the left before he flashed her his signature grin. This time, she wasn't buying it.

"Bree! Hey!"

"Hello, Simon," she said wearily as she stopped behind an elderly woman buying a single tube of toothpaste, bottle of whiskey, and a bunch of bananas. She felt only a moment of panic when she saw her future flash before her eyes, but she pushed that firmly back into place. She was only thirty-two. And she'd wasted enough time on the man who had come to stand beside her.

"I've been meaning to call. I mean, I meant to call. About the tree lighting. I was really sick and—"

"The tree lighting?" Bree tipped her head. "Not sure what you mean."

"You know . . . When I saw you at the club . . ."

Bree pretended to ponder this for a moment. "Oh. That. I didn't think much of it. So, sick, huh? Shame." She smiled, but her gaze she knew had turned withering as she stared through those wire-rimmed glasses and straight into his lying eyes. Maybe he'd been there. Alone, with friends, or with another girl. It didn't matter.

Yes, she was thirty-two. And single. But she had a house. And a business. And a life full of friends and family and people who actually cared about her enough to be straight with her.

And Simon didn't fit into any of that. And looking back, he never had.

"Well, I should probably get going," she said as she inched her way along in the line.

His eyes turned quizzical and then perhaps knowing. She wasn't in the mood to try to figure it out. "Have a merry Christmas, Bree."

Oh, she'd have a merry Christmas all right. The best one yet, if she had anything to do with it.

★ ★ ★

The tea shop was already filled by the time Charlotte and Kate pushed through the door, only ten minutes after the designated start time. Fiona had her favorite Christmas carols playing from the speakers overhead, and she'd set up a Christmas tree near the bay window, filled with all her favorite ornaments from Ireland.

Charlotte stopped to admire the tree while Kate took their cookies to the table. There were beautiful glass ornaments, many hand-painted. Collected over time. Treasures, really.

She smiled sadly as she let one gently fall back against the branches. She didn't need to think about Greg now. Today she was going to focus on how many of her Christmas dreams had come true, even if that happy family life was still out of reach.

Her sister was waiting for her at the back of the room, a teacup already in her hand. "Better grab a box and start filling it before the good stuff is gone," she said with a wink. "I noticed Mrs. Moore already took three of the mini peppermint éclairs."

"Shameless," Charlotte said, and began laughing.

It felt good to joke with her sister again. Easy and right. She'd lived in knots for far too long.

"I suppose I have no reason not to indulge," Charlotte sighed. She picked up an empty bakery box from the table and began adding some homemade fudge.

"Just be sure you can still squeeze into your maid of honor dress," Kate remarked.

"My..." Before she could even reply, she was matching Kate's wide grin. "Oh, Kate. Me? Really?"

Kate winked. "Did you ever think I wasn't going to choose you?"

"Well, the wedding is next month, and you hadn't asked..."

"Believe it or not, even wedding planners fall behind. It seems like I'm a lot better at planning everyone else's special day and not my own." She gave Charlotte a look of understanding. "I just want this one day to be...perfect."

"It will," Charlotte promised.

"You know what? I really think so, too."

"Does that mean I'm a bridesmaid?" Bree asked, sidling up next to them. "Please tell me Alec has some gorgeous friends in Boston that you will pair me up with for my walk down the aisle."

Kate laughed. "Whatever happened to online dating?"

Bree wrinkled her nose. "I think I'd rather let things happen organically." She stopped when she saw their faces. "No, that is not yet another vegetarian comment, I mean, naturally. I want to meet the right guy at the right time."

Colleen scooted up next to them with an excited flush spreading over her cheeks. "Check out the man near the tree. Not too obvious, please."

So much for that. All three heads whipped around on cue, and Colleen let out a quiet squeal of horror.

Indeed, there was a sole man among them.

"Gay?" Bree asked.

"I thought this was a ladies-only event," Kate said uncertainly.

"I don't know what he's doing here, and frankly, I don't care. And nothing about him seems gay to me." Colleen stared over their shoulders. Her eyes were dancing. It was clear a plan was being concocted. "I'm going in," she announced.

"What?" Charlotte started to laugh with delight. It wasn't like Colleen to make a move or to show any interest in a man other than Matt.

"What can I say? It's not every day a handsome man walks into your mother's tea shop. Seize the day!"

"Hear, hear!" Bree said, holding up her teacup.

At once, Colleen's shoulders deflated. "I can't. I'm afraid. What will I even say?"

Charlotte glanced over to the tree. The man was standing with his hands thrust into his pockets, sheepishly regarding the swarm of women. And oh, he was pretty darn cute. "Why don't you offer him a box for some cookies?"

"Or ask him where he's from," Bree said. "I've never seen that man around town before."

"That's the man I was telling you about," Fiona hissed, wedging herself into their group.

Colleen's brow pinched. "What man?"

"The man I was telling you girls about the other day!" Fiona cried.

Now all the women fell silent. "That man doesn't have red hair or creamy white pale skin," Colleen finally insisted.

"No?" Fiona tipped her head, frowning, and studied him at length. "I suppose it's more of a dark auburn. And I don't remember seeing that scruff of beard last time, though it does suit him, doesn't it?"

Colleen slid her mother a look. "The bigger question is: What's he doing here?"

Fiona's mouth pursed into a pleased pinch. "I couldn't resist."

"For once, I'm glad you didn't," Colleen remarked.

★ ★ ★

Alec was already home when they arrived, tired and happy, and almost distracted from the events of recent days.

"You had a delivery while you were out," Alec said, opening the front door before Kate even had a chance to fetch her keys from her handbag.

"Wedding stuff?" Kate asked hopefully.

"Given the size of these boxes, I hope not!" Alec's brow shot toward the ceiling. He slid Charlotte a meaningful look as he opened the door wider. "Actually, they're for you."

Charlotte pulled the tape off the biggest box, opened the flap, and frowned. The two women stood in silence and stared down at the dolls and bears, the rocking horse and building blocks. It seemed that half of Toys on Main was now sitting in her sister's house, and Charlotte didn't like it one bit.

Her first instinct had been to think Jake had finally come around, finally started to care, and then she saw the delivery slip.

She closed her eyes for one brief moment and then promptly pushed the hope back into place. Greg was feeling guilty. That's all it was. And she would be a fool to wish for more.

"They'll have to go back," Charlotte announced.

Kate hesitated. "I think this was really nice of him."

"Nice? We can't be bought, Kate!" Charlotte cried. Her temper began to stir just looking at the pile.

"It's a pretty big gesture. And he hasn't pressed the arrangement you agreed to."

Charlotte stared at her sister, incredulous. "Kate! You almost sound like you're giving the guy a break. I told you what went down."

Kate shrugged and picked up the delivery slip. She glanced down at the note—*Wishing you and Audrey a magical first Christmas. Your friend, Greg*—and then set it aside. "It's your choice to make, Charlotte."

Charlotte narrowed her gaze. "What's that supposed to mean?"

"I mean that you have to do what's best for you."

"Oh, believe me, I intend to." She was done being played for a fool, being wined and dined by rich men who thought they could impress you with their money and then abandon you when they'd gotten what they needed.

"Charlotte—" Kate started, and then stopped herself. "Just . . . don't turn away something good when it comes along."

Charlotte widened her eyes. "I'm not a charity case, Kate."

"That's not what I'm talking about." Kate gave her a knowing look. "I talked to Greg yesterday, when I stopped by to check on the progress for the party. He cares about you, Charlotte. He cares a lot."

Charlotte shook her head. She didn't want to believe it almost as much as she did. "No. It doesn't matter. It wouldn't last."

"People can change, Charlotte." Kate gave her a little smile. "Look at you."

"Try to see it for what it is. Someone's trying to give Audrey a wonderful Christmas. And regardless of what was said, I just don't see how a man who supposedly hates kids would bother with this."

Her sister had a point. Still . . . "I can't take that risk. Not with Audrey."

"As your boss, I'm asking you to go to the party tomorrow." When Charlotte started to protest, Kate held up a hand. "And as your sister I'm asking you to please give this man one more chance. We all deserve that much, don't we?"

Chapter Thirty-One

⬦⬦⬦

Charlotte stood in front of the mirror and fastened her earring. She let out a nervous breath as she checked her reflection one more time. Still a solid fifteen pounds heavier than her pre-baby days, but the black dress was slimming, and besides, she was starting to like her new curves. Just like she was liking her new self.

"What do you think?" she asked Audrey, who was sitting on her play mat, stacking rubber blocks into a tower.

The little girl looked up at her with big green eyes and smiled until all four of her teeth were showing. "Titty!" she cried, and Charlotte almost choked on a breath.

"What did you just say?" she asked, aghast, but a little shiver ran down her arms.

"Titty!" Audrey cried again, pointing to Charlotte.

"You mean..." Charlotte blinked back the tears that threatened to ruin the very carefully applied makeup she didn't have time to redo. Baby's first word, and it wasn't *Daddy*. Or *Mommy*. It was...*Pretty*.

She knew she risked getting drool on the silk if she squeezed Audrey too close, but she didn't care. With a whoop of joy, she bent down and picked her baby up and twirled her around the room, stopping to stare at the pair of them in the mirror. "There we are," she said, pointing to the reflection. "Mommy and Audrey."

Enough. More than enough.

There was a knock at the door before the handle turned and Kate poked her head around, her blue eyes gleaming when she saw Charlotte. "Look at you. Greg won't know what hit him."

Charlotte shook her head as she set the baby back on the play mat. "No. Tonight isn't about Greg. It's about me. And Audrey." About being the person she'd set out to be. "And pulling off one heck of a party."

Kate tipped her head. "You sure you want me to bring all those toys to Goodwill?"

Charlotte looked at Audrey and reconsidered. "Maybe we'll hold on to them. At least until tomorrow."

Kate's mouth pulled into a slow smile. "I'm glad you're keeping an open mind."

"An open mind is one thing. An open heart . . . " Charlotte smoothed her hair one more time, but it did little to curb the butterflies that were dancing in her stomach.

"Sometimes there's more to the story," Kate said quietly. "Sometimes you owe it to someone to hear them out. I know I wish I'd heard you out sooner."

Charlotte nodded. Every word her sister was saying was true. She'd go to the party. She'd hear Greg out.

And then . . . She didn't know. The future was full of uncertainty. Her gaze fell on Audrey, and she warmed at the sight. And life was full of possibility.

★ ★ ★

Greg straightened his tie in the mirror, catching the reflection of the wall clock behind him. His mother would be here any second, followed shortly by the first guests. The caterers had already arrived, and Kate had been downstairs, overseeing them. He wanted to ask about the gifts. About Charlotte. But it didn't seem like the right place. Kate was working, and he respected that. It was professional.

Whereas everything with Charlotte . . . well, that was personal.

Disappointment settled heavily in his chest. He'd call her. After the party. Once he got through tonight.

The doorbell chimed, right on time, and Greg cursed under his breath. That would be his mother, and he had some explaining to do, and quickly. Would she go for his idea? Or really, would she think that Burke would go for it? Family values didn't have to stem from the traditional makeup of a family, and why should it? Love came in all forms, and this was what would set Frost apart and bring them into the future. At least, he hoped so.

He took the stairs quickly, observing the scene on his descent to the foyer: the bustle of uniformed waitstaff weaving through tables, the clink of crystal glasses being polished for spots and lined up in perfectly straight rows. Even the air smelled fragrant, rich with pine and a hint of chocolate from the overflowing dessert buffet.

Rita had decided that as part of hosting the party at their family home, Greg should personally answer the door for each of his guests, and the staff dutifully ignored the peal of the bell. Greg hastened his pace, reaching for the handle, knowing how much his mother hated the cold.

But it wasn't his mother standing on the doormat, staring back at him. It was Charlotte.

Her hair was swept back, and she wore just a touch more makeup than usual. Her lips, especially, were an inviting shade of red, but she didn't smile.

He could have stared at her all night, but that wouldn't do either of them any good. Was she here for the party? Or for him? "I'm happy to see you," he said. He cleared his throat and stepped back so she could enter, suddenly realizing he wasn't even sure she would.

She marched into the house without a glance in his direction and turned her head over the room, assessing the situation. "Good, it's all come together on time," she said, speaking to him in profile as she plucked a loose petal from the nearest table's centerpiece.

"I was hoping we could talk," Greg said, leaning closer to her. He could feel her posture stiffen. Deflated, he stepped back, giving her the space she so clearly craved. "Did you receive my gift?"

She whirled around to face him. He could see the hurt in her eyes. "Were you trying to buy the entire toy store, or were you just trying to buy my forgiveness? Or were you just trying to tempt me to continue with our arrangement?"

Her words stung. "Charlotte—"

But she held up a hand. "We made an agreement, and I'm a person of my word."

"And I'm a man of mine. I care about you, Charlotte. And Audrey. I sent her those toys because I want her to have a magical Christmas. But if I'm being honest, I think she already will."

Tears filled Charlotte's eyes, but he wasn't finished yet. "It's true that I never thought I wanted children before. I didn't think I could be a good father, since I never had one of my own."

"And what's changed?" Charlotte asked.

"You," he said with a smile.

"What's this?" a shrill voice cried out.

Greg whirled around to see his mother standing behind him, frowning in distraction as she looked around the room. She held up a Champagne flute, inspecting it closely, and demanded again, "What's this? Doesn't anyone around here know how to pick up a cloth?"

Greg held back as his mother looked around, her mouth a thin line as she assessed the setup for the event. "Well, I can't believe I'm saying this, but it's better than I expected. Still, the night's not over yet," she added suggestively.

Charlotte gave his mother a tight smile and said, "I'm so happy you like the way everything looks. I can confirm that the event planner worked very hard to make sure it would be to your standard."

Rita mewed at this, and Greg felt his temper stir. Charlotte had worked hard, in a short time frame, while taking care of a baby. She deserved some credit.

"Yes, I was just telling Charlotte that I'm thrilled with what she's pulled together."

Both women's expressions fell with surprise, and Greg grinned, turning to his mother with an affable shrug. "Oh, didn't I mention that, Mother? Charlotte here is an event planner. A local event planner."

Charlotte's cheeks flared, and for a moment Greg worried he had upset her, until he saw the light in her eyes when she glanced in his direction, however briefly.

"I hope the night will be all you want it to be," Charlotte said to Rita warmly.

At a loss for words, Rita tutted something under her breath and then walked away, murmuring something inaudible. Greg watched as she wandered around in a haze of confusion, her brow pulled to a point, and then turned back to Charlotte. He blew out a breath and slid his hands into his pockets, holding her stare.

He had done one thing right, however small, and it felt good to be honest, and fair. It was a small gesture, not nearly as grand as the toy delivery, but it was all he had left. There was very little else he could give her. There was very little else she wanted from him.

"I hope that didn't get you into trouble," she said, giving him a sad smile.

"Nah," Greg said, rolling back on his heels as he glanced in his mother's general direction. "She'll get over it. Besides, I have a new vision for the company, and one that makes this whole fake engagement thing unnecessary."

Charlotte frowned. "Oh. Does that mean—"

He reached out and took her hand before she had a chance to back away. "Stay. Stay because you want to. As my real date."

* * *

Charlotte's heart was pounding as she wandered toward the kitchen. She had told herself that she could handle this, that she would come here and do her job, thank him for the gifts, and be on her merry way, check in hand. But one look into those chocolate-brown eyes had unnerved her, and she'd lost her resolve. Worse, she'd lost her will. To fight. To resist.

Could she really be wrong about him?

It wouldn't be the first time she'd been wrong about a man.

She was still pondering this as she entered the kitchen, and she hesitated when she saw Rita standing near the window, sipping a glass of nearly finished wine.

Charlotte forced a bright smile as she began taking stock of the trays that lined the counters. "The guests should be arriving soon," she said, hoping her tone sounded light and companionable.

"The food looks lovely," Rita said, and Charlotte paused. That was unexpected.

"Thank you."

"You know this was my parents' house. I spent my summers here as a girl, and when Gregory was a boy. Holidays, too..." Rita smiled and looked out the back window onto the stretch of lawn and the lighthouse in the distance. "It's not easy to come here anymore, though. It doesn't feel quite the same. I've come to dread it, actually."

Charlotte frowned and paused from her task. "You miss your parents. I'm sorry."

Rita took another sip of her wine and lost herself in the window again. "Sometimes it's easier to resist the things you love the most than to accept the fact that you can't have them." She turned, giving Charlotte a tight smile. "I haven't been especially warm to you, my dear. I admit it's not my strength. But hopefully we'll have time for that soon, once my retirement is here. I buried myself in that company, to create some semblance of a stable life for us. It's hard to let it go."

Charlotte wondered if she should dare to say anything. "I hope tonight is a success for you. And Greg. I know how much the company means to him. And the promotion."

"Oh, he's worked hard. He's earned it." Rita smiled. "I have lived and breathed this company for thirty years." She shrugged and set her wineglass on the table. "Letting it go won't be easy, but knowing it will be in my son's hands is a proud moment."

Charlotte stared at her in confusion. "But—"

Rita arched a brow. "But what? Oh, that thing with Drew?" She brushed a hand through the air. "Greg has spent too much time alone. Sometimes men need a little push down the aisle. Greg never had a traditional family—I wanted that for him, something more than I had for myself. He's obviously crazy about you, but a little extra incentive never hurt." She gave a little smile. "Everyone has a different way of showing their love. I know I'm not the most traditional mother, but I do the best I can."

Rita patted her arm and floated through the room, out into the party, where guests had started to arrive. Charlotte stood in the middle of the kitchen, reeling from Greg's mother's words, desperate to run and tell Greg, to ease the pain he carried with him, to tell him that he was loved much more than he knew. She wanted that for him, to know how much he was cared for, to know that none of this mattered in the end, not the party, not the Burke's account, not the fake engagement.

She hesitated, realizing her emotions. She wanted Greg to be happy.

And she wanted herself to be happy. And wasn't the last week the happiest she'd been in a long time?

She had to make a decision, had to trust her instinct to do the right thing. And this time she knew she wasn't going to make the wrong choice.

Greg was standing near the tree in the front room, and Charlotte hurried to him, her stride long with purpose.

"I'll stay as your date," she said.

His eyes widened for a moment and then he grinned. "Good."

"But I have one condition," she said.

"What's that?" he asked, frowning.

"Tell me what you would have done tonight if I hadn't come. I want to know what you meant when you said that you had another way of showing them Frost is a family-focused company."

Greg grinned and tipped his head to the back of the room, where a collage of photos had been set up, of Greg, of his mother, of his grandfather, who had started it all. And there, next to each photo, was an ornament, a Frost ornament, that captured a moment in time.

"I always thought these were just ornaments," Greg said, picking up the one of the little boy looking at his grandfather. "But they're memories. My grandfather made sure of that. And I will, too." He patted his pocket. "That reminds me of something."

Charlotte watched as he pulled out one small pink ornament.

"Baby's first Christmas," she gasped.

"I want you to have this. So you'll always remember how Audrey's first Christmas was spent. And I was hoping...maybe we could hang it on the tree?"

Charlotte brushed away the tears that had started to fall, and only then did she notice her sister, standing near the fireplace, overseeing the waitstaff, grinning from ear to ear.

Event planner Kate Daniels thought nothing could be worse than learning her fiancé had cheated. Until she found out it was with her younger sister. Now Kate has just seven days to hide her heartbreak, host her best friend's wedding–and stumble into true love.

A preview of
One Week to the Wedding
follows.

Chapter One

⸺⬥⬥⬥⸺

If there was one part of her job that wedding planner Kate Daniels struggled with most these days, it was the dress fitting. She used to enjoy these appointments, finding it a true perk to sit in a beautiful, sun-filled boutique, surrounded by breathtaking gowns made of satin, lace, or tulle. What wasn't to love other than the occasional meltdown of a bride who hadn't had much success with that crash diet, or the long, patience-testing afternoon spent with a bride who tried on every dress in the store— twice—and still couldn't make a decision? The wedding dress was the focal point of the entire ceremony, a symbol of hope and happiness and dreams that had finally come true.

Except not all dreams come true, Kate thought as she wrestled with the overstuffed silk pillow wedged behind her back. Her stomach roiled with bad memories, and she tried to stay focused on the reason she was here at all. Her best friend was getting married. She could have a good cry about her own misfortune when she went home, and if recent history proved anything, she probably would. But right now she would hold herself together, show her support, and not let her self-pity taint what should be a very special moment.

"Do you need any help?" she called out. It would be easier to make herself useful, assist with a zipper or buttons or a train. Anything would be better than sitting on this too-stiff velvet love seat, trying not to let her gaze drift too far to the left, where another bride was trying on the very dress Kate had chosen for herself not so long ago, her girlfriends fawning over her selection.

"I'm fine. I just... Well, let's see what you think." Elizabeth stepped out from behind the pink satin curtain of the dressing room wearing the classic strapless ivory gown she'd selected months back when William first popped the question to her, and despite the ache in her chest, Kate couldn't help but smile.

"You look stunning," she whispered. She had known Elizabeth since they were five years old and placed next to each other in Ms. Richardson's kindergarten class, bonding over their love of Barbie dolls and their mutual affection for Ken. She had been there every step of the way that had led to this day. How many summer afternoons had been spent twirling in their mothers' lingerie, clutching dandelion bouquets, Elizabeth's reluctant younger brother bribed with candy into playing the groom, even though he always took off across the lawn before the vows were complete.

Elizabeth turned uncertainly in the gilded three-way mirror that anchored the small store. "I was planning on wearing my grandmother's pearls, but now I think a necklace might be too much."

Kate nodded her head in agreement. "They're too formal for a beach ceremony. Besides, the gown speaks for itself." And it did. Some gowns could be heavy or overly formal, but this one gave just enough of a nod to the bride's classic style while still feeling summery and light. With its low back and subtle details near the waistline, it was perfectly pretty; there was no other word for it.

"I think you're right." Elizabeth scrutinized herself in the mirror and released a nervous breath. "I just want everything to be perfect."

Kate smiled tightly. Every bride said the same thing. She'd said it herself at one time not so long ago.

She frowned. It felt like a lifetime ago. In fact, it felt like another person altogether. Some strange alternate reality where she was the blushing bride pondering menus and color schemes and the band list. Now she was back to doing it for other people.

"It *will* be perfect," Kate said, standing up to fluff the back of the dress. "I'm seeing to it myself."

"You know why I'm so nervous, don't you?" Elizabeth turned to face her properly, her eyes clouding over as her mouth thinned.

Kate squeezed her friend's shoulder, saying nothing. Elizabeth was still recovering from her first and only meeting with William's family, which hadn't gone very well. It had been a bit of a disaster, really, not that Kate would be saying that today. No need to bother with the wedding just a few days away!

"I'm sure it will be different this time," she assured her, even though she wasn't so sure about that. "They were probably just surprised is all. You and William hadn't dated very long," she pointed out, not that an engagement after six months was entirely unheard of, though it was quick. Six months to plan a wedding on the other hand . . . that was rushing it a bit, if anyone asked her.

"I'm just worried that they'll come to town and make trouble. Especially William's brother." Elizabeth gave her a long look.

Every wedding Kate planned had some element of familial tension, and in this case, the source was rooted with the best man. Oh, she'd dealt with her share of unruly wedding party members—groomsmen who hit the bar a little too hard during the cocktail hour, bridesmaids throwing hissy fits over their ugly dresses, mothers-in-law showing up in white—and Alec Montgomery was no different, really. Though she hadn't met him yet, she knew enough about him to know that he'd show up and play the role as dutiful brother. He and William were close, after all. And society weddings didn't leave room for public outburst or noticeable drama.

No, that was usually left behind the scenes, she thought, chuckling to herself when she considered all she heard and saw.

She checked the row of satin-covered buttons on the back of the gown, making sure none were loose. "You'll be so caught up in the excitement of the day, you won't even notice he's there," Kate assured her, knowing this was true. People claimed they barely remembered their wedding days, that it was all a blur. That it was too surreal to capture. Too overwhelming in its emotion.

Kate released a soft sigh. Not that she would know firsthand. "I emailed with him a few times about the rehearsal dinner. He was very laid-back about the whole thing."

"Probably because he was too busy to care," Elizabeth said. She shook her head as she stared at herself in the mirror. "I'm still amazed he even agreed to come to town for the bachelor party tonight, what with how glued to that office he is."

"Well, it's a Saturday," Kate said.

Elizabeth turned to face her. "So? That man works seven days a week. William used to, too." Elizabeth tutted as she took her veil from the sales associate and set it on her head. "I know I sound dramatic, or like some anxious bride, but I'm nervous, Kate. He really doesn't like me; I can tell. It's like I'm not good enough for him or something. It's hard enough knowing your new family doesn't like you, but given how he disapproves of William marrying me or, should I say, marrying into my average American family, I wouldn't put anything past him."

If it were any other bride, she'd chalk it up to high emotions, but Elizabeth was levelheaded and not prone to exaggeration. When she'd come back from Boston, weeping into her Chardonnay and recounted the chilly reception she'd received from William's father and brother, Kate had known that there was no drama or enhanced details for the sake of telling a better story. Kate had seen the red flags then, braced herself for a time when William might call the whole thing off, but time moved forward and now she didn't see that happening. William adored Elizabeth and their life in Misty Point. There was no reason to project her own disappointment onto her friend's situation, even if there were some unsettling parallels.

"You've been watching too many of those reality shows again," Kate said now, and a sharp pain hit her at the thought of their beloved weekly tradition of wine and bad television and endless laughter. They'd been doing that in some shape or form all their lives, really. It was soap operas and pints of ice cream as teenagers—two spoons, no bowls—and later coffee and tabloid magazines. Once they hit their twenties, and even lived together for a brief time after college, it was wine and dating shows.

Would that tradition end now that Elizabeth was getting married? Maybe not right away, but eventually...Elizabeth and William would want to start a family. They'd find other couples to hang out with. And Kate was single. Again. Maybe indefinitely. After all, there'd only been one real boyfriend in her entire life, and the whole town knew how that had ended.

"If you're referring to the season where Tiana, who was kicked off in episode one and had to be removed by ambulance for her hysteria, returned for the final flower ceremony and hovered ominously in the background, hiding behind a rosebush, then, okay, maybe I have been a tiny bit swayed." Elizabeth laughed, but she soon frowned again. "I mean it, Kate. I'm worried. I can't stop thinking about the way Alec just stared at me through that entire dinner. He doesn't like me."

"Well, you're not going to be best friends. It's more common than you think." Kate laughed nervously, wishing she could better disguise her growing alarm. There was no way that anything or anyone could upset this wedding. If that happened, Elizabeth wouldn't be the only one in tears on Saturday. Kate would be crying all the way to the unemployment line. "It will be the happiest day of your life. I promise."

Elizabeth looked unconvinced. "If you say so."

"I do say so." If she had any control over it, at least one of them would have the wedding day that she deserved. Kate turned her friend's shoulders to face the mirror, admiring their reflection. "I still can't believe you're getting married," she said, feeling that tug in her chest again.

"Me neither," Elizabeth said, her tone laced with wonder. Kate recognized the sound of it—the disbelief that all your dreams could actually be coming true. That years of hoping and waiting were over. That you could be so lucky. That your entire future was decided, and bright.

It echoed the emotion Kate had felt once. She blinked quickly, then smoothed Elizabeth's veil, trying to not think about everything that had happened instead.

An hour later, Kate triumphantly scratched the final dress fitting from her to-do list and said goodbye to Elizabeth, waving cheerfully from her perch on the cobblestone steps outside the bridal salon. She held her smile until her friend was safely out of sight and then fell back against the wrought-iron railing with a frown. For months she had obsessed over every detail of this wedding—right down to spending an excruciating amount of time holding various invitation samples to the light to determine the closest shade of pink to the bridesmaid's gowns—but not everything, she knew, could be controlled. An inebriated guest, she could handle. A sniffling flower girl, sure. But a stubborn man who didn't support the wedding? He'd require a tight leash.

And that was why she, as best friend, maid of honor, and wedding planner extraordinaire, was going to personally greet him upon arrival.

But first, she had a haunted house to visit.

★ ★ ★

Bree was sitting behind the counter of Rose in Bloom when Kate reached the end of Harbor Street, the main drag in their small Rhode Island town. Even before her fingers could reach for the handle, she watched as her cousin shot up off her stool and darted to greet her.

"Thank God you could make it," Bree gushed, fumbling to turn the sign on the door to CLOSED.

"That's what cousins are for," Kate said with a smile.

"Well, I still can't thank you enough. The thought of going into that house. Alone." Bree shuddered as she turned the key on the shop door and dropped it back into the pocket of the denim jacket she wore every day from April through September. Even in the flower shop she owned and operated, she was rarely without it, claiming the refrigeration made her cold.

Now, though, the shivering had nothing to do with the warm summer afternoon temperature and everything to do with Bree's paternal grandmother's house.

"What are we checking on this time?" Kate asked as they walked down the block to Bree's station wagon, a modern one, but still a purchase solely made for the sake of her flower deliveries.

"It's not supposed to rain, at least not according to the five-day forecast," Bree explained.

Kate climbed into the passenger seat. She could only hope that the weather held up until at least next Saturday. A hurricane could hit Sunday for all she cared. But for Elizabeth's big day, the sun had to shine.

"I need to air the place out for a bit."

"Does that mean in a few days you'll be calling on me for a favor again?" Kate asked.

Bree gave her a pleading look. Even though she was older by a year, she had always looked up to Kate. And Kate had taken her under her wing, welcomed her into the fold, away from her brother and strictly boy cousins on Bree's other side of the family. A rowdy lot from which Bree clearly needed saving.

Kate laughed. "Fine. You know I'm always here for you when you need me."

Bree gave her a small smile. "And you know I'm always here for you, too."

Kate looked away before she turned emotional. Bree, like Elizabeth, had always been there for her. And that was why today, her first Saturday off in more than a month, Kate was choosing to help both of them out rather than grab her towel and hit the beach.

Rose Callahan's house was not far from the center of town, but too far to walk. Still, they arrived within minutes and, as usual, sat in the driveway with the talk radio that Bree preferred filling the car.

Finally, because time was a tickin', Kate said, "So, ready to go in?"

Bree drew a long breath. "I wish I didn't have to."

"But it's your house!" Kate exclaimed. She looked up at the beautiful Colonial, not quite old enough to be registered with the historical society, but full of history and charm all the same. Rose had kept the house impeccable, right up until the time of her death last fall.

Grumbling something under her breath, Bree released her seat belt and popped the handle on the car door. Kate hurried to catch up with her, knowing there was little sense in running in her heels, considering that Bree wouldn't cross that threshold on her own.

Her cousin took her time fishing around in her handbag for the key, still kept on a crocheted ring most likely made by Rose herself. They'd discussed the fact that she couldn't bear to put the key on her regular keychain just yet, back at the visit where they had to hurry over on a particular cold winter day to make sure no pipes had frozen and burst or anything else catastrophic that came with a mostly abandoned house.

"Have you thought any more about moving in?" Kate asked as she stared down at the half-dead perennials in the planters that anchored the front door.

"No. I can't do that!"

"Because it would upset your cousins?" It had been a sticky situation, of course, when Bree, the only granddaughter of a woman who had borne six sons and never a daughter, was given not just the flower shop but also this house.

Bree said you could hear a pin drop in the room. If ever the boys had managed to convince themselves that somehow Rose wasn't the favorite grandchild, the reading of the will was bitter confirmation of pecking order.

"Oh, they're over it now," Bree said tersely, leading Kate to think they were no closer than they'd been last Christmas, when apparently every Callahan had snubbed her vegetarian contribution of a butternut squash side dish.

Bree wrestled with the key and finally managed to jimmy open the door. "This thing is solid wood," she said, giving it a sound knock. "Swells in the heat!"

"They don't make them like that anymore," Kate agreed, wondering if her own door was solid wood. She hadn't considered it before—she'd simply fallen in love with the sunny front room and back stone patio—but now she had the sudden urge to check.

Maybe this was her problem. She didn't inspect things closely enough . . . at least not when it came to matters of the heart.

They wandered into the hall, which remained intact, exactly

as it had been the morning of Rose's fatal stroke. Even her handbag still sat perched on the console, its zipper open, as if at any moment Rose herself would come around from the kitchen, wiping her hands on her apron, to riffle through it for a stick of gum.

Kate would never admit it to Rose, but she wasn't exactly comfortable in this house. Not when it was like this—frozen in time. No wonder Bree was too freaked out to deal with it herself.

Bree marched into the living room and wrestled with the window, finally managing to crack it a few inches. Without pausing, she marched back into the hall, brushed past Kate, and disappeared into the kitchen. From the sound of her grunting, the back windows were just as challenging.

"It really is a beautiful house," Kate said, admiring the built-in shelves that framed the fireplace. "But I understand it would be hard to move in, with all the memories..."

That handbag! She had to stop staring at it! Was it open on purpose? Was Rose coming or going?

Just stop thinking about it, Kate.

"I can't move in here," Bree said firmly as she appeared in the hall again. She turned into the dining room and threw back the curtains.

"Of course. It's hard to let go—"

"If I move in here, then what kind of message would that send to Simon?" Bree demanded, officially silencing Kate.

Kate stared at her cousin, hoping she wasn't hearing what she thought she was hearing. Did Bree actually think that she and Simon had...a future?

"I think that would send a message to him that you are a smart, independent woman," she said carefully.

But was that what Simon was looking for? Of course not! Simon was looking for a sweet, easygoing girl who went along with whatever he wanted, no questions asked. And unfortunately for her, Bree was currently that girl.

"I recently bought a house," Kate pointed out.

"Yes, but you've given up."

"I have not!" Kate blinked at the wall. Had she? Sure, she hadn't gone on any dates in a year, but that wasn't the same as giving up. She was busy. With other things.

Better things.

Christ. Maybe she had given up.

Bree shot her a pointed look. "He'll never propose if he thinks I've made commitments that don't include him."

Kate pressed a finger to her forehead. There was a lot she could say in response to that, but she decided to pick her battle. "But you own this house. Outright. Why continue to pay rent when you could live here for free?"

Bree hesitated, but only for a moment. She shook her head as she flicked the metal latch on the window and reached for the handles. "I don't think it sends the right message. Simon and I have been dating for almost a year. Now isn't the time to do anything that would mess up our plans."

"Oh." Kate hadn't realized that things had become serious with Bree and Simon. Last she knew, Simon had still refused to spend a Friday night with her cousin because that was "guys' night."

Bree set her hands on her hips. She was slightly out of breath. "I just . . . I just need to tread lightly."

Kate counted to three, willing herself not to overstep. She could tell Bree that it was obvious that Simon was not thinking of rings or white weddings, but then she'd just be accused of being bitter. And maybe she was. Maybe Simon was a wonderful, devoted, adoring boyfriend worthy of her cousin's affection.

And maybe the sun was blue.

"Are you seeing Simon tonight? Before the bachelorette party, I mean?" It was Saturday, but the festivities didn't start until seven thirty.

"It's his bowling league tonight," Bree said, frowning. "He's there all day."

Ah, right. His Saturday activity. Co-ed league. Bree wasn't invited. "Team only" was the excuse.

Kate opened her mouth to give a heavy dose of tough love and then shut it again. Some lessons just had to be learned the hard way. After all, hadn't she overlooked the warning signs with Jake? The wandering eye, the disapproving family, the way they had drifted further and further apart at a time when they should have been coming together, planning their wedding?

Right. No more thinking about that. It was time to focus on the present. Not the past. "Well, I'll help you with the upstairs windows, but then I have to get back to town. Elizabeth's future brother-in-law is arriving for the bachelor party tonight, and I want to go over a few things with him beforehand."

"The best man?" Bree's eyes lit up. "Is he cute?"

"Why? Are you thinking of breaking up with Simon?" Kate asked hopefully.

Bree frowned. "Of course not! I was thinking of you."

"Ha." Kate shook her head as she reached for the banister rail. "I have enough to worry about without romance complicating matters."

READING GROUP GUIDE

DISCUSSION QUESTIONS

1. When Charlotte is visiting with her single, childless cousin, Bree, she gets a little bit jealous of Bree's life, thinking, *Oh, the luxury. To live without a care in the world. To live only for yourself and your own whims.* But Bree is lonely and heartbroken. Can we ever really tell how happy another person is? What strategies do both Bree and Charlotte use to hide their sadness from their friends and family?

2. As Charlotte struggles to stand on her own two feet, she worries that she's not independent enough to be a good role model for Audrey. Is she right about showing Audrey the value of independence, or is it also important for her to show her daughter how (and when) to ask for help? What makes a mother a good role model?

3. Charlotte agrees to pretend to be Greg's fiancée for the Frost holiday party to land the account for Kate's event planner firm. Was this the right move, professionally? How would you feel if your employee made the same deal? Would you

have reacted the same way Kate did, or would you have handled it differently?

4. Greg's mother, Rita, was also a single mother with no support from Greg's father. How was her approach to single motherhood different from Charlotte's? What other events and obstacles may have influenced her more reserved style of parenting?

5. Charlotte is not a great cook, and yet she's able to pull together a somewhat decent meal for Greg and Rita at the last minute. Have you ever had a similar "fake it until you make it" moment? What was that like? If you were in a similar situation, what would your go-to recipe be?

6. In what ways did motherhood change Charlotte? In general, how does becoming a parent shift a person's identity?

7. Later in the book, Charlotte and Greg debate whether the Christmas holidays bring out the best or the worst in people. What do you think? How do the holidays change the characters in the story, for better or worse? What are some examples from your own life of people behaving exceptionally well or exceptionally badly around the holidays?

8. Charlotte spends so much of the book worried about making Audrey's first Christmas special. What do you think is the ideal "baby's first Christmas"? If you have kids, what was your first Christmas with them like? If you don't, can you

imagine what kind of traditions you'd like to introduce to your children, should you choose to have them?

AUTHOR QUESTIONS

1. The book opens with Charlotte making a "Thanksgiving Day resolution." Have you ever made a resolution at a nontraditional time? If so, what prompted that resolution?

I don't tend to make New Year's resolutions, but instead, randomly promise to change and grow as things pop up throughout the year. As in Charlotte's case, some things just can't wait until year end!

2. This novel is filled with wonderful Christmas traditions, from the town tree lighting to the cookie swap at the local tea shop. What are some of your favorite holiday traditions?

One of my favorite holiday traditions is high tea with my daughter, and she also participates in the *Nutcracker* (on ice!) every year. Christmas through a child's eyes is so much more magical, and this was something I tried to tap into with Charlotte and Audrey. The holiday is no longer about Charlotte, but in trying to make it special for her daughter, she is able to relive some of her fondest memories and traditions and create new ones, too.

3. There are so many different, vibrant characters in Misty Point. Do you have any favorites? Are there any characters you relate to more than others?

I relate to Bree quite a bit. I'm a vegetarian, as is she, and I've been known to tackle home remodeling projects that I then wished I had never started. But in fairness, I'm also impulsive like Charlotte and a perfectionist like Kate, so I relate to each character in my own way. While I couldn't say that one character is my absolute favorite, Charlotte holds a special place. She's very real to me.

4. What's your favorite holiday book?

I always read my daughter *'Twas the Night Before Christmas* around the holidays, and I'd have to say it's a personal favorite.

5. Over the course of your last book, *One Week to the Wedding*, and in this novel, Charlotte really comes into

her own and grows as a person. Is your writing process for character development different when it happens over the course of two books instead of one? Why or why not?

Yes, my process is different when a character is developed over multiple books rather than one, because it affects the pacing and allows me to build up their backstory in a more present and impactful way. I enjoyed having the time to show the two sides of Charlotte and better explain her conflict and choices in a way that I think makes her more relatable to my readers.

About the Author

Olivia Miles writes women's fiction and contemporary romance. A city girl with a fondness for small-town charm, Olivia enjoys highlighting both ways of life in her stories. She lives just outside Chicago with her husband, young daughter, and two ridiculously pampered pups.

You can learn more at:

http://oliviamilesbooks.com/
Twitter at @MsOliviaMiles
Facebook at https://www.facebook.com/authoroliviamiles

Sign up for Olivia's newsletter to get more information on new releases and insider information!

http://oliviamilesbooks.com/newsletter/